SOULSNATCHER

BY

KERRY ALAN DENNEY

To Valerie;
Thank you so much for
all your support & encourgement!

Kerry Denny

Soulsnatcher paperback edition published by Kerry Denney Enterprises
ISBN-13: 978-1-49925-177-7
ISBN-10: 1-49925-177-7

Soulsnatcher e-book edition published by LazyDay Publishing
www.lazydaypub.com
ISBN-13: 978-1-61258-129-3
ISBN-10: 1-61258-129-3

Front cover design by Anthony Walsh
Back cover and spine design by Nicolle Brown

To my great friend and fellow writer and dog lover Lynda Fitzgerald. We faced the crashing waves together, and earned our passage with tails wagging and wind-in-fur.

ACKNOWLEDGMENTS

Many thanks to Staci Taylor and all the excellent staff at LazyDay Publishing, Michael Wilson and Holly Pisarchuk at Permuted Press, Earl S. Wynn at Thunderune Publishing, Nancy K. Wagner at Page & Spine, Becky Haigler and Barbara B. Rollins at Silver Boomer Books, Jim Czajkowski, and Anthony Walsh for the excellent cover.

Special thanks to my critique group, The Atlanta Writers' Collective, the most perceptive and demanding beta readers: Lynda Fitzgerald, Ken Schmanski, Lorraine Norwood, Natalie Watts, Glenn Emery, Richard Bowman, Kristine Ward, and Michael K. Brown.

To my friends, for their constant support, encouragement, and for understanding that true friends don't tell you what they *think you want to hear*, they tell you what they *think*: Mike and Shirley Marjenhoff, Gary and Sandy Rosenberger, Carla Brooner Hayden, Jeanne Berinato Duncan, Barrie and Linda Hicklin, Melissa Sue Aderhold, Karin Johnson, Lauretta Hannon, Cecil Hutchins, Sherrie Storm, Jack Chastain, Irene and Tom Noden, Jeffrey Egan, Kevin and Lisa Denney, Reggie Barton, Nicolle Brown, Clay Ramsey, Valerie Connors, George Weinstein, Bettye Jarrell, Shannon Clute, Michael Varga, Polly Iyer, my parents Scott and Madelyn Denney (I miss you both so much), and my dear departed and sorely missed little brother Kolan Denney. A big part of the reason I was able to create this crazy story is because you all can do amazing things just like the kids in this novel do.

And although she can't read, thanks to my furry four-legged friend, my Golden Retriever Holly Jolly the rock star Therapy Dog, who makes loneliness and ravenous monsters magically disappear in the way only a loving dog can. She knows how to fly better than Superman, and how to make good friends better than any of us humans ever will. If we can all learn just a small piece of that magic, what a wonderful world it will be.

Chapter 1

August – Helen, Georgia

Chaz Tandy laughed as he struggled to keep up with the other boys while the girls giggled, watching them. They chased Dante around the gently sloping hillside of his back yard. Chaz was celebrating his ninth birthday, which was supposed to be amazing. According to Mother, who didn't keep secrets from him about his condition, his doctors had said he would likely never see it.

"Well, we'll just show them, won't we, Binky?" Mother had said, her pretty smile winning the battle against the tears pooling in her eyes. He loved her so much. He loved Dante too.

Mother said Dante was his guardian angel. Chaz had found the German Shepherd two years ago in the woods, dying from malnourishment and abuse. Dante was his best friend for life. Dante had saved him every bit as much as Chaz had saved Dante.

Chaz looked over his shoulder toward their house to see if Mother was looking. She watched him like a lioness guarding a newborn cub, always worried he was overdoing it, but he didn't mind. He knew how much she loved him.

He had the best mother of anyone in the entire universe.

She turned, laughing and chatting with the other kids' mothers, her short, raven-black hair glistening in the afternoon sunshine. She looked so pretty, so free of worry, even though Chaz knew she constantly worried about his frail heart.

But she wasn't watching him at the moment, and he picked up the pace.

Dante scampered and avoided the boys, the drool-streaked Kong ball clamped in his teeth, his tail wagging. He spun around at the edge of the slope that dropped off into the valley below, slowed down just long enough to tease the boys into believing they could catch him, and darted off again. He dashed past Chaz and leaped at the girls, who shrieked with delight disguised as fear.

Chaz saw Mother look his way, and he slowed to a trot. Sometimes he could actually feel her eyes on him, as if they had some supernatural connection. When she was satisfied that he was pacing himself, she returned her attention to his friends' moms.

They rarely had guests since they'd moved to the North Georgia mountains—adults or children—but this was a very special occasion.

Dante dropped the ball at Jerome's feet. Jerome picked it up and ran with it, and Dante growled and nipped at his heels. Jerome laughed and chucked the ball toward the back end of the property. Dante sped after it, and was just about to snag it when it hit a root poking up out of the ground beneath a huge maple tree and bounced high.

Dante leaped for it, twisted in mid-air like a canine acrobat, and missed. The ball hit another root, bounced and flew over the lip of the hill, and careened down toward the valley. Dante sprang after it and disappeared past the drop.

Jerome, Billy, Dale, and Ramon laughed and ran after him, and the girls squealed, hot on their heels.

"Dante!" Chaz called. They weren't supposed to go down there. "Too far!"

Dante ignored him or didn't hear, and the boys and girls followed and disappeared down the slope. Chaz glanced back to see if Mother was watching, and hurried after them.

A crash of broken branches and an unmistakable canine yelp ripped a chunk out of Chaz's heart. The kids started shouting and screaming, Dante let loose an agonized howl, and Chaz's chest ached as he raced down the hill.

"Dante! No!"

"Chaz!" Mother called, already sprinting toward him.

Chaz reached the others and dashed past them. Dante lay in a partially hidden thicket of broken branches, alternately howling and whimpering. A sharp, pointed branch about an inch thick protruded out of his chest. His fur was covered in blood; some of it spurted out of the fresh hole in his side. Chaz approached him, feeling like his heart was going to explode. Dante's pleading eyes locked onto his.

"Chaz, hold up!" Mother yelled.

Normally Chaz listened to her. But something broke inside him when he saw Dante's sad eyes begging him to make the bad pain go away. He got down on all fours and crawled toward Dante, heedless of the pain in his chest or the danger lurking in the thicket of broken branches.

If Dante died, Chaz would die too. His frail heart pounded, way past the critical danger level. He scrambled toward his friend, knowing he had only seconds before it was too late.

With Chaz's *special gift*, as Mother called it, Dante still had one chance left.

Fighting tears, Chaz slid and scampered down beside his suffering buddy, breaking rotten branches and scraping his hands and arms on sharp rocks.

"Dante. Hang on, boy, I'm coming."

*****

"Chaz, slow down!" Jasmine Tandy—Jazz to her father and the few friends she had—called, her heart racing. She ran past the screaming children and scrambled down the ravine, bruising and scratching her arms and legs. She crouched down beside Chaz, who was reaching out for Dante.

Dante's wails receded as he became weaker. He was definitely dying. The helpless look in his soulful eyes was the third most heartbreaking thing Jazz had ever seen or experienced. She knew how much Chaz loved him. She loved the goofy dog too.

The second most heartbreaking thing was the dying children in the cancer ward of St. Jude's Children's Hospital in Atlanta, which Jazz and Chaz visited once a week ever since they moved here eight months ago.

The first was when Chaz's doctors told her he had catecholaminergic polymorphic ventricular tachycardia, which basically meant he had an incurable and usually fatal heart disease. Jazz made sure Chaz understood it didn't mean he had a *bad* heart; he just had a *fragile* heart.

In her estimate, especially considering what Chaz did when they visited the cancer ward, he had the biggest, strongest heart she'd ever known. And she made sure he knew it, every day of his life.

She grabbed his arms before he could touch Dante and pulled him to her. He looked back at her, tears streaming down his cheeks. Tears poured out of Jazz's eyes too, and she swallowed a sob, needing to stay strong for his sake.

"Chaz, no."

"Mother, please. I have to."

"It's too soon, baby."

"He's dying. I can't let him die!"

"Binky, it could kill you. I can't lose you." She would die without him.

"I can't lose Dante!" he blubbered, breaking her heart for the umpteenth time.

All the children were crying and shouting. Their mothers came up to join them along with Manny, Ramon's grandfather.

"Dante!" the children called, a mantra intended to some- how magically spare him.

In Jazz's mind, no one was there but her baby boy and his guardian angel. On one hand, if she let Chaz do it, it could kill him. It was too soon after the last time. On the other hand, if she didn't let him do it, the loss of Dante could break his fragile heart, effectively killing him anyway.

She made up her mind. Chaz was her only child, her precious baby, but it was his life, and his choice how much of it to give. She nodded.

"Okay, Binky." It was probably pointless to ask, but she did anyway. "Try not to give him everything you've got, okay?"

"Okay, Mother." His eyes glistened with hope and tears. "I love you."

Jazz bit back another sob. "I love you too, Chaz. Stay there while I get him out, okay?"

Chaz sniffled and nodded, and Jazz scrambled down toward Dante. He whimpered, gazing at her with such a meaningful look that she was certain he knew what they were going to do.

After all, they already did it once before, when they found him.

Jazz crouched, wrapped her arms around Dante's torso, and planted her feet against hard dirt beneath him. With a mighty tug, she grunted and yanked Dante off the wicked branch, smearing her blouse and arms with his blood. Dante didn't even yelp. He just licked her neck and cheek. Huffing with his limp weight, she carried him up to stable ground. He panted, a hoarse gurgle. She gently set him down beside Chaz.

"Okay, Binky," she whispered. "It's now or never, baby. Do your stuff."

Chaz knelt beside Dante, put his hands on his heaving bloody chest, laid his head against Dante's, and whispered to him.

"It's gonna be okay, boy. You're gonna be okay."

Jazz looked around at the others. They watched in rapt silence, and she knew that no matter what happened, this was going to come back to haunt them. They might have to move again.

There was no flashing ethereal light from the heavens, no magical glow, no bizarre static crackling in the air, but in what seemed like an agonizing eternity that was merely moments, Dante's breathing evened out. His tail thumped the ground, and he licked Chaz's face. No more blood poured or even oozed out of the hole in his side.

In fact, the hole was no longer visible. The only evidence that he'd been mortally wounded was the drying blood matting his coat.

Chaz keeled over.

"Chaz!" Jazz reached down and scooped him up. The trees and the hillside and the people spun around her as she listened to his chest. She detected the faint beat of his heart. She put her face next to his and felt his breath against her cheek, coming shallow but steady. He was unconscious, but alive. For the moment.

Gasping and praying to a God she often cursed in the dark nights when hope seemed forever lost, Jazz struggled to her feet, her baby boy cradled in her arms.

"Chaz, Binky, come on, come back to me. You can't leave me." She hustled up the hill, her legs suddenly powerful pistons endowed with superhuman might. "I need you. Dante needs you."

The whole world needs you, baby.

Chaz didn't move.

Dante kept pace with Jazz, wobbly but determined. They passed the others, who stood silent and frozen, bug-eyed with their jaws hanging open as if they had just witnessed a miracle.

Jazz had no time to worry about what the future would bring once the rumor mill got cranked up. Nothing mattered now but Chaz. He was far too precious to her and this world— and to suffering children he had yet to meet—to leave it so suddenly.

Jazz didn't pay attention to the other kids and adults as they followed her. At the house, she climbed the wooden deck steps, Dante right beside her. She tugged the storm door open, rushed into the living room, and gently laid Chaz on the couch. Dante sat on the floor beside Chaz and pushed his snout against Chaz's face. He let out a little whine and looked up at Jazz, who ignored him.

The children, their mothers, and Manny straggled in, gaping like zombies. Jazz sniffled, knelt on the floor, and brushed Chaz's dark, sweaty locks out of his eyes. Jerome's sister Janelle leaned over Jazz's shoulder and handed her a cool, damp washcloth.

"Is he going to be okay, Ms. Tandy?"

Jazz took the cloth. "I hope so. Bless you, sweetie." She brushed Chaz's sweat-soaked brow with it, willing him to wake up. He seemed to be breathing okay. Dante whined.

Chaz finally stirred, blinked several times, and opened his eyes. He saw Jazz hanging over him and Dante panting beside her, and smiled.

"Dante. Good boy." Dante's tail thumped the floor as he licked his master's face. Chaz giggled and rubbed Dante's neck.

Jazz wrapped her arms around Chaz and squeezed him, kissing his cheeks, eyes, lips, and neck. "Oh, Binky, don't ever scare me like that again. I thought I was going to lose you."

"Don't worry, Mother. I still have some things left to do, remember?"

Fresh tears flooded her eyes. "Yes you do, my special boy." She squeezed him tighter, oblivious to the others crowding around them, to what they had witnessed.

If they had to move again, then so be it. At least they would do it together, their little family intact. The room seemed to breathe a collective sigh of relief, and everyone started talking at once.

"Chaz, my man!" Jerome smiled and stuck an open palm out. Chaz lifted a shaking arm and high-fived his friend.

"It's a miracle," Billy's mother said, and the others echoed her.

"Praise God," Manny said, and crossed himself.

"How did you do that, Chaz?" Dale asked, his eyes bugging out.

Their buzzing voices transformed into the comforting hum of a hive hoarding a treasure, and Jazz's heart finally started beating again. There was no way they were going to keep it a secret this time. She looked back at the others and her eyes met Manny's, and he nodded.

"Come on, folks. Party's over," Manny said. "Ms. Tandy and Chaz need to rest for a while." He waved his arms and started ushering the small crowd out.

"Thank you, Manny," Jazz whispered, not certain if he heard her. She picked up Chaz and carried him into his bedroom. She stretched him out on his bed, took his shoes off, and lay down beside him. Dante jumped up on the bed and nuzzled them.

Jazz dared to hope they would be okay this time. She snuggled against Chaz and just held him and watched him for a while, afraid that if she took her eyes off him, he would drift away and leave her.

Thirty minutes later, her eyelids drooped and closed, and as she nodded off she prayed that Chaz would still be here when she woke. Then she let the dreams take her—along with the recurring nightmare where sinister, shadowy figures stole her son and left her to die.

Chapter 2

A week and a slew of amazed phone calls later—most of which Jazz let go to voicemail, and didn't return—Chaz wanted to go back to the children's hospital.

The few calls she did answer were either work-related or alarming enough that she felt the need to quash the rumors personally. She did her best to laugh them off as wishful presumptions and children's overactive imaginations.

The testimonies of the parents who had attended the party would be harder to dismiss. Jerome and Billy's mothers hadn't been able to keep quiet about it. Jazz spent a good part of the week waiting for the media vultures to swoop down upon her and Chaz again.

She tried to talk Chaz out of another hospital visit, but he insisted he was strong enough. When he gave her that sad, brown-eyed penetrating gaze, she sighed and gave in.

Anxious about the incident with Dante, she called the hospital and asked to speak with Dr. Lloyd Petrokovich. She identified herself, and the operator quickly patched her through to him. He said he'd be there until six that evening, which gave them plenty of time.

If he'd gotten wind of any wild rumors, he didn't mention it.

Jazz worked in the research department at Wilson Pharmaceuticals. When she and Chaz had to move last year, the company had transferred her from Houston, Texas. They didn't want to lose her, and she couldn't afford to lose her job, so they relocated her near their plant outside Helen, Georgia. She used her profession as a convenient excuse to visit the children's ward, ostensibly to observe the results of the company's latest revolutionary drugs.

Dr. Petrokovich was like an old friend from the moment they'd first met, and knew about Chaz's gift. In the eight months they'd known each other, he'd told no one but his wife about it. Because of his lifelong struggle treating children with leukemia, Jazz knew neither Lloyd nor his wife had told a soul about it. Jazz loved him, and trusted him with their lives.

Chaz loved Dr. Lloyd too. He was a big teddy bear of a man with the heart of a saint and the face of Santa Claus, minus the beard.

At the hospital, Chaz carried around his iPod and pretended to be bored and annoyed with his mother for taking him to work with her. But Jazz knew he was scoping out the patients and deciding who would be next.

In the hallway, Dr. Lloyd approached them, wearing a big smile on his ruddy face. Chaz ran toward him, and the big jolly ox scooped Chaz up in his arms and laughed.

"Chaz, my boy, how are you?"

"Hey, Dr. Lloyd." Chaz hugged him and kissed him on a rosy cheek.

Jazz approached him, saw that no one was watching, and rose up on her tiptoes and kissed his other cheek. "Hey, big guy."

"Ahh, Jasmine, far sweeter than the fragrance, more beautiful than the most glorious sunrise," he boomed in a baritone voice, and winked at Chaz. "You know, my boy, if I was still in my thirties like your mother, and single, and in much better shape…" He sighed, set Chaz down, and looked at Jazz. "Well, I suppose I'd have to take a number and get in line, and hope if nothing else that she'd merely grace me with the gift of her gorgeous gaze."

Chaz giggled, and Jazz blushed.

"So, how's it going?" she asked, pulling an iTouch out of her purse.

Dr. Lloyd whipped his own handheld computer out of a coat pocket. "Desperate but ever hopeful, as always. How else could a cancer ward be? And how's my favorite surrogate family?"

Two nurses approached them from down the hall.

Jazz sighed. "Depends. Have the rumors started circulating this way yet?"

Dr. Lloyd frowned and lowered his voice. "Well, a few. But I did my best to remind the more loquacious gossipmongers of the dangers of such preposterous wishful thinking."

The nurses averted their eyes and stopped talking when Jazz looked at them. They started whispering after they passed the trio.

Jazz chewed her lower lip. "I hope we don't have to move, and change our name again. We really like it here."

"Me too. We like having you here, believe me. But rest assured, my little man's special gift is just as desperately needed no matter where you may be."

"I don't doubt that. But I'm tired of running and hiding, and Chaz is too."

Chaz beamed up at the doctor. "Yeah. I love it here, Dr. Lloyd. And I love you too."

Dr. Lloyd grinned, puffing out his chest. "And I love you, my boy." He leaned over and spoke softly. "And don't tell anyone, but you're my favorite."

Chaz practically glowed. Jazz figured Lloyd probably told all the children that, but seeing Chaz happy made her happy.

She and Lloyd turned and started down the hall, and she leaned over Chaz and whispered, "Okay, Binky. Remember you're supposed to be bored, and pick one. Just *one*."

Chaz nodded, wiped the grin off his face, and started straggling behind them.

They walked around the ward for fifteen minutes. Jazz and Lloyd discussed the incident with Dante, and the conditions of some of the children on the ward. Chaz pretended to play with his iPod and slyly watched the children in their rooms as they passed them. Lloyd would have suggested certain children for Chaz's magic, but he and Jazz knew Chaz had a sixth sense about which child was the most deserving of a second chance.

Of course, Chaz wished he could save them all. But he knew his limitations better than anyone, and was careful about whom he selected.

When no one but Lloyd and Jazz were watching, Chaz slipped into a room. Jazz and the doctor stopped by the door-way and discussed the treatment that Charisse, the little girl in the room, was undergoing.

A few minutes later, Chaz wandered out, sleepy-eyed but smiling. Lloyd picked him up and carried him against his shoulder. No one should think that was unusual. Lloyd loved all his children, and showed it.

"Do you know what a special little man you are, Chaz?" he said as they headed toward the exit.

Chaz sighed and leaned his head against Lloyd's shoulder. They'd picked a time of the afternoon when the hall-way was mostly empty except for the staff. When they passed by the nurses' station, they caught several nurses whispering as they watched them.

Jazz gave them the withering glare she normally reserved for her worthless ex-husband, who'd left her four years ago, unable to deal with Chaz's condition and Jazz's single-minded efforts to care for their son. The glare silenced the gathered nurses, who seemed to get busy suddenly.

Jazz silently cursed as they approached the exit. The word was already out. After the incident with Dante, it was bound to happen. Too soon the newshounds would come snoop-ing around, wanting to know the truth of the rumors, and things would get sticky again.

"Damn," she exhaled, and Lloyd set Chaz down and turned to her. She took Chaz's hand to steady him, tears pooling in her eyes.

"Now, Jazz." Lloyd wagged a finger at her. "Don't jump ship yet. I've already planned a stern lecture for the staff about spreading unsubstantiated rumors. Let's give it a little time, and see how things work out. I have a pretty good handle on things around here, so hold your horses and don't do anything rash just yet."

"Okay. But if it's anything like last time, then we're pretty much toast around here."

Lloyd chuckled, a determined gleam in his eyes. "It's not over till the fat lady sings, and I plan on ramming a pretty for-midable cork down her gullet. So let's just wait and see, okay? Doctor's orders."

Jazz shook her head and mustered a smile for the best doctor she'd ever met. She wrapped an arm around his neck and kissed him on the cheek. "You're the best, Lloyd. These chil-dren are lucky to have you for their doctor."

He chuckled again. "That's what my patients' parents keep telling me. Maybe there's something to it after all." He turned to Chaz, who was blinking, half-asleep. "You get some rest now, Chaz, and I'll call you in a day or so and let you know how Charisse is doing."

"Okay," Chaz mumbled. "Bye, Dr. Lloyd."

Jazz gave him a hopeful smile. "I'll let you know if any-thing... unusual starts happening."

"You do that, Jazz. You know where to find me if you need me." Lloyd nodded, smiled, and headed back into the ward, whistling a happy tune.

Outside, Jazz picked up Chaz, carried him to the car, and gently laid him down in the back. "Go to sleep now, Binky. I'll wake you when we get home, and we can have some ice cream and cookies."

"Okay, Mother." Chaz closed his eyes. "I love you."

Jazz wiped tears from her eyes and hopped in the dri-ver's seat. "I love you too, honey. So much."

They got home at four o'clock, and Jazz retrieved the mail and parked in the garage. In the living room, she saw the message light blinking on the answering machine, but she didn't check it. Chaz was too conked out to do anything but sleep, so she put him to bed. Dante jumped in bed with him and lay still beside him. Jazz put a pillow against the head of the bed and sat beside them, her heart troubled, and went through the mail.

Bills, junk, and more bills. She came to a hand-addressed letter in a child's script and opened it, wondering if it was from one of the rare children who'd figured out the miracle Chaz had performed for them. They occasionally got one of those. Twice after they did, they'd had to move and legally change their last name to avoid the subsequent unwanted attention. Jazz was sick of running and hiding, but she would do anything to protect Chaz.

The return address on the envelope was smeared and unreadable.

When she read the handwritten letter, her heart started pounding, and fear made her break out in a sweat.

It wasn't from one of the children Chaz had saved.

And it wasn't good news.

Chapter 3

March – Haven, Kansas (five months earlier)

"I told you and told you, don't ever let anyone find out, you little witch!" Carson Fleming threw Mara against the wall by the kitchen table. His voice rasped, his breath reeking of cigarettes and whiskey. "How many times have I told you, Mara?"

He ground his fingers into her shoulders, and she gasped. He leaned over her, his face inches from hers. "The letter said, Mara: *Tell no one!*"

Mara whimpered, almost gagging from his rotten breath. "I didn't mean to Poppa, I swear. Josh and Jonas were tellin' mean lies about us in front of everybody, and I—"

"What did you say to them?" Carson shook her and pushed her against the wall again. His fingers squeezed tighter. Tears rolled down his leathery cheeks.

"Poppa, you're hurting me."

"Goddammit, what did you say?"

Before Mara's mother died last year, her father hardly ever touched the bottle, and his goofy smile and raspy cackle came easier. But he'd started drinking early today, ever since the phone began ringing off the hook. Rumors traveled fast in small towns. Mara fought tears, but they came anyway, in a deluge, long overdue.

"Please, Poppa. I didn't mean to give away the secret." She cringed, waiting for lightning to strike. She'd seen her father angry and even mean plenty of times in the past year, but the violence lurking in his hard eyes had always simmered beneath the surface before.

It finally boiled over, stoked by the wild accusations

hurled at them that afternoon. Pandora's Box had been opened.

He let go of her shoulders and backhanded her, striking her cheek. She crumpled to the floor on her hands and knees.

"Poppa, I'm sorry, I—"

"What did you tell them, you little freak?"

That's what Josh and Jonas Thorne had called her. Mara knew she was a freak, and she hated it.

It's not my fault, don't you understand? I can't help it!

As Mara struggled to rise, he kicked her in the thigh, knocking her to the floor again. He sneered and leaned over her, fists clenched, and she thought he was going to start punching her.

"No, Poppa, please don't hurt me. They said we killed Momma. They said we pushed her down the stairs together."

Carson wheezed. "Did you tell Josh and Jonas their daddy was gonna die today? Dammit, Mara, did you see that, and tell them? In front of everybody?"

"I had to, Poppa. I'm sorry!"

"Sorry doesn't cut it anymore. Did you make this happen, Mara? Is that how your power works?"

"You know I can't *make* anything happen, Poppa."

He reared his leg back, and she kicked a chair at him. He tripped and fell over it. Mara screeched and struggled to her feet.

"You did kill your Momma! You could've seen it, could've stopped it!"

"I told you I can't control what I see!" She stumbled away from him through the kitchen doorway and ran into the hall. He regained his feet and hurried after her. His boots clomped against the hardwood floor, sounding like the deadly tread of an enraged giant.

"Mara!" He dove, grabbed her foot, and yanked it. She tripped and crashed to the floor. Her face smacked into the hard wood, and stars blazed in her eyes as she turned her head and stared at a man she no longer recognized.

He scrambled toward her on all fours, and she shrieked and kicked him in the face. Her heel smashed into his upper lip and knocked his head back against the wall. He lost his hold on her leg, and she leaped to her feet and dashed toward her bedroom as if she could find safe refuge there.

Nowhere was safe anymore, at least according to the damn letter.

"Mara, what have you done to us?"

That, more than anything else, cut like a blade in her mind. It was all her fault. If only she'd kept her stupid mouth shut, hadn't told Josh and Jonas that their father was going to die today in a horrible accident.

She couldn't take it back. Even though she was only thirteen, she already knew you never could, once the mouth blurts.

"I'm sorry, Poppa!" She dove through her bedroom doorway, her heart hammering, blood pounding in her ears. Carson snagged her jeans and tripped her again, and she tumbled into her bedroom.

"Do you have any idea how hard I tried to keep the farm and what's left of our family together? How hard I worked to keep you safe?" He staggered against the doorframe, his face scrunched up in a tortured grimace. He barked out a harsh sob and advanced toward her.

She scrambled backward, trying to regain her feet. She bumped against her bed, and slowly rose and glared at him. She was cornered, but fight conquered flight in her heart. Her mother would have been proud, even though Mara trembled and her legs felt like crackling twigs. The man her father had once been—the one she'd lost the day her mother died—would have been proud too. He had always taught her to stand up for herself.

He stopped short, fists clenched, teeth grinding, and lungs heaving.

Why, oh why hadn't she seen *this*?

He tensed to strike a moment later when the madness resurfaced.

"Touch her again, and I'll break both of your arms," a soft but commanding voice rang out in her bedroom.

Mara and Carson froze. The voice seemed to come from everywhere.

"It's *them*, Mara," Carson said. "They're here. Just like the letter said. It's all your fault."

"No." She sucked in a sharp breath as she glanced into the corner of her dim bedroom. Her hands flew to her lips and Carson turned to follow her gaze.

The man stood there immobile, so dark except for the whites of his eyes and the flash of his teeth that he almost fused with the gathering gloom. He wore a waist-length black leather jacket, black jeans, and black Rockports. His hands clenched into fists at his sides. He might have been waiting there for hours, days, even years.

Maybe he'd been waiting there all Mara's life.

Carson sneered. "You see what you've done now, Mara?"

"I'll break both your legs too." The man's voice was quiet but firm.

"Are you with… *them*?" Carson asked. "Because if you think you're taking my baby girl…" He stepped between Mara and the dark man. "You got another thing coming, buddy. This blood runs true here, asshole, and—"

"Oh, shut the hell up." The dark man looked around, maybe searching for someone else. He glared at Mara. "You should have done what the letter said, Mara."

She looked down. It all came back to the damn letter.

Carson growled again. "See, Mara? I told you, but no, you—"

Glass shattered and sprayed inward through the window, and a whirlwind in the shape of a man followed it. Carson grabbed Mara's arm, pushed her behind him, and leaped toward

18

the new intruder. Hard steel stabbed into his throat, cutting his howl short. The invader ripped the blade out, and a crimson spray shot from Carson's torn neck. He gurgled and clutched at it, trying to stem the flow of life pouring out.

"Poppa, no!" Mara screamed.

The new intruder spun toward the dark man. Mara's father lay on the floor, retching. He reached a bloody hand toward Mara, and she took it in both of hers.

"Mara," he rasped, one hand gripping his throat. Something broke inside her as she realized she couldn't help him. "Poppa... loves his... baby girl."

Mara fell to her knees and cradled his head in her lap, oblivious to the pooling blood and the battle raging in her bedroom. "No, Poppa, no, no, no."

Something metallic flashed out of the killer's hand toward the dark man. The dark man raised his right arm to deflect the flying blade, and dove and rolled. The spinning blade glanced off his bicep with a wet tearing sound and *thunked* into the wall behind him.

He landed on his feet in a crouch and jerked his wrists forward. Two sleek black pistols shot out of his loose jacket sleeves, and flames spat out of the barrels as he fired. The reports were deafening in the small room.

The killer moved like chain lightning. He kicked the dark man's right hand before he could fire again. The dark man's pistol flew from his hand, and he barely ducked a deadly kick to the head. He rolled and fired his other pistol again, and again.

The killer jerked, clearly hit, but he kept on coming. He snatched a pistol from a shoulder holster as the bloody blade in his other hand flashed. He fired one shot and the dark man fired again, twice, three times.

The killer staggered backward and tripped against the bedpost. He fell onto the mattress and dropped his gun and blade, gasping as blood sprayed out of his neck. Mara couldn't breathe. She was too scared to move, even though her mind screamed at her to run.

The killer bared his teeth, watching the dark man move toward him. The barrel of the dark man's pistol didn't waver as he spoke.

"Mara, move away from the bed. Now."

The killer laughed. "You guys are getting... quicker, sea-jay."

He was dying. Most of the dark man's shots had hit their mark. Mara's mattress was soaked with blood, and her world was crumbling. The killer laughed again, a horrible gurgle. Incredibly, he sounded victorious as crimson fluid sprayed out of his mouth.

Mara whimpered. If she screamed, she might never stop. Her father was motionless, his eyes open but empty. Mara looked at her father's killer with a dark fury blazing inside her. He stared at her, grinning as if he'd just single-handedly won the war, and laughed again.

"Mara, dammit, get away from him!" The dark man's right arm dangled at his side, blood dripping from his hand. But the pistol and his left arm stayed on target.

Was he afraid the killer would leap up and start fighting again? Mara didn't know what to do, who to trust. Everything was wrong. Then something far stranger than anything she'd ever seen or imagined happened.

The killer *shimmered*, and Mara screamed.

"No!" the dark man shouted. He fired four quick shots into the killer, two in the head and two in the chest. The killer's body jerked with the shots, and he died smiling.

"Damn," the dark man muttered. His pistol arm dropped to his side.

Mara stood and stumbled backward, her feet slipping in blood. She smacked into the wall beside the doorway.

The dark man sneered. "You see what you've done, Mara?"

"N-no." *I didn't do this. Not this.*

"You should have heeded the goddamn letter," he muttered, his shoulders slumping.

He wasn't going to hurt her, wasn't one of the bad people, wasn't with *them*. He sighed and held out his injured right arm to her. He wasn't a spook. He was real, a man. He bled, could be hurt. And somehow, he'd saved her from something awful.

"Mara, you don't want to be here when they come looking for you. Come with me."

"No!"

His fathomless eyes scared her the most, telling the tale of a man with nothing left to lose. He moved toward her.

"You can either stay here and suffer the consequences of your decision to ruin your lives—and it'll be painful, Mara, trust me, they'll make you beg them to let you die—or you can come with me and strike back at them for what they've done to you. Your choice."

She couldn't breathe again. This crazy stuff only happened in bad horror flicks.

The dark man turned aside. He ejected the clip from his pistol, caught it and pocketed it in his jacket, and replaced it with another one. He picked up his dropped pistol and shoved both into his jacket.

"Decide, Mara."

No. She couldn't move, couldn't think. *No. Not fair. Poppa...*

"He would have taken you, and they would have used you up until there was nothing left. I'm giving you a choice. Come with me and live and fight, or stay and die."

She whimpered. "No."

He pulled something out of his jacket and crouched in front of her father. She couldn't see what his hands were doing. He turned his head toward her and sighed.

"Go get your father's truck keys and bring them to me.

Now."

She staggered out of her bedroom and hurried down the hallway. She had no reason to trust him, but something in his voice and eyes compelled her, was impossible to refuse. This wasn't happening. Her father wasn't dead. It was just a bad dream, like her mother tumbling down the stairs.

Mara sobbed and stumbled into the kitchen. She snagged her father's keys off the hook on the wall and hurried back down the hallway. The dark man stopped her in front of her bedroom and snatched the keys out of her hands.

"Go, girl. Move it."

"I have to get some of my stuff and—"

"There's no time, Mara."

She hesitated, scowling. "What were you doing in there while I got the keys?"

He spun her around. "Go, Mara!"

"Why are we taking Poppa's truck? You couldn't have walked here." She suddenly understood the farm's isolation, despite the fact that gossip traveled faster than a neck-snapping jolt out of a nightmare.

"They may have sabotaged my ride, or be waiting for us there," he said, propelling her down the hallway. They raced into the garage and jumped into her father's Ford. The dark man jammed the key in the ignition and twisted it. Mara hit the door button on the remote mounted on the visor, glowering at him.

The pickup rumbled to life, and the dark man threw it into reverse and mashed the accelerator. The tires spun and squealed as he backed out. The bottom edge of the rising door scraped against the roof of the cab, and the passenger side mirror tore off against the garage doorframe as they cleared it. Mara shrieked, and the dark man spun them around in a one-eighty in the gravel driveway.

Thirty seconds later he pulled out past the gates of the Fleming farm and onto the dusty road and floored it. The pickup backfired and belched a cloud of smoke out of the exhaust as they sped away.

Mara felt like she was outside her body, and knew she was in shock. Ten seconds later, she heard a muffled *whump* over the roar of the engine. She looked back and saw billowing clouds of smoke and flying, flaming debris. She turned and glared at him.

"You blew up my house! That was my home, asshole!"

He glanced at her, then back at the road. "Sorry, Mara. Had to burn the evidence."

So that's what he did while she got her father's keys. "Who *are* you?"

"Somebody you can trust."

"Why should I trust you?"

He turned to her and sneered. "Because I just saved your ass."

"Why didn't you save Poppa too?"

"I tried to, dammit."

"Didn't look much like it to me."

"Jesus. You have no idea how lucky you are." He studied the rearview mirrors. He even looked up in the sky, and that was just weird.

"Expecting someone?"

"You'd damn well better hope not, girl."

"You're not very good with people, are you?"

"And you are?"

"Obviously better than you." When were the tears going to come? "Who was that man, and why did he kill Poppa?"

"You'll find out soon enough."

"I wanna know *now*."

"Jesus, kid, cut me some slack. I almost got killed in there too."

"And that's my fault how?"

He looked at her and shook his head. "You were given a friendly warning to keep your ability a secret, Mara. The letter told you the bad people would come for you if they found out about it, and guess what? They found out because you couldn't keep your big mouth shut."

"Damn your stupid letter, and damn you!"

"Too late for that, kid." He frowned and watched the road, the rearview mirror, and the sky again. "Did you burn the letter after you read it, like it said?" He waited while she seethed. "Mara?"

She thought her father might have kept the letter, and hidden it somewhere in the house. If he had, it was gone now. "Where are you taking me?"

"Away from *them*." He glanced at her, and his brow smoothed out. "Some place where you'll be safe. I promise."

She looked back toward home, and the rage boiled over past her shock. She punched him in the arm right where his jacket was split open. "I want Poppa back! And I want my life back!"

"Oww, Mara. Dammit, that hurt. Why'd you do that?" He flexed his arm, shook his hand.

She looked at her fist. His blood was on her knuckles. "Why'd you do this to me?"

"I didn't do anything to you. I'm the one who saved your ass, remember?"

"Yeah, you keep reminding me."

"Look, Mara… I can't give you those things back. But I am taking you to some people who'll… give you a new life. A better life, where you'll be safe, and won't have to hide your ability."

"Yeah? What if I liked the one I had just fine?"

He turned to her, his eyes smoldering. "You liked hiding your talent, Mara? You liked getting beat by your father?"

"He never hit me before, never! He may have seemed mean to you, but he loved me, and I loved him too. You people took that from me. And I never asked to be able to… see things before they happen."

"Yeah, well, welcome to the real world." He opened and

closed his right fist. "It chews you up and spits you out. Lots of people don't get the lives they wish for. Why should you be any different?" He shook his head and sighed. "Why didn't you just do what the letter said?"

"Because Josh and Jonas told everybody that me and Poppa pushed Momma down the stairs and killed her, and that's a lie. So I told them their daddy was gonna die in an accident today."

"Jesus. Do you have any idea what you've done?"

"I messed up, okay? They just made me so mad. I didn't know this was gonna happen."

"So you saw that, but didn't see this?"

"No. Duh. If I did, I wouldn't be riding here with you, running for my life, would I?"

"Huh. Good point. Maybe not."

Tears rolled down her cheeks, and she wiped them away. "So what was happening to that guy on my bed? When he started... flickering?"

"I'll explain later, when we're safe. Or someone will. Look, Mara, I have to ask. Do you... *see* what's going to happen to us?"

"No, but if I did, what makes you think I would tell you?"

"Jesus, kid. I'm not the enemy here."

Mara sighed, reached behind the seat, and pulled out a first aid kit. "Pull over and I'll bandage your arm."

"There's no time. I have to get you as far away from here as fast as possible."

"Yeah, well, you're not gonna be much good to me if you bleed to death."

He looked at his arm and grimaced.

She shook her head. "At least take off your jacket and let me clean and dress it while you drive."

He sighed and carefully removed his jacket, wincing. Mara helped him take it off while he kept one hand on the wheel. He gazed all around them as if he expected aliens to abduct them.

She looked at him in his short-sleeved black tee shirt and gasped at all the scars on his arms. White lines, scratches, burns, and punctures stood out against his dark skin. Was the rest of his body this ravaged? "Oh my God."

He grunted. "God didn't have anything to do with it."

She shook her head and tutted, just like her mother often had. This she could handle. Her mother had taught her how to patch a man up. The scars were scary, but she wasn't afraid of a little blood. She cleaned his wound, concentrating on her task, and talked to stay distracted.

"So, why is your jacket so heavy?"

"Because it's got Kevlar sewed up in it. That's—"

"I know what Kevlar is. Just because I grew up on a farm doesn't mean I'm stupid. We gots the Internets and satellite TV even all the way out here in Nowheresville, Kansas."

He took a deep breath. "Look, Mara, I'm sorry—"

"Be still. Looks like your Kevlar didn't stop that bullet through the armpit. You're luckier than you think. Coupla more inches to the left…" She clucked her tongue.

"Huh?"

She picked up his jacket and showed him the two holes, in and out, four inches apart.

"Whoa."

"Yeah. Be still." She set the jacket down and resumed her task.

He watched the road, the sky.

"So you know my name, dark man," Mara said. "What's yours?"

"That information is given out on a need-to-know basis. And right now, you don't need to know."

She pressed her cloth against his wound, and he gasped. "Hey!"

"Don't be such a baby. What's your name?"

He alternated his gaze between her, his arm, and the road. "Cody. Jackson. Not that it matters."

She'd heard "sea-jay" when her father's killer had addressed him. Now she knew it was his initials. She nodded. "Well, maybe it doesn't. But if you've been telling me the truth, then thank you for saving me, Cody Jackson."

He grunted. "You're welcome."

She finished dressing his wound. "You're gonna need to get that sewed up."

"It'll have to wait." He looked at her work and flexed his fingers. "Good job. Thank you, Mara."

"You're welcome." She curled up against the door, wrapped her arms around her shins, and let the tears come. Cody left her to her grief.

She missed her mother. It wasn't Mara's fault that she couldn't control what she foresaw and what she didn't. Her mother had understood her talent, and had called it a gift. Her father had too, until her mother died and the music stopped playing in his heart.

After that, Mara's gift had become a curse in his eyes.

Now everyone would think she was a killer and a freak, and there was nothing she could do about it. But she would have done anything, would have given her own life to prevent her mother from tumbling down those steps and breaking her neck, if only she'd seen it. She would have saved her father, too, but she hadn't seen that either. It was *so* not fair.

She eventually cried herself to sleep.

When she woke, it was twilight. Cody looked eternal, like a statue, his eyes dark, intent. At the same time, he looked like he could just melt into the landscape, as if he wasn't even there.

Mara yawned and stretched, and groaned when it all came back to her. She barely glimpsed the sign welcoming them to Oklahoma as they passed it in the encroaching darkness.

"I don't think we're in Kansas anymore, Cody."

Cody chuckled humorlessly. He glanced at her, then back to the road.

"Damn straight."

Chapter 4

May – Bowling Green, Kentucky

Kaylee Daley smiled, the secret hers for the moment. Her parents always said God meant for us to share the love we have, so why not share the gifts too?

Well, what her mother and father didn't know couldn't hurt them. Could it?

Besides, ever since Kaylee had started sharing her gift, Daley's Delights Floral and Gardening Specialties had blossomed. They couldn't stock the shop fast enough to satisfy their happy customers, and her parents were cheerfully running themselves ragged trying to.

At least so far, they hadn't yet attributed their success to Kaylee's special talent. They would be so all up in her grill if they made the connection. And if they figured out what she was doing, then others who must not discover her secret might also.

Last week, after they tallied up their substantial earnings, her mother had said, "I just can't believe how good God's been to us this year."

"Spring is in the air!" Kaylee had twittered, hoping they wouldn't ask any tough questions.

Friday afternoon in late May, just before closing time, Kaylee sat at the front counter beside the cash register. She was admiring the bouquet she'd specially prepared for Ms. Kennedy, inhaling the sweet fragrance, when Tom Grainger walked in. He grinned, gripping two stuffed plastic bags in his hands.

"Hey, Mr. Grainger," Kaylee said, smiling.

"Hey, sweetheart. I told you to call me Pops. Everybody does."

"Whatcha got?"

Grainger plopped the bags on the counter and chuckled. "Best dadgum produce I ever growed, honey. And that's saying something, 'cause I been around a awful long time."

"Oh." Kaylee's smile faltered. *Oops.* She glanced toward the back of the shop. Had her parents heard the bells on the door jangle when he entered?

"Yep," Grainger said. "All my years, ain't never seen the like. Still can't believe it. Take a gander at this, young lady." He chortled and pulled a couple of bell peppers out of one bag, a pair of tomatoes out of the other. "Whaddaya think of them apples?"

"Wow."

"Yessiree, Bob. You betcha. And wait till you taste 'em."

God, please don't let Mom and Dad come up and see this. She had to run Mr. Grainger off and hide the evidence.

"And you oughta see my squash." He pulled one out of the bag. "Look at that. Have you ever… what's wrong, girl?"

"Umm… nothing. It's epic. Stellar." Kaylee swallowed a lump in her throat. The produce even *smelled* delicious.

Holy crap, if Dad sees this, he's gonna know, and shit liquid fire. And rake me over the coals.

Ken and Darlene Daley took that precise moment to pop out of the back.

"Tom!" Ken said, smiling. He took off his gloves and offered his hand. "Good to see you. How is every little thing?"

"Hey, Pops," Darlene said. "How's crops?"

"Things couldn't be better." Grainger shook Ken's hand. "Darlene, you're looking as pretty as ever. And your little girl, well, she's all growed up now, seventeen and probably breaking every young man's heart in Hawkins County. She's the spittin' image of ya, praise the Lord."

Darlene blushed. "Sweet talker. Are you angling for a discount on fertilizer?"

Grainger laughed. "No, ma'am. But if I was twenty-five years younger and we weren't both already married..." He beamed and showed them his prizes before Kaylee could hide them.

Kaylee avoided her parents' eyes. How was she going to talk her way out of this?

Grainger proudly displayed his yield. "Y'all ever seen anything like this?"

"Wow." Ken hefted a tomato in one hand, a pepper in the other. Kaylee felt his gaze burn into her skull. "Amazing."

"Yeah," Darlene muttered. "Unbelievable." Her amazement was directed at Kaylee, who felt daggers piercing her.

Dammit!

"Ayuh." Grainger nodded. "And just wait till you take a bite of them tomatoes. You won't even care about the juice dribblin' down your chin, they're so tasty."

"I'll just bet." Ken glared at Kaylee, and offered the produce back to Grainger.

"Oh, no. These are for y'all. I can't pluck 'em off the vines fast enough."

Kaylee wanted to disappear, but her talent didn't include that slick trick.

"Well, thank you kindly, Tom," Ken said. "Guess we'll be having stuffed bell peppers and sautéed squash-n-onions for dinner tonight. I'm sure Kaylee will be happy to rustle up our grub, too. Won't you, Kaylee?"

"I guess." *I'm screwed. Thanks, Mr. Grainger.*

"Yeah, and just you wait," Grainger said. "You won't believe how tasty they are."

"I don't doubt it for a second," Darlene said. "How'd you get 'em to grow like that, hon?"

"Aw, hell, it wasn't nothin' *I* did. More like your magic fertilizer, I reckon."

"Yeah, right," Ken muttered. Kaylee was melting under his glare.

"Nothing magic about our fertilizer, Tom," Darlene twittered, her voice quavering.

It was stifling in here. Kaylee and her parents were sweating. Grainger smiled and winked.

"Well then, it must be Kaylee's magic touch that did it, 'cause I didn't do nothin' different than what I always done."

Kaylee grimaced, and her parents tensed.

Ken snorted. "That's ridiculous."

Darlene forced a laugh. "Magic touch. That's just silly."

"Think what you will, but I'm convinced of it ever since she came over three weeks ago." Grainger winked at Kaylee.

Kaylee closed her eyes. *Isn't it your naptime, Pops?* "I don't know what gave you that crazy idea, Mr. Grainger."

"Don't you worry none, sweetie." Grainger touched her arm. "I won't tell a soul. It'll be our little secret."

It was a furnace in here. A cauldron.

The phone rang. Kaylee grabbed it after the first ring, but Ken snatched it out of her hand.

"Well, I'll get out of your hair now," Grainger said, nodding. "You folks have a nice evening."

"Thanks again, Tom," Darlene said, waving. Kaylee noticed her hand shook. Darlene clenched her other hand into a fist.

Ken nodded at Grainger. "Good afternoon, Daley's Delights."

Grainger finally left, and Darlene turned to Kaylee, frowning with her arms crossed.

"How are you, Ms. Campbell?" Ken said. Kaylee heard his voice quaver, and couldn't look in his eyes anymore. He never got this angry. She couldn't help but notice that he looked frightened too.

"Yes, ma'am. I'm *delighted* you're so happy with your rose garden." Ken grimaced. "Yes, ma'am. It is amazing they're blooming so fast, and in such dry weather." He nodded. "Well, I have a feeling it's going to be an especially green summer."

Darlene sighed, her shoulders slumping. Ken winced.

"No ma'am, we didn't put anything special in our fertilizer. I reckon you just have one heck of a green thumb." Ken looked like he was about to cry. "Oh, she did, did she?" He looked first at Darlene, then Kaylee. "Well, yes ma'am, Kaylee's always had a special touch with flowers. Especially roses. Yes, ma'am, you're very welcome. I'll be sure and tell her. You have a blessed weekend too, Ms. Campbell." He set the receiver down softly, closed his eyes, and shook his head. Gripping the edge of the counter, his knuckles turning white, he glared at Kaylee again.

"*Kathryn Leeann Daley,*" Darlene said, squinting.

"I didn't *tell* 'em anything, Mom. I just… touched their stuff, and whispered to it. They can't know."

Tears rolled out of Darlene's eyes, breaking Kaylee's heart.

Ken groaned. "Kaylee, how long?"

"Dad—"

"How long?"

Kaylee slumped. "Only a couple months, Daddy, but nobody really knows, I swear it."

"Apparently Tom knows. 'Magic touch'? And Ms. Campbell? You may as well have painted it on a billboard."

"Oh, Kaylee," Darlene whispered.

"I'm sorry!" She couldn't stand to be the cause of their pain. They had done so much to make her happy.

"Kaylee, honey, the letter was very explicit," Ken said, his voice husky. "It was meant for your protection. And you're practically advertising your talent to the whole county."

Kaylee's tears burned her eyes. "You always said before that my gift was meant to share. Now all of a sudden I'm supposed to—"

"You were supposed to exercise some personal restraint." Ken huffed. "How much clearer could the letter have been, Kaylee? It said they would stop at nothing if they found out."

Kaylee pouted. "They? Who are 'they' anyway, Dad? How do we know for sure any of it's even *real*?"

Ken smacked his palms against the counter. "The very fact of its existence means it has to be real, Kaylee. Somebody had to know about you to write the letter in the first place. How many times have we gone over this?"

"Every single day for the last two months, ever since that stupid letter came in the mail." Kaylee couldn't stop the tears rolling down her cheeks.

"Dammit, Kaylee."

"Ken," Darlene said, putting her trembling hands on Ken's arms. "It's too late to put the genie back in the bottle now, baby."

Ken sighed and nodded. "All right. We have to think this through." He turned to Kaylee. "Okay. If Ms. Campbell knows, or even suspects, then no doubt half the state of Kentucky knows by now, or will by dinnertime."

"She's a nice lady, but that woman couldn't keep her mouth shut about this if her life depended on it," Darlene said.

"Right. Which means we have to assume the worst." Ken closed his eyes, took a deep breath. "Kaylee, get the bags Pops brought and ride your bike home, and don't stop for anything. Get dinner started. Your Mom and I'll close up. We'll be home in twenty minutes, thirty tops. Then we'll figure out what we're gonna do."

Kaylee grabbed the bags of produce and bolted. She needed to get away from the tension and paranoia, even if only for a short while. She left, silently screaming, *It's not fair, not fair!*

"Be careful, honey!" Darlene shouted after her. "And lock the doors when you get home, and don't answer if anybody knocks or calls. We love you!"

"So much," Ken croaked, but Kaylee barely heard him.

Outside the shop, she stuffed the ridiculously oversized

produce in her backpack and jumped on her bike. She hurried home, letting the artificial breeze blow the tears off her face. She wasn't sure if she believed what the stupid letter said would happen if she publicly revealed her talent, but she glanced over her shoulder on the way home as if slavering hellhounds were hot on her tail, ready to rip her to shreds.

When she got home, she threw her backpack on the counter. She considered leaving the door unlocked in defiance of her mother's wishes, but a nagging fear that the letter's warning was true made her turn and lock it.

"Stupid damn letter. Ms. Motormouth Campbell is the biggest gossip in the southeast, but there's no way anybody could find out about it this quick."

She washed her hands, then the bell peppers, squash, and tomatoes, and set them on the countertop. She got some ground beef out of the fridge.

No snarling demons with razor-sharp talons leaped out at her.

"Mom, Dad, you are *so* way overreacting!"

She went into the pantry to get the rice and a couple of onions. The boogeyman wasn't hiding in there, waiting to pounce on her and take her to some hellacious place where they would torture her and try to squeeze her talent out of her for some sinister agenda.

Her nerves were already frayed, and it just made her angrier.

She crouched, opened the cabinet beside the dishwasher, and pulled out a baking pan and the skillet. No slithering tentacles with poisonous serrated spikes reached out and clamped around her arms.

She tossed the pan and skillet on the counter, and listened to them clang in the empty house. Her brown-and-orange-striped tabby, Tigger, wandered in. He meowed and looked up at her as if complaining about the commotion.

He didn't transform into a vicious Bengal tiger, didn't

gore her with metamorphosing claws. He rubbed against her legs, and she picked him up, cooed at him, and stroked his soft fur.

The phone rang, and Kaylee screeched. Tigger's claws raked across her forearm, drawing bloody furrows as he flew out of her arms. He sprang out of the kitchen with an angry *mwrowr!*

"Dammit!" She was angry at herself, not Tigger. She grabbed some paper towels, pressed them against her arm, and went to the kitchen phone as it rang again.

Her mother had said not to answer it or the door.

Kaylee sneered, her heart thumping. "God, this is freaking ridiculous."

The caller ID display read *S. Daniels*. Probably Robbie. Her parents didn't like him. She answered the phone out of defiance.

"What do you want, Robbie?" It was important to pretend like he was annoying her.

"Hey, Kaylee. What're you doing?"

"Mopping up the blood where my stupid cat just scratched me." The pity ploy was always good too.

"Ouch. How bad is it?"

"Hurts like hell. Bleeding all over the place. What do you want?"

"Well, I was wondering—"

Someone yelled in the background over the line. She looked out the window. When were Mom and Dad coming home? "What, Robbie?"

Robbie sighed. "Mom wants to know if you'll come over and look at her stupid plants tomorrow morning." Another shout, another sigh from Robbie. "She said she'll pay you. What the hell have you been telling everybody, Kaylee?"

"I didn't tell anybody anything."

"Yeah? Well, everybody seems to think you're like some plant fertility goddess all of a sudden. What did you do?"

Damn! Somebody blabbered. "Is that all you called me for?"

"Well, no. I was wondering if you wanted to go hang out at the lake with me tomorrow after you get off work."

"Robbie, there is no way my parents are gonna let me go out with you. You know that." *Especially now, because of the stupid letter.*

"That's cool. Carla can pick you up, and you can tell 'em you're going to a movie, then we can hang out together. They don't have to know."

"I doubt they'll even let me come over in the morning before work. They're all, like, paranoid all of a sudden." She scowled. They especially wouldn't let her go if they knew what Robbie's mother wanted. Maybe she would go over there any-way, because this letter bullshit was starting to piss her off.

But she was getting worried too. Her parents should have been home by now, and ragging on her for using her damn talent.

"Well…" Robbie sounded desperate. "Will you at least think about it?"

Teasing boys was sweet. It made the misery she was going through a little more bearable. "All right. But that's all I can promise."

"Okay. So I'll talk to you tomorrow?"

"Yeah." *If they don't ground me forever when they get home. Or if the boogeyman doesn't get me first.*

They hung up, and Kaylee went into the bathroom and cleaned and patched up her arm. No extraterrestrial lizard monster was hiding in there, waiting to bite her head off.

She hurried back into the kitchen and watched out the window while she started dinner. Maybe the shop had some late customers. That's all it was. The letter was a prank, some overgrown kids having a little fun at her expense. If she found out who it was, she'd make them pay.

Thirty minutes later, dinner was almost ready, her

parents still weren't home, and it was getting dark outside. Kaylee eyed the phone. They should have called by now.

She dashed toward the phone and snagged it, her hands shaking, certain that if she didn't call them *right now* it would be too late, and a giant ungodly worm would devour them all. She stopped before she punched the speed-dial number.

No dial tone. She randomly punched buttons, a scream building up inside her. She'd just spoken to Robbie. A line had to be down somewhere. Some Department of Transportation idiot screwed up and cut into a cable. That's all it was.

She screeched and dropped the phone when she heard a car engine outside.

"Thank God, finally!" She ran to the door, twisted the lock, threw the door open, and ran outside.

The van from the Presbyterian church was parked in the driveway. Reverend Thatcher hopped out of the passenger side, a somber look on his face. Darrel Clayton, the owner of the hardware store, stepped out of the driver's side. He didn't meet Kaylee's eyes.

Parasitic aliens gnawed on her insides, trying to eat their way out.

"Where's Mom and Dad?" She ran toward Reverend Thatcher. His eyes told a terrible tale, and she stopped a few feet from him, her heart about to explode.

"Oh, Kaylee, I'm so sorry," the Reverend said.

"No!"

Reverend Thatcher shook his head. "They never stood a chance. The fire was just too—"

"No! They can't be dead! I was just with them—"

"They're in God's loving arms now, Kaylee."

"So hot. So incredibly hot," Mr. Clayton rasped, tears spilling from his eyes. "We tried, but nobody could save them. *Pfft*, and it was gone, just like that."

Kaylee crumpled to her knees, finally noticing the pall of smoke drifting over the hillside, coming from town. With the light breeze came a whiff of burnt wood and plastic, and she realized everything the letter said was true.

She heard a sound like a hammer striking a melon, and Reverend Thatcher lurched forward and smacked face first into the dirt in front of her.

"Holy—" Mr. Clayton started, and Kaylee heard the thwacked melon sound again. Clayton jerked, fell against the van's hood, and slid down to the ground.

Kaylee looked up, trying to see through her tears and a thick fluid that ran down her face. A figure stood behind the van, pointing something. His teeth glimmered in the gloom as he leered at her.

It was the boogeyman.

She crawled backward and scrambled to her feet. The ground seemed to give way beneath her, and her licorice-stick legs almost betrayed her as she whimpered and stumbled toward the house.

She looked back over her shoulder when she reached the front door. The boogeyman grinned at her.

"Boo."

She shrieked, and he laughed and sauntered toward her as if he had more than the weekend to kill and wanted to taste her terror buffet-style.

She bolted inside and slammed the door shut, her heart hammering. She fumbled the doorknob, her hands slipping on it. The dark fluid on her hands was blood, and something else.

Reverend Thatcher's brains.

She twisted the lock and turned and staggered toward the hallway, wheezing. Glass shattered, and she looked over her shoulder as she ran down the hall. A hand reached through the front door's broken pane and turned the lock…

…and she crashed into a wall of black leather and dark unyielding flesh. A brown-skinned hand clamped over her mouth before she could scream.

"Shh! Kaylee, you gotta come with me."

His pupils and irises were black, fathomless, but something glinted in his eyes that spoke of salvation and made her want to trust him. Praying this dark man wasn't going to kill her, Kaylee looked back down the hall.

The front door was open.

The dark man tossed a cylindrical object down the hall toward the front door, grabbed her arm and jerked her into her bedroom, and slammed the door shut behind them.

"Kaylee, get down!"

He pulled her to the floor, and something exploded and blew her bedroom door off its hinges. The dark man flicked his right wrist and a pistol sprang out of his sleeve into his hand.

"Motherfucker!" somebody screamed from the hall. There was a popping sound, and another, and wood chips flew from her doorframe.

"You're not getting this one, CJ," the voice from the hall said with a strangled laugh.

The dark man stuck his arm out into the hall. His pistol boomed once, twice, three times, spitting flames. The boogeyman in the hall gagged, a horrible gurgling sound, and Kaylee heard two more pops. More wood splintered off her doorframe.

The dark man fired his weapon twice more, its reports deafening. He took a step into the hall and fired two more times. He turned to her, his black eyes gleaming.

"You have to come with me now, Kaylee. They'll be coming."

"No," she whimpered. Mom and Dad couldn't be dead. This was all a bad nightmare. She just had to wake up.

He dragged her down the hall to the back door, and she stumbled beside him. He threw open the door, practically carrying her. She could no longer resist. Her limbs didn't respond to her commands.

He pulled her outside and thrust her into the passenger seat of an older model black Camaro, shut the door, vaulted over the hood, and hopped into the driver's seat. He twisted the key in the ignition, and the beast rumbled to life.

"Why did you disobey the letter, Kaylee?"

"I didn't know! How could I know it was all true?" *Wake up, dammit, wake up!*

He peeled out of the back yard and sped down the street, away from town. The black beast growled, its powerful engine pushing her into the seat as its tires screeched against the pavement.

"Mom! Dad!

"I'm sorry, Kaylee. It's too late for them, but it's not too late to save you."

"No!"

"You should have done what the letter said!" he shouted over the engine's roar. His words echoed in her mind, *the letter, the letter, the letter...*

"Where are you taking me?"

"Somewhere safe."

"My parents—"

"Your parents are dead because you disobeyed the letter."

"No! This is just a nightmare. I just have to wake up."

"I'm sorry, Kaylee, but it's not."

"How do you know my name? Who are you? What are you?"

"I'm a friend."

"You're the boogeyman!"

"Hey, if that's what you wanna call me."

Tears poured from her eyes as the Camaro sped away into the darkening twilight, away from everything she knew and loved. They raced down the road, and she heard a faint *whupping* sound. It grew louder with each second.

"What's that noise?"

"Shit!" The dark man pounded his fist against the steering wheel, and fastened his seat belt. "Better strap in,

Kaylee. I got a really bad feeling about this."

"What's happening?" She clicked her seat belt and pulled it tight. The *whupping* sound battled with the noise of the Camaro's engine.

"They found us. Hang on. Ride's gonna get bumpy."

"Who found us? What's going on? Tell me!"

She heard several *pocking* sounds, like someone striking metal with a hammer, and the Camaro's rear tires blew out. The dark man growled, trying to keep the vehicle under control, but it slid sideways. The noise was deafening, and Kaylee screamed.

"Hang on, hang on!" the dark man shouted.

Her world was a sudden roller coaster ride, and she was jerked around hard in her seat. The Camaro rolled three times, twisted, and flipped end over end. Metal shrieked and glass shattered as the front bumper slammed into the pavement, and they ended up sliding across the asphalt backward on the driver's side. The car finally stopped moving and rolled over onto its top in the dirt of the roadside.

Disoriented and badly shaken, Kaylee tried to regain her wits. Her body hung upside down, still in her seat, held tight by her seat belt. She felt mauled, and smelled gasoline and smoke. The *whupping* sound grew louder as metal creaked and ticked.

She coughed and looked at the dark man. He wasn't moving. His body hung limp upside down beside her.

With a sudden *whump*, flames spat out of the wreckage of the hood. She screamed, and reached over to the dark man and shook him.

"Wake up, wake up!"

He coughed, shook his head, and groaned. Blood dripped from a gash on his forehead.

"Mister, wake up! We're on fire!"

He opened his eyes and turned his head toward her, groggy and bleary-eyed. "Kaylee... get out. Of here. Hurry."

"Why?" She tried to help him as he fumbled at his seat

belt.

"I'm sorry, Kaylee. So sorry."

"Who *are* you?"

"Get out. Run."

They finally unhooked his seat belt, and he fell against the roof and grunted. He reached toward her, and something infinitely strange happened to her.

She *shimmered*, and shrieked. "What's happening to me?"

He grappled at her, his arms flailing, trying to help her undo her seat belt. "No! Kaylee!"

Everything went dark on her, and her world turned upside down like her body.

She felt like she was going to vomit. There was a blinding flash, and when she could see again, she rested against hard metal, her body swaying as if gravity no longer tethered her to the Earth. She groaned and gazed blearily at her surroundings. The *whupping* sound was deafening.

When she regained her senses, she realized she was in a helicopter, of all things, and she almost hurled. A little Asian boy of about eleven lay beside her, his face drenched in sweat. He looked like he was about to hurl too.

"What happened?" She gasped and retched, and the little boy did too. He looked at her, his eyes full of misery.

"I teleported you," he said.

"What?" *Not possible. That's science fiction stuff. This is just a nightmare.*

"I'm sorry." The boy gagged, clearly in pain. "They… made me do it."

She sat up and shook her head. A sledgehammer pounded the inside of her skull. She could barely hear herself think, and felt faint, sick, confused. A pretty Asian woman sat in a seat in front of her and the boy. The woman gazed down, studying them as if they were mice running panicked in a maze.

The little boy started crying, wrapped his arm around his

head, and stuck his thumb in his mouth and sucked on it. Kaylee looked out of the window and watched the wrecked Camaro recede below her as they rose. Flames and smoke belched out of the undercarriage.

A figure struggled out of the driver's side of the Camaro. It was the dark man, her failed rescuer. He crawled away from the car and gazed upward at her new ride.

"No!" She screamed, feeling her guts wanting to spew out. Her parents were dead. Everything was wrong, all wrong.

The nightmare was real.

The Camaro exploded right as the dark man rolled into the roadside ditch.

Kaylee screamed again.

Chapter 5

August – Helen, Georgia

Jazz reached over and touched Chaz, just to make sure he was still there. Even though she could see him, she wanted to feel him, smell the sweet scent of his innocent youth in the light sweat beading on his brow. Dante eased forward across the comforter on Chaz's bed and licked her fingers. Her hands shook as she read the letter again.

Dear Ms. Tandy and Chaz,

Hi. My name is Amanda. I can't tell you my last name. You'll understand why soon. I'm fifteen years old. I have a special ability too, like Chaz. I can do something amazing that would make some people want to take advantage of me and use me for their own gain if they knew about it. My new friends told me I can't tell you what it is. I can only say that it is both wonderful and scary, just like I'm sure Chaz's ability is for both of you.

It's wonderful because my new friends who are protecting me and keeping me safe help me use it to do good things and help people.

It's scary because there are some very bad people in this world who want to kidnap me and make me use it for some very bad things. They would make me use it to hurt good people, and to make the bad people richer and more powerful. They are already very rich and very powerful, and very dangerous.

If they kidnapped Chaz, they would use him to heal their people who kidnap children like us so they could hurt more people and kidnap more children like us.

The bad people who steal children like me and Chaz and some of my friends here are called Extractors. I can't tell you where here is, because my new friends are protecting me and all my friends like me and Chaz from the bad people.

One of the Extractors tried to kidnap me, and murdered my mother and father.

It still makes me very sad, but it makes me very angry too. I am angry at the bad people for what they did to my family, and for what they do to other families like yours and mine. I still miss and love my parents very much, even though they have been dead for three years.

The reason I am able to write you this letter is because a very special kind of friend saved me from the Extractor who murdered my parents and tried to kidnap me.

The special people who save us are called Guardians, and they are our friends.

The Guardians watch over us, but they don't show themselves unless the bad people find out about us. They leave us alone to live our lives, and protect us from the bad people. They try to keep the bad people from finding out about our special abilities. With the help of my friends here, they also try to find more children like me and Chaz so they can protect them too.

But it is <u>very</u> important for you and Chaz to understand that it is <u>your</u> responsibility to keep the bad people from finding out about him.

The Extractors and the bad people are <u>ruthless</u> and <u>merciless</u> (my friends told me that these are the right words), and they will stop at <u>nothing</u> to take Chaz away from you forever and use him for their own purposes.

If they take Chaz away from you, they will probably kill you. If they don't, you will wish you were dead, because they'll make sure that you <u>never</u> see Chaz again. If they steal Chaz, whether they kill you or not, they will use him up until he wishes he was dead too, or until his heart can no longer take it.

I am very sorry about his heart condition. Sometimes life just doesn't seem fair, does it? It often seems like God punishes the good people, and rewards the bad people.

I am not saying all this to scare you. I am saying it because it is the <u>truth</u>. If you don't believe me, then ask yourself, how do I know what Chaz can do?

I am very sorry to tell you these terrible things, but my new friends told me that I <u>must</u>. Please try to understand that it is for your and Chaz's own safety. Do anything and everything you can to protect Chaz, and don't let <u>anyone</u> find out about his special ability.

The Guardians are only human, like all of us, except that they don't all have special powers like me and Chaz, and they can only do so much to protect us. I don't know if the Extractors are human or not, but I <u>do</u> know that they are heartless killers.

If you have a gun, keep it with you always, and be prepared to use it. If you don't have a gun, get one and learn how to use it.

If you see an Extractor, <u>kill</u> them. You will know them if you see them, because they are not like us. They don't have any feelings, and they don't care if you live or die. They only want Chaz. If you do not kill them, they will certainly kill you, and take Chaz.

I want you to understand that there is good news too. The people who are taking care of me and protecting me and my friends are very kind and generous. They are helping me learn how to use my power for good things, and they <u>never</u> ask me to use it to hurt people. They have given me a good life after the bad people stole it away. They helped me write this letter, but it's mostly my words, and they are home-schooling me since I can't go to a normal school anymore. Even though I'm sad because my parents are dead, I am not lonely. I have made many good friends here.

They are my new family.

Finally and most important, the reason they don't want to take you and Chaz and bring you here is that unlike the bad people, they understand that your life is <u>yours</u> and belongs to <u>you</u>, and that no one should ever try to steal it from you.

I hope that God and the Guardians keep you safe and happy, and that you are able to keep helping Chaz do good and wonderful things.

If the bad people find out about Chaz, I hope that the Guardians can save you both and bring you here to live with us. I would very much like to meet Chaz and you, and I'm sure that we would be good friends.

It is very important that you destroy this letter after you have read it. Burn it! If the bad people find out about it, your lives will be over. I don't want that to happen, and I'm sure you don't want it to happen either. Please protect Chaz and keep him safe and happy.

Beware of Soulsnatcher and his hunters. God bless you both.

Your New Friend,
Amanda

After Jazz read the letter a third time, she held Chaz for a while and quietly cried tears that burned away the good life she thought they had. Dante watched her, whining softly with a soulful look in his eyes. When she was done with the tears, she left Chaz and Dante and went to her bedroom and let the fury come.

It came with a vengeance.

Her ex-husband Jack left her and Chaz four years ago, when Jazz had turned twenty-eight and Chaz celebrated his fifth birthday. Consequently, Jack missed the discovery of Chaz's gift a year later.

Six months after he left, Jack had surprised his abandoned family with an unannounced visit. He'd shown up drunk and angry, and in the kitchen right in front of Chaz, Jack had cursed the day their son was born. He'd also made out-rageous demands of Jazz.

"Dammit, Jasmine, when are you gonna grow the hell up and realize you're not capable of raising a child in his con-dition?" He was in her face, his fists clenched and a mad look in his eyes. Jazz thought he was going to hit her, and do God knows what with Chaz.

That finished it between them for Jazz, but then Jack dropped the bomb.

"Jazz, when are you going to see that you belong with me and he doesn't belong with us?" His voice suddenly oozed with what he probably believed was sincerity and indisputable logic. "Baby, if you'll just turn him over to the state's care, we can be together again. They'll take much better care of him than you ever can. I'm sorry, but you know it's the truth. State of the art medical technology—"

"Get out." Jazz felt the first spark of the fury then.

"Baby, think about what's best for Chaz instead of you for once."

"Get. The fuck. Out. *Now.*" Jazz scowled and clenched her fists.

He punched her in the nose, apparently giving in to a monster that had dwelled beneath the surface for some time. The blow knocked Jazz to the floor, and Jack stood over her, tense and breathing hard.

Jazz kicked him in the groin so hard it bruised her heel

and left her hobbling on it for a week. He recovered moments later, and howled and sprang at her. She hit him in the head with a stainless steel, two-quart saucepan.

She called the police, debating how sorry she wanted to make him, but he took off like a Great Dane at the crack of the starting pistol. She got a restraining order against him a few days later, but the fury told her that wasn't enough.

When Chaz had said, "Mother, he scares me now. I don't want him to hurt you anymore," she bought a gun, and learned how to handle and fire it. If Jack threatened them again, she was fully prepared to kill him if she had to. They hadn't seen or heard from him since.

After that, it seemed like she and Chaz stayed on the run, moving from place to place every time their secret leaked out.

Jazz was through with running and hiding.

She undressed and took a quick shower, then dressed in jeans, a denim shirt, and a pair of running shoes.

Her mind whirled with the implications of the letter. She went to her walk-in closet and retrieved her Glock 17C nine-millimeter semiautomatic, holster, a spare magazine, and a box of rounds from a high shelf. She sat on the bed and loaded the pistol and the spare magazine, slipped the pistol into the holster and clipped it to her waistband, thrust the spare magazine in the back pocket of her jeans, and returned to Chaz's bedroom.

She stood in the doorway, watching Chaz and Dante for a minute, trying to steady her racing heart. Dante looked up at her and held her gaze as if demanding an explanation for the sudden change in the air, and she sighed.

The letter lay on the nightstand beside Chaz's bed where she'd left it, refuting her disbelief. It could be someone's idea of a very sick joke.

But she didn't know anyone that imaginative, other than her father and Lloyd, and they didn't have anything to do with this. Jack could never come up with such a tall tale.

As incredible as it was, if the story that the letter told

was real, they were potentially in danger. The incident with Dante had seen to that.

On that cool, late August evening, Jazz thought only of Chaz, and made up her mind. She wasn't taking any chances. She told herself that she wasn't running; she was only regrouping until they could come up with a plan.

She went to Chaz's bed and sat on the mattress beside him, turned the nightstand lamp on to push away the gathering gloom, and gently shook him.

"Chaz, wake up."

He fluttered his eyelids and squinted. "Mother, what? I'm sleepy."

"Get up and take a shower and get dressed in your traveling clothes."

"Where are we going? Are we moving again? I don't wanna."

"No, we're not moving. We're going to visit your grandfather."

Chaz perked up. "Grandpa's! Yeah!" He sat up and rubbed sleep out of his eyes.

"Yes. So go get ready now."

Chaz's brow furrowed. "Why are we going now? It's like *dark*. It'll be *tomorrow* before we get there. And I'm still sleepy from today."

"You can sleep on the way. Consider it a late surprise birthday present."

"That was a week ago, Mother."

"You do wanna go see Grandpa, don't you?"

"Yeah!" Chaz slid his feet over the edge of the mattress, then looked at her and frowned. "Can Dante come with us?"

"Of course Dante's coming with us."

"Yay!" Chaz jumped out of bed.

"Yes, yay. So go get ready now, mister, while I pack your bag."

By the time Chaz showered and dressed, she had a suit-

51

case packed for each of them, with a backpack stuffed full of Dante's food, bowls, a bone, and a couple of toys, all packed up in her Toyota Forerunner.

She pocketed the letter, though it instructed her to burn it. She wanted her father to see it first.

"Come on, honey. Time to go."

Chaz did a little dance, happy about going to see his Grandpa and oblivious to her plan. "C'mon, Dante. Go for a ride?"

Dante recognized the word, and pranced beside Chaz as they entered the hall. They both stopped outside the bedroom door, and Dante barked and growled as they focused on something down the hallway.

"Uhh, Mother, somebody's here."

Chapter 6

Jazz's heart lurched. She drew her pistol and jacked the slide back, chambering a round, then dashed out into the hall. Holding the pistol in both hands, she aimed it down the hall at a dark figure.

It was a man. He stood motionless, his hands at his sides, palms open. Dark skin, short dark leather jacket, dark blue jeans, and scuffed black Rockports. He looked like he could unleash Hell in the blink of an eye.

"Chaz, stay where you are." Jazz advanced toward the dark man, the barrel of her pistol steady on his center mass.

He didn't budge or flinch. He stood watching her while her heart hammered a crack in her sternum.

She tried to avoid his eyes after looking into them. Surrounded by the gleaming whites of his eyes, his dark orbs were penetrating, almost hypnotizing, as if they'd seen things she couldn't imagine. She focused on his chest, her finger gently squeezing the trigger and releasing the internal safeties.

"Give me one good reason why I shouldn't blow your ass away right now," she growled. Her voice sounded steadier than she felt.

The dark man nodded. "Because right now I'm your only hope for keeping Chaz safe and getting *your* ass out of here alive."

Dante stood beside Chaz, tense and growling.

Jazz's trigger finger was relaxed but ready to squeeze. She needed answers, and a way out. She had apparently waited a few minutes too long to leave.

She snorted. "So you say. Why should I trust you?"

The dark man shrugged. "You didn't hear me come in. I could've already killed you and taken Chaz, if that's what I was here for."

Neither she, Chaz, nor Dante had heard a thing before they found him standing in the hall. Jazz smirked. *You failed your duties as our watchdog, Dante.*

"So why are you here?"

"I'm here to help you and Chaz get away from some very bad people."

She thought of the letter in her pocket. "Are you a... Guardian?"

"Yes, and we have to leave. Now."

It was all true, everything the letter said. Somebody had found out about the incident with Chaz and Dante last week. Somebody *ruthless* and *merciless*, according to the letter.

She bit her lip. "How can I believe you?"

"When did you get the letter?"

"I asked you a question, mister."

"You don't have any choice. When did you get the letter?"

Jazz sighed. "Just a couple of hours ago. In today's mail. It's all true, isn't it?"

"I'm afraid so."

Her heart sunk. This wasn't some elaborate joke.

She was going to ask him how did she know he wasn't an Extractor, and was going to kill her later when it was more convenient and he didn't have a deadly weapon aimed at him, but she decided against it. Something in his calm voice and unfathomable eyes made her want to trust him. But she couldn't lower the pistol. She wasn't letting anyone take Chaz.

He sighed. "Look, Jasmine, either shoot me now or let me help you. Your choice. But decide now, because they're coming."

They. He was talking about the bad people the letter warned about. She lowered her pistol and shuddered. "If you hurt Chaz—"

"I'll die before I let Chaz get hurt. Or taken."

She eased her finger off the trigger. "Okay. So what do we do now?"

"We get the hell out of here, pronto, and—"

"Mother, something really weird is happening behind us," Chaz said.

Jazz spun, the dark man crouched and flicked his right wrist forward, and Dante barked and charged toward the back of the hall as if he intended to dive into the mirror mounted on the wall.

Something *shimmered* at the end of the hallway. Jazz aimed her pistol at it, and Dante dove toward the bizarre flickering light as Chaz shouted.

"Dante, wait! No!"

A figure materialized. It was a man. His feral eyes flashed a look of triumph as he drew a pistol out of a shoulder holster. The look turned to alarm when he saw the dog flying straight at him. Dante bit into his wrist, and the man dropped his pistol and cursed as bone crunched.

"Chaz, get down!" Jazz advanced toward the man, her pistol aimed at his chest.

Chaz dove to the floor. The intruder kicked at Dante's belly. Jazz fired, hitting his kneecap, and it splattered blood and bone. Dante growled and tore at his hand, and the man clenched his fist and tried to punch Dante.

Jazz fired again. The bullet ripped through his shoulder, throwing him backward to the floor. Dante let him go and backed up beside Jazz, snarling with fangs bared. The intruder choked out a laugh, and Jazz bore down on him, ready to blow his brains out.

He held up his hand and rasped, "Wait." He looked at the dark man, who advanced toward him beside Jazz, holding a black pistol aimed at his head.

"CJ," the intruder rasped, a grim smile on his face as blood poured out of his shoulder and shattered knee. "We all got a... pool. On you." He coughed. "Whoever gets you first gets—"

The dark man fired, and the intruder's skull shattered behind him in bits and pieces, splattering the floor and walls. Jazz spun toward the dark man and raised her eyebrows. He nodded, saying nothing. She hurried toward Chaz, who was suddenly *flickering*.

"Mother, what's happening to me?"

"Grab Chaz and hold him!" the dark man shouted, and Jazz dove toward Chaz.

There was a whisper of movement at the end of the hallway by the living room, and the dark man spun as a whirlwind attacked. Jazz scooped Chaz up and squeezed him against her pounding chest, her pistol still clutched in her hand. Dante whined and jumped at them.

"Mother," Chaz rasped, squeezing her. He stopped shimmering.

The whirlwind spat fire out of its hands, and two more pistol shots rang out in the cramped hallway. It was another man, moving lightning-quick toward them.

The dark man absorbed the blows of the shots and flicked his left wrist forward as he fired the pistol in his right hand. He staggered, but he stayed between Chaz and Jazz and the new attacker. He fired again with the pistol in his right hand, simultaneously firing the one that appeared in his left hand as the whirlwind fired twice more at him.

The dark man jerked backward, clearly hit, but still stood and fired again from each pistol. One shot blew the new intruder's head apart and spattered the walls with gore. Before Jazz could figure out what was happening, their dark Guardian dashed toward them and grunted.

"Car. Now."

"What?"

"Your SUV. Let's go," he rasped, and something sounded broken inside him. He grabbed Jazz's arm and stumbled as he steered her and Chaz down the hallway toward the living room. Dante was hot on their heels.

"What was *that*?" she asked as they ran. "What was happening to Chaz—?"

"No time. Jesus, two. More will be coming. They want Chaz bad."

Bad*ly*, Jazz thought crazily, struggling to keep her feet while they headed through the living room and into the kitchen toward the garage.

She stumbled, and the dark man pulled her up and bore her along. His hand clenched her arm, still strong despite the fact that he was wheezing and clearly hurt. Jazz kept her fingers wrapped around her pistol and her arms wrapped around Chaz.

"Why?" she asked as they staggered into the garage and headed toward her Forerunner. So many questions…

"Keys!" the dark man shouted.

"In the ignition. Why?"

"Because he's a healer." He helped her buckle Chaz in the back seat. Dante jumped in and sat beside Chaz. "Do you still not know how incredible that is?"

"I didn't think—"

"You didn't have time to, Jazz." He pushed her into the front passenger seat.

"Don't call me that."

He slammed the door on her, hurried around the front bumper, and hopped in the driver's seat and started the engine.

"Only my friends call me that," Jazz said. She looked back at Chaz, worried about his heart. He gazed wide-eyed at them while Dante licked his cheek.

The dark man pushed the garage door remote on the visor, and peeled out of the garage when the door rose.

"And you're not my friend," Jazz added. *Although you did just save our lives back there.*

"Fine with me." The dark man spun the wheel at the end of the driveway, turned onto the road, and floored it.

Jazz saw her next-door neighbors standing out on their

front deck, watching the spectacle. They apparently heard the gunshots and rushed outside to see what had happened.

They had no idea, but she did. Everything the letter said was true. Chaz was in danger. According to Amanda and the dark man, some very bad people wanted Chaz, and *badly*, because he was a healer.

She reached for her cell phone at her waist while the dark man drove. He looked up at the darkening sky, as if expecting more intruders to swoop down on them.

"What are you looking for?"

He glared at her and ground his teeth. "The enemy."

"What, can they *fly* too?"

"Huh. They can do lots more than that."

She fumbled her cell, her hands shaking. She had to call her father. He had to know what was happening, and that they were coming incognito again. She felt the fury rising, and scowled at the stranger driving her car.

"Where are you taking us?"

"Away from here."

"Where?"

He looked out the windows, in the mirrors, up at the sky. "A safe place, Jasmine."

She looked at the pistol in her white-knuckled hand, raised it, and pointed it at him. Her hands trembled, and the barrel shook. She knew she couldn't shoot him. He had just saved their lives.

"No." She took a deep breath. "You're taking us to my father's."

He shook his head and sighed. "Jazz—"

"I told you, don't call me that. Take us to my father now." She put the pistol's barrel to his temple.

He turned his head toward her as they flew down the road. His forehead rested against the barrel of her Glock. She worried that he would drive them into the ditch as he glared at her. Demons and angels waged a war in his strange eyes.

58

"If you're gonna do it, do it," he said, his voice thick with gurgling liquid. "Put me out of my misery. Please."

She stared at him and lowered her pistol.

He looked back at the road and sped off into the darkness. Elsewhere, families were sitting down to dinner, enjoying some precious time together. Here, she and Chaz were running for their lives again, in the hands of an unpredictable stranger.

"Look, Jasmine," he said, and some kind of fire burned in him, something that made her realize he was a haunted soul. "We *can't* go to your father's. He's a target now. Surely you understand that. In fact, you should call him before—"

Her phone vibrated, and she flinched and yelped. She fumbled it, then gazed at the display. It read *S. Steadman*, and she breathed a sigh of relief. It was her father.

She answered the call. "Daddy?"

The voice on the other end was neither Daddy's nor male. It was accented, maybe Chinese, and something slithered beneath its silky purr as it ripped a new hole in her world.

"If you want your father to live, Jazz, you'll bring Chaz now."

Chapter 7

Jazz couldn't breathe. She gaped at the dark man, and he grimaced. The smell of his blood left a metallic taste on her tongue, burning her nostrils. She looked back at Chaz, who quietly petted Dante. Dante's tongue lolled, his eyes closed.

Her voice shook when she spoke. "Who is this?"

"You know who this is, Jazz."

She looked again at the display. The call came from her father's house.

"You bitch, I wanna talk to my father right now."

"Mother!" Chaz started. "You said—"

"Put him on the phone *now*, or I'm hanging up." Jazz's hands shook, and she set the pistol on the seat and clung to her cell.

"It's your choice whether he lives or dies, Jazz," the woman droned, sounding like she was discussing the weather. "His life is in your hands now."

"Fuck you, bitch. Put him on now or we're finished."

"Mother!"

"Fine," the woman said. "So you know he's still alive. For the moment."

Jazz heard her father's voice over the line, and something in it sounded broken but not defeated.

"Jazz, they won't hurt me until they get Chaz. Do whatever you have to to protect him—"

"That's enough," the woman interrupted. "So, Jazz—"

"Only the shadow knows, Jazz!" her father yelled in the background. The phrase was a prearranged code—from previous times when they were hiding from the media—for Jazz and Chaz to stay away.

"Shut him up," the woman snapped. "He's going to pay

for that, Jazz. Maybe we'll cut off his tongue, hmm?"

"You listen to me, you stupid bitch. You better start looking over your shoulder everywhere you go, because I'm gonna find you, on my terms, and when I do, you're going to be *so* sorry."

The woman laughed, making it clear she loved this game. "You have no idea who you're messing with, Jazz. It shouldn't take you more than two hours to get here. If you call the police, your father dies. If you're not here in two hours, your father dies. If you come with anyone else but CJ and Chaz, your father dies. Bring Chaz to me, and all of you will live. And before you go getting any crazy ideas, neither your little pistol nor CJ can save you. You have exactly two hours. Don't dawdle. Ta-ta!"

"You're the one who has no idea who she's messing—" Jazz began, but the line was dead. "Dammit!"

While she'd been on the phone, the dark man had turned down a dirt road. A quarter mile farther, he parked in the grass behind a Ford Mustang.

"What are they going to do to my father?" she asked as he hopped out.

"No telling." The dark man opened the rear door. "He's compromised now. Come on, grab your stuff. Hurry. We have to ditch this ride."

"CJ?" Jazz said. She picked up her pistol, holstered it, and jumped out of the passenger side.

"Don't call me that," he rasped, holding his belly as Dante leaped out.

"Mother, he bled all over your seat." Chaz was staring at the dark wet stains.

"Well, what do you want me to call you? *Dude?*"

"My name is Cody. Not that it matters." He grabbed Jazz's big suitcase, grunting with the effort.

"Mother, his neck's all bloody and half his ear's gone. He's hurt bad."

"Come on, Binky." How many times had Cody been hit in the hallway? There was a *lot* of blood on her front driver's seat. Chaz got out on her side, and she grabbed his bag and the backpack.

"Are we still going to Grandpa's?" Chaz asked.

"Later, sweetie. Grandpa needs us to stay away right now. Get Dante in the back seat of Cody's car."

Chaz groaned. "We're gonna have to move again, aren't we?"

"Chaz, hurry!"

Cody had the Mustang's trunk open and threw Jazz's suitcase in it. Jazz tossed in Chaz's bag and the backpack while Chaz climbed in the back seat. Dante jumped in after him. Cody slammed the trunk shut and staggered toward the driver's side door.

Jazz grabbed his arm. "I'm driving. You're in no condition."

"Huh." He grunted, turned back toward the door, and almost fell as he leaned against it. Sweat dripped down his face. "Not on my shift."

His legs buckled, and Jazz caught him and held him up against the car. "You're crazy if you think I'm letting you drive. You'll kill us all."

"*I'll* kill us all? I'm not the one who let Chaz heal your damn dog in front of God and everybody. You sealed your fate when you did that. You should have let the stupid dog die."

"Fuck you! That wasn't your decision to make."

"Jesus, lady. Whatever. It's too late to go back and change it now. Unless Chaz is a time traveler too, which would be unprecedented." He coughed, spat up some blood. "We gotta get out of here now."

She wanted to slap him for the comment about Dante. Instead, she took his arm and wrapped it over her shoulder, and put her arm around his back and under his armpit. "Come on, let's get you in the passenger seat."

"Fine. But you have to go where I tell you."

"We'll see."

He stopped. "I mean it, Jasmine. Nowhere else is safe for you or Chaz."

Stubborn male. "Fine. We'll go where you say."

"Damn straight," he mumbled, and let her guide him to the passenger side.

She helped him get settled in the seat, and ran around the front and hopped in the driver's seat. Cody glared at her and handed her the keys. She shook her head and started the car, and its powerful engine rumbled.

She spun the wheel and headed back down the dirt road the way they'd come in, the tires kicking up gravel and dust. "So. Cody. What's going to happen to my father?"

"Left out of here. And hurry."

She turned the wheel and kicked it when she got back on the highway, and the Mustang responded with a throaty roar. "What are they going to do to him? Just how ruthless and merciless are these people?"

He frowned and looked away. The look in his haunted eyes told her all she needed to know.

Oh, Daddy!

Chaz and Dante were quiet in the back, both watching Jazz and Cody.

"Did the woman you spoke to have an Asian accent?" Cody's voice was thick.

"Yes. Why?"

"Shit. That's Taja Ling." He mumbled something else under his breath.

"What? What does that mean?"

"It means your father's screwed, Jasmine."

"Damn, Cody. Are you always this charming to everybody? Or did I just catch you on a really bad day?"

"Jesus, lady. I'm just *so* sorry you got stuck with me." He grunted as he shifted in the seat. "And no, this is about as good as it gets. Too bad for you."

She snorted. "Some knight in shining armor you are."

"You aren't exactly an enchanting damsel in distress yourself."

"Mother, is Grandpa in trouble?" Chaz asked.

She looked in the rearview mirror and saw the worry on his face. "I don't know, Binky. We'll talk about it later, okay?"

Chaz slumped, looking like the tears were about to come. "Okay."

Was she ever going to see her father alive again? The combination of shock and adrenaline put her in a zone where emotions seemed alien and inaccessible, and helped her hold the tears and anguish at bay for the moment. That would come later, an inexorable tide that could whisk her away and drown her.

She let the fury override that specter and turned to Cody. "So just what the hell was that with that guy materializing out of thin air into my house?"

"Huh." Cody took a deep breath, and she heard it rattle over the engine's noise. "He was teleported there, by one of the... bad people's little tools."

"Teleported? That's impossible. Science fiction bullshit."

"If you say so."

"Dammit, Cody, is that what they were trying to do with Chaz? *Teleport* him?"

"Damn straight."

"Jesus! What do you mean 'little tools'?"

He glanced at her, and something about the fire in his eyes diminished. "The special talented children they steal. Little tools. Like Chaz." He mumbled something else.

"You mean—"

"Yeah, I mean that every god damn thing the letter said was really true, Jazz. Sorry, *Jasmine*." He struggled and turned toward her. She saw blood on the seat behind and underneath him.

"What did you just say?" Her heart still pounded, and she was overdosing on adrenaline. Her father was in danger. They were all in danger. If the bad people could fly and freaking *teleport* people, they were screwed.

"I said, everything that the letter—"

"No, I mean right before that."

"Oh, that. I said, 'And like me.'" He glared at her, challenging her with his dark eyes.

She was unable to bear his haunted gaze, and turned her eyes back to the road. "So what's your... talent?"

He huffed, coughing up something nasty. Dante barked, and Chaz stuck his head between the front seats and stared at Cody.

"Mother, I think he's like dying or something."

"I should be so lucky, kid," Cody muttered.

"Chaz, don't say that. What can you do, Cody?"

Cody chuckled, a wet miserable sound. "I smell trouble."

"You mean now?" He didn't answer. "Cody?"

He smiled and slumped in the bucket seat. "No, I mean ever since I met *you*."

"Dammit, Cody, what does 'smell trouble' mean?"

Cody shook his head and coughed. Maybe Chaz was right. The bright crimson spray ejected from his mouth looked fatal.

"I mean I smell trouble. Usually right before it happens." His voice was growing weaker. "Not that I can ever... do anything but react to it. Crystal ball's broken, in the shop." He gazed at her and smiled, his eyes unfocused. "They never call back about the status of repairs."

He closed his eyes, and she knew they were losing him, and they couldn't afford that. They needed to know where to go and what to do, and right now only Cody held the secret.

"I think he's like dead or something," Chaz said.

She touched his bloody neck beneath his mangled ear

and felt for a pulse. It was still there, faint but persistent. She drew her hand back, sticky with blood.

"No, he's still hanging in there, Binky."

Cody's eyes snapped open, and he fumbled in a jacket pocket. He drew out an object the size of a flash drive and pressed the only button on it.

"What's that? Self-destruct button?" Jazz's voice quavered.

"Calling for reinforcements," Cody wheezed, offering it to her. "No matter… what happens... to me... keep it."

She reluctantly accepted the object. "Cody—"

He pointed at her and closed his eyes again. "Pocket. Now. Remember… Quintrado."

Jazz put it in her jeans pocket, realizing she'd decided to trust him. She was about to ask why she should remember *Quintrado*, but his head nodded, and he was out again. A part of her wanted to take her frustration out on him, blame him for their predicament. But a larger part understood that he might have given his life for her and Chaz.

You took a bullet for us, maybe several bullets, and still stood and fought for us.

At first she didn't know what to do. Then Chaz spoke.

"Mother, can I… help him a little?"

"Oh, Chaz."

"I still got some. Pinky swear."

She sighed. "Okay, but only a little. Until we can find some help."

"Okay. Are we going to Doctor Lloyd's?" Chaz gently placed his hands on Cody's chest.

She stared at Chaz's reflection in the rearview mirror, her eyebrows raised. She grabbed her cell and punched in a pre-set number.

"Yes, Binky." She waited, cell to her ear. Her heart still hammered. Come on, come on…

Lloyd's wife Tanya answered before it kicked over to

voicemail, and Jazz breathed a sigh of relief and asked for Lloyd. Tanya put him on.

"Jazz? What's wrong?"

Jazz took a deep breath and told him a fantastic and terrifying story.

Chapter 8

When Jazz finished her tale, Lloyd insisted that she bring her crew to his residence. Jazz resisted, not wanting to endanger him or his wife. When he said he would treat Cody's wounds, she realized she didn't have a choice. If Cody didn't get medical attention soon, he would die.

She couldn't let that happen. Cody was the only person with answers to her questions. Chaz's magic touch helped. Cody's breathing evened out afterward, but he was still in bad shape. And Chaz was worn out. He assured Jazz he was okay, and passed out in the back seat.

She had to risk going to Lloyd's. She had no one else to turn to, and no way was she taking Chaz to her father's, no matter what his captors did to him. He would never approve of that. Besides, he had insisted they wouldn't harm him until they had Chaz. She had to believe that.

Lloyd gave her his address and told her to park in the garage. The Mustang had GPS, as well as some other unidentifiable gadgets, and Jazz punched in the address. She told Lloyd she could get there in an hour and a half, and risked getting a speeding ticket on the way.

She felt untethered from the world she'd known, plunged into a nightmare where merciless killers materialized out of thin air, wicked women threatened to kill her father, and some very bad people wanted to kill her and steal her son.

"Oh, Daddy," she whispered, biting her lip. She had an unscheduled future appointment with this Taja Ling. It wouldn't be a friendly visit. Ms. Ling was going to be so very sorry.

Jazz glanced often in the rearview mirrors, wondering if the occasional car behind her bore cold, ruthless men called Extractors. Sometimes, she found herself gazing up in the sky, maybe searching for swooping winged demons.

A grueling hour and fifteen minutes later, she pulled into Lloyd's driveway and open garage. She had no idea if she'd lost Cody on the way. He hadn't moved.

Lloyd and Tanya were waiting in the garage. Beside them was a gurney. Jazz shut off the engine and jumped out and hugged Tanya, then Lloyd. The tears finally started, and they came in a flood. Lloyd squeezed her, his eyes on his wife as Jazz let it all go and cried against his shoulder.

"Jazz, you've been unfairly handed an ominous burden. But God means for you to bear it. This I know."

She nodded, unable to speak. Tanya had wheeled the gurney around to the passenger side, and Lloyd and Jazz rushed over beside her. Together they wrestled Cody out of the car and onto the gurney.

Chaz woke, yawned, and smiled. "Hey, Dr. Lloyd."

"Hello there, my boy." Lloyd smiled back. "That furball beside you must be Dante."

Dante barked, tail wagging as if he knew he was among friends.

"Yeah." Chaz beamed. "He saved our lives."

"I'll bet he did." Lloyd grunted as he assessed Cody's condition. He and Tanya wheeled the gurney out of the garage, and Jazz, Chaz, and Dante followed. Tanya clicked a remote to shut the garage door, and they hurried into the house. Dante stayed by Chaz's side as he stumbled, trying to keep up.

Inside, Tanya and Lloyd rolled Cody past the foyer and down a long hallway into a room with swinging double doors. Jazz stared at all the medical equipment clogging the room, her eyebrows rising, and she looked at Lloyd.

He smiled. "Had this room ever since I started as a general practitioner, my dear." In a practiced familiar move, he and Tanya slid Cody off the gurney and onto the operating table in the center of the room. A whiff of pine-scented fragrance battled in Jazz's nose with the acrid tang of blood.

Tanya patted Jazz's arm and moved her aside. "I'm a retired nurse, Jazz. Let us help your new friend."

Jazz found an unexpected strength in Tanya's smile, her confident eyes. *Yes, my new friend.* She looked at Chaz. *Our new friend.* Chaz watched Lloyd and Tanya, looking like he could fall asleep standing up.

Jazz didn't want Cody to die, and Chaz clearly didn't either. Cody was willing to give his life for them, and she wanted to say it, but she bit it back when Lloyd and Tanya cut his jacket away.

Cody hadn't been shot in the arms, so Lloyd and Tanya didn't bother with the rubber, plastic, and metal spring-loaded pistol rigs on his forearms. Jazz flinched at the scars on his arms, but when they cut off his black tee shirt and started inspecting his injuries, she gasped.

Lloyd glanced up at her, then returned to his work. "You know, Jazz, when I took the Hippocratic Oath, I took the part about 'do no harm' seriously, and I still do." He poked and prodded Cody, grunted and mumbled here and there as he and Tanya treated him, and Jazz finally found her voice.

"Jesus, Lloyd. What the hell happened to him?"

Lloyd worked on his patient and talked to Jazz in a soothing voice while Tanya cleaned up the blood. "Well, it appears that he's been shot, four times. Here." He pointed. "Here, and two here. But there's no indication that the amount of blood loss should be associated with such superficial wounds. See? They've closed up." He looked up at Jazz. "Did Chaz help him?"

Jazz nodded. "Yes. But... Lloyd. What the hell *happened* to him?"

Lloyd continued working on Cody. "When I decided to do no harm, Jazz, I figured it included helping some friends in need at one time or another along the way. By law, I'm supposed to report gunshot wounds, and these are clearly gunshot wounds. However, I believe doing no harm encompasses the needs of my patients first and foremost. And considering the strange tale you told me, I have no doubts that reporting these wounds would not only endanger my patient, but it would endanger you and Chaz as well." He put his hands on some bloody spots on Cody's chest, hemming and hawing to himself, then turned to gaze into Jazz's eyes. "And that, precious lady, I cannot do."

Jazz wanted to scream. "Lloyd, please."

He chuckled and waved his hand at her. "Trust me, Jazz, the patient's going to live, thanks mostly to Chaz. He's lost a lot of blood, but he'll make it." He pointed at Cody's chest and torso. "These appear to be old blade wounds, here and here, and these too. And these look like old gunshot wounds. The others... well." He glanced up at Jazz again, maybe evaluating her ability to deal with the horribly scarred man who lay before them. "The others appear to be an accumulation of cigarette burns, along with some other unidentifiable burn scars."

Jazz drew a deep breath. Chaz stood beside her, mesmerized. "Are we talking some kind of ritual self-mutilation psychosis here?"

Lloyd hummed, appearing to consider her diagnosis. "No, I don't think so. They appear much... *older* than that. Except for the fresh bullet wounds, of course, and they all passed through clean, so I don't have to dig for fragments." He glanced up at Jazz again, meeting her eyes. "He appears to be in his early thirties. These burn scars were sustained as a teenager, or a child."

Jazz gasped again. Chaz grabbed her hand, and she held on tightly. "You mean he was abused?"

Lloyd grunted and rose. "Possible. Likely."

Jesus, Cody. What happened to you? Who could do this? Your parents? Or someone else, maybe some very bad people?

Chaz sighed and leaned over Cody and put his arms around him.

"Chaz, baby, no."

Chaz looked up at her and smiled. "It's okay, Mother. I got enough."

"Binky—"

"You always said it was my choice." Chaz nodded at her until she nodded back, and he closed his eyes and leaned his head against Cody's chest. "Just let me sleep for a week after I'm done, okay?"

She tried to swallow the lump in her throat. "Okay, sweetie."

A minute later, Chaz slumped, and Jazz caught him and picked him up and cradled him against her shoulder. She turned and gazed at Lloyd and Tanya.

Lloyd gasped. "I've let him do it to some of my patients, but never watched him do it."

"It's a gift from God, sweetheart." Tanya put her arm around Lloyd's shoulder and gazed at Cody. His breathing was no longer harsh and raspy. His chest rose and fell naturally, and his wounds had completely closed.

"It certainly is, my love," Lloyd whispered, embracing Tanya.

The doorbell rang through the intercom system, blaring in the enclosed space of the makeshift operating room. Dante barked and darted out into the hall. Jazz, Lloyd, and Tanya stared at each other as Cody blinked and struggled to sit up.

Tanya hurried out into the hallway toward the front door. Lloyd dashed out right behind her. Jazz set Chaz down in a chair in the corner, drew her Glock, and ran after them, her heart pounding again.

"Tanya, wait up," she called.

Tanya stood by the front door in the foyer and looked at Jazz, who froze in a shooter's stance ten feet away with her pistol aimed at the door. Dante growled softly and moved beside her, his hackles raised.

Jazz scowled and nodded at Tanya. "Open it and step away fast."

72

Lloyd stood beside Tanya as she opened the door. They stepped aside, and Lloyd moved in front of his wife as they gazed at the smiling man standing in the doorway.

He was as big as a linebacker, and was mostly muscle. Bronze-skinned and of indeterminate race, maybe part Hispanic. Could be in his late thirties, or he could be fifty. Olive green uniform and cap, each with a rectangular white "Quintrado's Plumbing" logo patch sewn into them. He nodded at them, eyeing Jazz.

"Evening, folks."

"We didn't call a plumber," Tanya said, frowning.

"No, ma'am," the huge man said, and winked. "But my friend Cody did. I came as quick as I could." He turned to Jazz, still smiling and relaxed, his hands palms out at his sides. "And you must be Jasmine."

"Remember Quintrado," Jazz said, lowering the pistol. He didn't have the empty eyes of an Extractor. In fact, he had a perpetually amused gleam in his gentle eyes. She trusted him on sight, even though it went against her nature.

"Yes, ma'am, that's the code word." The man nodded and looked at Tanya and Lloyd. "May I come in?"

The couple looked back at Jazz, who nodded. They stepped aside as the big man entered, and Tanya shut the door.

"I'm Kino," the man said, pronouncing it *key-no* and offering his hand to Lloyd, who shook it.

"Dr. Lloyd Petrokovich," Lloyd said. "My wife Tanya. I assume you're the reinforcements Cody called?"

"Yes, sir, that's me. Pleased to meet you both." Kino turned to Jazz. "How are Chaz and Cody?"

Jazz holstered her pistol. "Well, thanks to Cody and Dante, Chaz is okay. And thanks to Chaz and Lloyd and Tanya, Cody's going to be okay."

"Thank God for that," Kino said.

Jazz squinted at him. "That was a tracking device Cody gave me, wasn't it?"

"Yes, ma'am." Kino crouched, holding his big hands out to Dante, who approached him and sniffed his hands.

"That's Dante," Jazz said.

"Dante!" Kino said, and Dante's tail started wagging. Kino rubbed Dante's neck, and Dante panted, apparently satisfied the new stranger was a friend. "So you're the poor fellow who accidentally started all this madness, huh, boy?"

Dante leaned into Kino's hands, and Kino laughed. "He's a good boy."

"He saved our lives back at the house," Jazz said. "He stopped one of the Extractors."

Kino hummed at Dante and stood. "I bet he did, Ms. Tandy." He rubbed his hands together. "Now, I hate to be rude, but we have to get you, Chaz, and Cody out of here fast. So where's Grumpy?"

Jazz laughed and gestured down the hall. "Back here with Chaz."

They entered the operating room. Cody sat on the edge of the blood-stained table, holding his head. Chaz snored softly in the chair, his head leaning against the wall.

"Hey, Beavis," Kino said, looking at Cody and shaking his head. "Can't you do anything right?"

"Hey, Butthead," Cody muttered. "What took you so damn long?"

Kino picked up Chaz and held him in his arms. Chaz didn't wake up. "Quit your bitchin', Grumpy. If you were better at dodging bullets, I wouldn't've had to come at all." Kino winked at Jazz.

"Maybe you should try doing my job next time," Cody grumbled.

Kino scowled at the blood on Cody's jeans and jacket. "Holy crap, dude. Did you *try* to dance into the path of every bullet they fired at you?"

Cody smirked at him. "Listen, dickless—"

"And put a shirt on. You're scaring the women."

Cody's eyes widened. "You do know I got shot, right?"

Kino smiled at Jazz. "Ms. Tandy, if you'll get any bags you need out of the Mustang, I'll put Chaz in my van. Please do it quickly, because we must get out of here immediately." Kino turned at the doorway and glanced at Cody. "If Grumpy'll get his lazy ass up and stumble after us, he can come too."

Cody mumbled something under his breath, and Kino laughed.

Jazz liked the sound. It was effortless and hearty, and reminded her of all the good things she was striving to hang onto. She looked back at Cody, wondering if he could even stand, and she touched Kino's arm as they headed down the hall.

"Kino, is he—"

"Don't worry, Ms. Tandy." Kino chuckled and raised his voice so Cody could hear. "If he can't crawl out to the van by himself, I'll pick him up and carry him." He winked at her again, and Jazz knew they were in good hands.

Lloyd and Tanya were already headed out the front door toward the garage, and Kino, Jazz, and Dante hurried after them.

A white van was parked in the driveway. A magnetic sign stuck on the door had "Quintrado's Plumbing" printed on it in embossed letters. Jazz suspected the phone number and website address below it were fake.

Tanya opened the garage door and Lloyd rushed to the front door of the Mustang and popped open the trunk. He helped Jazz with the bags, and they all hurried toward the van.

Kino had the sliding door open and was buckling Chaz into the back seat. Cody staggered out the front door, his leather jacket draped over one arm. Dante jumped in beside Chaz.

"Hey, Slowpoke Rodriguez!" Kino called out, glancing back at Cody with a stern glare. "You wanna pick up the pace a bit? You're holding everybody up. *Ándele, amigo!*" Kino grinned at Jazz, and took her and Chaz's bags and Dante's backpack and tossed them in the van.

Jazz studied Cody, still worried about him. He had taken four bullets for her and Chaz. But despite her fear and worry, despite not knowing if her father was dead or alive, she chuckled when she saw the flabbergasted look on Cody's face.

"Yo, Godzilla," he called out. "Cut me some slack. I've just been to the other side, and they told me something about you."

"Yeah? What's that, you crippled wimp?"

"They said your fat ass was too big to fit through the pearly gates, and that you have to go to the other place instead when you're done here."

Kino threw his head back and guffawed. Jazz laughed too, feeling safer just knowing she still could.

In the face of danger, there was courage in humor.

Kino turned to Jazz as Cody staggered toward them. "If you'll hop in the front, we'll get you and Chaz outta here and to a safe place, Jasmine."

Jazz smiled. "Call me Jazz." She smirked at Cody, who climbed into the back of the van. "All my friends do."

Cody sighed and plopped into the rear passenger-side seat. Kino closed the sliding door and climbed into the driver's seat as Jazz rounded the front of the van. She hugged Tanya, then Lloyd, and hopped in the front seat beside Kino. Lloyd closed the door and stood at the open window.

Cody leaned forward and nodded at Lloyd. "Thank you."

Lloyd nodded back. "You're welcome. And thank you for saving my friends. You're a lucky man."

Cody nodded again and fell back in the seat.

Lloyd looked at Kino. "Take good care of my friends."

"Yes, sir. Count on it."

"Hey, Goliath," Cody said. "Are you gonna start driving sometime this week? Or do I have to get out and start pushing?"

"Quiet in back," Kino said, starting the van. "And put a shirt on. Your spare gear bag's in back, with some fresh clothes and your toys. You smell like a slaughterhouse."

Cody grumbled, got up and moved to the back of the van, and fumbled around in the dark.

Lloyd touched Jazz's arm. "Call us as soon as you can."

She nodded, and Kino pulled out of the driveway. Lloyd and Tanya waved, and Jazz waved back as she wiped away fresh tears. While Cody changed into clean clothes in the back, Kino looked at Jazz.

"Jazz, I'm sorry, but you're gonna have to chuck that cell phone. Just toss it out the window when we get on I-85 up ahead."

Jazz looked at her cell like it was a snake coiled to strike. "They can trace us through it, can't they?"

"Yes, ma'am." Kino took a sharp turn onto the express-way, and there was loud bumping and banging in the back.

"Hey!" Cody growled. "Gargantu-boy! Where'd you get your damn driver's license? Disney World?"

"Pipe down, Grumpy." Kino winked at Jazz. "And watch your language, son. There's a lady present."

Cody returned to his seat and buckled himself in, eyeing Kino. "Yeah, I thought we were supposed to be saving her, and here you are trying to get us all killed."

Dante lay on the floorboard beside Chaz's seat and watched the exchange.

"Complaint department's closed." Kino looked at Jazz and snickered. "I think Grumpy must have missed nap time today."

Cody grumbled something under his breath, settled back in his seat, and closed his eyes.

A minute later he was snoring, in dreamland with Chaz. Dante decided to join them. On the expressway, Jazz tossed her cell out the window. She gazed ahead into the suddenly perilous night, wondering what the future would bring.

If they had one.

Chapter 9

Jazz turned and watched Cody while he slept. She bit her lip, and turned back to Kino. "Is he going to be okay?"

"Yeah. He's a lot tougher than he looks right now, believe me."

"I don't know. He looks pretty tough to me."

"Huh. Trust me, Cody's been through much worse than this, and still come out standing, and fighting."

What could be worse than almost dying? "He seems so bitter, and angry."

Kino laughed. "Would you believe you got the jolly Cody?"

She raised her eyebrows and shook her head. "Imagine how lucky I feel. He's just not the type to make friends, is he?"

He looked at her, and she saw something hard and dangerous lurking behind his gentle eyes. "If you knew what he's been through, you'd be more understanding why he is the way he is."

She frowned, pondering the nightmare she and Chaz had plunged into, and worrying about her father. Kino quietly watched the road, and she worried that she had shut him down. She couldn't help but like and trust him, and wanted to hear him laugh again.

She smiled, hoping he would open back up. "Are you two always like this with each other?"

He laughed, and she breathed easier. "That's how you know he's all right. If he'd been all serious on me, I would've been worried. Because he was jackin' me around, I knew he was okay."

"I think I understand what you mean. So are you two... friends?"

He looked at her, this time without the hard edge. "Cody's the best friend I've ever had. Best friend I could ever hope or ask for."

The power in his gaze stunned her. Between raising Chaz alone, fighting Jack, and all the running and hiding, she had apparently missed out on making a friend like that. Other than her father and Lloyd, she had no real friends, and the loneliness made her ache inside.

"Cody seems like he needs a good friend like you, Kino."

He gave her his penetrating stare again. "I love Cody. He saved my life several times. In fact, between him and the professor, together they saved my soul."

"The professor?"

"Yeah, you'll get to meet him soon. You'll like him, trust me."

"Strangers keep asking me to do that."

He laughed. "Hey, I'm no stranger. Not anymore. And you'll definitely like him. Everybody does."

"I like *you*, Kino," she said. "And I'd like to be your friend too."

"Everybody needs good friends," he said, and his grin pushed away some of the darkness as he offered his hand. "Anakino Guillarmo. All my friends call me Kino. Nobody's called me Ana since I busted up a senior for it when I was in eighth grade."

She grinned and shook his hand. "Jasmine Tandy. All my friends call me Jazz."

"Jazz it is. And I can definitely see what Cody sees in you." He laughed again. "Man, when I saw you standing there with that pistol pointed at me, I knew you were one tough lady. Chaz is lucky to have you for a mother."

"Wait. What do you mean, 'what Cody sees in me'?"

He frowned. "Maybe I said too much."

"No, we're friends now, right? So you can tell me."

He thought for a few seconds. "Cody's been watching over you and Chaz for some time now. Ever since you were in Houston, and the rumors started about Chaz. Dr. Ben—the professor—wanted to assign Roberta to you. Said Cody was way too personally involved. Roberta's another one of our Guardians, and a damn good one too."

He smiled, and had a faraway look in his eyes. "Man, when I see her in action, she's just incredible. Amazing." He shook his head. "Anyway, Cody insisted on staying assigned to you. And you're both lucky you got him. Don't get me wrong, Roberta's one tough and talented lady, but Cody's the best. And the... bad people want Chaz something awful. They'll do any-thing to get him. Don't doubt it for a second." He gave her his penetrating stare. "This isn't over yet, Jazz. Not by a long shot."

"Cody saved our lives tonight, and almost gave his in the process. Thanks to Chaz, he didn't."

"I don't doubt it, especially considering the way he... Well."

"The way he what?"

"Never mind. You'll figure it out soon enough. You're a smart lady."

"You think? I just wish we'd met you both before tonight. Then maybe my father would still be..." She sighed. "Alive, or at least not—"

"Your father? What happened?"

She told him about the phone call. "Cody said the Asian woman who held him was Taja Ling."

"Ouch. Damn."

"That bad?"

Kino pursed his lips. "I'm not gonna lie to a friend, Jazz. The devil himself might be more merciful." He saw the hope-less look in her eyes, and winced. "But I bet he's still alive. They'll use him to get to you and Chaz, I'm sure of it."

She wiped her eyes. "So are you a Guardian too?"

He chortled. "Heck, no. Guardians are highly trained

lethal weapons. Stealthy as a mouse, and almost invisible when they need to be. Me, I'm pretty hard to hide, and not very quiet."

"So what do you do?"

"I'm the backup squad, called a Fixer. Reinforcements. Wheel man. Guardian's gopher. Jack of all trades, master of none."

"Somehow I doubt that. I bet they wouldn't know what to do without you. So what happened to Cody? I mean, all the scars all over him."

Kino looked in the rearview mirror at Cody, and Jazz turned in her seat to watch him too. He looked peaceful sleeping, but his face twitched a few times.

Because of Cody's gruff demeanor, odd vocation, unusual appearance, and willingness to give his life for her and Chaz, he was an enigma to her. With the combination of his dark clothes, dark chocolate skin, Caucasian facial features, and wavy black hair, he seemed almost otherworldly. He truly was the dark man.

Kino winced. "I think that's something you should hear from Cody personally."

She checked on Chaz and Dante. They still slept peacefully, and she turned back around. "Okay. Why does he hate being called CJ? I assume those are his initials?"

"Huh. You're definitely going to have to drag that out of Cody."

She wasn't going to get Cody's secrets from Kino unless she pried them out of him, and she wasn't about to do that to her new friend.

"Okay." She smiled and let it go for the moment. "So what's your story then, big guy?"

"That I'll be happy to tell you, 'cause it starts out bad— really bad—but ends up good."

"How's that?"

"Well, I'm here with you, Chaz, and Cody, aren't I? And

Dante. I'm on the good guys' side now."

"Okaaay…"

"I was left on the doorstep of a hospital as an infant with a note that said, 'Please take care of Anakino Guillarmo. His daddy died in the war, and I just can't do it.' Pretty crappy, huh? I guess they meant 'Nam." Jazz figured that made Kino somewhere between forty and fifty. "Anyway, despite the odd last name, they never found out who my parents were. And no one adopted me, so I was raised in an orphanage. And because of my size, I was always getting into trouble. I was an incorrigible child. I got into fights a lot. And rarely lost." He smiled. "Still, I managed to finish high school, and because I played some football and my grades were excellent, I got a scholarship with Florida State University."

"Yeah, I thought 'linebacker' when I first saw you."

"Defensive tackle. But that all went to hell when I blew my knee out. After that, I was *persona non grata* on the gridiron."

"Ouch."

"Yeah. Anyway, that left me with jack. I dropped out of college, and cadged a job out of a local nightclub owner as a bouncer. I won't kid you, Jazz. I busted some heads, and I enjoyed it and didn't give a damn who suffered because of it. I wasn't a nice guy."

"Now that I find incredibly hard to believe."

"Well, it's true. I didn't even give a damn about myself. Hit the sauce pretty hard after the big NFL dream died. Got involved with some pushers, and they decided to use me as their strong-arm guy, their punisher. Busted a lot of heads there too, until this twenty-year-old kid I beat the hell out of died. Little bastard just wouldn't stop trying to fight me. Turned out the kid's dad was rich and powerful, so I did some hard time. Mostly circumstantial evidence, so I got a light sentence for manslaughter. Nobody messed with me because of my size. Five years, and they let me out because of exemplary behavior and prison overcrowding. After I got out, I found my future in the bottom of a bottle."

Because it felt right, Jazz reached a hand over and touched his arm.

"Well," he went on, "I managed to get another job as a bouncer. Even managed to show up sober a few nights. Turns out my boss was connected with some... uhh, very bad people."

Alarm bells went off in her head. "What?"

"Yeah, you heard me. What I didn't tell you is I have this unusual thing I can sometimes do when I'm not stone drunk. Boss found out about it, and told these people. Then they just came and got me, and tried to brainwash me. Damn near succeeded too."

"What, Kino? What can you do?" Her heart raced. Here was yet another one.

He frowned. "I don't want you to not like me or distrust me because of it. I did some bad things with it."

"Kino, tell me. Please. We're friends, right?"

He looked at her and nodded. "Yeah, we are. So here it is: I can often tell with certainty when people are telling the truth, and when they're lying."

"Whoa."

"Yeah. May sound all romantic and philanthropic, but try living with it for a while. The human truth machine. After a while, nobody trusts you."

"Oh, Kino. I'm so sorry."

"So was I. About the sorriest thing you've ever seen. Stayed drunk all the time, just to avoid the... knowing. Pretty soon, they decided I was worthless to them. But did they just throw me out on the street?"

"Something tells me *no*."

"Damn right. They don't play that way. No loose ends. So, one night when I was too blind ass drunk to even say my own name, three of 'em tied me up, gagged me, and took me to an abandoned warehouse. Put a gun to my head, laughing at me like I was nothing but a cockroach to squash. And to tell you the truth, I was too messed up to care. But just as they were about to put me out of my misery, guess who I saw standing behind them, snuck up on 'em just as quiet as a mouse?"

Her hand flew to her mouth, and she turned to the Guardian behind her. "Cody."

"Yep. You should've seen him. He tore their asses up before he killed 'em. And I just laid there laughing, not even caring what was happening. Next thing you know, I'm in a new place, with good people who cared about me and wanted to rehabilitate me. After that, well… here I still am. Working for the good guys now."

"Wow."

"Yep. I owe my life to Cody and Dr. Ben. And all the others, too. Who you'll meet pretty soon, if all goes according to plan."

"My God."

"Mine too. I think that's pretty much it. God must have had a plan for me. And now I know what it is: helping the Guardians, and people like you and Chaz. I haven't touched a drop since, and never will again. Honed my talent, and been working with these guys for six years, and ain't quitting until my crusty old heart gives out, or somebody kills me."

"That's an amazing story, Kino. And you're an amazing man."

"I don't know about that. But I'm happy now, whatever happens. I got a second chance that lots of people don't get."

Kino had exited the expressway a few minutes ago, somewhere south of Atlanta, and was headed down a dark, deserted two-lane road. No buildings or homes were in sight. Jazz felt like they were the sole inhabitants of another world.

As she absorbed Kino's story, a slew of unanswered questions assaulted her mind. She tried to assemble them cohesively, but they spilled out in a jumble.

"Kino, what is this teleporting thing? Chaz started

shimmering, and Cody told me to grab him. Did that stop it? And who are these very bad people? What do they want Chaz for exactly? And where are we going, and—"

"Whoa there, little filly. One question at a time. My poor pea-brain can't handle more than that."

She smirked. "Oh, please. How many people know what *persona non grata* or incorrigible or philanthropic mean? C'mon, Kino. I need answers."

"Okay. I'll give you as many as I can, except for the stuff about Cody." He slowed, turned onto a dirt road, cut off his headlights, and drove down the tree-lined road with just his parking lights on. "We're about to hop on a plane here, so let me—"

"A plane? Where to?"

"Homestead. It's safe there, and—"

"Homestead? Is that the place where…" She stopped and looked at him. The scowl on his face looked so alien that she laughed. "Okay, okay. Sorry."

He grunted. "Yes, Homestead is where all the talented kids the Guardians rescue are relocated to. And it's safe. It's an isolated fortress, in fact, and a good and happy place. I promise you and Chaz'll love it, and everybody there." He gave her his hard stare again. "I gotta tell you, Jazz. You're one of the lucky ones. Extractors usually kill their targets' parents. They don't want any angry witnesses determined to get their kids back." He looked back at the road and continued as he navigated the rough terrain.

"And yes, teleporting is real. But teleporters are limited in what they can move, and how far. And it takes an awful toll on the ones who do it, just like Chaz with healing, but much worse. And thank God for that. Otherwise, we'd all be in big trouble. That's why holding Chaz prevented it. They couldn't move you both. Thank God they only have one, as far as we know. They used to have another, but they used her up 'til it killed her. *They* killed her. And no, we don't have one."

"These people are soulless barbarians, aren't they?"

"Damn right." He turned the wheel as the bumpy road took a sharp turn, and the van jolted when he hit a big pothole. Cody grumbled in his sleep as Kino continued.

"As for what they want Chaz for, I'll let the professor tell you about that. You won't like it, if he's right. I *can* tell you that everything Amanda said in the letter is true. As for the kids, you'll meet them soon enough, and find out what they can do. They're really good kids too, Jazz, all because of the professor and Tinga. You'll meet her too."

Jazz nodded, soaking it in and keeping her lips zipped.

"As far as Extractors go… well, one is ten too many. We have no idea how many there are. They're the most dangerous people you'll ever meet, unless you have the misfortune of meeting Taja Ling, or… *him*."

She ignored the "him" comment and gritted her teeth as the fury resurfaced. "I plan on meeting her, and she's not going to like it. In fact, she's going to be very sorry when I get through with her."

He grunted. "I have no doubts you're a tough and resourceful lady, Jazz, and I'm really sorry about your father. We're going to do everything we can to help you get him back. But don't ever underestimate Taja, or any of them. In case you haven't figured it out yet, there's a war going on here, underneath the radar, but a war nevertheless. Our side's goal is freedom. Theirs is domination and subjugation. Don't ever forget that."

"Okay." She wanted to ask more about that, but he kept talking.

"We had seven Guardians, but an Extractor killed one of them last year, so now we only have six. They go all over the world, wherever they're needed. And their Fixers—guys like me—go wherever they go."

"Wow. I had no idea the… scope of this thing."

"Yeah." He took another turn. "One of our best Fixers

got killed in Japan a year ago during a botched rescue. Stephan was our genius. Technical wizard. Built a lot of our toys. Marco, the Guardian, was lucky to get out of that one alive. Blames himself for Stephan's death, even though nobody else does, not even Roberta. Stephan was a huge loss, in more ways than one." Kino couldn't hide the sadness in his voice. "He was Roberta's husband. Great man. Big heart. Funny guy too. The kids loved him. Everybody loved him. Roberta, she's so amazing, so strong. She's working through it, but she…"

He sighed, and she put her hand on his arm again. "You got a thing for her."

He snorted. "Who, me? Nah. Roberta's way out of my league."

"Kino, you may be the truthseer, but we women have this thing. And friends aren't supposed to lie to each other."

He sighed again, glanced at her and then away, and his eyes told the tale.

"Oh, Kino. You're in love with her."

His shoulders slumped. "Hopelessly."

She rubbed his arm. The big man had already touched her heart in a way she hadn't expected could happen. "There's always hope."

He looked at her as he pulled into a camouflaged building no larger than a six-car garage. "Please don't tell her."

The building was hidden so well she wouldn't have even seen it if they hadn't stopped. "Of course I won't. Where are we?"

"We're here," he said, and hopped out. A woman dressed in camouflage fatigues ran toward the van as Kino slid open the back door.

The woman rushed up to Kino, placed her hand on his arm, and gazed up into his eyes. "Hey, Kino. It's really good to see you all safe. Even Cody."

"Hey, Roberta. Cody's gonna be okay—"

"I'm especially glad to see you safe, big guy," the

woman said softly. She rubbed his arm and let go. "Did you see any tails on you?"

He shook his head. "Didn't track any."

Jazz exited the van, studying Roberta as she and Kino sprang into action. Roberta was five-four tops, maybe one-hundred-thirty pounds. Her medium-length blond hair was tied back in a ponytail. She was attractive in a plain Jane way, but her eyes gave her face an unnatural beauty that struck Jazz when Roberta rounded the front of the van and confronted her.

"Hi, Jazz. I'm Roberta."

"Hi, Roberta."

"Glad to see you both made it." Dante barked, and Roberta chuckled. "All three of you. Four counting Rip van Winkle here. Wake the hell up, Cody. Let's get you guys out of here, Jazz, and on the plane, as quickly as possible."

Roberta handed Chaz's bag and Dante's backpack to Jazz, and grabbed Jazz's suitcase. She passed by Cody and smacked him gently on the shoulder. "Hey, sleepyhead. Wake up."

Cody grumbled and gazed blearily up at her. "Okay, okay. Hey, Roberta. What the hell do you want now?"

"Come fly with me, tough guy." Roberta stopped and gazed into Cody's eyes. She reached down and squeezed his shoulder.

Jazz saw them nod at each other, an unspoken signal passing between them.

"Better you than Gargantuoid over there." Cody grabbed his bag, struggled out of his seat, and stumbled out of the van. "We'd all die for sure."

Dante jumped out and pranced around Jazz, apparently liking this new game.

"Hey, Grumpy!" Kino called out as he unbuckled Chaz's seat belt. Chaz mumbled something and wrapped his arms around Kino's shoulders. "Try to keep up this time, crip. I don't wanna have to fill out all the paperwork stating why we had to leave you here."

Cody mumbled as he staggered out of the building and into the woods behind Roberta, who was heading down a wide trail that led down a slope. Kino came around the van with Chaz in one arm, his gear bag in the other, and stopped beside Jazz.

Jazz lifted a hand and rubbed Chaz's back. "Chaz, honey? Binky?"

Chaz lifted his head off Kino's shoulder and smiled, his eyes half closed. "I'm okay, Mother. Don't forget Dante."

"He's right beside me, baby."

"Okay. Are we going to meet Amanda?"

"Chaz! Did you read the letter while I was in the shower?"

"Mother, you left it on my nightstand."

"I thought you were asleep."

"I was, then I woke up, and read it."

She shook her head. Clever *mischievous* boy.

"So are we going to meet her? And her friends?"

"I think so, baby." She looked at Kino. He nodded and took off behind Cody. She slipped her arms in Dante's backpack and grabbed Chaz's bag, and hurried after Kino.

No matter what happened, she knew they were in good hands. It helped that Chaz felt safe in Kino's arms. She ran behind Kino, hoping and praying to a God that she wasn't sure existed that her father was still here, still somehow okay.

They hustled down a slope through the trees and came out on a grassy field. The nearly full moon was rising over the horizon, an ethereal luminescence guiding their way. Cody was almost invisible, but he looked stronger as he rushed down the hill. He turned and glanced back at her, the whites of his eyes almost gleaming, seeming to float independently in the darkness.

She spotted the little plane at the floor of the valley, backed up against the slope's incline. It had pontoons. And a propeller. Even from only a hundred yards away, it looked like a toy.

"Get the lead out, boy!" Kino called, laughing as he hurried past Cody. "Damn, am I gonna have to come back and carry your sorry ass too?"

Cody shook his head, saving his breath for the mad dash toward the dinky aircraft. Jazz ran up beside him right as he stumbled to one knee. She grabbed his arm with her free hand.

Cody jerked his arm away. "I got it. Just go!"

Jazz snorted, shook her head, and hurried after Kino.

Roberta reached the plane and tossed Jazz's bag in the back. She hopped in the pilot's seat and started the engine right as Kino and Jazz arrived. Kino buckled Chaz into one of four seats behind the pilot. Dante jumped in and stood in the doorway and barked at Jazz.

Jazz looked at the short, open field and threw Chaz's bag and the backpack in behind the seats. How were they possibly going to take off and clear the tree line ahead? She jumped in behind Kino, who hopped in the copilot's seat while she strapped herself in the seat behind him and beside Chaz.

Cody staggered up the steps, pulled them up, and locked the door behind him. He tossed his bag in with the others, pushed Dante out of the way, and fell in one of the two rear seats. "Sometime today, Roberta!" he shouted over the engine's growl.

"Pipe down in back!" Kino called out, chuckling.

Cody shook his head and buckled himself in. "Hey, Roberta. I hope you got a fresh, extra-heavy-strength rubber band wound tight for that prop. It's gonna take a miracle to lift your lardass copilot off the ground."

Kino looked back at Cody as the little plane started moving. "Jesus, Grumpy. What died in here? You stink to high heaven."

"Yeah, well, I didn't have time to stop and shower at the Holiday Inn Express, smartass."

Their banter didn't calm Jazz as they sped up. She

watched the approaching tree line, her heart in her throat. Dante lay beside Chaz, who was watching wide-eyed.

"Mother…"

She grabbed his hand. "It'll be okay."

The trees seemed to grow taller. *We're never going to make it. This is crazy…*

"You can pull up anytime, golden girl!" Cody shouted.

"Quiet!" Roberta barked.

Kino stared ahead. "Roberta—"

"Quiet!"

They finally started rising, but it was too late, Jazz knew it, too late…

The trees seemed to rise with them, and she swore she heard pine needles brush the pontoons as they cleared the tree-tops. She released a breath she hadn't realized she'd been holding and wondered when her heart was going to start beating again.

Kino turned around and looked back at them, all grinning teeth. He raised his open palm at Chaz as they soared away into the night. He looked so goofy that Jazz and Chaz grinned back at him. Chaz high-fived him.

"My man!" Kino laughed. Chaz laughed too, unaccountably happy.

Dante barked, sat, and raised one paw at Kino. Chaz had taught him this trick. Kino laughed again and slapped his palm against Dante's paw. "High-five, Dante. Good boy."

Cody leaned forward, his face in his hands, and shook his head.

Kino snickered. "Soil your britches back there, Grumpy?"

Cody snorted, fell back in his seat, and stared out the window into the darkness.

Jazz took a deep breath. It was time to go meet the psychic geniuses.

Oh, Daddy, I'm coming. Somehow I'm going to find you,

and Taja, and when I do, she's going to be so sorry. They're all going to be so very sorry...

They were off into the unknown, to try to start a new life among strangers in an extraordinary place called Homestead.

Chapter 10

August – location unknown

Kaylee Daley leaned her head against the window and sighed. From the padded ledge of the alcove in her spacious bedroom she gazed two floors down at the mansion's sculptured architecture and admired her handiwork adorning it. Even though it was almost September, every plant and flower she had "touched" was in full bloom, a cornucopia of vivid, bright colors.

Why had she done it?

She didn't know. Taja and the men she called "body-guards" let Kaylee walk the grounds at her leisure anywhere within the fifteen-foot-high walls of the enclosed and well-guarded property. They encouraged her to exercise her power, and she did because it was the only joy she had left.

Organic life blossomed everywhere in her new world. The only place life didn't reside was in her heart.

Although she'd been here—wherever here was—over three months, the grounds were extensive enough that she'd only explored half of them. Much of it was foraged with an unbearable truth shadowing her.

They gave her, without hesitation, anything she asked for, except for the four things she desired the most: Mom, Dad, home, and freedom.

She was free to roam the property any time of the day or evening, but a taciturn bodyguard always accompanied her when Taja wasn't with her, and she was kept apart from the other children she occasionally glimpsed. It made her feel like a prisoner, and very lonely.

She sometimes wondered if Taja and the bodyguards

were there not to protect her, but instead to prevent her from escaping or getting into some forbidden mischief. Or maybe they just wanted to stop her from meeting the other children, and finding out about their special powers. She had certainly tried that, without success—so far.

Were these the *good new friends* the letter had promised?

These people, whether they were who they said they were or not, didn't know how determined and stubborn Kathryn Leeann Daley was.

Taja had been gone for two weeks on a business trip. She hadn't told Kaylee what it was about. She'd just flashed that angelic smile and promised Kaylee she'd be back as soon as possible.

Kaylee didn't miss her.

The chimes sounded, announcing a visitor to her extravagant four-room suite. Through the open door of her bedroom, Taja's singsong voice rang out.

"Kathryn! I'm back, sweetie. Where are you?"

Kaylee got up from her post in the alcove and shook her head. She still didn't like the idea of them walking in on her any time they pleased. Even Mom and Dad had always respected her privacy. Here, although they told her otherwise, she had none. Hidden eyes were everywhere, constantly watching her.

"I'm back here, in the bedroom."

Taja waltzed into her room, grinning. "Kathryn, sweetheart, what are you doing cooped up in here on such a pretty day?"

Kaylee sighed, feeling rebellious again. "My name is Kaylee. I told you. Why won't you call me that?"

Taja grimaced. "Kaylee sounds so hick, so gauche, honey. It makes you sound like an uneducated hillbilly. Kathryn is so much more classy and sophisticated."

"I don't like Kathryn," Kaylee mumbled.

"What?" There was that authoritative snarkiness in Taja's voice again. It made Kaylee nervous, despite Taja's almost irresistible beauty. She had the face of an angel.

"Nothing."

"Well, never mind that. I have a surprise for you."

"What, you're letting me go home?"

Taja sighed and rolled her eyes. "Kathryn, honey, you know why we can't do that. I explained it when Jhin and I rescued you from the bad people and the dark man. That took a lot out of Jhin, because he hasn't learned yet how to control his power. You should appreciate the sacrifice he made to save you."

"Yeah, but the dark man said that's what *he* was doing." Kaylee had no idea what had happened to her dark man. Although he was gruff and blunt, something in his eyes had made her trust him. The last she'd seen of him was when he rolled into the ditch beside his exploding car.

Something lupine flashed in Taja's eyes. "I told you, Kathryn, he's one of them. He was lying to you, deceiving you for his masters' purposes. It's the way they work, to fool you into compliance."

Kaylee frowned. Although the argument was old and tired, she couldn't resist rehashing it. "So you say, but how do you really know? What if he—"

"Because we've seen what he's done, what he's capable of. You have no idea how many people he's killed, how many families he's destroyed."

"But what if he had no choice, and did it to save me? The other man killed Reverend Thatcher and Mr. Clayton." *The real boogeyman.*

"Kathryn, why do I have to keep telling you? It's a masquerade. The dark man would have killed them too if the others hadn't beaten him to it. They saved him the trouble. There's more than just one group of bad people kidnapping children like you and Jhin. And they're all equally as ruthless and deceptive. You should be more appreciative of everything we've done for you. We've given you everything you asked for."

"Not everything," Kaylee mumbled.

"What more do you want, Kathryn?"

"I want my parents back!"

Taja closed her eyes and took a deep breath. At an unusual six feet tall, she leaned over to gaze into Kaylee's eyes. "Kathryn, when are you going to get it through that thick head of yours? We tried to rescue them, but we were too late. I swear, we did everything we could to save them. The fire was just too much."

Kaylee wanted to cry, but she wouldn't let Taja see her tears. She no longer knew what to believe. The story Taja told her about different warring factions fighting against each other, trying to steal her and others like her and use them for their own wicked purposes, was certainly plausible. It was no stranger than teleportation.

She had personally experienced that oddity. Thinking about it still made her feel ill. But the last time she'd believed anything a stranger told her was when her dark man had gazed at her with soulful black eyes. Now, she had a policy of not trusting anyone.

It was an unbearably lonely feeling.

"Kathryn, you have to believe me. We're doing everything we can to protect you from these people."

Were they? Kaylee missed her parents, her life, her home. Someone had stolen it all from her. She just didn't know who. Yet.

"Do you believe me, Kathryn?"

"I guess," Kaylee mumbled, letting it go for the moment.

Taja rose, smiling. "Well, never mind that now. You'll understand one day. In the meantime, how would you like to take another little trip with me?"

Kaylee really didn't want to go on another excursion with Taja, but it was a chance to get out of this strange place. She'd done it three times since she arrived, and even though it required a little work, anything was better than being stuck here.

She had no idea what would happen if she refused. One day, she was going to try, just to see what Taja would do.

"Okay," she said.

"Good." Taja clapped her hands and grinned. "Pack your bag for an overnight trip, and meet me down in the foyer."

"Are we taking the helicopter?"

"Yes. You like riding in the helicopter, don't you?"

She did, despite her first disconcerting trip in one. She wasn't about to let Taja know that she used these airborne trips to try to determine where they were. It could be useful knowledge when she escaped.

Because one day, she was going to escape, and find out who really killed her parents. And then she would get her revenge.

"Yes," she said, grinning for Taja's sake.

"Good. I'll meet you downstairs in… say, one hour?"

"Okay."

Taja left, apparently satisfied, and Kaylee started packing. What ostentatious mansion or prince's palace would they visit this time?

*****

Kaylee gazed out the helicopter window, pretending to be bored. She studied the terrain zipping past below, trying to guess their general location.

She'd met Taja downstairs a little after eleven a.m. A limo had driven them the half mile to the heliport next to the hangar where they kept their private planes, which Kaylee hadn't seen yet.

The sun was directly overhead, so she couldn't tell what direction they were moving. The sprawling vineyards below them implied that they were in wine country. She figured they were somewhere in California.

They'd been traveling over an hour. Because of the rocky foothills and the mountain ranges behind them when they took off, she thought her new home might be somewhere in Utah or Colorado, or maybe Nevada. Regardless, it was a long way from Kentucky, and in more than just miles.

"We're here," Taja said. "Isn't it beautiful?"

Kaylee looked at her. Not for the first time, she wondered if everything Taja told her was a lie. Was she involved with the people who killed her parents? Kaylee hated not knowing. But playing along couldn't hurt. Besides, making Taja Ling angry might not be a good idea.

"Yeah," she answered, stretching. "Where's here?"

"Our destination." Taja beamed at her. "Wine country."

Kaylee wrinkled her nose. "Yuck. You want me to help grapes grow better so people can get drunker? What's charitable about that?"

Taja sighed, losing the smile as the helicopter descended to a grassy field at the foot of a hill. "Kathryn, it's harvest wine season. The Montreneau Vineyards donates fifty percent of profits from their harvest wines to very worthwhile charities, like orphanages, children's hospitals, and cancer research. We're helping a lot of people with this little adventure. So cheer up."

Kaylee recalled their first excursion. They'd gone to a lavish estate boasting the finest flower gardens in the northeastern United States. With Taja's assurance that much of the profits went to charitable organizations, Kaylee had used her magic to make them even more fertile and bountiful. She didn't like the arrogant owners—the husband and wife team had treated her as if she were an ignorant child. But she did as she was asked.

On their second excursion, Taja took her to a series of apple orchards, claiming the rich owners donated a substantial portion of profits to research on rare children's diseases. Kaylee took Taja's word for it and did her job, hoping and praying that she really was helping people.

The third trip they went to a palace. The owner was some Arabian prince or something. His tropical gardens were his public pride and joy. Kaylee had a good idea what his private pride and joy was. She hadn't liked the way he'd leered at her, and kept touching her. But after one narrow-eyed glare from Taja, he kept his hands and eyes to himself. Taja told Kaylee he funded the upkeep on the mansion and the care of the other "talented" children where they kept her—none of whom she'd met yet—and the rescue operations when they found another talented kid in danger. Kaylee only half-believed it, but she had made the prince's gardens grow.

It was a far cry from the happy home and friends the letter had promised. Taja said the letter was a wicked lie. Kaylee ached to know the truth.

"Kathryn? Hello?"

Kaylee smiled, resigned to playing her role in this performance. If the possibility of escape arose, she didn't know what she would do or where she would go. How easily could they track her down? She didn't want to see Taja's angry side. And she definitely didn't want to be teleported again.

Sometimes she would envision her dark man gazing intently at her, and remember his eyes. With his dark skin, clothes, and hair, the whites of his eyes had gleamed in the shadows. His black pupils and irises had held a promise of a better world, of goodness and strength. She'd trusted him from the start. She didn't want to believe he was all the horrible things Taja said he was.

Sometimes at night when she couldn't sleep and was aching for Mom and Dad, she would pray to God to bring her dark man to come rescue her. Then she would realize how unrealistic and unlikely that was, and she'd turn her head into her pillow so the night-vision cameras she knew were watching couldn't record her tears.

Taja had to be lying about her dark man. And if she was lying about him, then what else was she lying about?

Kaylee shook herself out of her reverie and forced her smile into a grin.

"Okay. Let's do it."

"That's the spirit." Taja clapped her hands, smiling. She and Kaylee stood as the bird landed, and Taja put a hand on Kaylee's shoulder. "Are you ready to do your magic, sweetie?"

"I'm ready to kick it. Let's rock this joint."

"That's my girl."

Yeah? We'll see about that...

Chapter 11

August – The Everglades, Florida

Jazz woke and glanced at her watch as the plane descended. Almost midnight. She gazed out the window. The light of the nearly full moon revealed ghostly cypresses, mangroves, and sawgrass marsh.

Roberta put them down smoothly in a clear patch of water, and Jazz understood the reason for the pontoons. Chaz and Cody woke, and Dante nuzzled Jazz.

She ruffled his fur behind his ears. "Good boy, Dante. Kino, where are we?" She suspected Florida, probably the Everglades.

Kino turned to her. "How about we wait to tell you until you decide to stay with us?"

You mean I have a choice? Jazz nodded. "Okay. I understand."

Roberta taxied through the swampy waters until they came to an impenetrable barrier of tangled melaleucas. At forty feet away, Roberta shut off the engine and let them coast toward the interwoven mass of white, grey, and beige paperbarks. A small motorboat chugged out of an unseen break between the trees.

Chaz yawned, stretched, and scratched Dante's hindquarters. "Where are we?"

"Looks like we're in the swamp, Binky." Jazz watched the motorboat.

The driver wore a miner's helmet, and maneuvered his craft underneath the plane's propeller. By the light of his helmet, he attached two segmented bars to the plane. Then he attached the other end of the bars to either side of the boat's stern, and smiled and waved at the cockpit window.

"Hi, Raj," Roberta said, smiling and waving back.

"Kino, what's going on?" Jazz asked.

Kino smiled. "Watch this, Jazz. You too, Chaz."

Cody grunted, unhooked his seat belt, and fumbled around with the bags in the back. "Good job, Roberta. At least Godzilla wasn't flying us."

Kino laughed. "Better me than you, Grumpy. You'd have killed us all." He winked at Chaz, who grinned.

Jazz looked at Kino, her eyebrows raised. "So all three of you can fly?"

Kino snorted. "Well, I can. But you don't wanna fly with Chuckles the Clown as your pilot unless you have a death wish, trust me."

"Keep it up, tubby," Cody said. "Good thing for you I have such a great sense of humor."

Kino guffawed. "Okay, now that was funny!"

Jazz watched as Raj towed them toward the tangled melaleucas. He turned on the boat's prow lights and drove through a break between the interwoven branches. Jazz would never have seen it if it hadn't been revealed to her as it was now, and she realized it was undetectable from an aerial view.

They entered what had to be a manmade tunnel through the trees, barely wider than the plane's wingspan. Raj flicked on some brighter lights, revealing the tunnel's structure. The boughs of the trees overhead appeared to be woven together, so thick that Jazz could barely spot stars twinkling above them.

"Wow," she whispered, marveling at the unnatural construction.

"Neat!" Chaz said. He leaned forward and watched through the cockpit window. Dante barked, watching beside him.

They chugged through the channel for about a quarter of a mile before the tunnel opened up, revealing a small lagoon a third the size of a football field.

Raj towed them to a dimly lit dock at the opposite end of the lagoon. He tied the boat to the dock with some ropes coiled on the ledge, while Kino and Roberta hopped out onto the dock and did the same to the plane. A plane almost identical to theirs was tied up to the other side of the dock, with two large swamp boats tied up at either end of it.

"Okay, Jazz. Chaz." Kino offered his hand while Cody tossed the bags up to Roberta. "Ahoy, mateys. Come on up."

Jazz held Chaz's hand while he stepped out onto the pontoon. Dante leaped onto the dock and stood beside Kino, tongue lolling and tail wagging. Chaz grabbed Kino's hand, and Kino lifted him up onto the dock. Jazz stepped onto the pontoon, and Cody took her arm to steady her.

"I *got* it," she huffed, and pulled her arm out of his grasp. She looked up at Kino, smiled and took his hand, and stepped up onto the dock.

Cody shook his head and leaped up. He stumbled when he landed and barely caught himself before he fell. Jazz saw Kino look back at him, and noticed them nod to each other.

Roberta grabbed her gear bag and Dante's backpack while Raj took Jazz and Chaz's bags. Dante ran ahead of the group to dry land and stood beside an old Chevy pickup truck. He looked back at them as if he already knew the plan. Kino grabbed his gear bag, winked at Jazz, and put his arm around Chaz's shoulder.

"Come on, my man," he said. "Whaddaya say we go meet some new friends?"

Chaz looked up at him and grinned. "Okay."

After tossing the bags in the pickup's bed, Raj hopped into the driver's seat. Roberta sat beside him in the passenger seat. Jazz, Chaz, Dante, and Kino climbed in back, followed by Cody. Raj started the truck, and Cody winced as he leaned up against the metal siding.

"You gonna make it there, tough guy?" Kino asked

softly.

Jazz heard the concern in his voice, and watched Cody. He just nodded, closed his eyes, and his head sagged.

They rode down a dirt road through spooky-looking overhanging trees laden with Spanish moss. Jazz felt as if they were traveling through another world.

She hadn't forgotten about her father's predicament. She intended on asking these people to help her find him, and rescue him too. If he was still alive.

Kino must have read her mind. "Don't worry, Jazz. They won't hurt him. They'll want to use him as a bargaining chip to get Chaz."

That solidified her resolve. Nobody was taking Chaz from her. She nodded at Kino.

A few minutes later, they passed a dozen quaint cottages surrounded by overhanging trees that effectively camouflaged them. Beyond the cottages were several brick buildings, and Raj parked beside the largest one.

Everyone hopped out, leaving the bags in the pickup, and walked up the brick porch steps. Raj smiled, held the door open for Jazz and Chaz, and gestured them inside. Jazz followed Chaz through the doorway, with Dante right behind them.

She was pleasantly surprised by the unpretentious interior of the twenty-by-thirty-foot front room. A few well-worn sofas rested against three of the walls. A threadbare tan carpet covered the floor. At the far end of the room, a doorway led down a long hall. Two ceiling fans circled lazily overhead, gently stirring the air. Framed pictures hung on three of the walls. All appeared to have been drawn, colored, or painted by children. The only anomalous décor was a giant flat-screen monitor against the fourth wall. It appeared to display a visual of the grounds outside the building.

But all of this barely registered. Jazz was too busy watching the nine children sitting on the floor in the middle of the room. Beside them stood a tall, beautiful, raven-haired

Asian woman in a flowery blue, green, and violet kimono. She looked to be in her late twenties. Everyone was smiling and watching Jazz and Chaz. Roberta, Kino, Cody, and Raj followed them inside, and the smiles became delighted grins.

"Kino!" several children cried. They jumped to their feet, and the others took up the chorus. "Kino!" they called, and dashed toward the big man.

"Hey, guys!" Kino roared, grinning.

The children grabbed his arms and legs. Two of the smaller kids climbed up him, wrapped their arms around his neck, and kissed him on the cheeks. They all started laughing and chattering.

"We missed you, Kino!"

"Why'd you have to be gone so long?"

"You're going to stay for a while this time, right?"

"I missed you guys too!" Kino said. He laughed and poked one in the belly, tickled another. They tackled him, dragged him to the floor, and started jumping on top of him and wrestling with him. He grunted, wincing in obvious pain. When he caught Jazz watching, he hid the look, winked at her, and smiled.

Jazz looked back at Roberta, Raj, and Cody, her eyebrows raised. Roberta and Raj grinned. Cody glanced at her, rolled his eyes, and shook his head. He walked toward one of two older girls standing beside the Asian woman, an attractive brown-haired girl of about thirteen. She smirked at him, and he punched her gently in the arm.

"Hey, Mara. It's good to see you. You look good."

The girl punched him back harder, but she was smiling. "Hey, butthole. Wish I could say the same about you."

While the other children giggled and wrestled with Kino, Cody walked toward the other young girl. The Asian woman nodded to him and approached Jazz and Chaz, smiling.

Jazz watched Cody and the girl while Chaz stayed by her side. Dante rubbed up against Chaz's leg and watched everything, his tail revving up to takeoff velocity.

Cody stood before the second girl and smiled. She looked about fifteen, and was all arms and legs. Her medium-length blond hair was stringy and fell in her face. Jazz thought she would be very pretty one day, whenever she grew into her body and matured some. The girl looked up at Cody, her face glowing.

Cody lifted a hand, gently stroked her hair out of her eyes, and said something Jazz didn't hear. The girl reached up and hugged him, and kissed him on the cheek. Cody looked stiff and awkward as he hugged her back. When she let him go, he said something else, and left her and headed down the hall.

The Asian woman was watching Jazz watch Cody, and Jazz turned to her. The woman had the face of an angel, and her smile lit up the room.

"Hi. I'm Tinga." She looked down at Chaz and put her hand on his shoulder. "Welcome to Homestead."

"Hi, Tinga," Chaz said, beaming at her.

Jazz relaxed a bit. "Hi, Tinga. I'm Jazz, and this is my son Chaz. And Dante."

Tinga put a hand to her lips and giggled. "Yes, I know. Welcome to you all. I let the children stay up past their bed-times because they all wanted to meet you."

Jazz laughed. "Looks like most of them are a little pre-occupied at the moment."

Dante barked, and Chaz waved his arm. "Okay already! Go play, boy."

Dante jumped into the fray, and the children welcomed him as if he were one of the gang. Kino howled as one child jumped on his belly, and Tinga turned to the revelers and scowled, her hands on her hips.

The gangly blond girl approached Jazz and Chaz, nodded at Jazz, and smiled at Chaz. She stuck her hand out.

"Hi, Chaz. Welcome. I'm Amanda."

Chaz's eyes widened, and he grinned and shook her

hand. "Are you the one who wrote the letter?"

"Yep. That's me. I'm so glad you're okay, and so happy to meet you." Amanda turned to Jazz. "All three of you."

"I'm pleased to meet you too, Amanda," Jazz said. "I have… umm, a lot of questions."

"I'll be happy to answer any that I can, Ms. Tandy."

"Jazz, please."

"Okay. Jazz." Amanda offered Jazz her hand, and Jazz shook it.

One of the smaller girls approached Roberta, leaped into her arms, and kissed her on the cheek. Raj headed out the front door, and Tinga put her fingers to her lips and let out an ear-piercing whistle. The children eased up on Kino and watched her. She gestured to Chaz and Jazz.

"Children, I want you all to meet our new friends. As you know, this is Chaz. Make him feel welcome."

"Hi, Chaz!" the children called out in unison, and Chaz waved.

Tinga nodded. "And this is his mother, Ms. Tandy."

"Jazz, please. Everyone call me Jazz. All my friends do."

"Hi, Jazz!" the children shouted together. Dante barked, his wagging tail a dangerous weapon.

Tinga grinned. "And this is Dante."

"Hi, Dante!" the children cried out amid giggles. Dante barked again and pranced around them, as full of energy as Jazz and Chaz were drained of it.

The children started chattering at once, and Tinga whistled again.

"Enough!" She waggled a finger at her charges. "We had a deal, remember? They've had a long, hard trip today. There will be plenty of time tomorrow and the days ahead to get to know our new friends, *if* they decide to stay with us. Now it's bedtime."

The children grumbled and moaned good-naturedly, and Kino stood and squinted at Tinga. "Tinga, do I need to go get my whip?"

The children shrieked and giggled, and dashed to the hallway and down the hall.

Dante lingered, and Tinga turned and bowed to Chaz and Jazz. "Goodnight, Chaz. Jazz. Amanda and Mara will show you to your room. I'll talk to you more tomorrow, and answer any questions you like."

Jazz nodded, and Chaz smiled and said, "Goodnight, Tinga."

Kino roared at a couple of straggling children, and lumbered toward them like a B-movie monster. The kids squealed and ran. Amanda and Mara stayed and Tinga headed down the hallway. Roberta followed, waving at Jazz and Chaz. Kino turned at the doorway and winked at them.

"I'll see you guys in the morning, okay?"

Jazz walked up to Kino and hugged him. "Thanks, Kino. You don't know just how much—"

"Don't worry, Jazz." He squeezed her. "We'll come up with a plan, okay?"

Jazz sniffled and wiped a tear away. "Okay."

Kino nodded and turned and headed down the hallway. He roared again, and the kids squealed.

Amanda took Chaz's hand and smiled at him, winning Jazz over for good. "Come on, Chaz. Mara and I'll show you and your mother to your room for the night. I bet you're all pretty tired. Raj already got your bags and took 'em to your room."

Amanda led Chaz down the wide hallway, and Jazz, Mara, and Dante followed. Jazz watched Chaz as he looked up at Amanda. The girl showed leadership capabilities as well as maternal instinct. Judging by Chaz's starry-eyed gaze, he was already as smitten as a nine-year-old boy could be.

"This is my newest best friend, Mara," Amanda said.

"Hi, Mara." Chaz looked over his shoulder and smiled, still holding Amanda's hand.

"Hi, Mara," Jazz said, grinning at Chaz.

"Hi," Mara said.

Jazz asked the first question that came to mind. "Mara, Amanda, was Cody your Guardian?"

"Yes, ma'am," Amanda said. Her eyes twinkled as she looked over her shoulder. "The dark man saved us both."

"Oh, you call him that too?"

Mara smirked. "Everybody does. What else would you call him?"

"Oh." Jazz realized Mara didn't mean it as a racial slur, whatever mixed race Cody was. *He* is *the dark man*, she thought. Then she thought of something else. "Mara, did your umm... parents... I mean—"

"One of the Extractors killed Poppa," Mara said, scowling. "Five months ago. Then Cody brought me here. Momma died in an accident a year and a half ago."

From Mara's tone of voice and expression, Jazz could tell the wounds still cut deeply. "Oh, honey. I'm so sorry."

"*They're* going to be sorry," Mara said. "When we find them."

Jazz felt Mara's rage. Thinking of her father, she realized she shared it. "So where's the professor? Dr. Ben?"

"He went on a little trip," Amanda said. "With a couple of the children, and another Guardian and a Fixer. That's what Kino is." Amanda turned and smiled at Jazz. "I like Kino. A lot."

"I do too," Jazz said, remembering their conversation in the van.

"Everybody does," Mara said, nodding.

"You'll meet Dr. Ben tomorrow," Amanda said. "He'll be back sometime tomorrow afternoon. You'll like him too. He's a good man. And a good friend."

"He's richer than God," Mara said, still nodding.

"Yeah, he invented some... stuff," Amanda said. "I can't explain it. It's quantum physics stuff. He's really smart."

"Genius," Mara said. "But he takes good care of every-body."

"Very good care," Amanda said. "He's like a father to us all. I love him very much."

"Yeah, me too," Mara said softly, as if she'd just realized it.

Jazz wanted to meet him. She had a lot of questions for him.

They had passed several doors. Amanda turned at one door mid-way down the hall and gestured at it.

"Here's your rooms for the night." She opened the door and waved her hand with a flourish. "I think you'll be pleased."

Jazz walked in first, and Dante slipped in behind her. Amanda and Chaz entered hand in hand, and Mara followed.

The room was a cozy but practical combo of living room and kitchen, with a dinette dividing them. A comfy-looking sofa rested against the far wall beside the dining table. A computer station on a wheeled cart sat opposite it, with a twenty-seven inch monitor mounted atop it.

The apartment's outer walls had three large windows with a view of unfamiliar flora that appeared otherworldly in the moonlight. Beyond the kitchen was an open door with Jazz's bag beside it. Dante's backpack rested against the sofa. On the right past the living room was another open door. Chaz's bag sat in the doorway.

Jazz wanted to know everything, and now, but she could hardly stand. Chaz finally let go of Amanda's hand and checked out their new digs. Dante followed at his side. Amanda turned and gestured to a keypad on the wall beside the door.

"Intercom and security system," she said. "For now, your security code is 'Chaz.' You can change it later if you decide to stay. Or not. I hope you decide to stay." She pointed to a button labeled "talk," and then to two green-lit buttons beside it with adhesive labels with the letters "C" and "J" mounted on them. "C is for Chaz, and J is for Jazz. For your bedrooms. There's one at each wall above your beds, and one in each bathroom."

Jazz's head swam. Everything that had happened, that was happening, was too much information, circuit overload, shutdown imminent.

C is for Chaz, she thought. *And J is for Jazz*. CJ.

Cody Jackson, a voice whispered in her head. Jazz stifled it, frowning and trying to concentrate on what Amanda was saying. She refused to think about Cody right now.

"...call anybody here you want to anytime by scrolling through the menu here. Hit the red button anytime you want *everyone* to hear. The red bar at the bottom is emergency, and sounds a silent alarm, and a siren if you punch it twice." Amanda turned to Jazz, smiling. "The computer is yours to use as you wish. Everything's routed through... umm..."

"Multiple anonymous Internet service providers," Mara said.

"Yeah," Amanda said, and turned and high-fived Mara. "That. So you're safe, wherever you surf. Even if you want to email your dad. Kendra and Malek are working hard on tracking him down, I promise."

In a brief moment of clarity, Jazz realized that while she and Chaz had slept on the plane, either Kino or Roberta must have radioed in a lot of information about them.

"They're awesome," Amanda continued. "They took over the whole system after Stephan... died. You'll like them too."

Right, Stephan, the Fixer Kino told me about. Roberta's husband, the Fixer who got killed. Widow Roberta. I'm dreaming. Daddy's safe at home. I'm gonna wake up soon.

"Yeah, they're like mega computer geniuses," Mara said. "They can see really abstract stuff in their minds. They think in like equations or something."

Amanda nodded. "Complex multi-dimensional spatial thinking."

"Serious computer wizard stuff," Mara said. "After the

Guardians found out about them and before Soulsnatcher tried to take 'em, the government tried to steal them. Use them for military and espionage stuff."

"The government tried to *recruit* them," Amanda corrected.

"Whatever." Mara smirked. "It's stealing their lives either way. And it's what gave them away to Soulsnatcher."

"Yeah, but the government would have at least paid them," Amanda said. "Soulsnatcher uses them. Sometimes until there's nothing left." She gazed at Jazz. "Like he would use Chaz."

"It's still slavery," Mara said, frowning.

Wait, what? Soulsnatcher? Who is that? You mentioned him in the letter. Jazz was sure she was about to keel over.

Amanda sighed. "Yeah, it is. But not like with *them*."

Mara shrugged. "So everybody tells me."

"Maybe you should ask Cody what the difference is, Mara," Amanda said with raised eyebrows.

"Okay, okay." Mara surrendered, waving her hands.

"Girls, please," Jazz said. "What... umm, who is—"

"All of your questions will be answered tomorrow," Amanda said, smiling. "A buffet-style breakfast is served every morning between seven and eight in the dining hall next door. There's food in the refrigerator and cabinets here, but I recommend not missing breakfast. It's yummy. They have fruits and cereals if you don't like meat, and lots of meat if you do. Sausage, bacon, country ham, eggs, hash browns, grits, toast, pancakes, biscuits and gravy—"

"They get the point, Amanda," Mara said.

"Yeah, you're both probably exhausted, huh? Well, there's a full bath in each of your rooms, and a couple at the end of the hall." Amanda frowned. "And if for some crazy reason you don't like it here, they'll take you anywhere you want to go."

"I recommend staying here," Mara said.

"Me too," Amanda said, nodding. "Now that Soulsnatcher and the Extractors know about you, there's no safer place to hide Chaz from them. You can look at the cottages that are unoccupied tomorrow, if you don't like your rooms. Either way, I hope you'll stay with us."

What choice did they have? Dante barked, and Jazz found her voice. "Girls, thank you both. So much."

"Good night, Jazz," Amanda said. She turned to Chaz and gave him sunshine in a smile. "Goodnight, Chaz. I'll talk more with you both tomorrow, and we'll figure out what you need to do, okay?"

"Okay." Chaz gave her a vigorous nod. "Goodnight, Amanda."

Mara turned and went out into the hallway. Amanda followed, grinning and waving at Chaz, and closed the door behind her. Jazz took a deep breath. It was all too much. She was crashing hard.

At least Chaz was safe. She felt good about their situation, even though unanswered questions made her head feel like it was going to explode.

"Okay, Binky. Let's get you in bed. We'll decide what we're gonna do tomorrow, after we find out more about this place."

"I wanna stay here, Mother. I like it here."

"We'll see."

"Dante likes it here too."

"You think? Well, it's too late, and I'm too tired to make any decisions right now." She had no idea what she was going to do about her job, her father, their possessions, her money, or anything for that matter.

"If we stay here, I'll be around lots of children just like me."

"Mmm-hmm." She steered him into the bedroom. "Get undressed, and in your pajamas."

"I could learn a lot if we stayed here."

My persuasive, precocious little boy. She plucked his pajamas out of his bag and handed them to him. "It's time to go to bed, sweetie. Get some sleep."

Chaz put them on and hopped in bed. Dante jumped up and lay down beside him. Jazz went into the front room, pulled Dante's bowls out of the backpack, filled one with food and the other with water from the tap, and set them on the floor beside Chaz's bed. She was hungry, but she was too tired to eat.

Chaz looked up at her from under the covers and grinned. "It would be a valuable learning experience for me, Mother."

She chuckled and sat on the edge of the mattress. She tickled him, and he laughed. "Go to sleep, silly boy. We'll talk about it tomorrow."

"Promise me you'll at least think about it?"

"I promise. Now go to sleep." She kissed him on the cheek.

"Okay. Is Grandpa gonna be okay?"

Jazz fought the tears that wanted to come, and lied. "I think so, Binky."

"Good. Goodnight, Mother. I love you."

"I love you too, Chaz." Jazz nearly choked on her emotions. It had been one hell of a crazy roller coaster day.

She went into her bedroom, kicked off her shoes, took off her jeans and shirt, and flopped down on the bed. She said a silent prayer for her father, and barely laid her head on the pillow before she drifted off.

And dreamed of whirlwind demons teleporting from one place to another and stealing children's souls.

Chapter 12

Jazz woke to the sight of fiery orange sunlight filtering in through her bedroom window. Confused by her unfamiliar surroundings, she shook her head, gradually recalling details. She glanced at the digital clock beside the bed. The display read 7:14.

She'd slept well, and felt much better. Her stomach rumbled, and she sat up. Chaz was probably starving.

A white bathrobe hung from a hook on the back of her bedroom door. She threw it on and went out to the front room. Chaz sat on the sofa, doing something on the computer. Dante lay beside him, panting and watching Jazz.

"Hey, special guy," she said, smiling. "How are you feeling?"

"Better." Chaz let go of the mouse. "I really like it here, Mother. And I'm *starving*. We're late for breakfast." His hair was wet.

"Did you already take a shower?"

"Yes, ma'am. Can we go eat now?"

She grinned. "Did you take Dante outside to do his business?"

"No. I was waiting for you to get up."

"Well, go take him now. I'm gonna jump in the shower, and when I get out, we'll go eat."

"Okay. Hurry, Mother, please. I haven't eaten since, like, yesterday."

She laughed. "Yes, sir. Now go take Dante outside."

Chaz got up and called Dante. Jazz went into her bathroom and took the most refreshing hot shower she could remember ever taking. When she finished, she dressed in a denim skirt, white peasant blouse with leather-stringed lacing, and ballerina flats. She felt reinvigorated, relaxed, and ready to meet some new friends and chow down.

And figure out how to rescue her father, and get some answers to a lot of questions.

She left their rooms and headed down the empty hallway. Outside, she found Chaz standing beside Amanda.

Dante scampered and pranced around them, his Kong ball clenched in his jaws. Chaz gestured, relating some story to Amanda. He didn't see Jazz. He was engrossed in his tale, and fixated on Amanda, who waved at Jazz as she approached them.

"Good morning," Jazz said, grinning.

"Good morning, Jazz," Amanda said.

Chaz turned around. "About time, Mother. Please, let's go eat before it's all gone."

"Let's." Jazz chuckled and winked at Amanda. Chaz grabbed Amanda's hand, and she led them to the dining hall.

It was a beautiful morning, full of bright promise. Wispy tendrils of fog dissipated with the dawn, revealing the coming day. The sun shone through the canopy of tree boughs, stippling the ground in alternating patterns of light and dark.

Chaz made Dante stay outside and they went in. The comfortable sounds of conversation and laughter instantly reassured Jazz.

At the far end of the long room was an enormous fireplace, its brass-paneled grates closed until winter returned. For now, several ceiling fans circled overhead, creating a soothing current that stirred up the humid air.

The scuffed hardwood floor amplified the happy chatter and sent it echoing off the light cedar-paneled walls. Jazz thought it sounded like the gentle rush of a fond memory, and smiled. In the corners of the room a series of colorful, exotic potted plants and miniature trees contributed to the ambiance.

Amanda led them to the buffet against the long left wall of the rectangular building. Two rows of tables seating twelve to a side were lined up lengthwise in the center of the room.

Twelve adults and ten children sat intermingled at the ends of the tables closest to the buffet.

Jazz was pleased that they hadn't separated into groups. There was no ostracism going on here. She already felt as if she was among friends.

Chaz let go of Amanda's hand so he could fill up a plate. Tinga, Kino, Roberta, Raj, and Cody sat at the closest table and waved, and Jazz waved back. Several children called out "Good morning!" and "Hi, Chaz!" as Jazz heaped food onto her plate. The enticing aroma of eggs, bacon, and pancakes permeated the air, and her stomach rumbled again.

When they went to the table, three people had moved so they could sit in the midst of the crowd. As Jazz dug into her breakfast, she noticed the deference all the children accorded Amanda, and wondered what her special talent was. Pitchers of orange juice, milk, and ice water were passed down the table.

"There's coffee too, if you want it," Amanda said. "Far end of the buffet."

"Sounds good, thanks," Jazz said. "Maybe after breakfast."

She watched and listened to the group while she ate. Chaz sat to her left, then Amanda, then Cody, who was trading cheesy insults with Kino across the table. Roberta and Raj sat on either side of Kino, laughing as they watched him and Cody.

Cody grumbled, but he was laughing too. He looked good, and healthy. He was recovering from his injuries well, thanks mostly to Chaz.

Had she been too hard on him? He *had* saved their lives yesterday. She was certain he would have given his life for theirs if necessary. He nearly did.

Cody glanced over at her, and she looked down at her plate, feeling like a shy schoolgirl caught admiring the quarterback on the sly. She noticed Amanda looking at Cody the same way, the way Chaz looked at Amanda.

A handsome, muscular, black-haired man entered the

hall and walked over to the buffet. Some of the children called out "Good morning, Marco!" The man nodded and gave a weak smile. He filled a plate and went to the end of the table, away from everyone else, and sat.

Kino and Cody stopped their banter and stared at each other. Roberta and Raj stopped laughing, and Roberta and Kino started to rise. Cody stood and patted a hand at them, and they sat.

Cody walked over to Marco and spoke with him, and Jazz realized who the man was. He was the Guardian Kino had told her about, the man who believed he was responsible for the death of Roberta's husband a year ago.

The group had quieted down; many of them watched Cody and Marco. Jazz watched too, feeling the tension.

Cody put a hand on Marco's shoulder, spoke again, and gestured toward the others. Marco looked down, back up at Cody, and nodded. He rose and joined the others with Cody, and the happy chatter resumed.

Watching Cody sit and nod at Kino, Jazz realized she had sorely misjudged him.

Roberta looked at Marco and smiled. "Hi, Marco."

Marco nodded to her, his eyes downcast. "Roberta."

Roberta looked at Jazz. "Jazz, Chaz, this is Marco, one of our Guardians. He just got back from an assignment yesterday afternoon. Marco, meet Jazz and Chaz, our newest friends."

Marco nodded toward them. "Pleased to meet you both. Welcome."

"Hi, Marco," Chaz said, and resumed chowing down and watching Amanda.

Jazz smiled. "Hi, Marco."

Marco nodded again, and returned his attention to his plate. Cody and Kino resumed ragging each other, and Jazz quietly finished her breakfast. The pain in Marco's eyes reminded her of the gravity of their situation, and of her father. Now that her hunger was appeased, she needed answers.

Chaz went back for seconds. Jazz smiled, pleased to see him replenishing his strength. He'd overextended himself yesterday, making her worry about his heart. But he looked happier and more at home now than she'd seen him in a long time, and that and her full belly helped her relax.

The table gradually cleared as everyone finished eating. Jazz watched Amanda, dying to know what her talent was. What to ask her first?

"Amanda, what—"

Amanda stood, plate and cup in hand, and so did Kino, Raj, Marco, and Cody. Roberta remained seated, smiling as she watched Jazz, Chaz, and Amanda.

"It's time for class," Amanda said, grinning. "We'd love for Chaz to join us. You can too, if you want to watch and see what we study." She glanced at Cody as he left. "See you at lunch, Cody." Her eyes sparkled, and Jazz finally figured it out. Why had it taken her so long?

Cody nodded and strode off, accompanied by the others. Jazz shook her head, trying to concentrate on what Amanda was saying.

"…but if you don't want him to," Amanda continued, "Chaz can ride with you on the tour. Roberta will be your guide. She'll answer your questions."

"I want to go to class with Amanda, Mother," Chaz said. "You can go on the tour without me."

Jazz glanced at Roberta, who smiled and nodded. That told Jazz all she needed to know. She'd known it would happen someday, but she still felt the sting of Chaz's rejection. She was suddenly superfluous. Chaz was willing to strike out, in this small way, on his own. She couldn't stand in the way of that.

Roberta's eyes held answers, and Jazz realized she needed to hear them without Chaz's prying little ears. She stooped over Chaz, fighting tears she hadn't expected.

"Okay, Binky. I'll—"

"Mother!"

119

Jazz nodded, stood, and mustered a smile, her heart aching. "I was just going to say I'll see you at lunch?"

Chaz smiled and grabbed his plate and cup. "Yeah. I mean, okay." He hurried after Amanda, who looked over her shoulder and smiled at Jazz.

"Whenever you're ready, Jazz," Roberta said. "Whatever you want to know, beyond personal stuff about certain people, I'm ready."

Jazz figured personal stuff about certain people meant Cody. "Okay. I'm ready."

Roberta led her outside. Dante scampered among the children as they headed toward the building adjacent to the main one.

Jazz watched Chaz go with them, filled with a yearning for something she couldn't define. She turned to Roberta, who stood by a Jeep Wrangler with its top off, parked beside the dining hall.

"They know about his heart," Roberta said. "He'll be fine, Jazz."

"How do they know?" Jazz hadn't told Cody or Kino about Chaz's heart condition.

Roberta shrugged. "Cody's your Guardian. It's his job to know everything about you both."

Jazz suddenly realized how overprotective she had become. With everything that had happened lately, it was impossible not to be. Everything was different now, through no choice of theirs. The rules had changed.

She nodded. "Okay. Well, I guess I'm ready."

Roberta smiled. "Hop in."

Jazz did, and they went for a ride.

Chapter 13

"The island is about forty acres," Roberta said as she drove. "The whole property is the professor's. Other than the main buildings, cottages, hangar, and docks, there are no free-standing manmade structures. Helps keep us hidden from prying eyes."

Roberta showed Jazz the well-hidden security cameras mounted in strategic locations throughout the island as they bumped along in the open Jeep. "They're monitored twenty-four- seven, three-sixty-five, on three eight-hour shifts with four very dedicated people each."

Jazz tried to get a word in edgewise, but Roberta kept up her spiel.

"Everybody here came from some kind of hard luck story, and everybody's here voluntarily. Everybody gets a pay-check too, including the kids. It goes into offshore accounts. Put away for a rainy day, if you know what I mean, and I bet you do, judging from your and Chaz's history. Before you ask, if you wanna know anybody's hard luck story, you'll have to ask them. I'll only tell you mine, if you wanna hear it."

"I do," Jazz said. She could learn more just by listening.

Roberta nodded as she navigated around a huge puddle. "The way we found most people here was through a com-plicated series of computer tracking programs. They were de-signed to filter the results from various media and prioritize them in order of the most likely prospects for the Homestead Guardian Project. That is, primarily children with unusual talents. My husband Stephan designed and created it. Did Cody tell you about him?"

"Kino did. I'm sorry for your loss."

"Ahh, Kino."

Jazz heard something wistful in Roberta's drawl, but she couldn't give away Kino's secret. "He's a remarkable man, with an equally remarkable story."

"That he is. I just wish he'd…" Roberta shook her head. "Never mind."

"No, tell me. Please."

Roberta glanced at her. "I know how he feels about me, Jazz. Everybody does, even though Kino isn't aware of it. You obviously already figured it out too. I would've loved to hear your conversation with him, but I'm not going to ask you what he said about me. I wouldn't ask you to betray that confidence. I just wish he knew how I feel about him."

"Maybe you should try telling him."

Roberta squinted at her, and laughed when she saw her smile. "God knows I have! Every time I try to get him to open up to me, he runs away. I think he believes he could never fill Stephan's place in my heart. But he can, and does. Sure they're different, everybody is, in some way. But I've learned to live with Stephan's death, because I—and he—loved his life so much. He gave so much of himself, just like Kino does." Roberta shook her head and chuckled. "Listen to me, I'm rambling, unloading on you with my love life. Or lack thereof."

"No, I'm listening. I wanna know."

"Thanks, Jazz. That means a lot to me. I've needed someone… like you, just to talk to, for so long. Kino won't let me in."

"I need all the friends I can get, Roberta. I'm just now realizing that's what's been missing from my life."

"I'd like to be your friend, Jazz."

"I'd like to be your friend too."

Roberta grinned, teeth gleaming in the bright morning sunshine. She laughed, then sighed. "It's just… sometimes I wanna shake him into a knot, and make him tell me what he thinks is wrong with him. If he'd just open up to me, I know I can help him. I know he doesn't think there's anything wrong with me. He thinks it's all him. I just wish he'd tell me what it is."

"If he means that much to you, then just give him time." Jazz chuckled. "Maybe I can help. We women know how to influence men without them knowing, right?"

Roberta laughed again, and it was a hearty and cheerful sound. Jazz laughed too.

"I like you, Jazz."

"I like you too. So tell me more."

Jazz meant about her and Kino, but Roberta came to a fork in the dirt trail, turned to the right, and reverted into tour guide mode.

"Okay. We have sonar and radar surveillance all monitored by computer, in addition to motion detectors, heat sensors, and camera. So any boat—including submersibles— plane, helicopter, hot air balloon, hang-glider, skydiver, surveillance drone, UFO, or alligator that comes anywhere near us, we know about it."

Roberta drove slowly by another secluded lagoon that sheltered two more planes and three boats. "That's cove number two of three. We call it the Blue Lagoon. We have a total of seven planes, nine boats, and four fully-armed helicopters."

"Can all of you fly?"

"Everyone except the kids, the kitchen crew, a few of the maintenance technicians—like Raj—and a handful of security personnel."

"Wow. Even Tinga?"

"Yep. And the professor too. Tinga's one of our best pilots. We're ready for almost any emergency evacuation or de-fense contingency." Roberta glanced at Jazz and smiled. "We'll teach you to fly too, Jazz. If you decide to stay with us."

"I don't see how I have a choice."

Roberta nodded. "At least you're realistic about it. You're lucky to be alive, you know."

"So I've heard, but keeping Chaz safe and finding my

father is all that matters right now. And I don't want to be a burden. If we decide to stay, I want to contribute. Somehow. I just don't know how yet."

Roberta drove them across a shallow creek. Mud and water goose-tailed behind them as she kicked it and headed up the rise past the creek. "I'm sure you'll come up with something!" she shouted over the engine's roar.

The front tires were airborne as they topped the rise and hurtled past it. They emerged from the trees and brush onto a wide sandy promontory. Roberta rolled up to the water line, stopped, and engaged the brake. She turned off the engine, and she and Jazz gazed quietly out on the still water. Patches of thick marsh grass led up to a line of trees spanning the horizon half a mile away. Sunlight glistened on the open water, creating the silvery illusion of a vast mirror.

Something about the vision was mystical. It was enchanting but treacherous, providing bountiful life, yet harboring furtive death.

"Wow," Jazz said, exhaling. "It's… strangely beautiful."

"That's exactly what I thought when I first saw it."

"It's so… eerily peaceful, but…"

"Dangerous."

Jazz nodded. "Exactly."

"Just like what you're going through now, Jazz. The unknown threat is the most volatile. I just want you to know how safe you and Chaz will be here. And maybe happy too."

Jazz frowned. "Do the… bad people know about this place?"

"If they did, one or the other of us would be gone by now."

Jazz took a deep breath, remembering what Roberta's job was. According to Kino, she was a highly trained expert in the art of killing, just like Cody. Her bare hands alone were lethal weapons.

Roberta continued. "But because of the professor, and

Stephan, and a few others, a protective web is woven around us. Here, the children are able to develop and control their powers in a safe environment, and learn restraint and compassion in using them."

"Yeah." Jazz sighed, understanding more than Roberta could ever know. "But Chaz is going to miss healing others. He's always excited about healing people, especially children. He says that since he can't use his power to heal himself, he should use it to help them."

"Yeah, I was going to ask you about that."

"Ironic, isn't it? God's cruel joke."

"I don't know about that, Jazz. Maybe it's God's way of healing him. He's an exceptionally amazing kid."

"I know. I'm so confused. I feel so lost. Adrift."

"Homestead can heal that for you. I've made some really good friends here, and you and Chaz will too."

"You're trying to talk me into staying." Jazz thought back on the morning's events. "You all planned this whole thing out, didn't you? Taking me alone on this tour, trying to persuade me to stay."

Roberta shrugged, smiling at her.

Jazz shook her head, smiling too. "It's okay. I understand why. But I won't be able to find *any* peace until I find out what they did to my father. Until then, the only thing that takes precedence is Chaz's safety."

"Believe me, Jazz, I understand. We're trying to find out where they took him. And Kino, Cody, Marco, and I are ready to go after him like cats on mice if we get any leads." Roberta took a deep breath.

"I'm not gonna lie to you, Jazz. The bad news is, these people are very good at what they do, and thorough. They're pros, and they took your father to use as leverage to get Chaz. They won't have left a trace of him, or themselves. They'll hide him away wherever their own version of Homestead is, which we're constantly looking for, by the way, and keep him there.

125

Until they figure out how to threaten you into giving up Chaz for him. But there's good news too."

"I'll never give up Chaz. No matter what they do to my father. Neither he nor I would ever forgive me if I did." Jazz felt the fury rising.

"Good." Roberta smiled and nodded. "I knew that, by the way. It's one of the things I like about you, Jazz."

Jazz bit her lip. Cody had been watching over her and Chaz without their knowledge for some time now, and because of that Roberta and everyone else here likely knew everything about her. "So what's the good news? I could sure use some."

"The good news is they want Chaz really bad, and they'll do absolutely anything to get him. You'll find out exactly why when you meet the professor. So they'll be keeping your father safe and healthy until they get Chaz. And we aren't going to let that happen."

"They'll have to do it over my dead body."

Roberta glared at Jazz. Her eyes were emerald and deep, shining with a fiery determination. "Don't doubt for a second that they will kill you to get Chaz."

"Yeah? Well, they don't know who they're messing with. They just stepped into a lion's den. And they have no idea how sorry they're going to be when I find them."

"I knew there was a good reason I liked you so much as soon as we met. But don't underestimate them, Jazz. They're everything the letter said and worse."

"Yeah, well, maybe I have a few tricks up my sleeve too."

"I'm sure you do, along with the strength you need to withstand whatever happens. I saw it in you right away. But there's more good news."

"Well, share it."

Roberta nodded, gazing out again at the glassy expanse of water. "Right here, we have the smartest, most determined, and most gifted people on the planet doing everything they can to help you and Chaz, and your father too. You can't buy friends like that. And we won't stop until we find these very bad people, and when we do, we'll finish this thing once and for all. Or die trying."

Jazz knew Roberta meant every word. "Well, I want to help too. I feel so helpless."

"You won't for long."

"I have over thirty-six thousand dollars in savings accounts. I'll gladly use it, every last cent, to find Daddy."

"You can't do that, Jazz. They're monitoring everything about you. Bank accounts, driver's license, cell phone, email, credit cards, anything you own that they can trace you with. As soon as you access any of it, they'll be on you, and it'll be over for you and Chaz. And I know Chaz is worth more to you than any amount of money."

"You're damn right he is. But… dammit, I just want to do something about it."

"I understand, believe me, and we're gonna help you do something about it. Have you met Kendra and Malek?"

"No, but Amanda and Mara told me about them. The computer geniuses?"

Roberta laughed. "Way beyond that. They're unbelievable. They took over the entire computer system from Stephan when they came here four years ago, and he was happy to let them. He was a computer guru too, but these kids blew him away. Malek is nineteen now, and Kendra's eighteen. I'll introduce you to them after lunch. You didn't see them in the dining hall because they ate breakfast in the control room so they could work on tracking down your father. And our common enemy."

"Four years ago," Jazz said, calculating. "How long have you been here, Roberta?"

"Going on seven years now."

"Wow. How old are you? Yeah, that's a touchy subject, but we girls can ask each other, right?"

Roberta laughed. "I'm thirty-two. Stephan and I got

married ten years ago. He was a very outspoken political activist at the time. Hard-core Libertarian-slash-Constitutionalist. We were both disillusioned with our ridiculously corrupt government, and looking for a better life. Or at least a better way to live."

Roberta took a deep breath. "One day a couple of black suits came to visit us. When Stephan wouldn't let them in, they forced their way in. Told us it would be wise if we 'shut the fuck up or else,' and got on with our lives quietly."

"They actually said that?"

"Word for word. Stephan laughed in their faces, but I knew they meant business. Couple of cold fish, hard men with empty eyes. Anyway, they didn't like being laughed at. Started pushing Stephan around, and one of 'em threw me up against the wall. Scared the hell out of me. I told Stephan to let it go so they'd leave us alone. I should have known better. Stephan wasn't the kind of man to let something like that go, and that's one of the things I loved so much about him. But he was no match for those assholes. They were the kind of government goons who were trained to inflict pain and eager to intimidate. One of 'em nearly punched my lights out, and kicked me when I was down—"

"Whoa! Government guys did this?"

"Well, they didn't *claim* to be government goons, but even an idiot could see they were."

"That sucks!"

"No shit. Anyway, when they hurt me, Stephan went ballistic. He took 'em on even though he knew he'd get his ass kicked, or worse. I was dazed, but at the same time that I was afraid for our lives, I was so proud of him. My man fought for me, against impossible odds. And I hated that I couldn't fight with him. Hated my weakness.

"Stephan got a couple of good punches and kicks in before they pinned him down. All I could do was watch, and I was afraid they were going to kill us both and stage it to look like a break-in." Roberta looked deeply in Jazz's eyes. "I can't tell you how much I hated that I was powerless to stop them, Jazz. If we had a gun, I would've killed them, and enjoyed it too. Stupid gun laws."

"I'm so sorry, Roberta. That's horrible."

Roberta smiled. "Yeah, I thought we were dead meat. For all I know, those bastards might have even raped me in front of Stephan before they killed us. If you'd seen their eyes, you would've known they were capable of it. But right as they started whaling on Stephan, guess who showed up, just in the nick of time?"

Jazz had almost felt it coming. "Cody."

"Damn straight." Roberta laughed.

Jazz shook her head and laughed with her. "He has a habit of doing that, doesn't he?"

"Yeah, he does. You should've seen him. He annihilated those goons, and never even drew a weapon. One tried to pull a pistol on him, and Cody broke his arm in one slick move. He was like Bruce Lee on steroids. Tore those guys up so bad they had to be hospitalized. I can't imagine what their plastic surgery and dental bills were."

"Wow."

"Yeah. Jazz, I *so* wanted to be Cody that day. I wanted to be the one hurting those assholes. So when Cody told us how he'd been looking out for us, and about this guy called 'the professor' and about Homestead... well, Stephan and I jumped at the opportunity. And when he invited us to come check out Homestead and we saw it and learned what they were doing, we fell in love with the place. We'd found our new home.

"Stephan fit right in, with his technical genius. I didn't have any real skills to speak of, other than that I was fully prepared for maternal bliss. We tried so hard to have a baby, but couldn't, and found out later Stephan was sterile."

"Oh, Roberta. I'm so sorry."

"Yeah." Roberta sighed. "But we had a lot of fun trying,

let me tell you."

Jazz laughed, and Roberta snickered.

Two Great Blue Herons flew past over the still water, their talons dragging the surface and creating ripples in the silvery-blue reflection of the sky. Roberta smiled and continued as they watched the birds fly away.

"I was sad, but Stephan was heartbroken. He so wanted to give me a baby, and be a father. But the story has a good ending. When we got to know everybody here, Stephan and I fell in love with the children. So we pretty much adopted them all, unofficially. In that small way, Stephan got to be the father he wanted to be. And you already know what I decided to do. I wanted to be a Guardian like Cody."

"Did he train you?"

"Yep. Him and Tinga, and Serena, another Guardian. She's awesome." Roberta turned to face Jazz again. "I swore that I would never again let anybody push us around or hurt us like those goons did. And I wanted to help kids like Chaz. So I became a Guardian, and it worked out perfectly for everybody. I've rescued and relocated three kids since then. You'll get to meet them soon. If you stick around, that is."

"So neither you nor Stephan have... had... any special powers?"

Roberta laughed, and faced the water as a couple of fish popped ripples in it. "Not unless you consider Stephan's brilliance a special power. Which I did. But I had some exceptionally talented trainers. And I've never hesitated to use what I learned, when the time came. I killed two Extractors on a couple of my rescue missions, and those fuckers are hard to kill. And when we finally find their hidey-hole, I'm gonna kill some more."

Jazz believed her. "How long has Homestead been here? Doing all this?"

"A little over fourteen years. There's more, but the professor will tell you about that."

"Wow. This is all just blowing me away."

"Yeah, it did me too, at first. But it's home now. I can't imagine living anywhere else."

"That's an amazing story, Roberta."

"So is yours, Jazz. I'm just glad you survived it."

"Me too." Jazz still heard the sound of gunfire, and smelled the smoke. And the blood.

A gentle, cool breeze swept across the promontory, stirring the marsh grass and ruffling Jazz's hair as she thought back on everything Roberta had told her.

"Amanda told me I could use email to try and contact Daddy, but you said I couldn't, that they'd track me down through it."

"Here you can. Outside, you're taking a huge risk if you do." Roberta turned in her seat, facing Jazz again. "Listen, Jazz. If for some reason you decide you just can't stay with us, we'll take you wherever you want to go. Anywhere in the world. And Dr. Ben will give you all the money you need to start over, much more than your net worth, savings, IRAs, whatever. No questions asked, other than that you forget about this place. But if you do go, there's no way we can keep you and Chaz safe out there, and protect you from *them*. Now that they know about Chaz, they'll never stop looking for him."

Roberta flinched, and snagged her cell off her belt. Before she answered it, she looked in Jazz's eyes again. "I really hope you decide to stay, Jazz."

Jazz was torn. On one hand, she did feel safe here, and believed she was among friends. On the other, the thought of her father getting hurt because of her and Chaz was unbearable.

"Yeah," Roberta said, and listened. "Figures," she said into the phone thirty seconds later. "Okay, let's do that." She hung up and sighed, looked at Jazz. "You ready to head back? We're three-quarters of the way around the island anyway, and it's almost lunchtime."

"Okay." Jazz wished she'd heard the other side of that

phone conversation.

"We'll come here again sometime, okay?" Roberta started the Jeep, backed up, and turned around.

"I'd like that," Jazz said.

Roberta took them the rest of the way around the island, and showed Jazz the third lagoon—Gilligan's Retreat—and told her the lagoon where they'd arrived was called Cameron's Cove. They headed back to the main compound, and she showed Jazz the heliport.

It was a hangar large enough to accommodate the four helicopters and the equipment necessary to keep them in good working order, with a machine shop in the back corner. The roof was a retractable series of long aluminum panels that slid aside in multi-leveled tiers at the push of a button, revealing open sky.

"There's an underground tunnel leading from inside the main building up to the machine shop, for emergency evacuation," Roberta said. "Because of the water table here, it was extra expensive to build so it wouldn't flood. But it's a necessary addition, in case the worst happens." She drove them back outside the hangar. "See how it looks like part of the natural landscape from out here?"

Jazz nodded. "It's almost invisible, if the entrance wasn't open."

"The roof's the same way. The panels are painted and textured, so that from an aerial view, it just looks like a big patch of sand and dirt."

Jazz marveled at the structure and thought of the tunnel of trees, realizing that someone had planned ahead in excruciating detail to preserve secrecy and near-invisibility. But where had the money come from to fund it all?

The professor must be a very rich man indeed, and that worried her. An excess of money always brought the potential for excessive corruption.

Back in the main compound, Roberta showed her the

infirmary, explaining that it had state of the art equipment and the requisite professional personnel to run it. She also showed her the power plant, a building housing all the generators that kept power flowing into the complex.

They finally pulled up between the main building and the dining hall, back where they'd started. They watched the laughing and chattering children exit the classroom building. Dante pranced around them, happy as a dog could be.

Jazz spotted Chaz walking beside Amanda. Tinga was several feet behind them, herding her flock. Chaz saw Jazz, and Jazz waved, smiling. Chaz grinned and waved back, and continued chattering at Amanda.

"Let's go eat," Roberta said, and hopped out of the Jeep.

"Let's." Jazz got out, feeling something tugging at her heartstrings.

My precious boy is growing up too fast. Too soon, Binky, too soon...

Chaz told her yesterday that he liked it here, and didn't want to move again. Jazz smiled as she followed the happy group into the dining hall and figured that, albeit unintentionally, they just had.

So why did she have the creeping feeling that something was about to wreck their happy new home?

Chapter 14

August, Montreneau Vineyards, wine country

Kaylee exited the chopper with Taja, a bodyguard named Gordon who spoke only when spoken to, and the pilot. A smiling Hispanic man who apparently didn't speak English loaded their bags in an oversized golf cart, drove them to an impressive sprawling estate built into the hillside overlooking the vineyards, and dropped them off. Inside, a stodgy valet greeted them, and turned to announce their arrival to the master of the estate.

"He was supposed to be waiting here for us," Taja said, frowning at the valet's back. He didn't reply.

A few minutes later a pudgy man in his sixties dressed in a white suit arrived. He glanced at Taja, who watched him with her hands on her hips, then he turned and gazed down his nose at Kaylee and spoke with a stuffy French accent. "It seems to me that I should be allowed to carry on with my important business without interruption, considering your outrageous fee—"

"*Your* donation," Taja said, scowling.

"Hmph," the man straightened his suit jacket and turned to Taja. "Fine. My *donation*. Considering its exorbitance, I expected someone other than a child to serve my vineyard's needs. I have very high expectations—"

"Enough!" Taja snapped. "Monsieur Montreneau, we can certainly leave now, and let you tend to your needs alone, at your leisure. But I assure you, you will be billed for our time. And our collectors are considerably more insistent than any you're accustomed to. We do not take these ventures lightly. And did I not tell you there would be no discussion of this in front of my colleagues, and warn you of the consequences if there were?"

"Surely you don't intend on doubling my fuh… donation, just because I—"

"Don't tempt me, Monsieur. Perhaps we should just leave now. This was apparently a mistake."

"No, no, no, don't do that. You have my apologies, Ms. Ling. I merely—"

"We will continue this discussion in your office, Monsieur." Taja turned to Kaylee. "Kathryn, are you hungry? Do you want some lunch before you get started?"

Kaylee nodded. She would need all her strength for the task ahead.

"Gordon, take Kathryn into Monsieur Montreneau's kitchen, and have them fix whatever she wants. Then take her to the vineyards and let her get started." Taja winked at Kaylee. "Kathryn, I'll join you later, okay? You know what to do, don't you, sweetie?"

"Yes, ma'am." Kaylee smiled while the pompous man fidgeted. She enjoyed watching Taja make him squirm. He didn't seem like much of a humanitarian, especially not the type who shared his wealth with needy children.

Gordon gestured to the valet, who sniffed and sneered at Kaylee. But he led them out of the entrance hall, and Kaylee heard Taja's clipped accent on the way out: "Monsieur, your office. Now."

Kaylee snickered.

After a sliced roast beef sandwich with a couple of pickles, some chips, and a banana, Kaylee waved a hand at Gordon. He nodded and led her outside, where the Hispanic man waited in the golf cart. He drove them to the vineyards, and Kaylee started doing her thing.

At first she considered faking it. The snooty owner made her feel like she was wasting her time and effort. But she didn't know how long it took to make the wine, or how long it had to age before it would be put on the market. If Taja discovered she hadn't performed her magic on the crops before she could escape, they might not let her out again. Or worse.

Kaylee didn't want to find out what would happen, so she did her job.

Having Gordon follow her around was annoying. He seemed more like a prison guard than her protector. But he quietly left her alone to do her job, and she soon became immersed in her work and ignored him.

There was something wondrous and magical about using her talent. It was like communing with nature, but on a much deeper, more personal level. When she whispered to the vines, they seemed to whisper back in her mind, and graciously bent themselves to her will as if they understood she was a friend and was helping them flourish.

She spent the rest of the afternoon and part of the early evening wandering the fields and whispering to her friends. Taja didn't put in an appearance, and when the sun began to set, Kaylee told Gordon she was tired and hungry.

Gordon made a call on his cell, and someone came and picked them up and took them back to the estate. Kaylee went to the kitchen, where the chef had prepared the dinner she had requested earlier: fried chicken, corn on the cob slathered with butter, broccoli smothered in cheese, and a slice of apple pie topped with vanilla ice cream for dessert.

She dug in, eating by herself while Gordon milled around the kitchen. She was famished—making things grow stirred up a hearty appetite. When she was finished, she was stuffed, content, and sleepy.

Gordon showed her to her room for the night and shut the door behind her. She went into the bathroom and changed into her pajamas, and when she lay on the inviting bed, her eyes closed. Her last thought before she fell asleep was of getting up and scoping out the estate, but she was too tired. Her door was probably locked from the outside anyway.

SOULSNATCHER

She slept soundly, no dreams, and woke shortly after seven a.m. She took a shower, and dressed in clean clothes. Gordon followed her downstairs to the kitchen, where she had a big, hearty breakfast. Gordon had apparently already eaten. Taja popped in, said good morning, and slithered back out, citing urgent business.

When Kaylee was finished, fortified for the work ahead of her, Gordon quietly led her back outside, where another man drove them to the fields she hadn't covered yesterday.

Kaylee got right to work, wanting to be done with this place. She worked quietly, enjoying the communion with the vineyard. When she got hungry around noon, she asked Gordon if they would bring her a picnic lunch, saying she didn't want to go back inside, that she wanted to hurry up and finish.

Gordon made another call, and thirty minutes later one of the estate's workers brought her requested lunch. Gordon didn't have anything, but just loitered while she ate. She considered trying to draw him into a conversation in the hopes that he might reveal some crucial information she could use when she finally escaped, but discarded the idea.

His wrinkle-free complexion told the tale. He never smiled, maybe never had, and he never instigated a conversation or engaged in idle banter. Unless some skilled interrogation team tortured it out of him, Gordon was taking his secrets with him to the grave.

Suddenly more alone than she'd felt since her parents had been killed, Kaylee started walking the rows again. She whispered encouragement and touched some of the vines, but she was tired and her heart wasn't in her task.

Although she was outside on a beautiful, sunny day, she knew that whatever she had with these people, it wasn't freedom. Maybe Taja was telling the truth. If she was, Kaylee might never be truly free again. The thought of always being hunted or chased and being used as nothing more than a tool left despair knocking on her door.

137

Please, God, bring my dark man to come rescue me.

A man in a golf cart came with Taja to get Kaylee and Gordon at four o'clock and drove them directly to the helicopter. It was parked with its rotors spinning at the foot of the valley. Kaylee's packed bag was in back with Taja's, and they loaded up in the bird and took off.

Kaylee tried to stay awake and survey the scenery, but she was too exhausted. When she woke, they were back at her new home.

"That mean old man didn't seem like the giving type to me," she grumbled as they walked inside.

Taja turned and winked at her. "No, he doesn't, does he? But don't worry, Kathryn. I made him sign a contract guaranteeing his charitable contribution."

How do you write something like that into a contract? *Guaranteed contribution of fifty percent of profits to children's cancer research in exchange for magical plant-growing services?*

Kaylee wasn't thinking clearly, but she felt like pushing her luck. She stomped her foot, deliberately putting a little frustrated whine in her voice.

"I wanna meet some of the other kids here."

Taja sighed. "Kathryn, I told you before. Whenever two or more talented people get too close, very bad things happen. You do remember what happened the last time you were close to one, don't you?"

Kaylee didn't know what she was referring to. Her brain felt like mush. "When? What do you mean?"

"You've forgotten Jhin's sacrifice to save you already? What it did to you both, being so close to each other?"

Kaylee's head spun. Taja hadn't told her this before. She had always believed her nausea during her first helicopter ride was due to teleportation. She never even imagined that it was because she and Jhin affected each other that way. "You mean…"

Taja nodded. "Precisely." She laughed. "Did you think that was the normal effect of teleportation? Silly girl."

Not fair! It couldn't be true for everyone like her, could it?

Taja's eyes gleamed. "You know, Kathryn, there was another incident before that when you were around another person with special abilities. And very bad things happened then too."

"What?" Kaylee racked her brain to figure out what Taja meant. Hadn't Jhin been the first?

"Think gunfire and car crashes, Kathryn."

No! Not my dark man! "But I didn't feel nauseous when I was with him."

Taja smirked. "That's because different talents affect the exposed differently. I seem to remember that between the two factions fighting to kidnap you, they both nearly got you killed." Taja raised her hands palms up and grinned as if she'd just explained life, the universe, and everything. "See? Very bad things. If it hadn't been for me and Jhin, you'd be dead now. Or worse, in the hands of some very ruthless and merciless people."

Kaylee couldn't speak. *No! You're lying about my dark man. He isn't bad. He tried to save me.*

Taja sighed and frowned, but her eyes twinkled. "Oh, Kathryn. You really don't know, do you? You haven't figured it out yet."

Figured out what? Kaylee wanted to scream. What was Taja trying to tell her? Something boiled upward from deep inside her, a monster clamoring to arise and wreak vengeance.

"Well, I don't care. I wanna meet somebody. Even if I have to talk to them from across the room. I'm lonely, Taja. I need a friend, somebody, *anybody*."

Taja pouted. "But Kathryn, I'm your friend."

"It's not the same." Taja had no idea. A friend would call her Kaylee, and treat her as if she trusted her.

Taja took a deep breath, and Kaylee dared to hope she was actually considering it. Kaylee let the tears come, deliberately blubbering as she looked up at her.

"P-p-please, Taja!"

Taja pulled her cell phone from her waist. "Wait right here sweetie, okay?"

Kaylee nodded, her heart pounding. As Taja walked away and spoke into her phone, Kaylee held her breath and prayed for something good for once. Less than a minute later, Taja came back to her, teeth flashing.

"Okay, sweetie. Good news." She reached out, wriggling her fingers. "Come with me."

"Where are you taking me?"

"To make a new friend."

Kaylee didn't want to take Taja's hand. But she grabbed it and prayed that whatever she was about to experience, it wouldn't have the same air of false freedom she'd felt yesterday and today in the vineyards.

And every night in her heart.

Chapter 15

Jazz inhaled the scent of grilled burgers and hot dogs as she entered the dining hall. Her stomach rumbled, and she approached the buffet. For those averse to meats, lunch featured a variety of fruits and nuts. One section had plastic-lidded trays of peanut butter, grape jam, and strawberry preserves for anyone who wanted a good old PB&J.

Jazz built a hamburger with lettuce, onions, tomato, pickles, and cheese, and a hot dog slathered with thick, beanless chili and a healthy smattering of onions. She tossed some chips on her plate and sat beside Roberta and across from Amanda, Chaz, Mara, and a little black boy of about ten or eleven.

Cody, Kino, Marco, and Raj entered the hall with four adults she didn't recognize. She was pleased to see Marco join them after he filled up his plate.

She had so many questions, and wanted to know what Chaz had spent the morning learning, but she was too hungry for conversation.

"Hey, Mother." Chaz grinned with a ketchup-sloppy burger in his hand. "Guess what Amanda can do."

"What can she do?"

"And Mara. You'll never believe what she can do, Mother."

"What can Amanda do, Chaz? And Mara?"

Chaz's eyes widened. "Mara can see the *future*."

"Not deliberately," Mara said. "I can't control it. It just happens, or not."

"Wow. That's..." Jazz shook her head. "That must be a terrible burden for you sometimes, Mara."

Mara stopped eating and looked at Jazz, her eyebrows

rising. "Wow. At least somebody finally gets it."

Jazz knew how that felt. "I'm a good listener, and you can talk to me about it anytime you want, okay?"

Mara nodded. "Thanks, Jazz."

Jazz smiled, feeling something new and exciting tugging at her emotions. She was about to ask Chaz about Amanda again when Chaz pointed to the boy beside him.

"This is my new friend Ezekiel. You can call him Zeke, like I do. All his friends do. Guess what he can do."

"Hi, Zeke." He waved and looked down at his plate, and Jazz smiled at him. "You can call me Jazz."

Zeke smiled and stared at his plate. "Hi, Jazz."

"Don't worry about him, Mother," Chaz said, his head bouncing. "He's just shy because he thinks you're so pretty."

"Chaz!" Jazz glanced at Roberta, Kino, Cody, Raj, and Marco. They watched her, chuckling and grinning. She sighed and looked back at Chaz. "That wasn't very nice, Chaz. That's giving away personal secrets."

"He didn't say not to tell you!" Chaz rolled his eyes. "Besides, it's true. You are pretty."

The adults erupted in laughter. Jazz's face was so hot she thought it would melt. "Zeke, don't you worry about them, honey. They're just jealous because you're such a cute and handsome guy. So what can you do?"

Zeke smiled at her. "I can—"

Chaz butted in. "He can make people see things that aren't even really there!"

"Not all the time," Zeke said, glancing at Chaz. He looked at Jazz. "But I'm getting better at it, thanks to Tinga and everybody here."

"Is that amazing or what?" Chaz blurted, and took a big bite of his burger.

Amanda and Mara laughed with the adults, and Jazz joined them. "Well, yeah, it is," she said. She looked at Zeke. "Zeke, do you know you have to be careful how you use such an incredible power, and not hurt people with it?"

"Yes, ma'am," Zeke said, his head bobbing. "I want to make people see good things."

"Good for you, sweetie." Jazz considered the implications of such a power, were it properly wielded. So what could all the other children do?

She looked at Amanda, who jumped up with her empty plate. Mara and Zeke stood with her. Amanda touched Chaz's shoulder, and Chaz crammed the rest of his burger in his mouth and joined them.

Amanda smiled at Jazz. "Well, back to class. Until three. Then we're free. And we'll talk." She nodded, and the children followed her to the waste bins.

Most of the adults and all the other children gathered their plates and cups and left the table. Cody, Kino, Roberta, Marco, and Tinga remained seated. They all watched Jazz.

"What, guys?" she asked. "Tinga, aren't you going to teach class?"

"No," Tinga said. "Amanda is taking over. She's very good with the children. They all love her, and mind her."

"Okay," Jazz drawled, and looked at Roberta. "Roberta, what?"

Roberta raised her eyebrows. "You know that call I got when we were out by the lake?"

"Yeah. What about it?" Jazz's stomach was doing flip-flops.

Everyone stood except Jazz as Roberta answered. "Kendra and Malek have been trying to track down information about your father. They went through your email, and found a video message from Taja Ling."

"We're taking you to the computer shack," Kino said. "And watching it with you."

"We won't watch it with you if you don't want," Roberta said. "But Cody, Kino, Marco, and Tinga think we should."

Something tells me you've all already seen it. Everybody

143

except me and Roberta. "Okay." Jazz stood, wishing she hadn't eaten the hot dog.

Cody led them to a small building across from the main one. Jazz's heart pounded, and her legs felt like twigs ready to snap. She stumbled as she headed up the wooden steps, and Roberta caught her arm and helped her along.

Inside, the front room constituted the majority of the building. The walls were lined with nine computer work-stations. In the center of the carpeted floor space was a three-by-six-foot console, with two high-backed padded chairs facing the wall at the far end of the room. The wall was one large flat-screen monitor, currently broken up into sixteen equal sections showing different views of the island.

In the chair on the left sat an ebony-skinned teenage girl with dreadlocks. The chair on the right spun around to reveal a smiling, teenage Middle Eastern boy with thick-lensed glasses. As the girl spun her chair to face them, Roberta spoke. "Jazz, this is Kendra and Malek. Guys, this is Jazz, Chaz's mother."

Kendra smiled and rose from her chair, and Malek stood beside her.

"I'm pleased to finally meet you, Jazz," Kendra said.

"Me too," Malek said with a big grin. "Very pleased."

"Hello," Jazz said, her stomach churning. "So how did you two hack into my email?"

The pair looked at each other and laughed.

"Passwords are no problemo," Malek said.

"Haven't come across one yet we couldn't crack," Kendra said, nodding. "Decryption software program. Me and Malek wrote it. It's epic."

"Malek and I," Tinga said.

"Yeah, that," Kendra said, and wiped the grin off her face when she saw Tinga's expression. "I mean, yes, ma'am."

"We got the video dialed up and ready to play," Malek said.

"We *have*," Tinga said, glaring at Malek.

"Uhh, yeah. Yes, ma'am, we have." Malek looked at Jazz. "Just hit enter. It was sent last night at 2:24 a.m. We're gonna get some lunch, so you can have a little privacy."

"We're trying to trace its origins, but I doubt we'll have any luck," Kendra said. "You can use the mouse to play, stop, forward, reverse, or pause it."

"Thanks, guys," Roberta said. She took Jazz's arm, steered her into the chair on the right, and sat in the chair next to her as Kendra and Malek left. Cody nodded at Jazz, his lips pursed. Kino winked at her, and Jazz felt the tension radiating from them all.

"You guys are scaring the crap out of me," she said. *What am I about to see? Daddy? Dead or alive?*

Roberta spun Jazz's chair to face the wall screen. "It's okay, Jazz. We're all here for you. Whenever you're ready, hit enter."

Jazz looked at the keyboard on the console in front of her. She took a deep breath, said a silent prayer for her father, and hit the enter key.

The wall screen cleared, and a video player popped up. Jazz's finger hovered over the mouse, and she glanced at Roberta.

"It's okay, Jazz. If it was something you couldn't stand to see, they would've warned us."

"There's some harsh stuff in it," Cody said. "We decided you should see it raw, like we did, without any explanations upfront. You already proved you can handle it."

Jazz nodded, acknowledging the unexpected compliment, and clicked play. A beautiful Asian woman's grinning face filled the screen. She waved, her eyes twinkling merrily.

"Hi, Jazz! How's my little healer's mommy today? I bet you've been wondering—"

"Oh!" Jazz gasped, fumbled the mouse, and clicked pause. She leaped out of her chair and spun to face Tinga, her mouth open and her eyes bugging out. The woman's voice was the same as the one that threatened her last night on the phone, but her *face*...

Although Tinga wore her raven-black hair in a bun and the woman in the video wore hers loose, their pretty porcelain faces were one and the same. Jazz gasped again, struggling to speak.

"Not me," Tinga said, shaking her head. "My sister Taja. We're identical twins."

Jazz remembered to breathe, and struggled to bring her pounding heart under control. She said the first thing that popped into her mind. "Your parents named you Tinga Ling?"

Tinga put her hand to her mouth and giggled. "Taja and Tinga were the names on our birth certificates. We were adopted by a Chinese-American couple named Ling."

Jazz nodded as her initial shock wore off. "Right. Well, no stranger than if the Mahals adopted you, I guess."

Cody grimaced and shook his head. Kino, Marco, and Roberta chuckled, easing the tension. Tinga frowned at Jazz, missing it.

Jazz raised her eyebrows. "Taja Mahal?"

"Oh!" Tinga giggled again, grinning. "Well, Jazz, we may look the same, but we're as different as the sun and moon, I promise you."

"I can definitely vouch for that," Cody said. "The dark side of the moon."

Jazz wondered what he meant by that, and realized he must know Taja. She filed it away for later, and turned and sat again. She looked at Roberta, who nodded, and she clicked on play.

"—and worrying about dear old Dad," Taja resumed. "Well, don't you worry that pretty little head of yours, Jazz. Daddy's doing just fine. Well, mostly."

Jazz scowled as Taja took a deep breath.

"Which raises an interesting question. Is your father left-handed, or right? He told me he was right-handed." Taja frowned. "I sure hope he was telling the truth. Otherwise, he's going to have to learn how to write all over again."

"You bitch!" Jazz spat. "What did you do?"

Taja's head tilted back and forth, and she winked at the camera and held up what was either a severed pinky finger or a convincing replica of one. "Check your mailbox tomorrow, Jazz. There'll be a little surprise in it for you. Oh, wait, you can't check your mailbox because you've run away from home. Oh, well. Maybe you can send CJ to check it for you. Are you there watching with her, CJ? Come back to the dark side, Luke. It's much more profitable. And I promise it'll be just like old times. Me and you, together again, the invincible duo."

Jazz twisted her head and glanced at Cody, who was scowling. She returned her gaze to the wall screen, seething.

Taja shrugged. "Oh, well. It's probably for the best that you don't. Even though the sex was sublime, wasn't it, CJ? I miss that big hard dick. Does it miss my pretty pussy? But wait, you probably wanna poke the pretty new girl with it now, don't you?"

Cody grimaced and looked away, and Jazz gasped. Roberta put her hand on Jazz's arm and squeezed.

Taja grinned and winked. "Don't worry, Jazz. Cody has grown weak, and probably impotent too. He lost his edge when he decided to embrace a *nobler cause*. So even if you're not hot for him, he probably can't even get it up to rape you, like he did so many other helpless women and little girls... right before he killed them. How do I know? Because I was there. I taught CJ everything he knows, Jazz. Look in his eyes if you don't believe me."

Taja held up the finger again and smirked. "On the other hand—or finger—nobler causes bore me. So here's the deal, if you want to keep dear old Dad intact... Well, minus his recent loss of a digit. It was regrettable but necessary, so you know who you're dealing with.

"We want Chaz. You will both be welcomed and taken care of beyond your wildest dreams. Far better than CJ or the professor can provide for you. Anything you ask for will be granted. All we want is for Chaz to perform his magic for us once in a while. However, if you don't reply to this email in the next forty-eight hours with a plan for us to meet, and let us take you and Chaz to a better place, then you leave us no choice but to take Daddy's ring finger next. Twenty-four hours later and we'll have to take his middle finger, and it'll be all your fault, Jazz. Your choice: the world at your fingertips, your every wish granted, flashy cars, private jets, money, exotic travel, your own home on the oceanfront or mountaintop of your choice, powerful and *potent* men, as many as you like, or… living in fear and hiding from Chaz's divine destiny like cornered rats.

"Make the right choice, Jazz, the only choice for Chaz. He'll be treated like a god. We'll research all the latest heart transplant and genetic technology with the best men and women money can buy, and *pay for* a cure for Chaz when we find it. That will be your gift from us, for helping Chaz realize his full potential. Don't let his frail little heart give out on him just for your own selfish desires. Don't let the anxiety and fear of always running and hiding from his talent kill Chaz. Your only child. You and only you have the power to—"

Jazz was fumbling the mouse, and she clicked pause and stood and screamed. She didn't bother fighting the tears as her fury rose to the surface again. She wanted to throw something at the screen, and smash that smug face. The freeze-frame frigid glare in Taja's eyes taunted her.

She shot a look at everyone. Roberta had tears pooling in her eyes, but a hardness was there too. Marco just nodded at her. Cody stood motionless, fists clenched at his sides. He glared at her with those dark fathomless eyes, where a deeper hardness than Roberta's dwelled.

Jazz didn't want to believe the horrible things Taja had said about him.

Kino stood at Cody's side, and nodded at Jazz. Her nails were digging into her palms. A sob escaped her, and Kino opened his arms. She practically leaped into them, threw her arms around his wide shoulders and rested her head on his chest. "Oh, Kino."

"We're right here, lady. For you and Chaz." He squeezed her.

She felt strength suffuse her. When Kino let her go and stepped back, their eyes locked, and she nodded.

Cody squinted at her. "Push play."

She took a deep breath, sat in the chair facing the wall screen, and clicked on play.

"—save him from a life spent in fear, and help him achieve everything he richly deserves," Taja continued. "Don't steal his glory away from him, Jazz."

Taja's eyes gleamed like a panther's stalking its prey. "And don't make the mistake of thinking I care about you. I only care about Chaz. I don't give a damn if you live or die, and if you cross me or fight us, I'll squash you like a bug. That's a promise.

"But if you and Chaz join us, you'll be protected and treated like royalty. Dr. Sössnocher gave orders that you're forever untouchable, if you join us. And his word is God here. No harm will ever come to you, Chaz, or your father by our hands, or mine, if you peacefully surrender yourself and Chaz. It's a no-brainer, Jazz. Reign like a proud lioness, or live like a frightened lamb.

"In fact, Dr. Sössnocher is so generous and compassionate, he told me to offer you a little deal. To give you a chance to think this through clearly, and make the right decision, he told me not to start the countdown until noon today. See how merciful he is? So you have until exactly noon two days from now to decide.

"The choice is all yours, Jazz. You can save yourself, your son, and your father. However, if we do not hear a decision from you at this email address, I'll just keep lopping off fingers until dear old Dad has to get someone to hold his Johnson for him every time he has to pee. I advise you to decide quickly."

Taja grinned and waved, the severed finger gripped between her thumb and index finger. She laughed. "Until we meet, Jazz. Ta-ta!"

The video ended. Jazz mumbled, "…so sorry, gonna be so sorry when I find you, bitch."

Roberta stood beside Jazz and put a hand on her shoulder. Jazz looked up at her, finished with the tears.

"Is it real, Roberta?"

"What, the finger? Probably. Kino?" Roberta looked at Kino, and Jazz turned to watch him, suddenly remembering his truth-telling power.

Kino slumped. "It's fuzzy, but I'm afraid so." Cody nodded once.

Jazz rose. "So. I have a decision to make."

Tinga approached her. "Knowing my sister, Jazz, it's all too real. She was always cruel, even as a child. A manipulator, too. Everything is just a game to her, psychological warfare, and nothing she says can be trusted." Tinga glanced at Cody, and back at Jazz. "*Nothing.*"

"She mentioned a Doctor… Sorshnocker?"

Tinga nodded. "The children call him Soulsnatcher. It's an appropriate name for him too, considering what he does with the children he abducts. The professor will tell you all about him when he arrives."

Jazz scowled. "Amanda and Mara mentioned him last night, and Amanda said 'beware of Soulsnatcher and his hunters' in her letter, but I didn't get a chance to ask them about him."

"Do not be deceived by my sister's promises, Jazz. Or her lies about how merciful Soulsnatcher is. They would appear to welcome you, just to make Chaz feel safe. But soon, you would have an unfortunate accident. Knowing Taja, she would stage it for Chaz to witness, and make it look like *we* killed you trying to steal him back. She's very good at deception, and brainwashing gullible children. Soon she would have Chaz doubting everyone but her."

Jazz looked at Cody, and he nodded once. "Damn straight."

She was amazed that Cody could maintain his composure in the wake of Taja's horrible accusations. She didn't believe he could do those things. Something in his eyes harbored a good and honorable man.

But Tinga was right: Taja's persuasive banter and demeanor had her doubting what her heart told her, and more than anything else, it pissed her off, and fortified her resolve.

There was no way she could ask these people to decide for her. But she could ask them to help her. "What if we set a trap? Used me as bait?"

Kino nodded. "Cody, Marco, and I were discussing that. But we weren't going to ask you to risk your life unless you were willing to try. And we need a good plan, which we don't have yet."

"Let's do it." Jazz scowled. "I can't leave my father in their hands. He's a good man, and a wonderful father and grandfather. Chaz and I love him so much."

"They'll be ready for us to try that," Cody said. "You know how deadly the Extractors are. You have no idea how deadly Taja is."

"I have to do something, Cody."

"The reason they're giving you forty-eight hours is to give us time to *plan* a trap, Jasmine," Cody said. "So they have time to devise countermeasures."

"Dammit, there's got to be something we can do!"

Cody nodded. "There is, and we are gonna do something about it. But we have a little time, so let us all talk it over. And when Ben gets here, we'll discuss it with him. He'll know what to do."

Something in Cody's eyes and voice told Jazz he trusted the professor implicitly. And something else was there, too. Maybe it was love. She wanted to know his story. Tinga approached her before Jazz could organize her thoughts.

"Jazz, would you like to come with me, and watch Chaz in class? See what he's learning?"

Jazz looked at Kino and Roberta, who nodded at her. "Okay."

Tinga grinned and headed toward the door, and Jazz followed her out.

"See you at dinner, Jazz," Roberta said, touching Jazz's arm as she passed her.

Jazz nodded, her head spinning, her stomach churning, and her heart aching, and she went to class.

Chapter 16

Taja took Kaylee down a series of long hallways where Kaylee wasn't permitted to wander on her own. A guard was always posted here and there. Though they pretended not to be guarding anything, they always made it clear that she was not allowed there.

No one was in the halls now but her and Taja.

Kaylee was frightened and excited and emotionally exhausted, but she dared to hope. Whatever happened next, it would help her decide what she would do hereafter.

She wanted more than anything to learn the truth about her parents' deaths. If necessary, she would dig up their graves with her bare hands to discover the answers. It wasn't like she would be resurrecting their ghosts—they already haunted her every night.

Taja finally stopped at a nondescript white door. The only item of color in the hallway other than the beige carpet was a security device with blinking lights at about chin height beside the door. A hooded lens was just above it.

Taja let go of Kaylee's hand and stood in front of the device, punched in a code, dipped her head, and put her eye to the lens.

Retinal scanner. Why didn't Kaylee have one of those over her door? They just locked her in at night, for her *protection.*

What were they locking in here, and who were they locking out?

Taja straightened up as a latch clicked in the door. She turned the knob and looked back at Kaylee with a smile.

"Come on, sweetie. I want you to meet Jai. He's from

South Africa. He's only a couple of years older than you."

Subdued lights came on, revealing a small anteroom, its only furniture a two-seater leather couch facing a window in the wall before it. Taja walked to the couch, sat, and looked back at Kaylee with raised eyebrows. She patted the seat beside her.

Kaylee shuffled around the couch and sat beside her.

The window started at waist height, and was about four feet high by twelve feet wide. A closed door with another security pad and lens was beside it. The interior of the room beyond the window was dark.

Taja glanced at Kaylee, smiled, and touched a button on the armrest beside her. A green glow suffused the room beyond the window, and Kaylee leaned forward and gazed within.

"Night-vision lighting, Kathryn. Do you see him?"

"Yes, by the chair in the corner. What's wrong with him?"

"Watch."

Kaylee waited and watched him closely. He was tall, muscular, and lithe. His skin and facial features appeared black. An anguished expression twisted his handsome face.

Something about him struck a deep chord inside Kaylee, and she struggled to hide it from Taja. She definitely felt something, and it didn't feel like a *very bad thing* to her. Despite his grimace and his strangely unfocused eyes, he called out to her in some primitive way that transcended words.

"Do you see, Kathryn?"

Kaylee didn't know what to think or say. She blurted out the first thing that came to mind. "Is he blind?"

Taja touched a button at her side. "Watch."

Blazing fluorescent light illuminated the room, but Jai didn't even flinch. He just continued glaring straight ahead.

Kaylee noticed there were no windows in his room other than the one in front of her. Jai strode unerringly past the scant furniture in the room, stood before the window, and scowled. Though his eyes gazed past the window, they saw nothing.

He was so clear and close. Kaylee wanted to reach out and touch him.

"He doesn't see us, does he?"

"No, honey. He doesn't see anything but what's in his mind."

"Taja! I want to talk to him."

"Patience, Kathryn." Taja turned to face her while Jai stared into the window. Kaylee found it hard to turn her gaze from him, but she managed to wrench her head sideways and glare at Taja.

"Kathryn, it's important for you to understand why we have a fee associated with our services." Taja glared back at her, making Kaylee break eye contact. Her eyes were drawn to Jai anyway.

"Okay, tell me why."

Taja sighed. "We're desperately trying to restore his sight. He had an accident when he was twelve. He hasn't been blind all his life. And if we can help it, and you can help us help it, we can continue to afford to try more new surgeries to give him his sight back, sweetie. Where do you think the money comes from to pay for these things?"

Kaylee stared at Jai, her heart pounding. Her surroundings showed extravagant expenditure. But were the bank accounts that funded this place bottomless? She suddenly knew the answer Taja expected her to give. "From excursions like ours?"

Taja grinned. "Very good. So do you see now that we're really trying to help all of you?"

Kaylee didn't know. She could only stare into Jai's fascinating eyes. He turned away from the window and shook his fists, his lips moving. Kaylee couldn't hear his words.

"Kathryn? Do you understand?"

Kaylee groaned. "Yeah. I wanna talk to him."

Taja nodded. "Give me a few seconds. Let me see if I can... reach him."

Wondering what Taja meant, Kaylee watched him shake his fists again, his shoulders tensed. He turned back toward the window, seeing nothing or everything.

"Taja, what can he do?"

Taja glanced sideways at her again, her finger poised over a button. "I'm not sure I should tell you. You may wish I hadn't if I do."

"Taja!"

Taja sighed again. "He can make everyone feel his rage. Do you see his rage, Kathryn? Do you have any idea how long it's taken us just to reach him? Do you want him to make you feel his fury? Could you stand it if he did? His power is very compelling. He rarely speaks to anyone. Are you sure you want to take the chance that he won't want to speak to *you*?"

Kaylee felt a lump in her throat. Looking at Jai, she nodded and whispered, "Yes."

"What if he decides to speak to you, but directs all his anger and bitterness at you? What if it becomes yours, Kathryn?"

My name is not Kathryn, woman. And you still have no idea the volcano of rage I have inside me.

"I can take it. Let me talk to him."

Taja nodded. "Let me try to bring him around first, and then I'll turn him over to you. I want you to understand that we're trying to help him focus his power. We believe that if he can learn to focus it in a positive way, he can quench his rage. We believe that he can use it for good things, with the proper encouragement and discipline. Understand?" When Kaylee nodded, Taja punched a button beside her. "Jai? Can you hear me? It's Taja."

Jai didn't flinch, nor did his head turn or twist. He gave no sign of having heard anything.

"Jai? Come on, honey. I have someone here I want you to meet. She's a friend. She wants to be your new friend. She's seventeen, and very powerful, like you. Won't you say hello to her?"

Still he showed no reaction. Either the intercom speakers weren't working, or he was ignoring Taja.

"She's *very* pretty, Jai. Emerald eyes, long, dark brown hair. She really wants to meet you." Taja turned to Kaylee and shrugged. "Your turn, sweetie." She hit another button.

Kaylee didn't know what to say. At the same time that she felt Jai was staring right at her, she felt as if his gaze was a million miles away. She cleared her throat.

"Jai? Hi. My name's Kaylee. I can make stuff grow. Like plants and stuff."

Jai didn't react. He appeared lost in his own private hell.

"Jai, please." Kaylee hated the tremor in her voice. "Please talk to me. I need a friend."

Nothing. No movement, no shifting of the blank eyes. Kaylee wanted to cry. Was this the best Taja could do to help her find a friend? She so wanted Jai to turn his gaze to her, to hear his voice.

"I'm lonely too, Jai. Just like you. Please talk to me." *Do you know the dark man? Do you dream about him?*

Taja sighed and punched another button at her side. "Sometimes he responds, and sometimes he's too far away. We can try again another time, okay?"

No! Kaylee didn't want to give up yet. "Wait—"

Taja shook her head and hit a button that cut off the light in the other room.

"Taja, please!"

"I think we need to leave him alone now, honey. And you look so tired, so worn out. You did so much for us all today and yesterday. For Jai too." Taja smiled, making Kaylee think of giant hairy spiders.

"Why do you have to keep him in there?" she asked.

"Can you imagine the destruction the rage in him could wreak, Kathryn? What if that fury were unleashed upon us all?" Taja rose from the couch and gestured toward the hallway.

Kaylee stood, feeling like a zombie. She looked long-ingly over her shoulder at the blank window when she exited the anteroom, not sure whether she should break down and cry, or just give up.

Out in the hallway, with the outer door closed, she stood with her head down, her eyes closed, and her heart aching. Taja reached down and took her hand. Kaylee was crushed, and so weary, and didn't resist.

Taja led her out of the maze of hallways and back to her room.

When Kaylee entered her room, Taja followed her, and Kaylee turned to her. She didn't want to hear any more sad stories tonight. "I'm really tired, Taja. I'm gonna take a shower and go to bed."

"All right. You did really well yesterday and today, Kathryn. We'll try again with Jai someday soon, okay?"

Kaylee nodded.

Taja left, and Kaylee took a long hot shower and tried to wash away some of the day's ills. Had her proximity to Jai caused her to feel this despair, as Taja had explained? Or was it just because Jai's story was so incredibly sad?

As she dressed in her pajamas, she wondered what it was that Taja said she "just hadn't figured out yet."

Although she was way beyond exhausted, she went to the alcove, sat on the padded ledge, and looked out at her handi-work. She needed something to stop her mind from spinning, something to calm her thoughts. Her green friends always helped.

In the wash of the outdoor floodlights, she saw the morning glory and Japanese honeysuckle's remarkable prog-ress. Melding with each other, the creeping vines had grown six feet since yesterday morning.

"Good job, guys," Kaylee whispered.

The Japanese honeysuckle sprouted a tendril from one of its vines a few feet beneath her window, and that tendril sprouted two more. As she watched, it grew a couple of inches. The tendrils quivered as if in ecstasy, reaching toward her like wriggling fingers.

She gasped. "Wow. Did I do that?"

The clinging vines sprouted a series of tendrils, many already bearing tiny buds. They extended toward her, as if in homage or supplication.

"Whoa," she muttered. Was this happening because she was exercising her power more regularly now, a case of practice makes perfect? Or was it something even more amazing?

Was she just beginning to develop a power that would continue to grow, like her green friends? Had she not even begun to tap her potential? What exactly would she eventually be capable of doing? She smiled and put her fingers to her mouth, and waved at the honeysuckle and morning glory.

"Hi, guys," she whispered. The vines writhed, appearing to celebrate.

Kaylee grinned with the thrill of bearing a new secret, and got up and turned off the lights and went to bed. This night, for the first night in a long string of desolate nights, her tears were of joy and hope. She closed her eyes, and drifted off.

In what felt like mere moments later, she felt a gentle touch at her forehead, something stroking strands of hair out of her face. She jerked awake and sat up with a vision in her mind of the plants having broken through her window and crept their way up onto her bed.

From the dim glow of her nightlight, she saw the window was intact. No vines surrounded her.

Taja sat on the edge of the mattress beside her. She'd been so quiet, Kaylee hadn't heard the slightest rustle, or even felt the mattress move.

"Taja!" she gasped, and leaned up against the headboard. "Don't sneak up on me like that. You scared the hell out of me."

Taja reached up as if to brush the hair out of Kaylee's

eyes, and Kaylee flinched backward, avoiding her touch.

Taja sighed. "Oh, Kathryn. I'm so sorry. I came in to check up on you, and saw your tears. You figured it out, didn't you?"

Kaylee was fully awake now, her heart pounding. She prayed Taja meant something other than her new secret. That was private. It belonged to her and her alone.

"Figured out what, Taja?"

Taja pouted, but it didn't hide the sparkle in her eyes. "Your dark man's secret, honey."

Kaylee perked up. "No. What is it?"

"Oh. You don't know yet. You should have figured it out by now. You're obviously in denial. Oh, honey, I'm so sorry. I didn't want to have to be the one to tell you, but now you must know. It's for your own good."

Please, God, no more nightmare stories. "What, Taja?"

Taja wrung her hands. "You really have no idea what he's done to you, do you?"

Kaylee's fists clenched her pillows. "Dammit, Taja! What can he do?"

"It's really a rather simple talent. But it's potentially horrible in its long-term implications. Especially if his victims never learn of it. I guess it's best that you learn about it from someone who *really* cares about you. A true friend."

"Taja!"

Taja sighed again. "Your dark man has the ability, with just a glance, to force strangers to trust him completely, and believe in him, and even believe he's their friend. And that's what he did to you, Kathryn."

"No!" *It can't be true. You're lying!*

"Oh, Kathryn. I'm so sorry, but it's the truth. You poor, dear, sweet girl. You probably even fantasized about him coming to rescue you, didn't you?"

Kaylee pounded the mattress with her fists, tears pooling in her eyes. "No, it's not true!"

"See? Even now he still has his claws in you. It's a powerful spell. But it's all just a sad little magic trick."

"No." It was all Kaylee could say or think.

"Think about it, Kathryn. You've put him up on a pedestal, assigned him hero status. That's nothing more than his power working on you. It's all a pathetic, cruel lie."

Kaylee didn't want to think about it, but she did. From the moment she'd seen him, though his sudden appearance in her house had frightened her, she'd trusted him... completely. She had seen hope, strength, and goodness in his eyes. And she'd fantasized over and over that he would come rescue her.

He had seemed invulnerable, even invincible.

For her to admit that everything Taja said about him was true would not just be admitting that a psychic spell had easily duped her. It would also be admitting that she had no friends. Or hope. Kaylee fought the tears, but they came anyway.

"I'm so sorry, Kathryn. I can see you need to be alone right now. You need time to think it through." Taja stood and gazed down at her. "But I want you to know I have faith in you. I know you'll cast the spell off soon, now that you know the truth. And I know you'll come out stronger and happier in the end."

Taja nodded, gave her a sad smile, and walked away. As she left the room, she looked back over her shoulder. Even in the gloom, Kaylee could swear her eyes were sparkling.

Kaylee felt as if her chest was being crushed. She didn't know what or who to believe. She just wanted to melt away, dissolve and leave this hard world.

Taja told such dreadful bedtime stories.

An anguished sob escaped her, and she turned and buried her face in her pillow so the hidden cameras couldn't see her lose it. Meeting Jai had seemed like it would start changing things for the better, and it had ended up crushing her spirit. But this felt like someone had gleefully plunged a blade into her heart and twisted it. Now all she had left was her gift, and a desire to use it to avenge her parents.

If she could just escape this never-ending nightmare.

Chapter 17

Jazz and Tinga ascended the steps to the porch of the schoolhouse, and Tinga stopped and gestured toward a cedar swing suspended by chains from the ceiling.

"Before we go in, would you like to sit and relax for a few minutes with me?"

Jazz knew Tinga meant she wanted to talk with her privately.

"Okay." She walked over to the swing and sat. Tinga joined her.

After a minute, while Jazz struggled with the implications of Taja's video and the ultimatum she'd given, Tinga spoke.

"It is hard to see her and not see me, I know. When we were children, she often tried to talk me into using our resemblance to play tricks on people. But perhaps you have already considered that either there is no Taja, or there is no Tinga, that we're one and the same, and are playing mind games with you for some reason."

"Perhaps." Jazz crossed her arms so Tinga wouldn't see her hands shake. "But if that was true, what would be the point? You would already have what you want."

"And what is it that you think we want, Jazz?"

That was easy, if the implausible scenario was true. "Chaz."

"No." Tinga frowned and shook her head. "No, we do not 'want' Chaz. We want to help him, and you, Jazz. Do you believe that I am her, and she is me?"

Jazz didn't have to think about that. "No. I know you're not her, Tinga. The emptiness in her eyes… it's not in yours. But why didn't someone warn me?"

"Cody said not to, and I agreed. We wanted you to see it the way you would have seen it were you alone. Which you are not."

"I don't feel like I am. I feel like I'm among friends."

"You are, and thank you." Tinga clasped her hands in her lap and gazed out into the maze of trees in the compound. "Jazz, what do you think they really want with Chaz?"

"Amanda said in the letter that—"

"Do not think of what you learned from the letter. Think instead of what you feel in your heart. What the letter didn't say."

Jazz considered it, hearing Taja's venomous voice, seeing the void in her eyes. What occurred to her was perverted, but it was the simplest explanation. She frowned at Tinga.

"Occam's razor. They want to use him to heal people who're willing to pay a shitload of money for it and keep their mouths shut about it. Get rich off him."

Tinga closed her eyes and nodded. "You're as wise as I suspected. And that, Jazz, is my sister for you. She thinks only of herself. The world is her playground, its inhabitants her toys."

"Yeah? Well, this toy fights back, and she has no clue who she's messing with, no idea what I'm going to do to her when I find her. She'll regret she ever even knew about me and Chaz for the rest of her life, however long or short that may be." Jazz felt the fury rising, and forced it back in its cage.

Tinga opened her eyes and gazed at her. "I admire your strength and determination. But do not make the fatal mistake of underestimating Taja. Domination and subjugation are her drug, and she is addicted for life."

"Yeah, that's basically what Kino and Roberta told me. And Cody, in so many words."

"Do you trust them, Jazz?"

Jazz didn't have to think about that either. "With my life. Kino is a wonderful man. It's no wonder the children love him so much. And Roberta… I feel like I've known her for years, and could tell her anything."

"And Cody?"

Jazz sighed. "It's hard not to trust him. He's got these… hypnotizing eyes. He's incorrigible, but there's something good and honorable in him, beyond the darkness." She realized she was crossing a bridge. "Yes, Tinga. I trust him with my life. I don't even know why. He's so damn bullheaded. But he saved our lives yesterday."

"Do you believe the horrible things Taja said about him?"

Jazz leaned forward and put her head in her hands. "I don't want to. It just doesn't seem like him."

"What does your heart tell you?"

Jazz sat up, watching Tinga. "It tells me that they're all horrible lies, meant to make me doubt him. But that bi… uhh, *woman* is just so convincing. I wanna smash her face in."

"That's my sister. The queen demon bitch from Hell."

Jazz laughed, not expecting that from this very proper and soft-spoken woman. Tinga laughed with her.

"I like you, Tinga."

"I like you too, Jazz. I have ever since Cody told us about your and Chaz's regular trips to the children's hospital. Cody believes you are a kind and strong woman, and I do too. We all do. And we all love Chaz."

Jazz sighed, thinking of Chaz's *faux pas* at breakfast, his innocent silly smile. "Yeah, he's an amazing kid, isn't he?"

"As are all the children here."

"So just what the hell is Cody's story, Tinga?"

Tinga dipped her head and raised her eyebrows at Jazz.

"Okay, okay." Jazz waved her hands. "I get it. If I wanna know his story, I have to ask him."

Tinga nodded. "I can tell you this: Taja did not teach Cody everything he knows. When he left her and joined us almost ten years ago, he was trained, but he was not the composed and adept fighter that he is today. He had to learn discipline. He had to learn when *not* to fight, yet stand true."

"You mean you taught him, don't you?"

Tinga tilted her head back and forth, lips pursed and eyebrows raised.

"You mean you can do all that martial arts stuff too? And the weapons?"

Tinga giggled. "A woman can keep some of her secrets, can she not?"

Jazz laughed. "That she can. But tell me one. How old are you?"

"I'll be forty-six in December."

"No way!"

"Way."

"Damn, girl."

"I look good for forty-six, don't I?"

"Woman, you look good for twenty-eight."

Tinga nodded, serenely watching the trees. "Thank you."

"I hate you." Jazz watched the trees with her.

"You are a beautiful woman, Jazz. Do not doubt it for a second, and don't think that the men here haven't noticed. Especially Cody."

Jazz snorted. "Yeah, right. What is his damn problem, anyway?"

"Ask him, Jazz. Maybe he'll tell you. It helps him to talk about it, and I believe it will greatly help him to tell *you*."

"I will." Jazz turned to Tinga. She didn't want to experience the helpless feeling she'd had yesterday ever again. "Will you teach me, Tinga?"

"Does that mean you want to stay with us?"

Jazz threw her hands up. "What choice do I have?"

"Roberta told you we would take you anywhere—"

"Yeah, but that's not really a choice, is it? If these people are for real, I'd be signing my death certificate, and effectively Chaz's too."

166

Tinga nodded. "Yes, Jazz. I will teach you. We all will."

"Thank you. Although I can't see Cody doing so willingly."

"Perhaps you'll be surprised." Tinga straightened out her kimono. "There is something I will tell you that Cody will not. It may explain where some of his anger and bitterness comes from.

"A few months ago, in May, Soulsnatcher captured a girl Cody was guarding. She's the first ward he's lost since he's been here. He blames himself for what he perceives as his failure. But they had their teleporter, so he never really had a chance to save her."

"Wow. Teleportation? Despite Chaz's ability, I'm still finding it hard to believe that's actually real."

"It's as real as what Chaz can do. The ward's name is Kaylee. She's seventeen, and headstrong and determined. But in Taja's clutches... I know my sister, Jazz. I have no doubt she's brainwashing that poor girl, and Cody is just as certain of it because, like me, he truly knows what Taja is capable of."

"What can Kaylee do?"

"Kaylee is an organic fertility thaumaturge. Which means she can make plants grow to unprecedented healthy proportions, at a speed similar to time-lapse photography. In a very big way, it's like magic. And I believe she may just now be discovering the magnitude of her power."

"Whoa. Different. What would they want her for?"

Tinga scowled. "Kendra and Malek keep tabs on these things with a tracking program they created. They recently discovered that a man with mob connections named Dimitri Dinelli won a big national garden show contest. We sent Serena—she's one of our Guardians—to check it out. Serena said there was no way it was natural growth. We believe Dinelli hired Dr. Sössnocher to use Kaylee to make it happen. We don't know what else they've made her do, or what they've promised her to make her do it. But Kendra and Malek are keeping a close eye out for similar anomalies. And if we can catch them in the act, so to speak, we may be able to rescue Kaylee."

Jazz sneered. "These people are twisted. Using children like that... it's just plain evil."

"Indeed. Remember how you told me Cody is hard not to trust?"

"Yeah. He's got this... look."

"Yes he does. But it isn't his power—it's something that just comes naturally to him. Even after my sister nearly ruined him. So Kaylee probably trusted him too. But knowing my sister, I imagine she told Kaylee that it *is* his special talent, so Kaylee would doubt him, and lose hope. Taja will try to convince her that she is her only real friend. It's how her warped mind works."

Jazz perked up. "You know, you just gave me an idea. She's arrogant, right? She thinks she has the upper hand because she thinks she's tougher than I am."

"What are you thinking?"

"I'm thinking she's not expecting us to play her game her way. So why don't we? We make a recording of me in her face, like she was in mine. I tell her I think she's full of shit, that the finger was a fake, and I don't even know if..." Jazz's heart pushed up into her throat. "If Daddy's even alive. Because she didn't show him, or let me talk to him, since the phone call. I tell her to fuck off until she's willing to show me my father, alive and well, even if he's minus a finger."

Tinga nodded slowly. "Not bad. If you can pull it off without showing fear."

"I'll laugh in her face. It could buy us some time before we come up with a plan. We could even wait to send it until the countdown is nearly up."

Tinga's eyebrows rose. "I like it. But let's talk it over with the others and the professor first."

Jazz nodded, scheming. Taja wasn't going to make her break down in tears and beg. Her father wouldn't approve of that, and Jazz just didn't roll that way. "Okay."

"I like the way you think, Jazz. But make no mistake: though she's playing mind games, my sister is a cold-blooded killer. If we do this, she won't back down. She'll consider it a challenge. You could make it worse for your father."

"Trust me, Daddy would approve." Jazz was already rehearsing her speech in her head, and it made her feel better.

"The more I think about it, the more I like it," Tinga said. "I'll back you up when we discuss it with the others. And help you with it."

"Thank you. So tell me about this Dr. Sorshnocker. Soulsnatcher."

"It would be best to let Benny tell you about him."

"Benny?"

Tinga grinned. "Dr. Benjamin Cameron. The professor."

"Uh-huh. Benny. I see. A woman's got to keep some secrets, right?"

Tinga blushed. Jazz chuckled, and then snapped her fingers.

"Hey, I remember that name. There was a Dr. Cameron who was famous for discovering some kind of medical breakthrough back in the early eighties. I remember learning about him in college. Won a Nobel prize for it."

"Yes he did. But that's not where all the money came from. It would be best if I let Benny tell you about it, okay?"

Jazz sighed, resigned to waiting for the rest of the story. "Okay."

"So would you like to come and observe our classroom in action?"

Jazz stood. "Let's."

Tinga rose and led her inside. The front room was one big classroom, with a huge computer screen divided into two sections of lesson plans mounted on the far wall. The desks had been moved to the walls, and nine children sat in a circle with Amanda and Mara, who sat side by side in front of the screen.

169

Amanda was grinning, and the children were laughing. When Amanda saw Tinga, she raised her eyebrows. Tinga shook her head and led Jazz to some folding chairs in the corner, where they sat together. Dante sauntered up to Jazz and nuzzled her leg. She patted his flank as Tinga spoke softly.

"We teach them the basics, of course: reading, writing, math, science, and history. But we also try to teach them to open their minds, and hearts. Listen."

The cute little girl who had jumped into Roberta's arms last night was speaking, her golden curls bouncing as she bobbed her head. Jazz figured she couldn't be older than seven.

"… but more than anything, I wanna use my power to help make sure nobody ever takes anybody's mommy and daddy away from them again like the bad people did to me."

"Me too, Andrea," Amanda said, nodding and smiling. "That's very good. And we're all going to help you learn how to do that, aren't we, everyone?"

The children's voices rose in a chorus of assent. Jazz realized they were discussing their powers and what they wanted to do with them for Chaz's benefit. She couldn't help but wish Amanda was next. Chaz took that moment to interrupt in typical Chaz fashion.

"Well, I want to use my power to help people too. So why won't you let me fix Lynette's bent foot? Or Anthony's broken arm?"

Amanda sighed and smiled. "Chaz, remember how Mara told you there's someone else we hope you'll help first? We'll discuss that with you and your mother later, okay?"

Chaz's shoulders slumped. "Okay."

Jazz glanced at Tinga, who nodded and closed her eyes.

"Thank you, Chaz," Amanda said. "Jenna, your turn."

A girl about eleven spoke next, but Jazz only half heard it. She was too busy watching Chaz and feeling his disappointment. She didn't know if he had recuperated enough to perform his magic again yet. She usually allowed him several days to a

170

week after a visit to the children's ward. But he clearly wanted to do it again, and now. She sighed, and Tinga touched her arm.

"All will be clear soon, Jazz."

Jazz looked at her and ruffled Dante's fur. "Okay."

A few minutes later, Amanda stood, and Mara and the other children stood with her. Amanda looked at Tinga, received a nod, and grinned and said, "Class dismissed."

Amid shouts and laughter, the classroom emptied except for Jazz and Tinga. Jazz stood, curious where everyone was headed.

Tinga grinned at Jazz. "Shall we go play now?"

Jazz smiled and shrugged off her worries for the moment. "Okay."

She and Tinga followed the chattering mob outside and around the back of the schoolhouse. They took a short winding path through the trees to a partially open field, where the children were already gathered. With the grass and other foliage cut back, the field was laid out in the form of a baseball diamond, complete with bases and a home plate with an aluminum stick poking out vertically in front of it. Several adults had already joined the growing crowd, and several stragglers followed, shouting and cheering.

Jazz looked up. The intertwining branches of the trees overhead shielded the field from a portion of the aerial view, but the late afternoon sun still shone through them brilliantly, illuminating the happy gathering.

Tinga smiled, watching Jazz. "Mondays and Thursdays are T-ball day."

Jazz nodded, soaking in the spectacle. Dante pranced around, as happy and carefree as if everything was essentially right with the universe, and the game began.

A grinning, gawky girl, maybe thirteen years old, hobbled up to the plate with a bat in hand. Her right foot was turned inward, causing her to limp. Jazz figured it was Lynette, the girl Chaz had asked to heal.

Kino, Cody, Marco, and Raj were out in the field, shouting encouragement. Roberta stood behind home plate.

"Come on, Lynette!" she shouted, clapping.

"Big hit, girl!" Kino howled.

Lynette hit the ball, and Jazz realized, as she watched Chaz smiling and laughing in the outfield, that nobody cared who was on whose team, or who won. They were all here to have fun. Lynette hit the ball over the shortstop's head, and she struggled toward first base and rounded it. Dante scampered into left field and snagged the ball before the outfielder could catch it. With a playful feint, Dante ran into center field. Instead of getting angry and shouting at Dante, the fielders laughed and chased him.

Lynette ended up with a triple before a fielder reclaimed the ball. She smiled as she stood atop the base, and nobody complained.

Jazz felt something clogging her breathing, and knew what it was. She had unwittingly found what she and Chaz had been looking for. It was communion on a scale that she had doubted even existed. It was exhilarating, and effortlessly celebrated here. She watched Chaz, and knew he felt it too.

It struck a chord deep inside her, and resonated with a feeling of independence and freedom. She fought tears as she clapped and cheered. Tinga cheered alongside her, making her feel like she was a part of something greater than herself or Chaz.

With numerous plays enhanced by Dante's participation, the afternoon seemed to last forever and was over far too soon at the same time. When they were done, nobody knew who'd won or lost. There was only the sense of camaraderie that had been absent from her and Chaz's lives for so long.

Everyone was family here, and she wanted to be a part of it. She saw the smile plastered on Chaz's face and knew he wanted it too, was already more a part of it than her.

Throughout the game, she never lost sight of the fact that

lives were on the line, and she saw it in the eyes of the adults and some of the children. Yet they played on as if it were every-thing that mattered, at least for this brief moment.

It broke her heart, and revived it.

She wanted to cry tears of loss and joy at the same time. At some point in the game, Roberta and Tinga hugged her, and then acted like nothing unusual had happened. Jazz and Roberta even took an at-bat, joining in the fun.

She didn't miss the fact that Kino, Cody, Marco, Raj, and the other adults never stopped encouraging the children, oblivious to any rules. Cody hustled back and forth in the field. And something else happened, something Jazz had never intended.

Her resistance broke down, she let go of her fury, and found peace.

It was profound to the point that it left her speechless. When Dante snagged the ball on the last at-bat, everyone laughed and chased him.

She ran after their silly dog, calling his name and laughing, tears of joy running down her cheeks. All the shields and barriers she had so carefully constructed over a period of long, hard, lonely years came crashing down, and their demise was welcomed, invited, joyously celebrated.

She was home. This was home.

Several adults gathered up the bases and equipment while Kino, Raj, and two other men herded the boys to the showers. Tinga, Roberta, and a couple of women rounded up the girls. When they left the field, there was no evidence that anyone had been there.

Only the spirit lingered.

Chapter 18

Jazz headed to their room with Chaz, and told him to feed Dante and give him fresh water before he took a shower. She took another luxurious hot shower, her mind full of questions and revelations. When she was done, she dressed in light blue jeans and a beige cotton blouse, slipped on her ankle-length moccasins, took Dante outside, and waited on Chaz.

When he came out with his hair wet and tangled, it was six o'clock. They followed the crowd into the dining hall, leaving Dante on the porch.

Inside, Malek's voice blared from the speakers: "Good evening, dudes and dudettes. This is your favorite console captain and computer guru with a public service announcement."

"I'm their favorite, Malek, you hopeless geek!" a female voice interrupted.

"Be quiet, impudent girl. I'm on important business here. The professor just called and said their arrival is delayed for a couple of hours, so they should be rolling in between eight and nine. Your camp counselors advise you all to just simmer down now, enjoy the in-flight meal and movie, and snuggle up to your sweetie. We now return you to your regularly scheduled programming."

"Malek, you doofus—"

The sound was cut off, and laughter filled the hall. Jazz stepped up to the buffet and inhaled slowly, savoring the mouth-watering bouquet wafting off the steaming array.

Dinner was beef pot roast with potatoes, onions, and carrots. Five vegetable dishes and a selection of fruits complemented the main course, along with the makings for a fresh garden salad. Jazz licked her lips when she saw lemon meringue pie and chocolate cake laid out for dessert. She filled her plate, sat down beside Roberta and Marco, and dug in.

Conversation was cheerful, mostly about the professor coming back or the afternoon's game. Jazz withheld her questions and enjoyed the meal. She couldn't remember the last time she and Chaz had eaten so well and with such regularity.

She wanted to spend some quality time with Chaz and hear about his day. She snagged his arm on the way outside after they finished dinner and dessert. He looked longingly at Amanda as she walked away with Mara and the other children.

Jazz briefly wondered if Amanda's special talent was making nine-year-old boys develop hopeless crushes on her.

They called Dante, walked over toward one of several wooden benches spaced around the perimeter of the buildings, and sat. Chaz picked up a stick, tossed it toward the surrounding trees, and Dante leaped after it.

"So what do you think, Binky?"

Chaz grunted and rested a hand on his belly. "I really like it here, Mother. A lot." He squinted up at her. "I really think we should stay here."

She chuckled. His wide-eyed innocence was endearing, and she would wrestle lions, tigers, and bears to help him keep it. So far, he'd handled the shock and stress of their situation much better than she'd expected. She agreed about staying, but she didn't let on.

"Hmmm."

"What?" He grabbed the stick from Dante and threw it again. "Mother, I don't think you understand how important it is that we stay here."

She laughed. "You know I love you so much."

"I love you too, Mother." He watched Dante play and let out a long sigh.

"What's wrong, Chaz?"

"I'm *stuffed*. They keep feeding me like this and I'm gonna turn into a lardbutt."

"Chaz! Don't say that. It's not nice."

"Yeah? Well, you better watch it too. They'll be turning you into a lardbutt before you know it."

"Oh, yeah?" She poked her belly out and puffed up her cheeks.

He grinned at her. "Yeah. If you're not careful." Then he sighed again.

"Come on, Binky. Talk to me. I know when something's bothering you."

He turned and faced her, his eyes pleading for under-standing. "It's just that… they keep telling us we should use our powers to help people, and I want to, but they won't let me. They wouldn't let me help Lynette or Anthony. It's not fair."

"Maybe they understand that you need time to recuperate from yesterday. Maybe they're just giving you that time."

"But I feel strong. It's like I can do it again and again now, more than before. I can fix them."

She'd never seen him so energetic and enthusiastic less than twenty-four hours after he healed someone. Before, he'd been sluggish and weak for days afterward. Something had changed. Maybe he *was* getting stronger, and she dared to hope, desperate to defy his doctors' unanimous prognoses.

"Chaz, what did Amanda mean when she said Mara told you there was someone else they hope you'll help first?"

Chaz took the stick from Dante, threw it again, and frowned. "I don't know. I think Lynette and Anthony want me to help them but won't ask."

Jazz didn't have time to decipher that riddle. Amanda walked up to them, a half-smile curling her lips. Close behind her were Mara, Tinga, and Cody.

Amanda stopped a few feet away, and the others stopped with her. "Hi, Jazz. Chaz. May I sit with you?"

"Yeah!" Chaz slid to the other side of the bench, opening up a space between them. Jazz smiled and gestured beside her.

Amanda sat between them. Mara sat cross-legged on the ground. Cody squatted and rested his arms on his knees, and

Tinga stood behind him. Jazz didn't know what was going on here, but it was something far more profound than Amanda discussing her talent.

"Chaz," Amanda said, "do you know how it feels when you want something so bad, not for yourself, but for someone you love very much, but you feel so lost because you don't know how to make it happen?"

Chaz watched her, and Jazz could tell from his expression that he knew something deeper was happening here too.

"Well, I want Mother to be happy. And safe. But I don't know how to make her happy and safe."

"Oh, Chaz," Jazz choked out. "You make me happy. So happy."

"I know, Mother. You make me happy too. But that isn't what she means. Is it, Amanda?"

Amanda smiled and took Chaz's hand. "You are so smart, Chaz. I knew it the minute I saw you."

Chaz beamed, lighting up the encroaching darkness.

Amanda looked at Tinga and Cody, who both nodded at her. "Chaz, there's a reason Lynette and Anthony didn't ask you to heal them. We've been taught here—and wisely, I believe—not to ask first what we want for ourselves, but what we want for others. People we care about."

Jazz leaned forward on the bench and watched Amanda's eyes. Amanda took her hand, squeezed it, and Jazz squeezed back.

What is going on here?

Mara snorted and waved her hands. "What are you waiting for?"

Amanda nodded. Cody stared at the ground.

"Chaz." Amanda looked at Chaz, and turned to gaze into Jazz's eyes. "Jazz. We want to ask something for a friend. A favor for someone we all love very much."

"Amanda, honey, what?" Jazz's heart pounded.

Amanda took a deep breath. "Kino has colorectal cancer. Colon cancer. It's almost always fatal. The doctors don't think he has much time left. Like, less than a year. You wouldn't think it, looking at him. He's so strong, like he could never do something so stupid and senseless as die. He doesn't let it show." Jazz thought of Kino's pained expression when the children climbed on him earlier, realizing now what it meant as Amanda continued. "And only me, Mara, Tinga, Cody, and the professor know about it, besides Kino. We only told Lynette and Anthony that someone here was very sick, so they would wait to ask Chaz to help them. And now you know. And Roberta definitely doesn't know. Kino made us promise not to tell her. He's dying, Chaz. And I... we were just wondering if—"

"I wanna help him!" Chaz stood up, still holding Amanda's hand. "Mother, I wanna heal him. I feel so strong now. I can do it."

Cody looked up at Jazz, and his eyes told the story. "He is my friend."

Tinga nodded. "And mine."

Jazz's heart broke all over again. "Chaz…"

"I can do it, Mother. I wanna do it."

Amanda closed her eyes and smiled. Jazz watched tears stream down her cheeks.

You remarkable and surprising girl.

"We understand if you can't do it now," Amanda said. "But if, maybe in a few days or a week—"

"I wanna do it now!" Chaz looked at Jazz. "Mother, I'm filled up with it. I can feel it. I love Kino, and wanna help him."

Everyone looked at Jazz, and she figured Atlas had no idea how light his burden was. To deny Chaz now would be to deny his gift, and his love of sharing it. But how much could his frail heart take?

She took a deep breath. "Okay, Binky. If you think—"

Chaz huffed and rolled his eyes. "Where is he? Take me

to him."

Cody nodded and stood. He turned and walked toward the compound.

Mara stood and brushed dirt off her jeans. "About damn time. You people take way too long to do the simplest things."

Jazz stood with Amanda, still holding her hand. Chaz tugged on her other hand.

"Come on, Mother, let's go!"

They followed Cody back to the central compound and toward the main building. In the front room, Raj, four other adults, and nine children sat on the floor, laughing as Kino did a passable impression of Shrek.

"Hey, guys," Kino said, smiling and looking at Chaz. "We're watching *Shrek 3* again tonight at seven-thirty. You wanna join us?"

"Yeah, Chaz, come watch with us," Zeke said, and the other children echoed him.

"I need to see you in your room," Cody said, glaring at Kino. "Now."

"Yo, Cody, what's—"

"Now."

Kino smiled for the kids. "Okay, guys. We got some business we gotta attend to. And stay off my property, or I'll eat ya!"

The children giggled nervously, and Jazz knew they understood something big was going on. Cody took Kino's arm and led him down the hall. Jazz, Chaz, and the others followed. At Kino's door, Cody gestured everyone inside. Tinga waited outside the door, and closed it behind them.

Inside, Cody glared at Kino and waved at the couch. "Sit down."

Kino frowned and sat. "Cody, what's—"

"Be quiet, you goofy-ass ogre." Cody turned to Chaz and Jazz.

Chaz looked up at Jazz, and she nodded. He went to the

couch, sat in Kino's lap, and put his arms around the big man's neck.

Kino gasped, started to get up. "Oh, Chaz, no. They told you. I can't let you risk—"

"Just sit still," Chaz said. "This won't hurt, I promise."

"Shut up and do as he says," Cody said.

"But Cody, what if he—"

"Please let him help you, Kino," Amanda said.

Tears leaked from the corners of Kino's eyes as he closed them.

A minute later, only hopeful hearts felt the change. The only physical indication that something momentous had just occurred was when Chaz slumped in Kino's arms, and Kino's body quaked with deep sobs.

"Oh my God," Kino whispered, opening his eyes and looking at everyone. "It's unbelievable. I think it's gone. I can't feel the pain anymore." He squeezed Chaz, kissed him on the cheek. "Thank you, Chaz."

"Welcome," Chaz mumbled.

Jazz grinned at Kino, her heart soaring. Cody stooped and took Chaz from Kino's arms, and Chaz rested his head on Cody's shoulder.

"Gonna sleep now, Mother," he muttered.

"Thank you, Chaz," Cody whispered in his ear.

Jazz stroked Chaz's hair out of his eyes and kissed him on the forehead. "My special boy."

Kino gasped as tears streamed down his cheeks. "I guess I just never really believed it could be possible. Until now. I feel so... *alive.*" He stood, his legs shaking, and looked at Jazz. "God, Jazz. Is he gonna be okay? Please tell me he's—"

"He'll be fine, Kino. Look at him, he's smiling. He said he wanted to do this, that he felt so strong tonight."

Cody looked at Jazz. "I'm gonna put him in bed now, Jasmine."

"Call me Jazz. All my friends do."

Cody nodded and turned to Kino. "Welcome back. You get a second chance. Don't blow it this time, doofus."

"God, Cody. I feel so... it's like... amazing. Like it was never even there. I think he really healed me."

Amanda and Mara sprang toward Kino and leaped into his arms. He laughed and squeezed them.

Jazz heard muffled voices from the hallway. They grew louder, and the door flew open. Roberta stood in the threshold, Tinga behind her.

"What's going on in here?" Roberta stepped into the room and glanced around. She saw Chaz passed out in Cody's arms, Jazz's tear-streaked face, and Cody's smile. Her eyes widened and flew to Kino.

Amanda and Mara stepped away from Kino as Roberta shuffled toward him. Mara nudged Amanda, and they left the room. Tinga smiled and put her arms around their shoulders and followed them.

Cody mouthed "thank you" to Jazz and left. Jazz stood still, watching Kino and Roberta. Her heart was suddenly full, ready to burst.

Roberta took Kino's hands in hers. "Dammit, Kino. Why didn't you tell me? What was it?" She let go of his hands and cupped his cheeks in her palms.

"Colon cancer. All gone now, I think."

"You were dying? Is this why you never..."

Kino bowed his head. "I couldn't make you go through that again, Roberta."

"Kino!"

"The pain. Of losing someone you... I know it hurt so much to lose Stephan. I just couldn't do that to you. Again."

"You stubborn, foolish... you should have told me. It wouldn't have changed how I feel. Kino, why waste what precious moments we have? Look at all the time we've lost that we could've been—"

"I love you too much, Roberta. I couldn't hurt you like

that."

"God, Kino!" Roberta hugged him, squeezed him as if it was all that mattered. "All this time. I love you too, you big… goofy…" She planted kisses on his cheeks, then kissed him on the lips.

Jazz smiled, walked out, and closed the door behind her.

Chapter 19

Jazz went to her and Chaz's room and found Cody tucking Chaz in. She stood in his bedroom doorway and watched them. Cody brushed damp strands of Chaz's hair out of his face and pulled the sheet up over his chest. Dante panted as he lay on Chaz's bed, his tail thumping the mattress.

Cody turned and nodded at Jazz, and they went into the front room. He took a deep breath and grabbed her hands, his eyes burning into hers.

"I don't know how to thank you. Chaz just saved Kino's life."

"Well," she drawled, smiling. "Thank Chaz. But you could start by telling me your story."

He grimaced and let go of her hands. "Maybe I will. Some day. But not today. Because you're not going to like it."

"Whether I like it or not is beside the point. I wanna know your story, Cody. Everybody else told me theirs, but they wouldn't tell me about you. So now it's your turn."

"Not now, Jazz. I feel too good, too happy right now, to be such a buzz kill. Leave it for another day."

"God, Cody. What's the big damn secret? I trust you, and I know you didn't do those horrible things Taja said."

"Not the ones she said, no. But I've done a lot of things I regret."

"We've all done things we regret, Cody. I know all about regret."

He glared at her. "Not the kinds of things that get innocent people killed."

She sighed and waved her hands. There had to be some way to get him to open up. "I know about Kaylee. It's not your fault. It sounds like you did everything anyone could have done to help her."

"She's only one of many." He shook his head and bowed it, and his voice lowered. "I knew Taja was in the copter. I can smell her from a mile away, just like I can smell trouble. Hell, she is trouble, with a capital 'T.' I should've killed her when I had the chance."

"Why didn't you?"

"Huh." He looked toward Chaz's bedroom, and back at her. "You've done a really great job with him."

"What?"

"Chaz. He's a good kid. You should be proud."

"Cody! Dammit… Yeah, I am proud. He's a great kid. And quit changing the subject. Talk to me."

"Why can't he heal himself?"

"God. You're impossible."

He sighed, held up his hands, and shrugged.

"I don't know why, Cody. Don't you think he would if he could? It's not fair." She hated the whine that had crept into her voice.

"I'm sorry, Jazz. Life's not fair. It chews you up and spits you out. I gotta stop thinking that, but it does. But I will tell you this: Chaz has two new friends for life. Because as long as we live, me and Kino'll die before we let anybody hurt him. Roberta too."

She nodded and pursed her lips. "Same here."

"Yeah. You were a lioness at your house. You nailed that asshole and had him down before I could even fire a shot at him. With Dante's help."

"Oh, Dante? You mean that dog we should have let die?"

He grimaced. "I didn't mean it like that."

"Dante saved mine and Chaz's lives just like Chaz saved Kino's life tonight."

He closed his eyes and nodded. "I'm sorry, Jazz. I was thinking of you and Chaz first, I swear it. Sometimes I forget. About stuff that means something."

"Jesus, Cody. What the hell happened to you?"

"Everything."

"Care to elaborate?"

"I never had a dog. I wasn't thinking."

He either didn't get it, or he was evading it. She didn't know how to reach him, and she realized just how badly she wanted to. She had questions in desperate need of answers. She needed to tell him about her idea of a video response to Taja. So many things...

"What does it take to get you to open up, Cody? I mean *damn.*"

"What do you want from me, woman? A signed confession?"

Her nails dug into her palms. "What is your problem anyway? Why can't you just—"

"I'm impossible? That's a laugh. You—"

"Good evening, ladies and germs!" a voice came over the intercom system.

"Malek, give me that!" The speakers popped, squawked, and Kendra's voice came back on: "God, you're so childish. Everyone forgive the dork, please. Folks, we have a happy announcement. The professor's boat is en route, and they should be arriving at the Blue Lagoon in about five minutes. You can meet him at the main building, and I encourage our new guests to be there. This is your *favorite* console captain, signing off."

There was a knock at the open entrance door, and Amanda came in when Jazz nodded at her. "I'll stay and watch Chaz while you go meet the professor."

"Thanks, Amanda," Jazz said, smiling at her. The girl had practically read her mind. Was that her talent?

Ignoring Amanda, Cody glared at Jazz and jerked a stiff arm at the door. "Well, this is the moment you've been waiting for. Shall we?"

He looked like a cornered wildcat itching to escape its

confining cage. Jazz shook her head and moved toward the door. "Might as well. Even if he's a deaf mute, I'll probably get more out of him than I've gotten out of you."

Amanda grinned and waved at Cody, and Jazz stomped out of her room and down the hall. Glancing back, she glimpsed Cody grumbling and shuffling out of her doorway. She stepped up the pace and strode into the front room, where several children waited. They chattered and watched the monitors, which were tuned in on one of the lagoons. The display showed a boat drifting into the secluded cove.

Jazz headed through the front door and onto the porch. Children and adults strolled toward the building, jabbering and smiling.

She headed down the steps and smiled at the people who passed her. When she reached the dirt of the compound, she spun around. Cody stopped at the bottom of the steps. She glared at him.

"What?" He waved his hands.

Jazz growled. "You know things you won't share with me. For all I know, you won't share them with anybody. You obviously have an analytical mind. But you can't figure out the simplest things of all."

Cody exhaled. "Explain them to me."

"Okay, Cody, since you haven't figured it out yet. You may be smart, but God, you're dumb. I want you to be nicer to Amanda."

"What?" Cody's face scrunched up.

"You heard me. You're so standoffish to everyone. Do you think that makes you tougher?"

"What are you—"

"You treat her like a kid."

"She is a kid!"

"Not in her mind she's not. Are you blind, Cody? God, men are so thickheaded where it counts the most. Can you possibly not know she's in love with you?"

"With... what? That's... I'm more than twice her age!"

"Oh!" She walked farther out into the compound, watching folks pass her and Cody. She spun around again, and he nearly bumped into her.

"Jazz, would you please—"

"Promise me you'll be nicer to her. That you won't break her heart."

He sighed and shook his head. He really had no idea. "Okay. I promise. But Jazz, if she really does..." He winced. "Do you know what she can do?"

He caught her off guard with that, and she suddenly had to know. "No. What can she—?"

The roar of a loud engine interrupted them, accompanied by a series of staccato bursts from a car horn. An extended-cab Dodge pickup rumbled up the dirt lane and into the compound, and parked outside the main building next to Jazz and Cody.

"Cody, what can Amanda—?"

"Boss man's here. I'll introduce you to him."

The rear and front doors opened. Raj hopped out of the driver's seat, and a Hispanic girl in her early teens and a boy of about ten or eleven climbed out of the back and approached Cody.

A handsome man probably in his early sixties got out of the front passenger side. Short, thinning gray hair, a weathered but friendly face, in excellent shape. He grinned at Jazz and Cody, a little beam of sunshine on a dark evening. Jazz returned the smile, realizing she'd missed out yet again on learning about Amanda's talent.

The little boy stopped in front of Cody while a gaggle of excited children poured out of the main building. They called out "Dr. Ben!" as they hustled around the Dodge pickup. The little boy frowned and looked up at Cody.

"Where's Kino?"

Cody squinted at the boy. "Hey, Cody. How are you? It's been a while. It's great to see you."

The boy smirked. "Hey, Cody, how are you, it's been a while, it's great to see you. Where's Kino?"

Cody chuckled. "He's temporarily indisposed. You can talk to him in the morning, Zane."

The children gathered around the elderly man, chattering all at once, and he chuckled and stooped over. Andrea, the little golden-curled girl, smiled at him and reached her arms up. He picked her up and hugged her, said something that made her giggle, and she kissed him on the cheek. He laughed and set her down and walked over to Cody and Jazz.

"Cody, my boy. It's good to see you safe and not full of holes. I gather you had some special help with your recovery?"

"Hey, Ben. Yeah, I did." Cody surprised Jazz by hugging him. He stepped back and gestured to Jazz. "Ben, I'd like you to meet—"

"Ahh, yes, Jasmine," Ben said, his teeth gleaming. He took her hand and kissed it. "Dr. Benjamin Cameron. Call me Ben. I must say, you're even lovelier in person than in your photos."

Jazz's hand tingled where his lips had brushed it. "Thank you. It's a pleasure to meet you, Ben, and call me Jazz."

"Jazz. It's a pleasure to finally meet you, my dear. Where's Chaz?"

"He's… recovering." She wasn't sure how much she should say yet.

"Ahh. Healing Cody took quite a toll on him, I suppose?"

"Not exactly, Ben," Cody said, raising his eyebrows.

Ben frowned. "No? Say, my boy, where is your over-sized shadow?"

Cody smiled, sharing a secret with his eyes. "He's with Roberta. They're celebrating. Privately."

Ben laughed, a hearty sound. "Wonderful! It's about time. Wait… what are they celebrating?"

Cody looked at Jazz, and back at Ben. "Chaz healed him,

Ben. I think he's going to be okay."

Tears glistened in Ben's eyes, and he laughed again, and Cody laughed with him. He stepped forward and embraced Cody again. "Praise God, Cody. That's the most wonderful news I've heard in years."

"Tell me about it," Cody said, and he and Ben parted. "So where's Serena?"

"She left the other site before us to check up on another special boy we just found out about," Ben said. "She'll fill us in tomorrow." He turned to Jazz. "Jazz, will you and Cody meet me in my study in thirty minutes for a glass of brandy? We'll get better acquainted, discuss what we're going to do about rescuing your father, and I'll fill you in on anything my friends haven't told you yet about our little operation."

"Of course, Ben. Thank you. I'm looking forward to it."

"As am I, my dear. I'm so happy you and Chaz arrived safe and sound."

"Me too. It was a bumpy ride."

Cody squinted at Ben. "So how was the trip?"

"Everything's mostly up and running at the other location. I'll fill you in when we meet up later."

A feeling of celebration was in the air, as if Santa Claus had just hopped off his sleigh with a huge sack of toys. Ben teased the children, and some of the excitement rubbed off on Jazz despite the worry crushing her.

They had to help her rescue her father, somehow. She was pinning all her hopes on these people. If they didn't help her with her sketchy plan, she was on her own. But if she had to go it alone, so be it. Nothing would be right until Daddy was safe.

The crowd worked its way inside the main building. Ben chatted with the children, and Jazz listened in on some conversations, even joining a few. The subject *du jour* was preparations for the backup location for Homestead. No one mentioned where it was, as if speaking it aloud would jinx them.

Twenty minutes later, Cody gestured for her to follow him. She broke free from the crowd, and he led her down the hall. She heard exclamations of disappointment from the front room, and turned to see Ben heading down the hall after them. He nodded and smiled, and gestured to Cody, who stood in front of a door with "25" on it.

Cody opened the door and went inside, and Jazz followed him. Ben entered behind her and closed the door.

Jazz expected Ben's study to be a sumptuously furnished room replete with state-of-the-art technology, but it was quite the opposite. The only furniture in the twenty-by-thirty-foot room, other than the four slightly worn sofa chairs facing each other in a circle around a coffee table, were the wall-to-wall bookshelves crammed with endless tomes. They made the room appear smaller, but it was still cozy and serene, and helped her relax.

Ben looked at her. "Have a seat. Make yourselves comfortable. Would you care for a glass of brandy?"

"Yes, please." She sat in one of the sofa chairs. Cody sat across from her.

Ben went to a small refrigerator built into the bookshelves, retrieved a bottle, grabbed three glasses off a shelf, and sat beside Cody. He poured each of them a half-glass of the chilled brandy.

"Janneau Armagnac, from France. One of my vices, I must confess. I think you'll find it delightful."

Jazz took a sip of the chilled liqueur. It tingled on her tongue, opening up her throat and sinuses as it went down. "It's fabulous, Ben. Thank you." Feeling her body relax while her mind remained in turmoil was a curious sensation.

She leaned back in her chair, took another sip, and an idea started sprouting tentacles in the musty shadows of her attic. She let the muse take her, and waited for Ben or Cody to speak.

"Jazz, out of necessity, let's dispense with the chit-chat,

shall we?" Ben leaned forward, and she nodded. "We can catch up and fill in the blanks later. Tinga called me while we flew in, and told me about your plan."

Cody nodded. "Yeah, she told me about it after dinner. Pretty bold. I especially like the part about you giving Taja the finger back, so to speak. You know your life is forfeit if they get their hands on Chaz, don't you?"

"I'm headstrong, Cody, not crazy. And I just had a great idea about my plan. Want to hear it?"

Cody shrugged. "Anything's better than the plan we have right now, which is none."

"Yes, Jazz," Ben said, nodding. "Can't be any crazier than my idea. Let's hear it."

She leaned forward. "Well, for starters, has anyone talked to Mara, and asked her if she sees anything about what's going to happen? It could help us figure out what to do."

"As a matter of fact, yes," Cody said, and frowned. "She was pretty cryptic about it. She said all she sees is trees. 'Big twisted trees everywhere, blocking out everything else,' was how she put it. She was pissed off that she couldn't see more. I don't see how that's going to help us any."

"Okay," she drawled, trying to think. The alcohol relaxed her, and she took another sip. "How about this then. We'd have to explain the situation and the danger involved to him before we ask him to help, but just how good is Zeke with his illusions?"

Cody raised his eyebrows and looked at Ben, and Ben chuckled and winked at her. "Exactly what I was thinking, my dear. He's very good. Real as life, until you try to touch them. And yes, he can do real people too. Only problem is, there's no audio. It's visual only."

"Okay." She stared at her empty glass, wondering where it all went, and Ben smiled and gave her a refill. "Thanks, Ben. This stuff is addictive." She took another long sip. "Okay. No audio. But we can still make it work, if Zeke's willing. We could arrange a meeting with Taja, make her bring my father. I go, but Chaz stays here, and Zeke creates an illusion of Chaz so they think he's with me."

Cody shook his head. "Too risky. They'd kill you on sight when they realized we tricked them."

"Yeah, but that risk is not yours to take, is it, Cody?"

Cody snorted. "No, Jazz, it's not. But how do we explain it to Chaz if we come back without his mother? 'Sorry, Chaz, but she's dead. They killed her, and we let them.'"

"I thought you said you wanted to help me get my father back."

"Yeah, I do. And I will. But we need a better plan than that."

"Well, I'm all ears. What's your brilliant plan, Cody?"

He smirked. "I'm still working on it."

"Yeah, and in the meantime, Daddy's in danger. If he's even still alive."

"It *would* be very risky," Ben said. "But I think we can make this work. Roberta, Marco, and Serena are all crack shots with rifles. We could plant them at the meeting site in advance, keep Zeke guarded and far enough away from the site that he's relatively safe, and have an escape contingency if things go haywire."

"And what about the other children?" she asked. "Are there any others who can use their powers to help? What about Amanda?"

"Amanda can't help us," Cody said.

"Why don't you let her decide that?" she said. "And why won't you tell me what she—"

"She can't. Help. Us." Cody glared at her, and they had a staring contest.

"I was just thinking the same thing, Jazz," Ben said. "Amanda can't help us, but maybe some of the other children can, if they're willing. Let me think about that."

"I don't know, Ben." Cody broke eye contact with Jazz.

"What if they bring their teleporter? We'd be screwed. And worst case scenario, they could follow us here. Then it would all be over."

Jazz thought about seeing Chaz shimmer in the hallway. It had definitely scared her. "Yeah, but Cody, how could they use a teleporter to follow us back here? They can only send somebody to a place they know, and only for short distances, right? The worst they could do is take me, but they wouldn't get Chaz, because he won't be there."

Cody shook his head. "They'd teleport somebody with us to some prearranged safe spot. Somebody who they could torture this location out of. And if they got me, they'd enjoy every moment. Even I couldn't hold out forever. Taja has ways. And then I'd be betraying everyone and everything I love. Whoever they got, it would be the ultimate betrayal. And then we'd all be fucked."

She exhaled loudly. "You're still burning because you lost Kaylee that way, aren't you?"

Cody looked at her, and she instantly wished she could take it back. The hurt pooling in his eyes cut like a dagger piercing her heart.

"I'm sorry, Cody, I—"

"Yeah, I failed her, okay? It's my fault they got her, my fault they're using her, and brainwashing her." Cody hung his head, and Ben patted his shoulder and rubbed it.

"Ahh, my boy. If we knew where she was, you'd already be gone after her. And then we'd lose you too, because even you can't go up against all of them. And they want you dead worse than any of us."

Cody looked up at Jazz while she wondered about that last comment. "I'd do anything to get her back. Anything."

Jazz bit her lip. "Cody, I'm—"

"No, you're right." Cody stood, took a swig of brandy. "I fucked up, and see what happens? One little screw-up, and people die. No. It's too risky."

Jazz set her glass down and stood and grabbed his arm. He flinched but didn't pull away. Her eyes bored into his.

"Cody, don't you think I feel the same way about Daddy as you do about Kaylee? Can't you understand that I have to try and help him?"

He took a couple of deep breaths, and nodded. "Yeah. I understand, Jazz. But we need a better plan than that."

"Then help me, dammit." She felt the tears coming, and realized she was squeezing his arm.

"Okay, Jazz." He gently pried her hand off his arm, reached up, and brushed a tear off her cheek. "Whatever you say, I'm with you. I'm all over it. But we still have a little time, so let's think this through a little better, talk to everybody else about it before we go off half-cocked and get somebody killed. I guarantee you they'll have a better plan." He squeezed her hand, and she squeezed back. Ben quietly watched them.

"Okay." Jazz let go of his hand, and they sat. She sipped her brandy and tried to find the eye in the hurricane of emotions swirling through her. Getting input from Roberta, Tinga, and Kino would help.

"You know, the whole idea of them believing I would ever even think about trading Chaz for *anything* is whack anyway," Jazz said. "And surely they know that I know they would kill me and Daddy, sooner or later. So why would they even keep him alive? He's a... liability."

Ben leaned back in his chair and crossed his legs. "Dear lady, I beg your pardon for being so blunt, but your father is worth something to them alive. He's worth nothing to them dead. I believe he's alive and safe, for now."

Jazz swallowed. He had to be right.

"I do too, Jazz," Cody said.

Ben cleared his throat. "Yes, my former business partner is certainly insane, and dangerous, but he's not stupid."

Jazz took the bait. "Former business partner?"

A knock at the door interrupted them. Tinga slipped in

and shut the door behind her. She glided over to the bookshelf above the refrigerator, grabbed a glass, floated like a whisper over to Ben's chair, sat on the armrest, and helped herself to the brandy. She leaned against Ben, and he smiled and put his arm around her slender waist.

"We were just discussing our rescue plan, my love," Ben said. "We'll hash it out together with Kino, Roberta, and Marco in the morning. It's late, we're all tired, and we need fresh, sharp minds for it. And two of those minds are currently pre-occupied, I'm happy to finally say."

Cody and Tinga grinned, and so did Jazz. Kino and Roberta probably had a lot of catching up to do.

"So, Jazz," Ben said, raising his eyebrows. "I'm betting you're ready to hear all about our little operation. And Soulsnatcher's."

Jazz looked at Cody when she answered. "Damn straight."

Chapter 20

Kaylee woke Thursday morning a little after seven, fuzzy-headed, her eyes puffy. She was hungry, and was going to head downstairs and eat breakfast after she showered, but at the moment all she wanted to do was curl up into a ball and disappear.

Despite Taja's awful revelation last night, she still wanted her dark man to come rescue her, now more than ever.

The disappearing trick wasn't working, so she got up, dragged the comforter off the bed, and curled up with it in her little alcove. The morning glory and Japanese honeysuckle were battling for dominance of her window seat outside, and obstructed the view at the window's lower half. She put her hand against the window and flinched when the honeysuckle and morning glory pressed their vines against the other side.

"Good morning, guys." Tendrils wriggled in response, and she smiled, finding some joy in her little secret.

She saw three figures walking one of the pathways around the grounds, and she gasped. She leaned forward, pressing both hands against the glass. Her green friends mimicked her and pressed against the panes opposite her hands. One figure stood apart from the other two. The oldest was a guard. She didn't recognize the dog, but she recognized the young man.

"Jai!" she shouted, and the honeysuckle and morning glory trembled. She knew the window was locked, and she couldn't open it. She stood and leaned her hands against the glass and the vines followed where she touched.

"Jai!" she howled. She was pushing hard against the glass, and eased up on it. The two panes cracked and burst inward where the vines pressed against where she'd placed her hands, and the vines crept in through the holes. One flying shard struck her left palm and sliced open a gash in it.

"Dammit." She grabbed her cut hand with the other and put her face up to one of the broken panes and shouted.

"Jai!"

He stopped and tilted his head in her direction, and she shouted again.

"Jai! It's me, Kaylee! Wait!"

He turned toward her, his blind eyes gazing upward at nothing. The man walking with him moved toward him, said something, and gently touched his shoulder and turned him. The dog led Jai away. He turned his head away as they moved down the path.

"No! Jai, wait!" Kaylee's cut hand brushed the honeysuckle vine, smearing blood on it. It quivered as if in ecstasy, and suddenly grew a foot, two feet, three feet, thickening and sprouting new tendrils as it flourished in a mad frenzy of growth. It twisted gently around her arms, caressed her.

"Oh my God," she whispered, realizing her blood had caused it. "Guys, you have to get out of here, now. They can't see you in here. It'll ruin our secret."

The vine loosened its grip, slithered off her arms, and slowly withdrew through the broken pane. It eased past the broken shards, and Kaylee gasped, torn between watching the amazing spectacle and watching Jai walk away.

Her heart pounded, and her hand stung and dripped blood on the comforter. She hurried into the bathroom, turned on the cold water tap, and stuck her bloody hand in the stream.

She moaned. "Oww." The shard had sliced a deep enough gash that it bled freely. She quickly dried her hand and wrapped a towel around it, picked up a brush, and looked at her reflection. Her hair was a tangled nest, her eyes puffy and red, her lips cracked and raw from chewing on them. She started to brush her hair, but looked at the brush and tossed it on the counter.

"Damn, what do I care what I look like? He can't even see me."

She didn't care if Jai made her "feel his rage," as Taja had warned her. It would only stoke the fire already burning brightly inside her, and she desperately wanted to meet him. He called out to her in a way she'd never felt before. She ran out of the bathroom toward the door to the hall, her cut hand pressed against her chest. Barefoot and still in her pajamas, she grabbed the doorknob and turned it. Surprisingly, it opened, and she flung the door wide and dashed out into the hall.

Gordon stood outside her door, and she jerked to a stop. She looked up at him, and he frowned. Before he could say anything, she darted down the hall and recklessly plunged down the steps two at a time.

"Hey! Kaylee!" Gordon shouted, and she heard his heavy tread behind her. Her heart was pounding, and her hand throbbed in time with its beat, but she bounded down the steps like a gazelle fleeing from a cheetah, and dashed through the lobby.

A man stood by the wide portico doors. He frowned when he saw her running toward him. He reached a hand toward her, palm open.

"Hey, Kaylee, you can't—"

She sprinted past him, threw herself against the portico doors, turned the latch, and sprang outside. She heard Gordon behind her, and the other guy right behind him, but she didn't look back. Her bare feet slapped against the cool ceramic tiles of the portico, down the steps toward the gardens, and into the soft grass. She flew toward the path where she'd seen Jai, shouting his name.

Gordon said something into his cell phone as she burst into one of the gardens surrounding the estate. She had spread her magic touch here, and a medley of lush fragrances assailed her. The flora thrived because of her. She let the aroma rush through her lungs, and turned a gradual curve in the path. She hoped to see Jai, but no one was ahead of her.

She looked back, saw Gordon yards behind her, and realized he could have caught her anytime. He had never touched her, and he was just pacing her now, so she slowed to a jog and tried to catch her breath as she headed down the deserted path, hoping Gordon would let her keep going.

She glanced around as she ran, and called out Jai's name a few more times. She saw no movement but the verdant foliage rustling in the gentle morning breeze. She burst out of the garden into an open grassy field, and glanced at the outer wall thirty feet away. The field was empty, and only Gordon was in sight, twenty feet behind her. The other guy hadn't even followed them into the garden.

She slowed to a walk, and stopped. Her lungs filled with the fresh scent of the grass as her pulse evened out. She'd lost Jai, taken too long when she'd watched her honeysuckle dance for her.

Still, she should have been able to catch up to him. The grounds were extensive, the paths long and winding. For him to disappear that quickly, especially since he was blind, he had to have help. Did he know it was her, remember her, and run because he didn't want to meet her?

Or maybe he did want to meet her, and they were preventing it. She turned and scowled at Gordon, and he shrugged.

"Dammit." She walked back toward the mansion, ignoring Gordon, who followed at a respectful distance. The dewy grass felt slick and cool against her soles, tickled her toes. Despite her disappointment and her throbbing hand, she enjoyed its gentle caress. Blades moved toward her as she walked, brushed her instep and ankles, and cushioned her tread. She marveled at the way her power was quickly changing, manifesting itself in new ways.

When she stepped back on cold tile, she sighed. In her mind she heard her friends sigh too, as if the parting grieved them. She would find Jai somehow, and she smiled as she headed up the portico steps and inside. Gordon left her alone after she started up the stairs. He hadn't said a word to her since she dashed off.

She returned to her room, figuring the reprimands would be left up to Taja, who could wield her tongue like the Grim Reaper's scythe and still sound just as sweet as a southern belle reciting her nuptial vows.

Kaylee went into the bathroom and took an awkward shower. She had to hold her towel-wrapped hand away from the streaming water. Her arm was tired and getting numb by the time she finished. When she stepped out of the shower and unwrapped her hand, the feeling started coming back, and she imagined she could visibly see it throb. It felt like Wile E. Coyote's pulsating paw after an anvil dropped on it.

She gasped, feeling woozy as fresh blood trickled out of the gash. In the cabinet under the sink, she found some hydrogen peroxide, gauze, and tape, and bent herself to the grisly task of cleaning and binding her wound. It needed stitches, but that would have to wait.

She didn't know if Gordon would tell anyone about her wound. He certainly hadn't asked her about it. She was busy cooking up a way to find and meet Jai. Not wanting anyone to find out about her injury any sooner than they had to, she clumsily got dressed, called down to the kitchen, and asked them to bring her breakfast up and leave it at the door.

Taja would come around soon enough, and try to sweet-talk her into feeling guilty and ashamed, as if trying to make a friend was a horrible sin.

While she waited for her breakfast—or for Taja to come in and ruin it, and her appetite—she went to the window and looked out at the grounds, hoping for another glimpse of the handsome, vanishing blind boy. She glanced down and saw her friends writhing, tentative tendrils reaching toward her.

"Guys, knock it off. You're gonna get me in trouble."

They toned it down to an almost imperceptible thrum,

and she smiled. This was a secret worth keeping, until the proper time came to reveal it. She planned on it being an unprecedented performance, one that would forever haunt those who witnessed and survived it.

She glimpsed something at the base of the alcove window, twinkling with a sparkling ray of sunlight, and realized it was a shard of glass. If Taja saw it, she would wonder why the glass broke inward instead of outward. *Details*, Kaylee thought, and she started picking up pieces of glass and tossing them out the holes in the broken panes. She felt like the perpetrator ditching the evidence at a crime scene.

She shook the comforter, turned it over, and spread it out on the alcove sill. She heard a knock at her door and hurried to it, hoping she'd covered any trace of her secret. Praying it wasn't Taja, she opened the door and hid her hand behind it.

It was her breakfast, on a wheeled cart. Gordon stood behind it. He looked at her left arm, then at her. She grabbed the cart handle with her good hand, pulled it inside, and shut the door.

Her stomach rumbled. She had to feed the machine that was performing such miraculous feats. She wheeled the cart over beside her bed and sat on the edge of the mattress. While she ate, she let the plan roam freely in her mind, and felt the seeds sprout tendrils as the idea grew like her little organic wonders.

Taja's unwanted knock hadn't come by the time she finished breakfast, and she wheeled the cart to the door and opened it. Gordon stood there, as silent and emotionless as ever. Kaylee pushed the cart out into the hall and shut the door.

She went to her bed, lay against the pillows at the headboard, and gazed out the window, pleasantly stuffed and scheming. Had Taja discovered her secret yet? Were recordings of her little morning adventure being reviewed and analyzed?

Paranoia crept in. She had to escape this prison, even if only for long enough to visit her new friends again. She decided to push her luck, and got up and went out into the hall.

She looked at Gordon. "I'm going for a walk in the gardens." She turned and started down the hall. He didn't try to stop her, and just quietly followed her.

Outside it was warm. The sun's rays beamed down through the upper boughs of the silent trees. Kaylee smiled, and at the border of cold concrete and bountiful greenery, she took off her shoes and socks, wanting to feel the cool grass tickle her toes again.

She giggled as the blades bent toward her hands and feet, desperate for her touch. "Shh, guys. It's a secret, remember?"

They quivered, and desisted for the moment.

She wished Gordon wasn't with her. Though he seemed passive, she knew he watched her with calculating camera eyes, recording everything within his scope.

She ignored him and sauntered into the garden with no particular destination in mind. She let her mind wander and soaked in the silent communion her new friends shared with her. It rejuvenated her troubled spirit, poured strength into her with the mighty flow of a raging river.

She practically floated through the garden, feeling the invisible magic touch her deep inside. Sometime in the past few days her power had jumped the rails, sprouted wings, and soared into the heavens. Something fundamental had been altered, and she wished she could share it with Mom and Dad, show them how her magic had transformed into something even more wonderful.

Tears leaked out of her eyes, but this time she found hope instead of despair. The sensation of being surrounded by silent majestic friends made her more determined than ever to grow her power and flee this dismal prison—and avenge her parents.

She held her hands out to her sides, softly brushing the leaves and vines. She felt them reaching out for her and shushed them with her mind, relaying the silent message that the time for the ultimate communion would come soon.

Gordon let her wander where she wished, keeping a respectful distance. There was no wind, but the boughs and branches and vines and petals swished and swayed as if a gentle gust blew through them.

"Tone it down a bit, guys," she whispered, giggling and wanting to join in the eternal dance. Flowery fragrances wafted past her, filling her lungs with their lively mélange of seductive scents, healing little pieces of her broken heart.

Gordon spoke into his cell, interrupting the symphony of rustling voices in her head. She heard other voices coming from nearby, and turned to look at Gordon. He watched her, shaking his head.

She tried to trace the origin of the voices, sending out a silent plea for her friends to be still so she could hear. They quieted their restless rustling, and she strained her ears. If it was Jai…

Her heart fluttered at the thought, and something achy pressed against her chest, something she'd never felt before. If it was Jai, she would catch him this time, and his power be damned. He couldn't fill her with any more rage than she already had. She was going to meet him and find out what this feeling was.

She heard the voices again, and sprinted after them as if the sensation inside her lent her wings. Gordon dashed after her, but he couldn't keep up, because this time she had a little help from her friends.

She darted through the brush, and where it would have impeded her progress, it moved aside and created a path for her. Gordon thrashed around as her friends closed up the path behind her. She snickered, picturing him tangled up in vines, and flew down the path opening up before her.

She burst out of the garden to the back of the mansion and another grassy field where children never played, danced, or sang. Two figures were hurrying toward the mansion.

"Hey!" she called, running toward them.

The taller figure—another guard—turned toward her and stopped to intercept her. The smaller figure wasn't Jai. It was Jhin, the teleporter. He watched her, frowning with such a sad look in his eyes that her heart broke for him.

"Jhin!" She tried to dart around his guard, but the man grabbed her arm and stopped her.

"Kaylee, you can't," he said. "You'll both just get sick again."

Her left hand throbbed with the pressure of his grip, and she watched Jhin as he watched her. He looked so forsaken and forlorn that something fierce welled up inside her, and she slapped the guard in the face with her good hand.

He didn't flinch. He was as emotionless as Gordon, and held onto her arm.

"Damn you!" she shouted. "I don't care! I wanna talk to him!"

"Kaylee, even if you don't care, you'll make him very sick. Do you really want to do that to him?"

She wanted to shout out that it was a lie, that they were all lying to her, but she had to keep her mouth shut and behave. She was already in danger of exposing her secret. For the plan brewing in her head to work, she had to pretend to be a good little prisoner.

Gordon approached behind her. Knowing she would get no help or sympathy from him or the other guard, she turned back to Jhin.

Another guard had come running up to Jhin from the rear portico, and was already leading him back to jail. The guard holding her arm loosened his grip as tears started rolling down her cheeks.

"I'm sorry, Kaylee," the guard said.

Sure you are. She watched Jhin as he walked away.

When he reached the steps, he turned and looked back at her. His face was scrunched up in a frown, his pouting lips poking out, and he nodded at her once, slowly, and turned away.

She felt the power and the hidden promise in his look. Letting the seeds of the plan blossom in her mind, she left Gordon and the other guard, and sauntered back to the mansion with a new hope filling her heart.

Chapter 21

"Tinga filled me in on everything you know, Jazz," Ben said. "So stop me if I ramble on about anything you're already aware of. And feel free to interrupt if you have any questions."

"Okay." She settled into her chair, almost a part of it now. The brandy had brought a smooth buzz.

"His full name is Larssen Thürgen Sössnocher," Ben said, and spelled the last name. "Several years ago, the children started calling him Soulsnatcher, and it stuck. He and I met in physics class in our university days. We were both still idealistic enough to believe we could change the world for the better. I knew he was tenacious, brilliant, and obstinate, but it took me a decade to find out how sadistic he is. His pathophobia was obvious from the beginning. That's an irrational fear of diseases."

"I actually knew that," Jazz said, slurring the words.

"Yes, you work for Wilson Pharmaceuticals, don't you?"

"I did until yesterday."

"Yes. I'm sorry for what you've been through the past twenty-four hours. Much longer than that, I imagine. You're damn lucky just to be alive."

"So everybody keeps saying." Jazz felt as if she was melting into the plush cushion.

"They're right, believe me. I, for one, am certainly glad you're here."

"Me too," Cody and Tinga said in unison.

"So am I," Jazz said, wondering where she could get a few cases of this exquisite brandy.

Ben smiled. "It's excellent, is it not? The brandy, I mean."

"I wanna live where they make it."

Everyone chuckled, and Ben continued. "Anyway, we worked well together, so I tolerated his eccentricity. He's an incredibly brilliant man. We did everything together back then, because our goal was the same: We wanted to rid the world of disease. We had the world by the reins back in those days."

Jazz tried to sit up, but her legs resisted. "Just how long ago are we talking about here, Ben?"

"Half a century."

"Really. How old *are* you?"

Ben laughed. "I'm seventy-three."

"Wow. You don't look a day over sixty."

"Thank you. I attribute it to clean living. And this brandy."

Everyone laughed, and Jazz felt something magical being here with these people. She and Chaz had lucked into hooking up with the good guys.

"We were happy at first," Ben said. "Stoked about saving humanity. Our wives were brilliant too. We met them our senior years, and decided to conquer the world together. But it didn't take long for things to fall apart.

"We got generous research grants straight out of university, and decided to pool our resources. Four short years and a handful of inventions later, Camille—Lars' wife—was diagnosed with an inoperable brain tumor. A year later she died, and that last year was pretty horrible. Dementia, bouts of suicidal depression, violent outbursts. And the accusations. I know Lars loved her, but I think she had already grown to despise him before she lost her mind."

Jazz tried to make her tongue cooperate. "What inventions, Ben?"

"One day I'll explain, Jazz. We cashed in on them big time, but they're irrelevant to this story."

"Oh." What kinds of wondrous things did geniuses invent? Maybe mad scientist stuff. Hopefully not *evil* mad scientist stuff. "Okay."

Ben nodded. "Lars became withdrawn, bitter, secretive with his research, and avaricious. We were offered a job together in an anonymous branch of the government, with an outrageous payoff, and Lars jumped at the opportunity. And God forgive me, so did I. I foolishly believed we could still repair the damages wrought by time and disease, and rebuild the dream."

Jazz's glass was empty, her belly warm, and her tongue tingly. Tinga refilled everyone's glasses.

"Thank you, Tinga." Jazz took another tasty sip. "What did you guys spike this stuff with?"

Tinga grinned, and Cody and Ben laughed.

"Nectar of the gods," Ben said. He had a sip and leaned forward. "Five years later, as I grew more aware of and disgusted with the applications our discoveries were being used for, I broke into Lars' files and found some unusual research documents. My wife Marlena and I pieced the puzzle together, and we were shocked, dismayed. Hell, we were horrified.

"Discovering that Lars had been diagnosed with a rare, fatal bone disease was just the tip of the iceberg. He was using government resources to track down child prodigies. Children blessed by God with wondrous psychic talents, and Marlena and I knew what he wanted them for. But we had little idea at the time how ruthlessly he was hunting them down. Or what he was doing with them when he found them."

Ben took another swig of brandy, maybe remembering a time of ideals and ignorance.

"Marlena and I wanted out. We'd made a handful of close friends over the years, and they wanted to come with us when we told them what we wanted to do. It was an audacious and unprecedented plan. We wanted to repair some of the damage we had wrought.

"I'm sure you've wondered where the capital came from to build and support this place. I'm not as proud of it as I was when I was a younger, more idealistic fool, but with our inventions, we were already multi-millionaires. Some of our financially savvy new partners knew how to hide and invest the money. So we cashed in our assets and flew the coop."

Jazz had to ask. "So what happened to Marlena?"

"I'm getting there, Jazz, but I guess you realize by now I do love to tell a story."

"Not you, Ben," Cody said, grinning, and Jazz realized what it was in his eyes that was echoed in Tinga's, what she hadn't identified earlier. They both loved Ben with all their hearts.

Jazz's face felt numb, but she smiled. "You tell it wonderfully. Please continue."

Tinga distributed the remaining brandy among them as Ben grinned.

"Well, we purchased some property in Texas, in the middle of nowhere, and built the first permanent safe refuge for Lars' victims. We called it Haven Home, and started searching for gifted children, just like Lars was. When we found those who were genuine, we tried to protect them from him, keep him from finding out about them, or rescue them if he did. Marlena called us The Guardians, and we liked it, so it stuck.

"Over time, we built up our forces. It was Marlena's idea that we recruit them from the human detritus, the lost souls who had given up hope. And that's what we offered them: hope for a chance at redemption, a promise of a second chance. It would at times certainly be a harder life, but it would be a better life." He raised his eyebrows at Cody. "Some of them we even found in a ditch."

Cody looked down and nodded, and Jazz perked up. She wanted to hear his story. Ben's eyes bored into hers as he seemed to read her mind.

"I'll let Cody tell you his story, should he choose to. But what Marlena wanted to do was help the children we rescued from Lars' Extractors, and provide them with a home. A nurturing environment where they could grow, develop their powers, and learn to use them to help others. She was a wonderful woman, Jazz. She became like a surrogate mother to the children.

"Over the years, we trained ourselves. Survival, weapons, self-defense, flight certification, you name it. Everything we needed to build, protect, and maintain a thriving community, one that brought and kept us all together with a common purpose."

"You do seem like one big happy family," Jazz said.

"We're happy, yes, thanks to Marlena, Tinga, and many others, including the children." Ben leaned forward, his eyes projecting something that looked like a blend of joy and sorrow.

"I believe that God blessed the world with Marlena. She rescued me from certain damnation. In fifteen years' time, we built a refuge from the world man made. And because of Marlena, we thrived, and the children grew into their powers, understanding their awesome responsibility."

Jazz frowned. "You keep talking about God. I thought quantum physicists didn't believe in God."

Ben smiled and nodded. "*I* do. A smart quantum physicist sees God in the details. Not just in the order, but in the chaos as well. Every choice we make in life is a chance to either stray or walk a closer path toward God. Some of us have strayed far off the path. I myself have a long way to go yet.

"But it is and always should be the ultimate goal of humankind to walk that closer path. Our mercy, compassion, and love are all we really have, other than free will. With free will, we either damn ourselves and spread sorrow, or find the path and learn to walk it. It's the only thing that can redeem us. And because God blessed me with Marlena, and she showed me the path, I walk it. When I lost Marlena and felt as if the path was lost forever, God blessed me with Tinga, Cody, and the children. Together they led me back on the path.

"*You* are walking the path, Jazz. In Chaz, God has blessed you with a bright shining beacon that summons others back onto the path. And you have walked it wisely, my dear. At the risk of everything you love and believe in, you have helped share an incomparable gift with kindness, mercy, and compassion. A gift that many weaker than you would call a curse and allow to defeat them."

Ben clasped his hands. "Bless you, Jazz, and Chaz too. For everything you've done together, every life you've helped Chaz save. But thank you most of all for Kino."

"Yes," Cody and Tinga said together.

Something pressed against Jazz's throat, chest, and eyes. She wanted to cheer, cry, and hug somebody all at the same time.

"Thank Chaz," she slurred. "I didn't really do anything."

"Oh, quite the contrary," Ben said. "You've done wonderful things with Chaz. You've helped him shine his beacon in the darkest corners, and shown others the path. *You* are his Guardian, Jazz. We are all in awe of you. Did you not know that? Rest assured, I'll be thanking Chaz in the morning."

Jazz didn't bother wiping off the tears rolling down her cheeks. She wasn't going to whine, and she wasn't about to tell these good people what her real curse was.

"That's one of the things I wanted to ask you all about," she said, her voice quavering. "Chaz is recovering faster lately, faster than ever before. But according to his doctors, he shouldn't even be here. Sometimes I go into his room after he does his magic, while he's sleeping, and lay down beside him and watch him. Sometimes I'm afraid he's going to go to sleep and never wake up."

Ben nodded. "That's something I wish to discuss further with you. Soon. You are a big part of the reason he's growing stronger. Without you, where would he be now? If you were gone, would he even still have the will to live? Those are questions for another day, and another round of Janneau. For now, I must answer your question about Marlena. You've been patient, and I've been far too long-winded."

"I can't even catch my own breath," Cody said. Tinga giggled.

Ben smiled. "A few years later—twenty-two years ago, for reference—our operation finally blossomed into the dream Marlena and I shared. We were happy, and loved the children so much, but we were so busy, and desperately in need of more Guardians. One day when they were all out watching over their charges, just four of them back then, we located another special child who was advertising his ability and in danger of being discovered by Lars' hunters. Only I, Marlena, and a Fixer were around to respond. I still don't know how I ever let her talk me into letting her go. I've cursed myself every day since for it. Stubborn damn woman, she wasn't about to let even one child slip through the cracks."

Ben grimaced, shaking his head. "It was a trap. Lars intended on his Extractors tailing Marlena back to Haven Home. They were trying to find us, and if they had, they would have destroyed us and taken the children. But Marlena smelled a rat, and spotted someone tailing her. She was flying one of our helicopters, and radioed in. She turned away from Haven Home to draw her pursuers away from us. The last thing she said to me was how much she loved me, and that if she didn't survive, I had damn well better keep the children safe and the dream alive, or she would come back from the grave and kick my butt.

"They must have known they'd given themselves away, because they shot her down out of the sky. I wonder if Lars ever knew that he'd gotten not one of our Guardians, but my beloved Marlena, his former friend."

"Oh, Ben." Jazz felt fresh tears roll down her cheeks. "I'm so sorry."

"As am I, my dear." Ben took Tinga's hand, squeezed it. "If I hadn't let her go, that would have betrayed everything we stood for. I would give almost anything to have her back." He sighed, his head drooping. "But then those aren't among the choices God gives us, are they?"

Tinga rubbed Ben's shoulder, her eyes on Jazz. "You have made many wise choices, Jazz. You've done much to heal Chaz's heart."

Cody nodded. "You are an amazing woman, Jazz. Impossible, stubborn as hell, but amazing."

"Indeed you are, my dear," Ben said. "Tinga says the children regard you as some kind of angel, because you're the first parent to survive an attempted extraction, and the first to kill an Extractor. To them, you've done what no other but a Guardian can: you have defied Soulsnatcher."

"Maybe so," Jazz said. "But technically, Cody's the one who killed him."

"Yeah, but you had him nailed down," Cody said. "I just shut him up."

"Okay, granted." Jazz had another swallow and set her glass down. "But I'm not done with Soulsnatcher yet, or Taja. I'm gonna get Daddy back. And when I find them, and that bitch... they have no idea how sorry they're gonna be."

Cody squinted at her, about to say something.

Ben nodded. "I admire your determination. But I do hope my friends and I have properly emphasized how dangerous these people are."

Jazz sighed. "Yeah, you have. Sorry. I blame the brandy. Please. Tell me the rest of the story."

Everyone chuckled, and Ben continued.

"The next few years were tough without Marlena. The last project we worked on together before she took that fateful flight was what ended up saving me. We wrote a cryptically worded advertisement to recruit more Guardians and Fixers, and published it in certain obscure periodicals. Two years after Marlena died, I interviewed a remarkable pair of identical twins, and found the other love of my life."

Jazz flinched and looked at Tinga. "You mean Taja tried—"

"Yes, the most evil woman I've ever met," Ben said. "I could tell them apart right away. It was something in the eyes. I knew instantly that Tinga was just as perfect for the dream as Taja was poison to it. Taja was seeking fortune and mayhem. Tinga sought a new life and a new path, and found it in Haven Home. She breathed new life into the dream, and made it home again. And became a surrogate mother to the children every bit as much as Marlena was. But Taja was infuriated that we didn't want her in the project. And she's a vengeful, malicious bitch."

"Damn straight," Cody said, nodding with Tinga.

"Indeed." Ben frowned. "That was a problem because of her and Tinga's little secret, which Tinga warned me about from the start. You see, whenever Taja and Tinga are within fifty miles of each other, they can sense the other's presence. But that was a risk I was willing to take. Tinga was vital to the project. Over the next five years, we built upon the dream. Tinga suggested we prepare another location, just like we have now. We did, and you're sitting in it. We practiced emergency evacuations in case the day ever came that we had to flee, and so we were prepared when Taja found us."

Ben leaned forward. "The bad part was that Taja continued answering unusual classifieds, like ours, and joined Lars' group. Consequently, when she came, she brought the Extractors, along with the best weapons money can buy. Thank God Tinga sensed Taja coming. With her advance warning, we were out of Haven Home and headed here in less than two hours, with all the children safely evacuated. And this place—I assume you realize we're in the Everglades—is remote enough that Taja could look for us forever and still not find us.

"Of course, since the advent of the Internet, people have become much easier to find, and consequently, so have children with special abilities. So we had to build up our forces and capabilities, because just as it became easier to for us to watch and keep track of gifted children, it became easier for Lars and his hunters to find them. It's a war when you get right down to it, Jazz. Silent war, but a war nevertheless."

"That's what Kino said." Jazz felt like she was floating separately from her body. She was as high as the clouds, nestled in their billowy folds.

Ben nodded. "I hate to think of us in such simple terms as good versus evil, but what better describes it?"

"Works for me," Jazz said. "I'm glad we're on the good side."

"As are we. So we made this our new home, continued recruiting members, grew our technology, started building our alternate location, and rescued a few more children from Lars' dogs. And ten years ago, we found the dark man nearly dead in a ditch."

Jazz jerked back into her body, looked at Cody. "Your turn, Cody. I wanna hear your story."

He stared at her with those haunted eyes, and damn if she didn't start falling into them. It was weird and different because this time it felt good, like it was where she was supposed to be.

"Maybe Ben should tell you what Soulsnatcher's real agenda is first, Jazz," Cody said. "What he really wants to do with Chaz."

"Wait... what? I thought—"

"Yes, Jazz. Perhaps I should." Ben's eyes shimmered, focusing on hers. "What exactly do you think Lars' ultimate intentions are?"

She thought that question had been answered. "To get rich. Richer. Sell Chaz's services to the highest bidder."

"Yes, my dear, and he no doubt intends to do so. But remember, Lars is a pathophobe."

Jazz tried to read between the lines, but her brain was turning to mush. "He's afraid of diseases." A beacon shone through the fuzz, and she perked up. "He wants Chaz to heal *him*!"

Ben looked at Cody, and back at her. "I'm afraid it's

much worse than that. He fears more than just disease. He fears everything associated with the dissolution of the body."

"Dissolution… body?" Jazz slurred.

Ben nodded. "I believe Lars has been searching for a *wunderkind*, and that he believes he has found it in Chaz."

"A voonder-what?"

"Wonder-child. The most rare of finds, a blessing from God. A child who can not only heal, but as he grows into his power, who can rejuvenate."

"Rejuvenate." She knew what that meant. "Oh, no."

"Yes," Ben said. "I believe, like Lars does, that when Chaz hits puberty—and yes, I believe he will—that even more miraculous things are going to be manifested in his power."

"Oh my God. Chaz."

Cody stood. "Soulsnatcher wants to live forever. And he wants to use Chaz to make it happen. The end."

Tinga stood as well. "Yes. And I guarantee my sister wants the same for herself."

"Can you imagine, Jazz?" Ben rose to his feet beside them. "Do I even have to say it? Neither believes there is a path, or a God. To them, there is only this playground to do with as they please, and after that, nothing, nonexistence."

"Immortality," Jazz whispered, free of her body again and afraid she might not make the journey back.

"A form of it, yes," Ben said. "And given all the extra years, who's to say he won't find a more permanent form of it? A reign where he steals God's greatest blessings. Enslaves them to do his will, and eventually finds the successor to Chaz. Where would it end?"

"Oh my God," Jazz said again. "No. Not my baby."

"No," Cody whispered in her ear. She tried to stand up, but she was so light, just a vapor. She realized Cody cradled her in his arms. They were warm and strong. He whispered again. "Neither our new little friend, nor his mother."

"What? Cody, are we floating?"

"Nor their damn dog," Cody said.

Ben and Tinga spun around her, smiling and waving. She would have waved or said something, but her arms were around Cody's neck, her face nuzzled into his chest. They floated into the hallway before she could emerge from her comfortable cocoon.

"Where we goin', dark man?"

"Home. To Chaz."

"Mmm. Good. Where's home, Cody?"

"Right here, Jazz."

"Mmm-kay. I'm glad you're here."

"Uh-huh."

"And Kino. I love him too. And Roberta. And Tinga." She nuzzled closer, letting the shadow float her through the halls. "And Ben is wonderful."

"Yep."

"Chaz gonna love him too."

"Mmm-hmm."

They turned a corner and glided down another spinning hallway, overhead lights strobing on and off as her shadow's dark profile obliterated them.

"Wanna hear yours, Cody. Story."

"Maybe later."

"No. Wanna know now."

"It's bedtime, Jazz."

They stopped, and Jazz hovered in the hallway beside the open door to her room, borne aloft by her impenetrable shadow. She followed Cody's gaze and saw a figure watching them. The glimmering fluorescence backlit her in a halo.

It was Amanda.

"Remember, be nice, Cody," Jazz slurred.

Amanda looked at Cody, then at Jazz. She sighed and raised an arm, wrapped her hand around Jazz's forearm, and closed her eyes.

When Jazz regained awareness, she was staring up at her

shadow as he lowered her onto her bed. She pulled him closer, kissed him on the lips, and lost control of her limbs. She floated on a cloud, watching him.

"Story. Please."

"Good night, Jazz."

"Mmm. Bedtime story. 'Boutchoo."

"Another time."

"Chaz…"

"I just checked on him. He's fine."

"'Kay. Thanks. Story now."

"Sweet dreams, Jazz."

They came, stranger than the one she'd just had, a shadow play of dark and light, and more vivid than any she ever had before.

Chapter 22

Kaylee walked inside, and the guard at the door made her wait for Gordon. Her mind spun with thoughts of Jai, Jhin, and other children here whom she hadn't met yet. She worried that Gordon was going to take her to Taja, and she *so* didn't want that woman all up in her grill right now. She felt euphoric from her revelations in the garden, and wanted to savor it.

Gordon strolled in, gestured for her to follow him, and kept on walking. When she didn't move, he turned to her and nodded.

"Gotta fix that hand, Kaylee. Come on."

She followed him to a room where a woman and a man waited. They removed her makeshift bandage, cleaned her wound, injected something that made it numb, stitched it closed, wrapped it with fresh gauze, and taped it up. They didn't speak while they worked. Kaylee kept her mouth shut too, concentrating on her plan.

When they were finished, they handed her two bottles of pills and instructed her how to take them. One was an antibiotic and the other was an anti-inflammatory, but Kaylee eyed the bottles with distrust.

She kept wondering when Taja was going to show up and lecture her to death. She hoped Taja was away on business, or too busy elsewhere, because she was afraid the nosy woman would see her plan in her eyes or read her mind, and try to stop her.

Kaylee's stomach rumbled as she left the mini-infirmary, and she told Gordon she was going to the kitchen to eat lunch. She had one of the chefs make her a sandwich and bring her some fruit, and ate alone at the table, as she usually did. Alone was better than with Taja, but she wondered why she never saw anyone else in the kitchen. This place was so big, maybe every captive here had their own private kitchen, replete with staff.

When she finished and went back to her room, she immediately noticed the difference. A new comforter was spread atop her bed, the old one was gone from the alcove, and the broken panes had been replaced. She paced her rooms, going stir-crazy. After fifteen minutes of that colossal waste of time, most of it spent worrying that Taja-ness was imminent, she put on a pair of sandals and went back outside.

Out in the garden, she pushed her luck and asked Gordon if she could have a little privacy. He shrugged, pointed to a bench about thirty feet away, and went over to it and sat down. Figuring that was the best she was going to get, she strolled to the grass bordering the path, took off her sandals, and sat cross-legged in it.

She closed her eyes, and in a matter of moments she was back in her private sanctum and communing with her new friends again. They whispered to her, and she whispered back, and it put her in a trance unlike any she'd ever experienced or imagined.

She had aural, olfactory, and visual hallucinations, and plunged her roots deep in the ground, tasted the nurturing soil. Spreading her branches high above her, she soaked in the life-giving essence of sunlight through her leaves and boughs.

She remembered an invented word from an old science-fiction novel she'd read for extra credit a couple of years ago. The word was *grok*, and she felt like the story's alien protagonist in *Stranger in a Strange Land*, by some famous dead guy named Heinlein. The word meant to intuitively comprehend something so completely that you not only empathized with it, you also understood everything about what it was to *be* it.

She grokked the trees, flowers, plants, grass, every living thing around her but people. In the story, at the end, the people crucified the protagonist because he was so different from them. They were jealous and hated him because he could grok things that they could not.

Even his friends hadn't been able to save him.

She cast aside the parallels and her paranoia, and embraced the grokking of her special friends.

When she opened her eyes, the sun was much farther down in the sky, and vines were entwined around her arms and legs. They gently pulsated, massaging and caressing her, and she jerked her head around and looked at Gordon.

He was watching her, as always, but he said nothing. She silently ordered her friends to chill and be gone, and they released her and slithered away. It creeped her out that Gordon had watched her all that time. She stood, turned away from Gordon, and started back toward her prison with her mind swirling with epiphanies and plans.

Back in her room, everything looked the same except her perspective and the clock. Nearly four hours had passed while she'd sat in the garden and communed with her friends. Her stomach rumbled again, reminding her of the need to feed her body just as her friends had fed her spirit.

Being like Valentine Michael Smith was exhausting work, and grokking things had its price.

Her legs and arms should have been cramped when she finally stood, prickling pins and needles warning her against sudden movement. But she had been refreshed, renewed, her limbs responding with strength and alacrity.

Her friends had done that. Her power had exercised itself in her trance, and simultaneously kept her body alert and prepared.

Taja should pop in any second now, and ruin the enchantment.

Kaylee went into the front room and picked up the remote and the phone. She dialed the kitchen and clicked on the wall screen. While she flipped around the channels she was allowed to watch, searching for some clue that pinpointed her geographically, she ordered dinner and asked them to bring it up to her room.

Click, click, surf, surf, and still no Taja. It was making her sweat. When she heard a knock, she tossed the remote on the couch and went to answer it, prepared to face Taja and get it over with.

It was just her dinner on a cart. Stone-faced Gordon wheeled it in and stepped back out into the hall without a word.

She channel-surfed while she ate, waiting for Taja's looming guilt trip sermon. An hour later she wheeled the cart back out into the hall, and Gordon took it. She looked up at him and frowned.

"Where's Taja?"

He shrugged. "Busy."

She closed the door, went to her bedroom, grabbed the new comforter, and spread it out on the alcove sill. She sat on it and watched her friends outside the window cavort and frolic, vying for her attention. The sun was setting behind her, and a deep purple haze limned the visible horizon.

Had Gordon tattled on her yet? Was Taja deliberately torturing her by making her worry, wonder, and wait? With her crazy plan taking shape in her head, Kaylee watched the room and the sky grow dark.

Something in her organic revelations today proclaimed a greater truth than she'd ever known, and convinced her that Taja had been lying to her. She thought of her dark man and closed her eyes, pictured his strength and the determined look in his arcane eyes. He had not deceived her with his power, and she prayed again that he would come rescue her.

Without him or another real friend from the outside, she would have no idea where to go when she escaped. She pictured Jai's handsome but tormented face in her mind, felt again the magnetic attraction that drew her to him, and thought of the enigmatic look Jhin gave her before he went up the steps. She wanted to take them both with her, and any other captives here who wanted to come along.

Taja would not be invited to join them. She was the reason for the sadness in Jhin's eyes, the anger in Jai's, and the bitterness in Kaylee's heart. Kaylee was as certain of it as she was that she'd been given a profound glimpse into her evolving power today.

In her mind, she replayed in detail everything that had happened since she'd taken that fateful bike ride home. She was thinking of the boogeyman and her dark man showing up when a queasy rumble in her belly made her taste bile. A familiar pulsating glow pressed against her eyelids and forced them open.

The glow was her. She was shimmering.

She gasped and almost shouted out loud, there was a blinding flash, and then nothing but the utter darkness of the deepest tomb.

Chapter 23

Jazz woke refreshed Friday morning a little after seven, not the least bit hung-over. She felt ready to take this whale by the tail and ride it like a bronco-bucking cowgirl. Stoked about recording her video reply to Taja, she was already rehearsing it in her mind.

She checked on Chaz, almost giddy with the revelations of the night before. He slept peacefully, with a smile on his face and Dante at his side. She figured he was having a good dream.

She'd had several herself.

While she took a shower, she reviewed them. Like all dreams, they had been strange, surreal. But some had been so vivid that she could easily envision the pictures they had planted in her mind.

Every time one of her dreams had turned a corner into dark and forbidding territory, a faceless shadow had been there to bear her back into the light. She knew that specter. It was Cody, their Guardian. Her dark man.

She vaguely remembered kissing him last night before the dreams commenced. Her soap-slick body tingled beneath the warm stream, and she hoped she hadn't made a drunken fool of herself.

There had been marvels and wonders too. In the brilliant light, she'd seen smiling faces, laughing children everywhere, and the atmosphere was charged with magic. And dogs: happy, scampering canines frolicked with everyone.

But most of the dreams were suffused with visions of Cody Jackson, along with an uplifting feeling that had been absent from her life for so long she could no longer define it.

Now more than ever she ached to know Cody's story. Something wicked had scarred him and molded him into the dark man, and she wanted to know who or what it was. In fact, she realized she wanted to make the hurt go away, and the thought surprised her.

More than that, she wanted to make those who had burned him pay, make them sorry for what they'd done to him. Taja had clearly been a part of it, and Jazz longed to be the one who made her regret it.

And she could do it, and would, if she got the chance.

After she showered and dressed, she checked on Chaz. He was in the shower, and she popped her head in the bathroom door.

"Chaz, I'm gonna take Dante out. Come join me when you're done, and we'll go have breakfast."

"Okay," he sputtered. Steam permeated the bathroom.

"Are you okay, Binky?"

"I feel great, Mother. I'm not even tired. It's amazing."

"That's good, baby. I'll be outside." She smiled and called Dante, remembering what Ben had said about Chaz's power manifesting itself in new ways, and they headed out.

Cody stood on the front porch, gazing at the sunlight-dappled compound as the morning activities commenced. He looked like he had stood sentinel there all night and never blinked.

He smiled when he saw her. "Good morning." He crouched and ruffled Dante's fur. "Hey, boy."

She smiled back. "It is a good morning, isn't it?"

"Yes, it is."

A loon brayed out its distinctive laughing call, and other birds joined in the chorus. A promise of good things to come seemed to linger in the still air, and made the brilliant morning sunshine appear brighter.

Dante ran off into the woods, and Jazz sniffed the fresh air, let it fill her lungs. She caught the pungent scent of peat and marl mixed with a flowery fragrance that was almost intox-icating. Pulling a stray strand of hair back over her ear, she grinned at Cody.

"Seen Kino and Roberta yet this morning?"

Cody laughed and stood. "Are you kidding? Those two are probably hibernating for the winter. I imagine we've seen the last of them 'til late March."

She laughed with him. Despite her worries about her father, hope blossomed in her heart as she thought of her two new friends finally, blissfully together, and Kino healthy again. In fact, they had probably both been exceptionally healthy throughout the night. Sometimes dreams did come true, and the thought made her spirit sprout wings. Somehow, she was going to rescue her father. And she had some very special friends who were going to help her do it.

Cody raised his eyebrows at her. "Hungry?"

"Famished. Waiting on Chaz."

"Afterward, you ready to make a video?"

She grinned. "Damn straight."

They turned together at a sound behind them. Roberta and Kino walked out onto the deck hand in hand.

Cody snorted and shook his head. "You big damn goofball, look at you. You're embarrassing yourself. You two look like Tinkerbell and Shrek together. What are you so damn happy about?"

Kino let go of Roberta's hand. He stepped toward Cody and embraced him, and Cody returned the hug.

"My brother," Kino said.

"Get off me," Cody grumbled after a telltale moment. He pushed Kino away. "And wipe that goofy-ass grin off your ugly mug before I have to bitch-slap it off you."

Roberta chuckled and looked at Jazz, and Jazz yearned to taste some of the dance sparkling in her eyes.

Jazz's hands flapped at her sides, her legs bouncing in a stationary ballet, and she just had to hug somebody, *now*. Roberta glided toward her and embraced her with a gasp.

"Oh, Jazz. Thank you. Bless you, and Chaz."

"I'm so happy for you both!" Jazz almost squealed.

"God, you're all so pathetic." Cody grimaced, but he couldn't hide the joy underneath his gruff bluster. He chuckled. "You worst of all, you gargantuan lunk. For the love of God, pull yourselves together."

They all laughed, and Chaz walked out grinning.

"What's so funny?" he asked.

"Chaz, my man!" Kino picked up Chaz and held him high. He hugged him, and kissed him on the cheek. "Thank you, little big man."

Chaz giggled. "You're welcome. I guess it worked, huh?"

"My man, I feel like a million bucks."

"Me too," Chaz said.

"Yeah." Roberta rubbed Kino's back and winked at Jazz. "I'd say he's about as healthy as a horse."

Jazz laughed, and Cody shook his head.

"And hungry enough to eat one," Kino growled, hoisting Chaz on his shoulder.

Cody smirked. "Good God. You look like one too. Let's go eat. Apparently we're having cheese and corn for breakfast."

Everybody laughed, and they headed to the dining hall together. Dante returned and barked and leaped at Chaz, and Kino set Chaz down and took Roberta's hand.

When they entered the hall, the children started giggling, some of the adults chuckled, and "good mornings" were tossed around everywhere. Ben was there, sitting beside Tinga. He stood and walked over to Kino, grinning, and hugged him.

"It's good to have you back, my boy," he said, just loud enough for Jazz to hear.

"It's good to be back, Ben. And it's great to see you back safe and sound. Sorry we missed you last night."

Ben said something else that Jazz didn't hear. She was already headed to the buffet with Chaz and Cody. Ben hugged Roberta, whispered something to her that made her laugh, and returned to the table while the others filled up their plates and joined them.

Amanda and Mara were sitting side by side. They looked at each other, grinned, and chanted in unison, "Roberta and Kino, sitting in a tree!" They giggled, and the other children joined in with the age-old limerick.

When they recited the last line, some of the children said "Then comes Roberta with a baby carriage," and some substituted Kino's name for Roberta's, and the room erupted into raucous laughter.

Kino and Roberta were rosy-cheeked, and took the ribbing in happy silence. Jazz thought their eyes twinkled when they looked at each other, and her heart fluttered.

Even Marco joined in on the teasing, maybe finding some private pardon and closure for his self-perceived failure with Stephan. Jazz felt like she and Chaz were part of one big, happy family. Only one important member was missing now— two if she counted Cody's lost charge, Kaylee, the organic fertility thaumaturge.

When they finished breakfast, Cody, Tinga, Ben, Kino, Roberta, and Marco stayed behind with Jazz while the children went to class with Amanda in charge.

"Well, you ready?" Cody asked Jazz.

"Damn straight," she said, and everyone laughed.

Kendra and Malek were waiting on them and frowning when they arrived in the computer shack. Malek looked at Ben and winced.

"Professor Cameron, before you get started on the video response—and we got everything set up and ready—we need to tell you something."

Kendra nodded and looked at Jazz, then Ben. "We got another email video from Taja this morning, through Jazz's address, like before. We just got it a few minutes ago."

"It's ready to play, like before," Malek said. "We're gonna go eat breakfast now." He and Kendra stood, and both nodded at Jazz.

"Call us if you need us," Kendra said.

"Thanks, Kendra. Malek," Ben said, and looked at Jazz. He gestured to the console chairs as Kendra and Malek left. Jazz sat in one, her breakfast suddenly weighing heavy on her butterfly-filled stomach. Roberta sat beside her while the others stood behind them.

Cody spoke before she could click play. "Jazz, if you want us to check this out first—"

"No." She swallowed something dry and coarse stuck in her throat. "No, let the bitch do her worst. Nothing she can do or say can stop me from making her pay when I find her."

She clicked the mouse, and the video started. Taja's angelic smiling face filled the screen, and Jazz flinched. Taja looked so much like her sister it was disconcerting.

"Hi, everybody!" Taja grinned and waved. "Hi, Jazz! How's my little healer's mommy doing today? Made up your mind yet? Well, no worry. Yet. You still have until noon tomorrow to decide before we lop another finger off dear old Dad. This message is for everyone.

"One of your Guardian bitches just snatched another special boy out from under us late last night. How she managed that with two Extractors on her tail is beyond me. Your people are getting smarter and quicker, Professor. Somebody's going to have to be punished for that."

Jazz let out a breath she hadn't known she'd been holding. This wasn't about her father. Maybe he was still safe for the moment. Taja continued.

"His name is Pablo, and we want him back. Just as bad as we want Chaz. He's a very special little boy. He can sometimes hear what other people are thinking. Yes, a genuine clairvoyant. So, here's the deal."

Taja grinned, a serpent's smile sans forked tongue. "I have some bad news for you. Pablo wasn't with his parents when your bitch snagged him, and your Fixer and the bitch had to split up. Mr. Fixer went after Pablo's parents. One of our

Extractors tailed him." Taja smirked, then chuckled. "Your Fixer is taking the eternal dirt nap now. It was pretty messy, because our Extractor let his emotions overcome him when he caught up to him. He's going to be punished for that, because we wanted your Fixer alive. I had some things I wanted to discuss with him. I think our Extractor was angry because he and his partner got bested by a woman. Would you like to see the results? Here, let me show you."

Taja grinned and held a severed head up to the camera, grasping it by the hair. Jazz gasped and Kino growled.

"Damn, Gunther," Kino said. "Has anybody heard from Serena?"

"Not yet," Ben said, holding up a hand.

Taja snickered. "He looks so sad, doesn't he? He's got that permanent look on his face like he knows how badly he fucked up. I guess you could say he lost his head over the matter. Or maybe he just wasn't headstrong enough." She set the severed head down and focused on the camera. She pouted, her brow furrowed. "Oh, come on! You didn't think that was funny? You people have no sense of humor. Well, never mind. The important thing is, we have Pablo's parents now. And let me tell you what we're going to do about it.

"If you don't make arrangements to return Pablo to us in the next twenty-eight hours—and Chaz too, same deadline, noon tomorrow—we're going to seat Pablo's parents down in front of this camera and I'm going to cut their heads off myself. I think I'll start with his mother, and make his father watch. And I'm going to use a dull blade, so the fun lasts. Oh, and there's more good news."

Jazz felt bile rise in her throat.

"Did I mention that Pablo is Mexican? You all know what that means, don't you? Those people just don't know when to stop hatching little ones. They spit 'em out like their race is in constant danger of extinction. So we'll have no short- age of relatives to make examples of, until you return Pablo to us."

Taja laughed, then forced a frown. "Aww! Losing the stomach for the war, Jazz? Daddy could be next. You don't know me yet, but your new friends do. I almost hope you don't bring Chaz, because I'm going to enjoy slicing Daddy up." Taja picked up the severed head and looked at it. "Okay, we're done for now. Say bye-bye, Mr. Dead Fixer." She grinned and looked at the camera again. "You have until noon tomorrow to decide. I suggest you make arrangements to do as we say. Otherwise, lots of innocent people are going to die, and it will be all your fault." She waved her free hand at the camera. "So until we hear back from you, ta-ta!"

The video ended, and Jazz buried her head in her hands. Comforting arms were suddenly around her again, touching and squeezing her and lending her strength. She slowly stood.

No tears were in her eyes. She was through with tears— for now—and looked at the others. "All right. Let's do this now. I'm ready."

Ben raised his eyebrows at her. "Do you know what you want to say, Jazz?"

She gave him a grim smile. "Yes I do." *Along with a promise.*

"Well then, my dear, come this way." Ben gestured to a video camera set up in the corner of the room. It was aimed at a blank white screen against the wall.

The group gathered in the corner. Roberta showed Jazz where to stand, pointed to the monitor displaying the camera's perspective, and stepped aside.

Tinga held up a remote. "Ready, Jazz?"

"Let's give that bitch the finger."

Tinga's approval shone in her eyes. "Lights, camera, action."

Jazz felt the fury stoke the friendly flames surrounding her, and gave Taja a taste of it.

Chapter 24

Kaylee retched and tried to sit up, her eyes wide open and seeing nothing but an imprint of the preceding flash on her retinas. Her belly gurgled, a dinghy in a storm-tossed ocean, wanting to kick dinner back out the way it had come in.

"Who's there?" the darkness asked in a British accent.

She felt soft carpet under her hands, and forced the bile back down. Something warm and wet lapped against her cheek, and she yelped and scurried backward until she bumped into something cushioned but stationary. She wiped her sleeve across her cheek, heard a soft whine, and the coarse wetness scraped across her face again.

"I said who's there?" the British darkness asked again, more urgently.

She reached up and felt something cold and wet, then something soft and fluffy. She heard the whine again, felt hot pungent breath against her face, and realized it was a dog. She pushed it away and struggled to stand, but the shipwreck in her belly wouldn't let her.

"Sadie, leave it," the darkness said. The dog moved away, and the darkness spoke again. "Who are you, where did you come from, and what do you want?"

"Where am I?" she finally choked out. "And who or what are you? And why can't I see?"

"I asked you first." Whatever it was, it was a demanding British darkness.

She groaned, losing the battle. "I think I'm gonna blow chunks."

"Here, let me help you fix that." There was a rustle, then, "Sadie, left side. Good girl."

A pair of hands brushed her breasts and she flinched. "Hey!"

"Sorry. Here we go."

The hands pressed gently against her belly, and something warm and comforting washed over her. The need to hurl passed, and she relaxed.

"How did you do that?"

The hands pulled away. "You're welcome. Now tell me: Who are you?"

"My name's Kaylee. Who are you, and where am I?"

"I smell blood."

"What? Hey!"

Hands touched her shoulders, trailed down her arms. One touched her bandage, and the other reached for it and held it. "Be still, Kaylee."

Something in the voice's cadence calmed her and helped her focus, calling out to her in some primitive way that she couldn't define. She relaxed as a warm, intoxicating rush spread through her. Her left hand tingled, and the pain gradually abated. In a few seconds it was gone, as if it had never been there. The hands let go.

She gasped. "Oh my God. What did you just do?"

"I healed your hand. Again, you're welcome. Now answer my questions."

She tugged on the bandage, her pulse quickening. She wished she could see it, didn't want to rip the cut back open, but it felt like it wasn't there anymore. She gripped the bottom part of the bandage at her wrist and yanked it off. The stitches had fallen out. She probed her smooth palm with her fingers, and knew if she could see, it would be unblemished, scarless.

"You made it go away. Completely."

"It's what I do," the darkness said, a laugh hidden in its inflection. "Now, Kaylee, tell me how you got here and what you want."

"Who are you? What are you?"

"Damn, girl, you're a cheeky one, aren't you? Okay, I'll make you a deal: I answer one of your questions, you answer one of mine."

"Okay. Deal." Her head spun. She couldn't orient herself in the darkness.

"My name is Jai, and I'm a healer. Now it's your—"

"Jai!" She reached out and felt him, wrapped her arms around his neck and hugged him. "It is you. Oh my God. Jhin must have teleported me here."

He gently unwrapped her arms from his neck and pushed her back. "How do you know me, who is Jhin, and what the bloody hell do you mean by teleported?"

Sadie chuffed softly.

"Wait a second," she said, and pieces of the puzzle finally clicked into place. "You know who I am. Why wouldn't you talk to me last night? And why did you run from me today?"

"What in the bloody name of—"

"And why aren't we making each other sick? And why don't I feel your rage?"

"That's a lot of questions. It's your turn to answer some. And for the record, I have no idea what you're talking about."

She scowled. "I'm talking about Taja lied, that's what."

Jai huffed. "Well, that's one thing we can certainly agree on. Now—"

"Oh, Jai." She took his hands in hers, her heart fluttering. It was about to fly out of her chest and soar away, and another mystery was solved. She knew what it was that she was feeling. "We have to be quiet. I think they watch us all the time. They can't know I'm here, or we're all screwed. You, me, Jhin, everybody."

"Okay," he said softly, and they started whispering. "So tell me—"

"I wish I could see you," she said, and squeezed his hands.

"They must keep the light off most of the time. And you can't imagine how much I wish I could see you. Here." He took her hands and placed them against his cheeks. "Now you can see me the way I see you."

She gently probed his face with her fingertips, then her palms. She pictured his face in her mind's eye, and felt the remarkable sensation of seeing him with her fingers and hands. Her heart pounded. Surely he could hear it.

"May I?" he asked.

"Yes," she said, trembling with revelations and an excitement she'd never felt before.

He touched her face, probed it, and a warmth flushed through her. Her face tingled where he touched it, and a new angle to the plan sprouted tendrils in her mind.

"You're a very pretty girl, Kaylee. I can see it with my hands."

"Oh, Jai." She pulled his face to hers and kissed him. He resisted for a heartbeat, but responded.

It was awkward at first, and new and mysterious, but oh, God, it felt so right. Kaylee didn't know if she had ever believed in love at first sight, but she did now.

What couldn't be seen could be felt on a deeper level, if your touch listened.

She finally drew back, though she didn't want to. Jai and Sadie panted in sync with her. She tried to think as more puzzle pieces fell into place.

"Why did you do that?" he asked. "Not that I'm complaining or—"

"Oh, Jai, this is wonderful." She threw her arms around his neck and hugged him again.

"Well, yes, it is, actually." He squeezed her back, then pushed away again and took her hands. "But what exactly—"

"It means she lied." She laughed and squeezed his hands. "She lied about everything."

"You mean Taja? Tell me something I don't know. But

what's funny about that?"

"You didn't even hear me last night, did you? Or Taja."

"What? No, I was here by myself all last night, with Sadie. Kaylee—"

"I knew it. That fucking *bitch*." She laughed again.

"Another thing we agree on. I knew that bird was trouble from the moment we met."

Kaylee smiled. Her dark man was coming for her. And they were getting out of here, and soon, if they didn't get caught first. She, Jai, Jhin, and anyone else who wanted to bust out with them were out of here.

"That's probably because you didn't see her face," she said. "She's beautiful, looks like an angel."

"Oh, I saw her face all right. I saw the face of the devil through the angel in her voice the first time I heard it."

Kaylee realized she should have too. If only she had closed her eyes and just listened. But that didn't matter now. Her heart was soaring, and she leaned closer to him.

"Your power doesn't have anything to do with projecting your rage, does it?"

"What? No. I told you, I'm a healer."

"Yes, you definitely are." *Taja never even intended on us meeting—ever. Bitch.*

"And Kaylee, there are so many questions, but first..." He let go of her left hand and tentatively touched her neck, moved his hand down over her left breast and placed his palm against her heart. "Your heart is... troubled. Burning. Bloody scarred. I can feel it radiate off you. Let me heal it."

She grinned, even though no one could see. "I think you just did."

He pressed his hand against her chest anyway, and suddenly Kaylee saw endless worlds of possibilities open themselves to her, wide-open blue skies inviting them to spread their wings and explore them together. After a short, blissful dream, she took his hand, kissed it, and held it to her face again.

She saw nothing in the darkness, but she felt him smile at her.

"You don't know anything about the other children, do you?" She struggled to concentrate, stop getting sidetracked, and still her pulsating heart. "The others like us, with special powers."

"What? Kaylee, you've got to catch me up. Other children... special powers?"

"Yeah. I don't know how many there are like us, but they're keeping us prisoners here. Using us. Using our talents for their own gain."

"Wait. Do you mean... Kaylee, are you... What can you do?"

She thought of her friends whispering to her today, telling her secrets only she could hear. "I make things grow."

"You certainly do."

Her face burned with her blush, and he chuckled and trembled. It felt like her friends caressing her, something new and wonderful, and she tried to swim back down through the majestic boughs and touch ground. She had to think clearly now.

"I mean, like plants: grass, flowers, trees, fruits, vegetables. Super-fast, and super-sized."

"Wow. That's amazing. And... unusual."

Wait 'til you see it, she thought, and was glad she didn't say it. "What did they promise you, Jai? To restore your sight? How many surgeries have they performed?"

"Surgeries? None yet. Taja said they're looking for a specialist who can do it, and waiting for a donor, and as soon as—"

"I knew it. That lying bitch." So many ideas and revelations were making her head swim. Not to mention the unique fluttering sensation she felt just being close to Jai. He didn't make her feel ill, didn't project rage onto her. In fact, he made her feel like she could conquer the world with him by her side.

There were so many things she wanted to ask and tell him.

"What do they make you do, Jai? Do they take you out of here to heal people?"

"Well, yes. A few times. How did you know?"

"Because they use me that way too. Only I heal plants instead of people."

He hummed. "After they rescued me from the bad people, when I first got here a little over two years ago, they took me to the old bloke that runs this place. Said if I didn't heal him, he was going to die. Called him the Doctor."

"Taja mentioned him, but I've never met him." The rage boiled just beneath the surface at the magnitude of the elaborate betrayal Taja had orchestrated.

"Wretched old codger, at least when I met him, before I healed him. He radiated sickness, bloody reeked of it. They said if he died, they couldn't keep me and protect me, and wouldn't be able to afford to try and restore my... Oh, bloody hell. She lied about that too, didn't she?"

"Oh, Jai. I think so." She hugged him again, realizing how educated and sophisticated he was despite his origins or handicap, and she yearned to hear his story. "Why would they restore your sight? That would give you power over them. And as long as they keep dangling the promise over your head, they have power over you. You'll do anything they say. I'm so sorry. For what they've done to you."

He squeezed her back, speechless for the moment. Sadie chuffed again, maybe wanting to share some of the affection lighting up the darkness. Kaylee felt another puzzle piece click into place when she thought of Jhin.

He had to know about her and Jai, and where they were, in order to have teleported her here. He knew what was really going on, and was sacrificing himself to nausea, and risking exposing them all so that she would know the truth. She thought of him lying green-faced on the helicopter floor when they'd first met, sick to his stomach like her, and realized he was probably about to puke his guts out right now because he didn't have Jai there to heal him.

"Oh, Jhin," she whispered. "Thank you."

"What?" Jai pulled away from her. "Wait... he's the one you said teleported you here. What the hell is that all—"

"Oh, Jai. We may not have much time. There's so much I want to tell you and ask you."

"Kaylee, I've got so many questions I don't even know where to start."

"I know. Me too." She touched his face, caressed it and tried to remember the feel of it and store it to strengthen her later, when the shit hit the fan. She took his hands and squeezed them.

Jhin would know he had to send her back to prevent their subterfuge from being discovered, and would make them both sick again in the process. He had done this for her, maybe because he saw something in her that could save them all.

Kaylee knew where to start, or at least her heart did. She leaned forward slowly, found Jai's lips by the feel of his hot breath on her face, and kissed him again. This time, it wasn't awkward. It was the way things were supposed to be, and it was so sweet, so fine. All the miraculous things she was feeling made her want to run away from this awful place with him, grow their powers together...

She started shimmering.

She pulled away from him and looked down at her glowing body, knowing he couldn't see it, but he must have felt something. Then the queasiness came again.

"Kaylee, what's happening?"

"Crap. I have to go now. I promise I'll come back for you. We're getting out of here together, you and me and Jhin and anyone else like us who wants to come with—"

There was a flash, and then the floodlights of the grounds limned her window. Her friends the honeysuckle and morning glory writhed against the panes, reaching for her, calling to her, whispering of an end of pain and anguish and promising unimaginable glory.

The raging ocean storm in her belly was about to overturn her dinghy. She turned away from the window, rolled over, and leaned her head over the edge of the alcove sill, ready to blow dinner chunks out on the carpet and paint it an unwholesome avocado mush.

The light over the headboard of her bed was on. Taja sat on the edge of her mattress, frowning at her.

Taja smiled when she saw Kaylee watching, and her angel-face lit up, but this time Kaylee saw the darkness in her eyes. Jhin had opened the door, and Jai, the blind boy, had taught her how to see it.

Blind man, she corrected herself. He would be a man soon, and soon she would be a woman. A man and a woman with awesome powers together, a combined force to be reckoned with. Unless some lying, wicked, evil bitch came along and ruined everything. Something unbearable gurgled downstairs, wanting out, and Kaylee groaned.

"Hi, Kathryn! Where have you been, sweetie?"

Kaylee hurled.

Chapter 25

"Hi, Taja!" Jazz wriggled her fingers at the camera and grinned. "In case you don't know it, I'm Jasmine, Chaz's mother, and Daddy's little girl. My friends all call me Jazz. You can call me Ms. Tandy.

"I'm also Chaz's Guardian, just like my father is mine. I'd try to explain that to you, but you'd never understand, even if I talked slowly and used really small words. And a book with pictures.

"You wave a finger at me, tell me it's my father's, don't even show him to me, and think I'm going to believe a damn thing you say? Hah. I got a finger for you, bitch. This one right here."

Jazz raised her fist in the air, her middle finger extended.

"Show me my father now. You have..." She looked at her watch. "I'll be generous, because I'm such a good sport, and give you four hours. It's nine o'clock in the morning now, so that means one p.m., in case your math skills are as retarded as your personality. Show me Daddy, alive and kicking, whether he's minus a finger or not. If he's minus two, you're too late. And show him with today's *USA Today* with the date and headline clearly readable. Bitch.

"You're so hopelessly lost in your over-bloated ego that you don't realize I mean more to Daddy than his own life, just like Chaz means more to me than mine. Daddy would never approve of anything that endangers me or Chaz, and I guarantee you he's willing to give his life for it. Just like I'm willing to give mine for Chaz. I understand that, and my *new friends* do too. But you'll never understand that. You're the one who's screwed, and you don't even know it yet. But you're going to find out.

"Remember that I've warned you how sorry you'll be for messing with me when I find you, Taja. Taste it. It's a piece of the future etched in stone by the fire you lit inside me when you decided to challenge me and threaten my baby. And you think you know me?

"Even if I wasn't here, even if you crushed me like a bug, hah. Do you really think they'd ever give up Chaz? Or Pablo, or any of the children for that matter? Can you possibly be that dimwitted? Fast cars and private jets? You have nothing but pretentious *things* to offer, and you're as totally devoid of substance as they are."

Cody stepped up beside her and put a comforting hand on her shoulder, squeezed it. Jazz felt his strength and support as he disgorged more words in one verbal explosion than she had yet heard him string together.

"Hi, Taja. It's me. She's right. You know as well as I do that if you really have Pablo's parents, they're already dead, or as good as dead. And you're never getting Pablo, or Chaz. Or Jazz. You're only getting me, and I can't wait. Dark side? You have no idea the darkness you fostered inside me, and wait 'til I share it with you. So until we meet again, I'm going to return the lesson you burned into me." Cody grinned and leaned forward. "I'm going to destroy your world, Taja."

Cody looked at Jazz, nodded, and stepped aside when she grinned at him. He was as full of surprises as life was lately.

"Did you get that, bitch?" she said. "You not only don't understand love, you don't understand the resolve it brings. Sacrifice is beyond your comprehension." She smirked at the camera, and stepped closer to it. "You say I don't know you? Well, you don't know me. And you don't know what regret is. But I'm going to show you when I find you. And it's going to destroy you, bitch."

She stepped back and took a deep breath.

"Your turn, Taja. Do you have what it takes to go up against me? You thought you did, but I doubt it."

Ben sliced a finger across his throat, grinning, and Jazz twisted the knife.

"Show me my father now, or suffer the consequences." It killed a little piece of her to say the next part, but she had to. "If you don't, then you leave me no choice but to accept that he's already dead. So until I teach you sorrow, Taja... ta-ta!"

She grinned at the camera and wriggled her fingers again. Silence reigned in the room for a heartbeat.

Then everybody started applauding and cheering.

Roberta hugged her and kissed her on the cheek. "That was a frickin' masterpiece, Ms. Tandy." She let her go and backed up, and Kino roared out a laugh, picked up Jazz, and spun her around.

"You slayed me, girl! God, that was a beautiful thing you just did." He kissed her cheek and put her down, and she looked up at him.

"Yeah, I just hope I didn't sign Daddy's death warrant with it."

"Maybe not, Jazz," Ben said. "You just put the burden of proof on her. Let's wait and see what she does now."

Jazz chewed on her lip and looked at him. "You don't think she's going to hurt Daddy for it, do you? Or kill him? If he's even still alive."

Ben shook his head. "Taja would never go to this much trouble if he was dead. And no, I don't think she'll kill him over it. Your father is the only bargaining chip she has right now, and she's not going to throw that away. So, shall I have Kendra and Malek post this when they get back?"

"Hell yes." Jazz nodded. "Let's shove it straight up her ass."

"Very well, then, my dear. It shall be done. Now, since what we currently have here is a stalemate until Taja makes the next move, let's all sit down together and come up with a plan to get your father back. And maybe even figure out a way to tail them back to the viper's pit."

Everybody agreed, and Ben started off by explaining Jazz's idea about using some of the children's powers to help them. While they discussed it, Kendra and Malek came back. Ben told Malek to upload the video and send it to Jazz's email, and had Kendra get started trying to track Serena down.

Two hours later they had the framework for a plausible plan, with two major obstacles: one, nobody believed Taja would fall for it, because the premise of Jazz giving up Chaz for any reason was just not credible, and two, everybody was certain Taja was already planning to double-cross them. Soon everyone started getting frustrated, and Ben called for a break. It was lunchtime anyway, and stomachs were rumbling.

Everybody hung around after Jazz asked if she could call Lloyd, and Ben had Malek hook her up with that. She tried the hospital first, and was quickly patched through. She summarized their situation and told Lloyd how Chaz seemed to be recovering quicker now, as if his heart was growing stronger rather than weaker.

Lloyd was delighted to hear they were okay, but worried about Jazz's father. Jazz said she would keep him posted whenever possible, thanked him again, and told him she loved him. He told her how much he loved her and Chaz, and they hung up.

Jazz smiled when she looked at Kino and Roberta. They were holding hands, and Kino grinned and winked at her, then turned to Ben.

"So, Ben. I hate to open up a whale-sized jar of cobras and stick a fork in the party, but what are we going to do about Pablo?"

Cody grimaced, then snorted. "You goofy-ass ogre, you just mixed more metaphors than is legally permissible. The American Authors Association would publicly hang you."

Everyone laughed, relieving the tension. Kendra interrupted the celebration.

"Dr. Ben, we have a call from Serena. You want me to

patch it through the speakers?"

"Yes, my dear, please," Ben said, and Kendra's fingers fluttered across her keyboard. The speakers rumbled with the throaty roar of an automobile's engine.

"Yo, Ben! I'm en route to one of our emergency evac birds with a new friend. Copy?"

"Copy, Serena, and it's delightful to hear your voice. Jazz and the gang are all here, listening in. What's your situation, and how's Pablo?"

"Sitch is good, boss man. All clear. Tell our new friends I said hi, and we'll see them soon. Rendezvous Homestead approximately five hours. Pablo's shook up, but otherwise seems okay."

"Any tails spotted?"

"One, sir. And you're not gonna believe this."

"Explain."

"Seemed like he was hardly trying. I backtracked on foot and surprised him in his car down a back street, and get this. He tried to evade, did not confront me or try to get the kid back, and you know me. He's Tango Uniform now. These guys are getting sloppy."

"Hmm. What if he was a decoy?"

"Not a chance. Swept the area for an hour and made a show of it, ready for a showdown. They're losing their edge."

"Keep a close eye, my dear. They could be playing you. I assume you checked Pablo for tracking devices?"

"Yes, sir. None. We're ready to fly home."

"Very well, then. We anticipate your arrival approximately five p.m., and respond as necessary."

"Roger that. Heard from Gunther?"

"Fixer is compromised. Head home now."

"Got it, boss man. See you all soon, over."

The sound of the roaring auto's engine cut out, leaving the room in silence.

"Well, folks," Ben said. "It appears we have another

special new friend coming to join us. Let's all go to class and tell the children about it, and then we'll have lunch while we wait to see what Taja's next move is."

Everyone agreed, and they headed outside.

"And for Heaven's sake," Ben added as they walked toward the classroom building, "if anyone comes up with any brilliant ideas how to make our plan work, please share them. Because I'm stumped."

Jazz was too. Was she ever going to see her father alive again?

Chapter 26

Kaylee finally finished dry heaving, groaned, and looked up at Taja, whose frown quickly became a smile when they made eye contact again. Kaylee moaned, rolled over, and looked out the window.

She couldn't think clearly. Her mouth tasted like she'd just eaten sawdust and dog crap, and her belly felt as if a vindictive mule had kicked it repeatedly. How cold-busted were she, Jai, and Jhin?

Her friends outside the window wriggled at her, and she shushed them with her mind and waited for the bad news.

"Well, Kathryn. It seems you've had quite an adventurous day. Maybe you should try and get some sleep now, hmm? I warned you what being around others like you would do to you, and that it affects each of you differently."

Liar, Kaylee thought. The teleportation effect made her sick, not being around Jai. That had been pure bliss. Getting there and back was what was ripping her insides out. Kissing and holding Jai had been so sweet.

"Well, go ahead and get some sleep, sweetie. I'll send someone up to clean this mess you made. I don't have time for it. I'm leaving on another important trip tonight. Plane's waiting."

Kaylee held her breath when Taja rose, listening to the receding clomp of her boot heels and daring to hope her secret was still safe for the moment.

"Oh, by the way, Kathryn. I'm taking Jhin with me."

Kaylee rolled over and looked at Taja, who stood in her bedroom doorway wearing that syrupy sweet angel's smile. Taja nodded when she saw Kaylee watching.

"So there won't be any more teleportation mischief for a while. Really, Kathryn. I want to help you, but I won't let you endanger the other children here any more than I'll let them hurt you. And besides, we need Jhin's talent to help some other children that are in danger of being kidnapped by our mutual enemies."

Kaylee suddenly realized why Jhin always looked so sad.

You're killing him. Piece by piece, a little bit at a time, but you're killing him all the same. You're using him up before he's even had a chance to grow into his power, like I am now. And you're going to use all of us up until there's nothing left.

She tried to respond, but her throat was on fire, and her swollen tongue was stuck to the roof of her mouth. Taja twisted the blade.

"Oh, and Kathryn. I almost forgot to tell you. I thought you should know. Because of his condition, we're relocating Jai tomorrow. It's regrettable, but necessary. He'll finally be among—"

"No!" Kaylee gurgled, heaved herself up off the alcove sill, and staggered toward Taja. "Not Jai!"

"I'm sorry, honey, but he'll be much happier where we're sending him. It's much more oriented for assistance to the blind, and there are others there like him that—"

"No! Taja, please, not Jai!"

"I'm sorry, sweetie, but it's not my decision to make. The Doctor insisted, set this place up specifically for Jai and others like him."

Kaylee tried to stop, but she blubbered. "Taja, p-please!"

Taja smiled sadly, and something vital broke inside Kaylee. She wanted to call her new green friends to come and stop this now. She'd only just met Jai, touched him, kissed him...

"It's out of my hands. The decision and the arrangements have already been made. I'm sorry, Kathryn."

"I hate you!"

"I know you feel that way right now, sweetie. But it's really for the best. You'll feel better soon, because I'm bringing some new special friends back with me when I return, and—"

"I don't want new friends, I want Jai!"

Taja smiled at her again, and Kaylee staggered backward. The witch looked like she was feasting on her anguish like a nightmare banquet celebrating the crowning of the queen vampire.

"I fucking hate you, you evil bitch!"

Taja nodded. "That will change. Good night, Kathryn. I'll be back in a day or so, and things will be better soon." She turned and headed out through the front room to the hall door.

Kaylee stumbled after her, her body hitching with sobs that felt like they were rupturing her shipwrecked stomach.

"Taja, wait—"

Taja didn't even turn at the door; she just walked out and shut it behind her. Kaylee staggered to the door and wrestled with the doorknob. It was locked.

She pounded on it, shouting "Taja!" over and over with the last of her fetid breath. She slumped against the door, slipped to the floor, and cried bitter, stinging tears that felt like they were emptying out her soul.

Sometime later, dehydration and her throbbing head made her swim back to the surface for air, and she heard the multitude of whispering voices calling to her. Her new friends felt her agony, wanted to heal her. It gave her enough strength to stand, and she stumbled into the bathroom. She flinched and grimaced at her reflection in the mirror above the sink.

"God, I look like a fried shit sandwich with maggot sauce," she mumbled, turning on the tap. She splashed her face with cold water, stuck her mouth under the tap, rinsed, and spat until the taste of bile didn't make her want to dry heave again.

She had to focus. She couldn't lose Jai now. Her friends kept whispering to her, and if her head wasn't pounding like a sledgehammer against an anvil, she might understand what they were saying.

Her resolve resurfaced with her friends' help. She brushed and flossed her teeth and rinsed with mouthwash. Her nausea was gone, but her gut and ribs ached. She washed her face with warm water and soap, glad to have two hands for the job. When she was finished she inspected her left palm.

She ran her fingers over the unblemished skin. It was like her injury had never happened, but she knew it had. She had witnessed the results of sharing her blood with her new friends.

Did Taja know about her wound? Had she noticed the bandage was gone and the cut healed? She'd shown no reaction.

"You're not getting Jai, bitch," she said to the mirror. "Or Jhin." She nodded and said it again, more forcefully, and liked the way her eyes reflected the embers smoldering inside her. The whispers of her friends fanned the flickering flames.

"Or any of the others, if I can help it," she said to her mirror-self. "We're busting out of here, whether my dark man comes for me or not."

When Kaylee was fully back and that whimpering, sniveling girl named Kathryn was finally gone, she nodded at her reflection, turned out the light, and went to bed.

Exhaustion claimed her the second her head hit the pillow. She dreamed of vampire queens, valiant blind knights in shining armor, bounteous flora flourishing in rampant rebellion over all creation, and forbidding castles with towering turrets that imprisoned angels.

And heroes.

She woke a little before eight Friday morning famished and feeling better despite her sore ribs and belly. With the lingering vestiges of her dreams and her escape plan swirling in her head, she went to the door to the hall. It was locked, just as she suspected.

"Bitch." How much did Taja know?

She called the kitchen and ordered breakfast. Then she

went back into her bedroom and headed to her alcove window, excited about sharing the plan with her green friends.

Sometime in the night, while she'd been dreaming, someone had come in and cleaned up the mess she'd spewed on the carpet. She looked out the window, and her heart felt like it quit beating and was lodged in her throat.

Somebody had been busy last night, or early this morning.

She dashed to the window, leaped up on the alcove sill, and looked down. She could barely breathe. Somebody had cut down the morning glory and Japanese honeysuckle. The wall below her was bare to the ground.

Now she really was a prisoner here. She screamed.

Chapter 27

At lunch, Jazz listened to the enthusiastic chatter while she replenished her strength. Challenging the queen demon bitch from Hell rustled up a hearty appetite. The hot topic was Pablo. Jazz smiled at Chaz as he discussed the newbie with the other children as if he was a veteran member of the group.

Jazz noticed Anthony's cast was gone. He was using his left arm as dexterously as if it had never been broken. She watched Lynette out of the corner of her eye. Lynette couldn't stop smiling, and kept looking at Chaz with wide, sparkling eyes.

When Lynette rose and went to the buffet for seconds, her right foot no longer turned inward, and she didn't hobble anymore.

Jazz caught Chaz's eye, and he grinned at her. She winked, and he winked back at her.

My special boy.

After lunch, she caught Amanda before she left. "Amanda, the suspense is killing me."

Amanda gave Jazz her little cherub smile and nodded. "I promise, Jazz, this evening. We have to go get ready for Pablo and Serena right now. After they get here and everybody settles down, I'm ready and all yours."

Jazz threw her arms up, but sighed. "Okay."

Amanda left with Mara and Chaz flanking her—as usual—and Jazz looked for Cody. When she didn't spot him, she looked for Kino, Roberta, and the others. They had already left, and the dining hall was emptying. Jazz hurried out, needing to talk to somebody.

Out in the compound, people bustled around with a purpose. Everyone except her was headed somewhere important.

She sighed, did a slow three-sixty, and scanned the scene. She didn't spot any familiar faces, and decided to head for the computer shack. She walked inside and found Ben, Tinga, Kendra, and Malek.

"Come in, my dear." Ben waved a hand, and Jazz walked over and stood beside him and Tinga. They faced the wall screen, with Kendra and Malek in the captains' chairs manning the console.

"Check this out, Jazz," Tinga said. Jazz looked at the screen, the shifting terrain. A rapid series of numbers clicked away in the bottom right section, and a complex signature of symbols, letters, and numbers remained stationary in the bottom left.

"It's a live satellite view, isn't it?" Jazz realized the running numbers were a clock, down to a hundredth of a second.

An electronically generated grid settled over the terrain, and Malek turned in his chair, grinned at her, and turned back to his work.

"When Serena and Pablo hop the plane," Ben said, "she'll be flying incommunicado. No traceable devices other than their physical signature."

"It's a satellite tracking program." Jazz looked at Ben, then at Tinga. "This is military, isn't it?"

Ben chuckled. "That would be highly illegal, wouldn't it, my dear?"

"Oh my God. Kendra, Malek? You guys hacked into a secure government site?"

Kendra turned and smiled at her this time, and spun back to the console.

Ben cleared his throat. "Well, we're trying to track Serena down. See if she's being tailed."

"Damn," Jazz said, impressed. "That's way rad. Kendra, you and Malek are the shizzle." She blinked and looked at Tinga. "Uh, do any of you know where Cody is? Or Kino and Roberta?"

Tinga grinned at her. "He's probably in the gym, playing basketball. Helps him think. He said he wants to figure out a way to make your plan work, Jazz."

Jazz nodded. "Me too."

"Us too." Tinga put a hand to her mouth and giggled. "Actually, he said 'make that crazy woman's whacked-out plan make sense,' but it's basically the same thing."

Jazz laughed and shook her head. Roberta had shown her the recreation building on the tour. She smiled and waved at Tinga and Ben, then headed for the main building and her and Chaz's rooms. There, she changed into a loose pair of shorts, tank top, and running shoes, and headed to the gym.

It was story time.

When she walked into the gym, she heard the echo of shouts, the squeak of rubber shoes on polished wood, and the unmistakable airy slap-back *thwack* of a basketball.

She headed toward the noise, breathed in the mixed tang of sweat, victory, and defeat, and walked through a set of double doors onto a basketball court.

Cody and Marco were battling Kino and Roberta in a game of two-on-two. They were working up a sweat, but the fierce competition didn't stop Cody and Kino from constantly ragging each other. Kino's height advantage offset Roberta's diminutive size, but Roberta seldom missed when she took a shot.

Jazz realized Roberta had probably played some high school basketball, as Jazz had, and the smells, sounds, and competitive atmosphere rushed back in a flood of nostalgia. Everyone waved hello, and continued the game while Jazz watched. She wanted to join in, but she was a fifth wheel for the moment, and she watched from out of bounds.

They finished the game with Cody and Marco winning by three points, and Marco tossed the ball to Jazz.

"Hey, Jazz, show these amateurs what you got, girl." Marco winked, and Jazz smiled, caught the ball, and dribbled it toward them.

"Aw, man." Cody huffed. "You know girls can't play basketball."

"Hey!" Roberta punched him in the arm.

"Well, present company excepted." Cody rubbed his arm.

Jazz took a shot from the three-point mark, praying for it to at least come within a foot of the basket, and got all net. She threw a leg up in a little kick and smirked at Cody.

"Lucky shot." Cody retrieved the ball as Marco headed toward the showers. "Yo, Marco. Where the hell are you going in such a damn hurry?"

Marco turned, grinning. "I'm getting ready for Serena."

"P-whipped wimp." Cody snorted and tossed the ball to Kino.

"Marco, my man!" Kino laughed. "I knew you two had a little somethin' somethin' goin' on." He threw the ball to Jazz, and he and Roberta followed Marco.

"Hey, you couple of chickenshits." Cody waved his arms. "Where the hell are you going? Can't stand getting your ass kicked?"

"Hitting the showers," Kino said. "And getting ready for our new little friend."

"Hitting the showers?" Cody snickered. "What is that, code for rutting like depraved monkeys? More like getting *your* little friend ready."

Kino laughed and waved as he and Roberta walked off. "See you later, shorty. You too, Jazz."

Roberta turned and smiled at Jazz, gave her two thumbs up, and mouthed, "Good luck."

"All right, Cody Jackson," Jazz said, and threw the ball hard to him. "Give it up. Story time."

"Uh-uh." He tossed the ball back to her harder, and she caught it. "You wanna get paid, you gotta play, woman."

"Fine. Twenty-one?"

"If you think you can last that long. Wanna play shirts and skins? I'll be shirts."

"Funny guy." Jazz dribbled, faced off against him. "I win, you tell me anything I ask. Deal?"

Cody laughed. "Looks like I'll be taking my secrets to the grave with me."

"That's what you think, buddy." Jazz faked left, spun right, and laid one up before he could catch her. "One to nothing."

"Enjoy it, because that's the last chance you'll get to cheat, woman."

"Put your money where your big mouth is, tough guy."

They faced off again, and the game of Jazz's life began. Cody was a good player as well as a fierce competitor, but Jazz was no slouch either. It all came back to her, like riding a bicycle.

They cut the banter and concentrated on winning. Jazz gave it all she had, but Cody beat her by a safe margin of twenty-one to fourteen. Breathing hard, sweating, and frustrated, Jazz watched him as he walked up to her and tossed the ball to her underhanded. She caught it, waiting for another cheesy, smart-ass comment, a little braggadocio, but he surprised her.

"Okay, you win, Jazz." He went over to some chairs lined up against the wall, pulled a couple of towels and two bottles of water out of a gym bag, handed one of each to her, and sat. He raised his eyebrows and gestured to the seat beside him. "Good game, by the way. You must've played some when you were in better shape, however long ago that was."

"Hah. You should do stand-up." Jazz wiped sweat off her face and sat beside him, her heart pounding for another reason now. "You're much better at it than basketball. You almost got beat by a girl."

"Yeah? Would you believe I gave up my regular gig at the Comedy Club for all this?"

"Seriously, Cody. I wanna know what happened to you."

"You just think you do. Remember that I warned you you'd be sorry."

"Making people sorry is my job," she blurted, and wished she could take it back. Now was not the time. "Come on, Cody. Try me. I'm a big girl now."

"All right. You asked for it." He took a long draft of water, looked off at something that existed only in his haunted past, and began his story.

Chapter 28

"By the time I turned fifteen—that was twenty years ago, by the way—I was too big and tough to molest anymore. And maybe I was just too old to appeal to his sick, twisted need too. But I wasn't so tough Pop didn't keep pounding on me with his fists, and one day I decided I'd had enough. He had this big, heavy brass ashtray that he got in the war, and while he was pummeling me, I grabbed it and walloped him in the head with it. When he went down, I couldn't stop. I hammered him until I caved his skull in."

"Oh, Cody. I'm—"

"Quiet, woman, and listen. I don't tell this story very often, for obvious reasons. Anyway, because I was a juvenile, and because of the abuse that became obvious once they arrested me—and because my mother was a worthless drunk, and a strung-out coke whore, too—they put me in a special home. Hah. J.D. prison is what it was. Put me through the wringer with a bunch of well-meaning but clueless social workers who called themselves psychologists. Thought they could solve my 'problems' for me. They didn't know shit about what I'd been through, even though I had a detailed roadmap of scars to show them the way.

"I wasn't the best behaved little bronco, and when I turned eighteen, they put me in big boy prison to serve out the last three years of my five-year sentence. When I came out of there, all I'd learned was that the world kicks you in the teeth when you're standing, and keeps on kicking you after you're down."

"Jesus, Cody."

He glared at her, and she mimed zipping her lips shut and tossing away the key.

"Believe it or not, there's not a lot of job opportunities for a twenty-one-year-old, half-honky, half-nigger convict fresh off hard time. After enough prospective employers laughed me out of the interviews, I hooked up with a dealer and started pushing drugs. Somebody higher up recognized my talent for bashing heads, and hired me as their enforcer. I was moving up in the world.

"I started dipping into the merchandise too. You name it, I tried it. Stayed pretty messed up most of the time. Drank more than my share too. Broke some bones here and there, put a few guys in the hospital, but I didn't kill anybody."

"Kino said he did that too, the enforcer thing," Jazz said, raising her eyebrows. Under any other circumstances, she would have laughed out loud at the squinting glare Cody gave her. "Sorry. I'm listening."

"You'd better. I'm not telling this story again. Anyway, two years into that nightmare, I made the mistake of trying crack. Huh. 'Sucking the devil's dick' is a perfect comparison. Got so strung out on the shit that I got fired the hard way. They found me in a bar one night and four of 'em took me outside and used their fists to explain why I was no longer on the team. Thought they were going to get in some practice and teach me a lesson at the same time.

"Funny thing is, fucked up as I was, the harder they hit me, the more I saw my father's face superimposed on theirs. They messed me up pretty good, but I hammered their asses. Killed three of 'em, and the fourth ran off. Hobbled off, I should say. I staggered as far away from the scene as I could, knowing that if the guy who ran off brought his buddies back with him, I was dead meat. After they had some fun with me, of course. Finally passed out in a dark alley somewhere, and when I woke up, guess where I was?"

"Oh, shit. Taja."

"Damn straight. I still don't know how she found me. But Taja made it clear they watched out for guys like me. New recruit material. Huh. New brainwashing material. Taja took me on as one of her special projects. Yeah, it was special all right. Kept me pumped up on whatever drug I wanted, as much as I wanted. For a while. Played games with my head, too. Damn, that woman can worm her way into your mind. She knows what buttons to push and when.

"And she knew how to push 'em. And I let her. I got where I couldn't wait for it, needed it worse than the drugs. Any kinky, whacked-out shit you can imagine—and plenty you can't, trust me—she played it for me, and played me. Bitch wielded pleasure like a weapon. And it's important you understand that I realize I let her. I'm not blaming anyone for my choices. I was in Hell and didn't even know because I loved the burn so bad.

"I'm not trying to be somebody or something I'm not. I know who and what I am. And I know I'll still be searching for Ben's path when I die, whenever that may be. That evil bitch showed me the dark side all right, and let me tell you, it's indescribably alluring. Thanks to her, my father, and my willing participation in her twisted fantasies, I wouldn't know the proper way to make love to a woman if my life depended on it. Or even kiss one. Or talk to one."

Jazz wanted to speak, but something was stuck in her throat. She watched him, willing the tears to wait so he wouldn't see her heart aching for him.

He watched her, and she loved that he held her gaze and didn't look away.

"Anyway, she weaned me off the drugs, a little at a time, so I didn't notice. I was too caught up in *her* drug. She started teaching me how to fight: weapons, hands, feet, teeth, whatever. Taught me all the killing strokes. I did whatever she asked because I wanted more of... Well, I was her puppet by then. She showed me Soulsnatcher's whole organization and the lie it perpetuated, that we were helping these children. Pretended for my sake that it was real, and one day she took me and two of

260

her veteran partners out on an extraction."

"Oh, Cody. What—"

"Hush. Let me finish. I'm almost done, thank God. By then, I would've happily killed anybody who had it coming, and enjoyed it and asked for more. I would've done anything she asked, except kill that little boy's parents. That's when I finally realized for the very first time that there was something inside me worth saving."

She blinked, swallowed a lump of dry dirt, and kept her blurring eyes on his.

"It was their eyes, his parents' eyes, that stopped me. I realized then that there were things in the world greater than I had the imagination to comprehend. Things far greater than me, and that saving them and their boy from Taja was what I was put here to do, if there was ever a purpose for anything. Either that or die trying. After that incredible moment, the drug *Taja* stopped affecting me."

Jazz felt tears burning as they ran down the sides of her cheeks, couldn't stop them.

"So I turned my pistol on her. I should have killed her right then, but I didn't. I couldn't, and it ripped another damn hole in me. She ducked and ran. I shot one of the Extractors who came with us before he could shoot me, then I ducked and ran too. I jacked a Porsche and tried to draw Taja and the other Extractor away. I was running for my life too, because they wanted my ass bad. They still do. I guess you already figured that out."

She wanted to speak, but knew that if she did, she would be all over him, trying to comfort him.

"They shot at me so many times it's amazing I'm still alive. I got four scars from the bullets that hit me. Kevlar doesn't stop everything. I thought I was going to die, and was driving half-blind with pain when shit started exploding everywhere. It was like there was a war going on around me, and my first thought was that they'd brought reinforcements. Turned out, it was my guardian angels. I never even knew they'd been watching over me."

"Oh, Cody."

"Yeah. Last thing I remembered before my life finally changed for the better was slamming into a ditch. I expected the angels to escort me to Hell, or to the pearly gates for a reckoning if I was lucky. But guess where I woke up?"

Jazz could barely even whisper. "Here. Homestead."

"Damn straight. Then I learned everything that was wrong about everything I'd ever learned. Then I started searching for the path. And I still am."

She could only nod as his eyes swallowed her.

"Look, Jazz. I told you you're an amazing woman, and I meant it. But don't kid yourself. If you ever go up against Taja and you haven't already blasted her full of holes or blown her head off with a grenade launcher, she will kill you, and she'll make it more painful than you can imagine. And there'll be nothing you can do to stop it."

"Yeah, everybody keeps saying that." She grabbed his hand and squeezed it. "But I'm not helpless, Cody."

"You don't understand, Jazz. We can't afford to lose you. Or Chaz. And he can't afford to lose you either. And... I can't afford to lose you."

He winced and stood, and she unlocked her shaky knees to rise and face him. She reached a tentative hand to his cheek, caressed it with her palm.

"Remember how you told me I'd be sorry about this?"

He closed his eyes and dipped his chin. "Yeah. I remember."

"Oh, Cody." She lifted his chin with her fingers, and felt the elegance of the moment like an angel that had just earned its wings. When he opened his eyes and looked at her, she saw beyond their impenetrable darkness.

"I'm so sorry." She leaned toward him and pressed her lips against his. He didn't flinch, but she felt him tremble. He resisted at first, then responded. When she drew back and took a breath an eternity later, his eyes revealed his worst fear.

"Jazz, you don't know—"

"Shh. I know enough. And I know how I feel."

She kissed him again, and it was just like it had been in her dream.

When they parted, the moment was gone, but the taste of it lingered. She drew back, worried about seeing rejection in his eyes. When he opened them, the pain was still there, and an indefinable longing, but no regret shone in them.

She was glad to see a hint of a smile curl his lips when he spoke.

"Jazz, I... why did you—"

"Because I wanted to." *Please don't make any cheesy comments, Cody.* She spoke again before he could: "Why do you not like being called CJ?"

He nodded. Apparently this was safer territory. "Because that's what Taja and everybody there called me. Pop did too. It makes me grind my teeth and wanna hurt somebody."

"And your scars? Your father did all that?"

"Most of 'em. Some are battle scars. Some are from... her. Please don't ask."

"God, Cody." She put her hands against his chest, felt his heartbeat. "Okay. Thank you. For sharing your story with me."

"You're welcome. So can we bury it again now?"

She ran her fingers up along his neck, his cheeks. "Okay." Despite his scars, in his tank top, gym shorts, and sneakers, he looked less like the unapproachable dark man and more like the man she wanted to kiss again.

She still tasted his lips, his tongue, felt his hot breath. And she still saw his face in her dreams, the face of her Guardian.

"For the record, Cody, I think you're walking the path admirably. And thank you for saving mine and Chaz's lives, and bringing us here. Dante too."

He smiled. "We'll see about that path thing after we get your father and Kaylee back. And you're welcome."

She nodded. They would do it together. A shout from Kino as he and Roberta walked back out on the court hand in hand interrupted her daydream.

"Hey! You two need to get a room for that. We have children around here."

Roberta laughed and winked at Jazz, Jazz grinned and blushed, and Cody winced. Jazz could tell he was struggling for a good comeback, but for once he refrained and just looked in her eyes again.

"I'm gonna hit the showers, Jazz, and get ready for our new arrival."

"Me too. And Cody—"

"We'll talk more about it later, okay?"

She nodded. A new feeling was growing inside her, and she didn't want to lose it. "Okay. I want to."

He grabbed his gym bag and headed for the showers, shook his head at Kino and Roberta, and mumbled something as he passed them.

Kino guffawed, and he and Roberta walked up to Jazz.

Roberta touched Jazz's arm. "I want a detailed blow-by-blow account later, okay?"

Jazz nodded, and the intercom crackled. Its announcement echoed in the mostly empty gym.

"Hey, all you happy little campers! This is your favorite camp counselor with a special public service announcement for all you kiddies."

"Malek, be serious or give it!" That was obviously Kendra.

"Quiet, girl. I'm busy. Folks, if you'll all direct your little peepers to Cameron's Cove, we have an ETA of about two hours—that's seventeen-hundred hours, or five p.m. for all you non-military personnel—for our sexiest Guardian and our newest little camper. For anyone wanting to greet them there, the trucks leave for Cameron's Cove at four-forty-five, so you snooze, you lose. This public service announcement has been brought to you by your favorite computer guru. End transmission."

Jazz nodded at Kino and Roberta. "I'll meet you by the trucks at four-thirty, okay?"

They nodded back, and Jazz went to her room, stripped, and hopped in the shower. When she finished, she spent some time on her hair, and applied makeup. She donned a pair of jeans and a loose, tan blouse and slipped into her ankle-cut moccasins, wondering why Taja hadn't responded to her video yet. She tried not to think about how it might mean her father was already dead.

She arrived out front at 4:30. Tinga, Kino, Raj, and another woman were loading the children in the beds of two pickup trucks. Cody, Marco, and Roberta were all armed and conferring in front of the trucks. Jazz walked over to them.

"You coming, Jazz?" Roberta asked.

Jazz looked at Cody. He was the dark man again, minus the leather jacket, and he was frowning. "Um, yeah. Cody, what's wrong?"

"I smell trouble."

"What? What do you think it—"

"I don't know." He shook his head. "Could be nothing. Maybe Chef burnt the Salisbury steak. Go ahead, Jazz. We'll see you when you get back."

"You're not coming?"

"Me and Marco are staying here. Roberta, Kino, and Tinga are going. Just be careful, okay?"

"Okay. Cody—"

"Go, Jazz. Nothing's going to happen with Tinga and Roberta with you."

She nodded, and piled in back of one of the pickups with Tinga and five children. Chaz was in the other pickup with Amanda, Mara, four other children, and Roberta. Dante leaped in before they shut the tailgate.

Raj drove Jazz's truck, and Kino drove Chaz's, and they headed out of the compound toward Cameron's Cove. Jazz waved to Cody, and was glad to see him wave back.

They arrived at the lagoon ten minutes later, and everybody piled out and gathered by the dock. The children were full of happy chatter, and Chaz was in Amanda-land, so Jazz sidled up next to Tinga.

"Tinga, did Cody tell you—"

"Yes. But until he learns to identify the source and degree, his talent is not very useful. It could be something as simple as a flat tire."

"Yeah, but what if it's something much worse?"

"We're on the lookout. Don't worry, Jazz."

Ten minutes later, all eyes turned to the far end of the cove, where a motorboat appeared towing a plane. The driver of the boat waved and smiled, and everyone waved back. He pulled up next to the dock, hopped out, and secured the boat.

Roberta, Kino, and Raj secured the plane, and an exotic, bronze-skinned woman in a jumpsuit hopped out of the cockpit and grinned at the gathering. She waved, and several of the children called out as they ran toward her.

"Serena!"

Serena hugged a few of the children, high-fived a few, and cheerful greetings were exchanged. Jazz figured she was in her late twenties, and wished she had a tight body with curves like that.

All the Guardians were in peak physical shape, even lanky Tinga and petite Roberta. Jazz hoped she lived long enough to get in shape like them. She wanted to be a part of this operation, and felt the rest of her old life shedding off her like a snake sloughing its dead skin. It already seemed like a memory of a distant past, in another incarnation.

Serena held up a hand in response to the children's requests and returned to the plane. She emerged holding hands with a frightened-looking Hispanic boy of about twelve. They hopped onto the dock together. Jazz was pleased to see the children give the boy, obviously Pablo, as warm a welcome as they'd given Chaz.

Pablo gave the children a weak smile and shook a few hands. As they all headed toward the trucks, he kept reaching a hand under his shirt collar, scratching his back, and wincing. Jazz's heart broke for him. She knew how it felt to be a stranger in a strange land. The poor boy flinched at each new sound as if he believed demons lurked in every shadow.

Excited chatter filled the air as everyone piled back into the trucks. Serena and Pablo climbed into the back with Jazz, Tinga, and the children who'd ridden to the cove with them, accompanied by groans of disappointment from the children not riding with them.

Jazz held out a hand to Serena. "Hi, Serena. I'm Jazz, Chaz's mother."

Serena smiled and shook her hand. "I know. It's a pleasure to meet you, Jazz."

As they rode back to the compound, Jazz noticed Pablo kept scratching his back under his collar. The children were asking Serena and Pablo about their adventure, happy little chatterboxes, and Jazz couldn't get a word in edgewise.

Serena raised her eyebrows and looked at Tinga while Pablo spoke in broken English about his rescue. "Gunther?" she asked.

Tinga shook her head, and Serena sighed and mustered a smile for the children. Jazz grinned at Pablo when he finally glanced at her.

"Pablo, did you get a bug bite or something, honey? What are you scratching?"

"It itches," Pablo said, frowning.

"Let me take a look." Jazz slid over beside him.

She saw Serena and Tinga exchange a glance. Serena sat beside Pablo and spoke softly in Spanish. He leaned toward her and pulled his collar aside so she could see his back.

Jazz looked with Serena, and Serena gasped. A puffy red sore about the size of a penny bulged between his left scapula and spine. Serena scowled at Tinga.

"Implant," she said. "Dammit, I missed it." She snagged her cell off her belt and punched a button. "Yo, Cody. Serena. We have a breach. I repeat, we have a breach. Pablo's got an implant, and I missed it. Sound the alarm now!"

"Oh, no," Tinga said.

"What?" Jazz felt a lump plugging her throat. "What is it?"

"Surgical implant," Serena said, shaking her head. "Tracking device. Dammit! I screwed up." She punched another button on her phone. "Yo, Roberta. Serena. We have a problem."

"Oh, no," Tinga said again.

"Tinga, what does this…" Jazz shook her head as it sunk in. "Oh, God."

Tinga held a hand to her mouth, her normally placid eyes wide.

"I can feel her. She's close."

Jazz's voice quavered. "You mean—"

"Taja's coming."

Chapter 29

Kaylee finished all of her big breakfast, even though she hardly tasted it. She would need all her strength for the coming ordeal. Taja was gone, off on another mysterious trip, and it was time for Kaylee to implement her plan.

First she had to figure out how to break out of her prison. She had no idea how she was going to do that now. Her friends whispered in her mind, calling her to come join them, but she couldn't get to them.

Nobody answered when she pounded on the door to the hall, so she left the cart where it was and paced her suites, trying to come up with a plan. Nothing came to her, and the volcano of rage inside her wanted to erupt.

After a while, she took a shower. She let steaming hot water wash over her, hoping for inspiration. She called out in her mind to her friends, promising them that somehow they would be together soon. After her shower, an idea started taking shape. She dressed in brown chinos and a loose, short-sleeved, green blouse, and skipped the shoes. She wanted to feel her friends' touch against her bare feet when she rejoined them.

Her breakfast cart was gone when she emerged from her bedroom. She knew she was being watched, and sat on the couch in front of the wall screen and channel-surfed. She pretended to be bored as the seeds of the escape plan sprouted in her mind. The best time to hatch it would be just before dark, so she mentally prepared herself for the agonizing wait.

She dozed off after a while. When she woke a little after one o'clock, she was hungry again. She called down to the kitchen and ordered some lunch, and waited and watched the door for the cart to arrive. It might be her only chance to talk to Gordon, or whoever was guarding her room, and see if they would let her go outside.

If they refused, it would be time for plan B.

When the door finally opened, a guard she didn't recognize wheeled a cart inside. Kaylee jumped up off the couch and confronted him before he could leave.

"I wanna go outside. I'm bored."

He shook his head. "Sorry, Kathryn. Taja said not until she gets back."

"Not even if you come with me?"

He shrugged. "Sorry."

"Well, when is Taja coming back?"

"Maybe this evening." He shut the door in her face before she could say anything else.

She'd figured they wouldn't let her out, but it had been worth a try. Because executing plan B was going to be tricky, and dangerous.

She stuffed her gut, not even thinking about what she ate. After she finished, she surfed the Internet on the computer in the front room, but the sites she was allowed to visit were so limited and boring that she zoned out for a while. As the afternoon waned and breakout time neared, she started getting excited and nervous. She kept running the plan through her head, searching for flaws.

When the shadows started encroaching and painted a gray gloom in the room, she went to pandora.com, one of the sites she was allowed on, and programmed an obnoxious death metal station. She hated that angry noise, but it was perfect for her plan. She cranked it up painfully loud, her heart pounding.

She wheeled the computer chair into her bedroom, shut the door, hurried over to the vanity desk across from her bed, and grabbed the chair in front of it. She dragged it over to her bedroom door, praying that no one was watching at the moment, and wedged it under the doorknob as tight as she could. She grabbed the computer chair by its backrest, swung it around in a three-sixty for extra momentum, and hurled it at her window with every bit of muscle she could muster.

The framework surrounding the panes buckled, glass shattered, and the chair crashed through the open gap and plummeted to the ground outside. She heard the chair break as it hit the hard tiles two stories down. She snagged her comforter off the bed and jumped up on the alcove sill.

Using the comforter, she pushed the jagged shards of glass and wooden framework out of the window, less worried about getting cut than being discovered and foiled. Getting cut was part of the plan anyway.

Someone pounded on her bedroom door, shouting "Kaylee!" over the blaring death metal, and she nearly panicked and fell out the window. She snatched a slender, finger-length shard of glass out of the side of the window frame and looked back at the door, hoping she wasn't too late.

"I'm coming, guys," she whispered, and drew the edge of the shard across her left palm. She bit her lip to keep from crying out, transferred the shard from the shaking fingers of her right hand to her left, and scored a gash in her right palm.

"Kaylee, open this door right now!" a deep male voice called.

"You're in big trouble, young lady!" another shouted.

Holding her hands out the window, she let the droplets of blood spray the shrubbery at the base of the building beneath her. She looked down, squeezed and released her hands, and watched the show below.

The result was instantaneous. Shrub branches wriggled and grew, straining toward her. The limbs thickened and elongated, a foot higher, two feet, three. She growled and splayed her hands open, nearly crying out from the pain.

The door behind her burst open, and she turned her head. Two guards rushed into the room. They stopped when they saw her standing at the window.

"Don't come any closer," she warned. "I'll jump. I swear it." She turned to face them and took a step back to the ledge.

"Kaylee!" one of the men shouted. "Get down from there now!"

She smiled, feeling the tremor of branches and leaves scrape the outer wall as the organic circus behind her came to town.

"Kaylee, don't be foolish," the other man said, patting his hands at her. "Come on down from there before you get hurt."

Hearing a rustle behind her, she clenched her fists to slow the flow of crimson life leaking out, smiled at the two men again, and took a step backward. The men leaped toward her, eyes wide and mouths open.

She dropped a foot, and strong vines twined around her feet and legs. They bore her downward and gently deposited her on the tiles of the walkway. She glanced up to see the astonished look on the men's faces as they peered out the window. Then she spun and dashed toward one of the gardens.

Kaylee heard shouts behind her, but she wasn't stopping for anything or anybody. When she plunged into the thick of the garden's lush foliage, she opened her hands wide and started brushing them against her friends.

The effect was swift and magnificent, just as she knew it would be. Everywhere around her, branches and vines and limbs flourished and grew as if they were soaking up her gift and sharing it with all their neighbors.

Angry shouts behind her confirmed that her pursuers were getting tangled up in the lively vines and cavorting limbs. She thought of the animated trees in The Wizard of Oz and giggled.

In moments the garden had grown a mighty, impenetrable wall around her, grokking her need. Daylight barely leaked through the entwining branches, and Kaylee sighed and smiled. Her escape plan was a success. Now it was time for the second act.

And it was going to bring the house down.

She held her hands out at her sides. Two slithering vines crept up her legs and twined around her hands. There was just enough light for her to see them fuse with the cuts on her palms and seal the edges of loose skin.

She would have felt it even if she was blind.

"Hey, guys," she said. "Welcome home."

She imagined the guards calling Taja and telling her what happened, and pictured Taja laughing and asking them, "Where can she go?"

Kaylee wasn't going anywhere but down to the roots. She still had some unfinished business here. She gazed into the dense thicket surrounding her and smiled.

"I'm coming, Jai," she whispered, and melded with the greenery.

Chapter 30

Tinga shouted at Raj, giving him the bad news. Above the engine's roar and the children's frightened shrieks, Jazz heard Roberta shouting at Kino in the truck behind them.

Serena turned to Pablo, drew a small knife, and said something to him in Spanish. He winced, nodded, and turned his back to her. With steady hands she made a cut over the sore, and he didn't even cry out. She withdrew a tiny object, held it in her bloody hand, and gazed at it. She dropped it and crushed it beneath her boot heel, then picked up the remains and tossed them into the brush whipping past.

Tinga yanked off her kimono. Underneath it she wore a tight-fitting jumpsuit like Serena's, along with full battle regalia: a holstered pistol at each shoulder, a pair of slender short swords in sheaths along her spine, and two knives and various devices clipped to a belt at her waist.

Jazz looked back at the other truck. Chaz peered at her over the cab's roof, his eyes wide. Amanda and Mara tried to calm the children while Roberta checked her arsenal. Kino had a determined scowl on his face as both trucks sped up. Jazz turned to Tinga.

"How long?"

Tinga pursed her lips. "Minutes. She's close. And she probably brought some heavily armed friends."

Roberta shouted at them over the truck's cab. "Tell Raj to get the damn lead out!"

"Haul ass, Raj!" Kino yelled out the window.

The truck raced ahead, and Kino matched their speed.

"Everybody up here, against the cab," Tinga ordered. The children crawled forward and crouched behind the cab. Tinga and Serena stood in front of them, facing the other truck.

Jazz crouched beside them in front of the children. She looked over her shoulder through the rear window of the cab and saw the compound come into view around the final curve.

And heard the unmistakable *whupping* stutter of helicopters behind them.

She turned back and looked for Chaz. Roberta and Amanda had collected the children against the other truck's cab. Jazz wished she were standing beside Roberta, protecting her baby.

She also wished she'd clipped her pistol to her waistband before she'd left her room. Maybe she should have even brought along a grenade launcher.

The helicopters soared into view, looking so ominous that a rush of despair nearly overwhelmed her. There were at least three of them, and they appeared to be heavily armed. She pushed her dismay deep down inside her, let it stoke the fury.

They couldn't get Chaz, mustn't get him. She would die first. The realization settled an eerie calm over her, preparing her for the coming storm.

Raj and Kino pulled into the compound and skidded to a halt sideways beside the main building. Security guards were waving everybody inside. Jazz figured they were directing them to the tunnel leading from the main building to the heliport. She hopped out, looking for Chaz, and chaos came to Homestead.

Something slender and hazardous-looking spat flame from the side of one helicopter, and it streaked through the air. It slammed into the dining hall quicker than Jazz could blink, and the building exploded. Flaming debris flew everywhere.

"Chaz!" she howled over the children's frightened screams. Smoke and ash obscured her vision. A moment later she spotted him running with Amanda and the other children toward the main building.

Another rocket shot out of a helicopter, zipped toward the computer shack, and blew half of it to pieces. The shock from the explosion knocked Jazz to her hands and knees.

Children shrieked as the adults shouted directions.

Jazz shook her head and staggered to her feet as ropes started trailing from the helicopters. Armed Extractors rappelled down them like giant flying spiders spinning their webs.

Marco stood in the dirt of the compound, pointing a long metal tube slung over his shoulder at one of the copters. Smoke spat out one end of the tube, and something whooshed out of the other end and flew into the cabin, a direct hit. The bird exploded, and flaming, smoking shrapnel flew everywhere. The Extractors dangling from the ropes were thrown howling to the ground and the surrounding woods.

Another security guard aimed the same type of device at one of the other birds. His head burst and he went down before he could fire. Jazz heard the crack of small arms fire from the crews in the birds and from the Extractors, who hit the ground running.

Her ears rang from the explosions and gunfire, and she spun around, looking for Chaz. One Extractor dropped the final few feet from his rope and dove and grabbed Mara, who was helping two of the smaller children toward the main building. He started dragging her back toward the dangling rope. Something dark and lightning quick slammed into his side and knocked him to the ground.

He let go of Mara's arm and drew a pistol from a shoulder holster, and Cody kicked it out of his hand. Mara shrieked and rolled away. Cody fired a shot and the Extractor's head blasted apart, and Cody shouted.

"Go, Mara, go!"

Jazz saw some Homestead security personnel drop from shots fired. Some of the Extractors grabbed children and ran for the dangling ropes. One clutched Andrea of the golden curls in his arm, snagged a rope, and started rising. Others did the same with some of the other children, but they had the fight of their lives on their hands.

Tinga, Serena, Marco, and Roberta darted here and there,

shooting and kicking and stabbing, and the dark man seemed to be everywhere at once. They dropped their adversaries when they could squeeze off a shot without hurting the children, and engaged them in hand-to-hand combat when they couldn't. Jazz saw Serena spin, sword in hand, and her swing lopped off an enemy combatant's head as Cody fired and dropped another Extractor.

In the swirling smoke and flaming debris, Jazz didn't spot Chaz. She saw Zeke stumble and fall, and an Extractor snatched him up and darted toward one of the ropes. Before he reached it, a razor-taloned winged dragon the size of a full-grown eagle flew toward him, talons extended, serpentine head coiled to strike, and forked tongue spitting.

The man shouted, let go of Zeke, and fired at the flying dragon. It kept coming, and he crouched and ducked. When it collided with him, it dissipated into nothing. He rose, looking stunned, and reached for Zeke.

Roberta was running toward him. She fired twice and the top of his head shattered and skull fragments scattered. Zeke huddled in the dirt as Roberta stood guard over him, and a dozen of the bizarre flying dragons swarmed through the compound. Several Extractors shouted in alarm and fired at the imaginary creatures Zeke created with his talent. Roberta brought two Extractors down with carefully placed shots.

Jazz frantically spun around, searching for Chaz. She finally spotted him right as an Extractor grabbed him and dashed toward another dangling rope. A security guard ran toward them, trying to get an open shot at the Extractor, who turned and fired at the guard and dropped him. The Extractor reached for the rope but got bowled over by a snarling, flying streak of brown and black fur.

He released Chaz, and Chaz hit the dirt and rolled. Dante dove for the man's jugular. The man cursed, drew his pistol, and tried to shoot Dante.

His hand went flying, still grasping the pistol after

Tinga's blade lopped it off. Sword in one hand and pistol in the other, she swung the sword at his flailing leg as he gurgled and tried to pull Dante off his throat. Her slash sliced his foot off at the ankle. Chaz leaped to his feet, and Jazz ran toward him, shouting his name. Dante ripped the one-handed, one-footed man's jugular vein open, and Tinga turned and engaged another Extractor.

In her peripheral vision, Jazz saw two Extractors rise on the ropes toward one of the helicopters. One held Lynette, the other clutched a child whose name Jazz didn't know. Two security guards fired at them, and a flying dark streak slammed into the side of one of them.

"No!" Cody shouted. "You'll hit the kids!" He dashed toward the other guard, but the woman went down from shots fired at her before he could reach her.

"Chaz!" Jazz shouted again. Chaz turned toward her, dazed. She hoped his fragile heart wasn't about to give out. He looked pale, disoriented. He started shimmering, and Jazz screamed. She dashed toward him, felt her arm jerk to the side, and she fell.

A female security guard dove at Chaz, snatched him up in her arms, and he stopped shimmering.

Jazz staggered to her feet, her left arm burning from the bullet that had torn through it. She howled "No!" as one of the copters descended to twenty feet above ground and hovered over Chaz.

In a stunning feat of aerial acrobatics, a black-clad woman who looked just like Tinga swung from a rope in a harness. She hit the ground running, fired one shot at the guard's head and dropped her, snatched Chaz up in one arm and clutched him to her chest, and fired at Jazz. It was Taja. She laughed as Chaz cried out.

"Mother!"

"Chaz, no!" Jazz ran straight toward them, heedless of the bullets flying at her. The rope bearing Taja started reeling her and Chaz in. Something ripped through Jazz's thigh, and she stumbled to her hands and knees. She got right back up and hobbled toward the rising bird, screaming Chaz's name, but she was too late and she knew it.

A few Extractors rose on the ropes toward the other bird, bearing a child each, but Jazz only had eyes for Chaz. She stumbled again and fell. Choking on the dust and smoke, she crawled toward Chaz as if she could sprout wings and save him if she only wished hard enough.

"No, Chaz," she sputtered.

Kino appeared, a juggernaut with a grim sneer and a scowl etched on his face. He was unarmed, with only a small black object poking out of one clenched fist, his arms and legs pumping for the gold. He growled and barreled toward Chaz and Taja like a linebacker who just snatched up a fumbled ball and was plowing ahead for the goal line.

He hurdled up onto the hood of the pickup he'd been driving and just kept going. Metal dented and creaked under his weight. He leaped from the roof of the cab and dove at the rising copter right as Taja and Chaz were lifted into its open side.

Kino grabbed the copter's strut and swung a leg up. The bird wobbled and Taja fired at him and missed. Taja stumbled in the doorway with one hand gripping Chaz's arm as the pilot corrected their pitch. Kino swung the hand carrying the object up and grabbed Chaz's foot, but didn't try to pull him out. Jazz saw a grim smile etched on Kino's face as Taja laughed and shot him. Blood sprayed out of his shoulder, and the bird swayed with his flailing weight as it rose. Taja shouted something, laughed again, and shot him in the chest. He lost his grip on the strut and Chaz's foot. His leg caught in the strut for a crucial couple of seconds as the copter rocked and ascended.

"No, Kino!" Jazz screamed. Kino's leg snapped at an unnatural angle and unwrapped from the strut, and he fell. Taja fired at him while he dropped like a huge sack of sand. Some of her shots tore through him and sprayed crimson blossoms as he fell and fell.

It was too far, too high up for anyone, even a minor god, to survive the fall, even if the bullets hadn't already done the job. Kino seemed to fall forever, in slow motion. He finally hit the dirt with a hollow *thunk* that sprayed blood and a cloud of dust around him.

The copters quickly rose together and flew away. A few security guards fired at them. Cody, Marco, and Serena shouted at them to stop before they hit the children. Jazz rose on her knees and watched the copters shrink as they soared off.

"Kino!" Roberta tore a path toward him, her boots kicking up dust and her face scrunched up in a tortured grimace. She seemed to move in slow motion, just like Kino falling. She dropped to her knees beside his body and folded herself over him and sobbed, "Oh, no, no, Kino…"

Jazz struggled to draw in air, coughed, and staggered to her feet. Her left arm was mostly numb, and her left thigh felt like someone was holding a lit blowtorch to it. Her heart was gone with Chaz and Kino. Something was stuck in her throat, choking her, and everything looked blurry. A sob broke out of her, and she thought she was going to die right there.

"Kino…" Roberta moaned, her body rocking back and forth over his.

Cody hustled up behind Jazz and touched her shoulder. "Jazz, you okay?"

She spun, almost fell. "No, I'm not *okay*. They got Chaz." She started to say *and Kino*, but choked on the words.

Cody just nodded, the inaccessible dark man again. He hurried over to Roberta and stood beside her, looking down at his dead friend.

Moans, groans, and haunting lamentations echoed through the compound, unbearably loud now without the roar of helicopters and exploding buildings. Smoke and flames rose from the fallen bird east of the main compound. Jazz heard a high-pitched keening behind her, and turned and looked.

Kendra stumbled out of the ruins of the computer shack. Tears poured from her eyes, and her ash-streaked face was wrinkled up in a silent scream, but nothing came out but a warbling whine. In one bloody hand she carried a pair of broken, cracked thick-lensed glasses. Blood and something thicker and darker dripped from them.

Jazz couldn't think. She slowly spun around, surveying the carnage. Bodies lay scattered about, both good guys and bad. None were children, but a silent voice told her Malek didn't survive the computer shack explosion.

At least five children, including Chaz, had been stolen.

Tinga was organizing the remaining children. Amanda and Mara helped, their eyes streaming tears. Serena and Marco wandered the compound, checking on the wounded and finishing off the few Extractors who were still breathing. They headed into the woods, apparently checking for survivors of the copter crash. Some of the Homestead crew were trying to help their wounded friends. Ben was nowhere to be seen.

Roberta kept moaning, "Kino, no…"

Cody shouted orders as if his friend didn't lay dead at his feet.

"Thomas, get a few guys and check the computer shack. See if Ben and Malek are still alive in there somewhere. If they are and you can, drag 'em out." He turned to some others as Jazz realized Ben had been inside with Malek and Kendra when the missile blew it up. "The rest of you not attending the wounded, get these kids on the planes and outta here *yesterday*!"

Jazz stared at him, her jaw hanging open, trying to think and figure out what to do now. Cody turned and faced her, his expression inscrutable. She wanted to slap him, shake him into a knot and make him shed a tear for Kino, but she couldn't move.

"What, Jazz?"

She waved a hand at Kino and Roberta, unable to speak. Cody stepped closer to her and glared at her.

"My best friend just gave his life to plant that tracking device on Chaz," he said, his voice husky. "And we're not wasting that sacrifice."

"Oh." Jazz staggered and almost fell as it hit her: Kino hadn't been armed because he needed to grab the copter's struts while hanging onto the tracking device. If he had been armed, all he could have done was shoot Taja and her comrades—which would have been good—but he would have gotten shot as well, and Chaz and the others would still be lost. The only way he could save them all was to slip the device in Chaz's shoe and hope Taja didn't notice in the heat of the battle before she killed him.

Jazz's body shook with sobs and she fell to her knees again. Kino had taken that final, fateful leap knowing he was going to die. He had willingly given his life for Chaz and the other children. Chaz had saved his life last night, and Kino had just given his to save Chaz.

Roberta stood and looked at Cody and Jazz. Nothing was left in her eyes but a dark fire. The fury rose inside Jazz, feeding her with its blaze, and she staggered to her feet, her pain forgotten. She wasn't the only one who'd lost something irreplaceable today. Dante trotted up beside her, looked up at her, and whined. He licked his bloody jowls, and she looked at the dark man.

"So... what are we gonna do, Cody?"

Cody nodded, lips pursed. "We're going to go get Chaz and the other kids, rescue your father and Kaylee, and kill Taja and Soulsnatcher. And make them all *so damn sorry* for ever fucking with us. And we're leaving now."

Chapter 31

Tinga and the Guardians quickly organized the rescue party, the evacuees, and the wounded into groups. Everybody worked together, as if they'd rehearsed such an impossible scenario and were prepared for it.

Jazz ached to do something as she waited while a woman cleaned and dressed her wounds. They were superficial, but her left bicep and thigh pounded with the desire for vengeance pulsating through her veins.

She noticed Pablo with Tinga, Amanda, Mara, and the other children. He was crying, as were most of the others. Kendra stood beside him, eyes closed, clasping the broken, bloody glasses against her chest. She swayed back and forth and moaned. Serena and Marco were back. Serena stopped by Kendra and Pablo, touched Pablo's shoulder and Kendra's arm, said something to them, and walked over to Jazz.

"We're taking the four choppers," Serena said. "They're taking the children in the planes to our other location. Tinga's going with them. If she went with us, Taja would sense her, and we don't want them to know we're coming. Besides, without Ben, Tinga *is* Homestead."

"Have they found him yet?"

Serena bit her lip. "Yeah. He's alive, but his legs are messed up bad, and he's lost a lot of blood. They're taking him with them, and doing everything they can to save him, but without Chaz… I don't know."

Jazz scowled. "Malek?"

Serena shook her head. "Gone."

Jazz started to say something, but Zeke walked up and stood beside them, his little fists clenched and a scowl on his sweet, ten-year-old face.

"I'm going with you."

Jazz knew Cody would have said "no" right away. Serena looked down at him.

"Zeke, there are going to be lots of heavily armed and angry people shooting at us and trying to kill us. You could die."

"I don't care." Zeke poked his lips out. "They killed my parents and stole my friends, and I wanna help."

Serena nodded. "Okay, Zeke. Stick with me." She turned back to Jazz. "They're headed due west. If they hold their course, we're all going to load up in one of our planes stashed in Mississippi or Louisiana, however far they're going. We won't lose them, Jazz. Unless Taja finds the locator Kino put on Chaz. When Tinga gets everybody to the new location, we'll have Kendra track them via satellite. She wants to hammer them as bad as the rest of us. As soon as we get her back online, we won't even need the tracking device. But we have to leave now."

"I'm gonna go get my pistol."

"You're going to need it. Bring extra ammo."

Jazz nodded, squeezed Zeke's shoulder, and hobbled toward the main building to load up. Tinga was piling the children up in the trucks, and stopped Jazz on her way and hugged her.

"I wish I could go with you and kill her myself," Tinga whispered in Jazz's ear. She stepped back and took a deep breath. "Go save your son, Jazz. And make Taja sorry."

"I will. Keep Ben alive, okay? I'll bring Chaz back and we'll really fix him up." Jazz clambered up the steps, and Tinga turned and did what she was born to do.

When Jazz emerged from the main building armed and ready for bear and dragon, loaded Jeeps were already speeding out of the compound. Dante stood at the bottom of the steps, wagged his tail, and whined when he saw her. Roberta waited for her in the driver's seat of a pickup truck loaded with four security personnel and various equipment in the back.

Jazz hopped in the empty passenger seat, and Dante jumped in with her. She and Roberta nodded at each other, and they took off for the hangar.

They were loaded up in the copters and ready to go thirty minutes later. Cody, Roberta, Marco, and Serena piloted the four birds, with three security guards aboard each. Jazz and Dante rode with Cody. Zeke stuck with Serena after Cody's half-hearted protest failed.

When they were airborne, Cody hooked Jazz up with a mike and headphone set. He let her ride beside him in the co-pilot's seat and explained the new plan.

"We're going in hard, fast, and silent as possible. We can't just go in there blowing shit up. Well, we might have to blow something up. But we can't kill the people we're trying to save. The more we have surprise on our side, the better our chances. They'll have an arsenal, and plenty of guys manning it, but if we can slip in while they're celebrating their supposed victory..."

He let the last part hang. Jazz watched him and saw the glistening streak finally crawl down his cheek. He turned to her and laughed, then gazed ahead again.

"You wanna know the last thing I said to him, before he drove off with you and the kids?"

Jazz could only nod and reach her hand out, touch his arm.

"I said, 'Try not to get anybody killed, you big goofy-ass lunkhead.'"

She squeezed his arm, her eyes on her dark man.

"And look what he went and did." Cody's face scrunched up for a second, squeezing another trail out of his eyes. Jazz reached up and wiped it away, caressed his cheek. He dipped his head into her palm for a brief moment. When he looked up, he was the dark man again.

He kept in touch with Roberta, Marco, and Serena while they flew. The security personnel spent their time checking and prepping their cache of weapons. Two and a half hours later, after they had refueled at a hidden depot, Tinga called and told them she was at the new location. Jazz listened in on the conversation with the four pilots.

"Yo, Tinga," Cody said. "How's Ben?"

"Unconscious, but hanging on. Barely. He needs a miracle, Cody."

"Copy. We're working on that. And the kids?"

"Safe, but worried. Kendra's at the console, tracking the signal. She has a lock on their jet, so even if Taja finds the tracking device, we won't lose them. They switched over from the copters in Alabama. I suggest you do the same before you run out of fuel."

"Copy that," Cody said. "Noticed the stationary signal there, wondered if it was target location until it started moving again. We'll rendezvous Mississippi location approximately thirty minutes and switch to wings there. They're still headed due west, so it may be a long flight. Will contact you on arrival. Whatever you do, don't lose them."

"Trust me, Kendra's all over it. It's her primary objective now."

"Roger that. Ours too. Over."

A half hour later, at 8:15 p.m. Central Standard Time, they landed next to a hangar somewhere outside DeSoto National Forest in Mississippi. While they loaded up the huge cargo transport plane in the hangar, Cody explained that Ben kept a handful of properties spread around the southeastern United States for just such an emergency. Jazz stood out of the way with her arm around Zeke's shoulder and Dante at her side, and looked at the two oversized trucks in the cavernous rear cargo bay.

"This stuff all looks military," she said as Cody and Marco passed by her with an armful of equipment each. "The

286

plane too."

"Shh," Cody said. "Don't tell anybody."

"Yeah," Marco said. "Lockheed C-5 Galaxy military transport aircraft. It's supposed to be a secret."

She looked at Cody, and pointed at the trucks and the gun turrets atop them. "What are those? Armored personnel carriers?"

"Israeli Wolf Armored Vehicles, converted with HOT missile launchers," he said. "Jews make the best military equipment."

"I think it's cool," Zeke said.

"Yeah?" Jazz took a deep breath and squeezed his shoulder.

"Yeah."

Roberta and Serena climbed into the pilot and copilot's seats and started a systems check. Roberta nodded at Jazz as she passed, and Jazz's heart broke again. She didn't think she would ever see Roberta's cheery smile again.

If they even survived this war.

They were loaded, fueled up, and ready to takeoff thirty minutes later. Roberta taxied them out to the runway, and they were off again.

An hour later, some of the security guys passed around sandwiches and drinks. Jazz refused at first. But she realized she was famished, and needed her strength for the coming ordeal. After they ate, mostly in silence, Cody went over the plan with everybody.

Shortly after eleven p.m. Mountain Standard Time, they were flying over the empty Arizona desert, and Tinga called in to confirm that their target was stationary. When they were several miles from the signal and it still hadn't moved, Cody turned to Serena and Roberta.

"Okay, ladies. We have found the viper's nest. Find a place to land this bad boy and let's do this thing."

Jazz worried that they wouldn't be able to find hard,

even ground to land on, but five minutes later Roberta put them down. It was a shaky landing, and rattled Jazz's already scrambled marbles. But the plane finally came to a halt in a giant cloud of dust, and everybody started loading up in the big trucks. The rear cargo bay ramp opened and touched ground.

Jazz and Zeke followed Cody to the trucks. Roberta started to climb in one of them with Marco, and Cody grabbed her arm and stopped her.

"When we deploy, you're our sniper. You're the best we got. Take out as many as you can."

Roberta frowned, and Jazz could tell she wanted to be in the thick of the battle, but she nodded. "Okay, Cody. But if I see Taja, I'm taking her down. And if anybody gets to her and you can just injure her and hold her, save her for me. I wanna kill that bitch myself."

"We all do, Roberta," Cody said. "But we go in as a team, and we come out the same way, with all our friends."

Roberta nodded again and climbed in the truck. Jazz and Zeke rode in the other one with Cody and Serena, and Dante jumped in with them. The twelve security personnel split up evenly in the trucks, and they rode down the ramps and out into the dark desert night with the witching hour fast approaching.

Cody held a tracking device slightly larger than a cell phone in his hand. He punched some buttons and the display lit up. Then he turned to Jazz and gave her the dark man look. Before he could say anything, she put her hands on his cheeks and kissed him.

"For luck," she said after they parted.

He licked his lips and nodded. "Let's go get our family back."

Chapter 32

They rode without lights and followed the signal. Jazz's eyes adjusted to the darkness, and she saw lights in the distance. A structure took shape ahead of them, clearly manmade and not of the desert. She made out the walls of a fortress against the skyline, lit up by outdoor floodlights, and saw various trees poking out above the walls, an anomaly in the mostly barren terrain.

The sprawling roof of an enormous estate was visible through the boughs of the trees, and Cody lowered the mike of his headset to his lips.

"Okay, Curtis and Lauretta, you're up," he said, speaking to the security guards operating the missile launchers atop the trucks. "On my signal, blow us a new gate fifty feet east of the southwest corner of that wall."

The trucks roared through the night, so loud Jazz was afraid they'd give their presence away, and moved closer to the wall. At a few hundred yards away, Cody spoke into the mike.

"Okay, everybody. We deploy immediately upon breaching the wall, otherwise we're sitting ducks. I knew we'd have to blow something up. As soon as the wall goes down, they're gonna know we're here, if they don't already. Curtis, Lauretta, on my mark."

Jazz put her hands over her ears, and Zeke did the same.

"Ready. Two, one, fire!"

The truck rocked with the roar of the missile launcher, and Jazz watched a portion of the wall crumble and spray rubble with the direct hits.

"Clear us a path guys!" Cody shouted. "Fire again!"

The second volley tore the rubble apart at the base of the wall, and the trucks raced forward toward the breach, Jazz's in the lead and the other right behind them.

"This is it, Jazz," Cody said. "Hang on, ride's gonna get bumpy."

Jazz wrapped one arm around Zeke and grabbed a horizontal bar overhead. They plunged through the new hole in the wall, got mired in the rocky debris for a heartbeat, but rolled over it. Bouncing and shaking like a spine-shattering roller coaster from Hell, they roared into the grounds of the desert fortress. The other truck barreled through the breach right on their tail, and they lurched forward together a hundred feet into the grounds and jolted to a halt.

"Deploy! Let's go, let's go!" Cody shouted into his mike.

Jazz wanted to make Zeke and Dante stay behind, but they both leaped toward the exit with the others. She drew her pistol, hopped out, and hurried after them with Cody at her side. He brandished a pistol in each hand.

"Stick with me, Jazz," he said, and they raced toward the forbidding mansion side by side.

The crack and echo of gunfire already surrounded her. Something flashed over her head, and she glanced behind her and saw their big truck explode. Thanking God that she hadn't left Zeke and Dante behind, she raced by Cody's side and tried to spot them, but couldn't.

A couple of men stood at the steps of the portico a hundred yards ahead of her, shouting and firing in their direction. One of them dropped, and the other turned toward the mansion and fled up the steps. He jerked to a halt, and tumbled backward down the steps.

Roberta was on the job somewhere in the dark night.

The Homestead crew fanned out and stormed the mansion amid shouts of alarm. Several men burst out of the front doors and around the sides of the estate and started firing as flashes of light flickered from some of the windows. Jazz saw three Homestead security personnel drop one after the

290

other, and wondered when she would feel the final jolt and join them.

She felt buzzing bees whistle past her from behind, and glanced up toward the southeast corner of the wall. A man stood atop it, flames spitting out rapid-fire from the short-barreled automatic weapon in his hands. He howled, and Jazz stumbled and recovered, then he pitched over the wall backward, his gun spraying lead into the desert night sky.

Go, Roberta, go…

Jazz pumped her arms and legs, willed the bullets to miss, and felt long blades of grass swish against her ankles and calves. They seemed to caress her as she relived part of her dream of the night before. She flew toward the mansion as if she was propelled by the lush greenery at her feet, and silently prayed, *Chaz Chaz Chaz…*

*****

Kaylee felt the rush. She shivered as the truth of her power flowed through her, and woke from her blissful dream of communion. She was a part of her friends now, as strong as their mighty roots that reached deep beneath the earth with persistent, probing tendrils. They rustled and caressed her as they woke with her at the sudden noisy intrusion.

The darkness held no sway over Kaylee. Her friends glowed all around her with an eerie emerald light, and she smiled. The sounds that had woken her were explosions and gunfire—signals that her dark man had finally come for her.

She snickered, picturing Jai in her mind, and silently whispered to her friends and called them to come out and play.

*****

Jazz stumbled again as the ground rumbled beneath her feet. She hadn't heard of earthquakes in the Arizona desert, but that's what it felt like. Cody fired one, two, three shots, and a man standing and shooting at them from sixty feet away dropped.

"Come on, Jazz, we're almost in!"

Jazz didn't waste any ammo firing at what she couldn't hit; she was saving it. She gasped as a ripple in the ground carried her and Cody forward as if they were surfing toward shore on a point break. This had to be an earthquake.

Cody shouted as the ground rose a foot beneath them. A man crouching behind the bushes beside the bursting tiled walkway sprang up and fired at them. Cody and Jazz ducked and rolled at the same time. Jazz got to her feet and fired twice at him and missed. Cody flew at the man, kicked out, knocked the gun out of his hands, and fired a point-blank shot between his eyes.

"I got your back, Jazz, go!" he shouted, and she hauled ass toward the portico steps.

Another man popped out from behind the banister beside the steps and shot at them. Jazz shrieked and fired at him. She kept squeezing the trigger again and again. He screamed and dropped his gun, flailing as the ground beneath him collapsed and sucked his six-foot frame down into it.

Jazz staggered up the steps with her pistol pointed at where he'd stood, and shook her head. *I did* not *just see that happen.* She kept waiting for him to burst back out of the pile of fresh, loamy soil and blow her away.

"Go, Jazz!" Cody howled. He fired at another man who popped out behind the doorway. The man gurgled and dropped. Cody shot him again and leaped over him and through the doorway. Jazz stumbled and followed. She gasped as several of the window panes on the lowest floor suddenly burst open. The last thing she saw before she plunged through the doorway was impossible, a hallucination.

There had *not* been wriggling vines and roots protruding from the broken windows when she dashed inside. She was having adrenaline-induced delusions.

The entire structure seemed to shudder as she followed Cody inside, and a mighty rumble shook it. The sound was deafening, as if monstrous chunks of brimstone were churning together beneath the earth's crust and spewing out the magmatic roar of the damned.

Something beyond her ken was happening, but she had no time to think.

Plaster and drywall, crown and molding, even the thick-tiled floor beneath her cracked and splintered, unable to restrain the beast clamoring to break through.

Cody shot at an approaching man who was firing at them from a hallway to the right of the expansive foyer. He missed, fired again, and dropped him. He holstered one of his pistols and grabbed Jazz's arm.

"Come on, Jazz! Let's go find Chaz!"

She tried to shut out the roar of battle and stifle the ringing in her ears, and hurried up the elaborate stairway beside Cody to the second floor. The whole place was falling apart, collapsing from within as if Mother Earth herself intended on swallowing it whole.

Jazz started shouting her son's name as she and Cody scrambled down the second floor hallway and pounded on closed doors.

"Chaz!"

*****

Kaylee heard the desperate panting whine from one of the smaller runners, and sympathized with it. She almost tasted the sweat and fear pouring out of the little one who ran beside the four galloping paws raking her outer skin.

She ripped her new arms out of the dirt, and her coiling roots wrapped around the desperate duo and lifted them off her. She didn't squeeze yet. Instead, she poked her face out of the fluid bark and glared at them.

"Are you with the dark man?" she asked.

The little black boy scowled at her, and a score of humongous bees with poisonous, dripping probosces suddenly appeared, ready to sting her and suck her honey from her veins. The dog whined and twitched in her roots' grasp. The boy sneered, ready to die but defiant, and she liked his bravado.

"Yeah," he said, unfazed by her magic. "Now let me go so I can help my friends!" The soundless, oversized bees surrounding him poised to strike. Kaylee laughed, her bark-face glistening with the umber, mahogany, and grays of pine, redwood, and oak.

"Those aren't real. Did you make them?" she asked, watching the whirly-winged creatures surrounding him.

"Yeah," the little boy said. "And I can make a lot worse, so let me go."

"Way cool. What's your name?"

"Zeke."

"Hi, Zeke. Who's your friend?"

"That's Dante. He's Chaz's dog, and Chaz is my friend. And we came here to rescue him, so kill us now or let us go!"

Kaylee grinned. Zeke had a lot of guts for such a little guy. "Hi, Dante. He's a good boy."

Dante quit thrashing and stared at her, and Zeke shook his head.

"Who… what are you?"

"A friend. My name's Kaylee. Come with me, Zeke. I can help you find your friends, and we can help them escape together. Will you come play with us?"

Zeke looked at her rippling bark-face, her twining roots and vines. He pursed his big lips, and smiled.

"Yeah."

*****

Jazz tried to remember how many shots she had fired as she and Cody hurried down the deserted hallway. She just remembered pulling the trigger over and over.

"Chaz!" she called out.

"Chaz! Kaylee!" Cody shouted.

They approached an adjacent hallway halfway down the one they were searching, and Cody put an arm behind him and pushed Jazz against the wall. He put a finger to his lips and crouched.

A man sprang out of the adjacent hall with a pistol aimed at them. Cody's leg shot up and kicked the gun out of his hands, then Cody spun and kicked him in the chest. The man grunted and went flying down the hall with the blow, and scrabbled for his pistol on the floor. Cody shot him in the back twice, ejected his spent magazine, and replaced it with a fresh one.

"Come on, Jazz, this way." He headed down the hallway where the man had popped out, and Jazz hurried after him.

They shouted for Chaz and Kaylee. Halfway down the hall a door flew open and a hurricane spat out of it. The man moved like greased lightning, and slammed into Cody's side. Jazz stumbled and fell, dropping her pistol as Cody spun and blocked a kick and a punch. Jazz knew this guy was an Extractor by the empty grin on his face and the way he moved, and she scrambled for her pistol.

Cody raised his gun arm, and the Extractor kicked his pistol out of his hand and pointed his own pistol at Cody and fired. Cody deflected the Extractor's gun hand and the shot flew past his shoulder, then Cody dove at him and engaged him hand to hand.

They whipped around, grappled with each other, and slammed into the wall. The Extractor's pistol went flying down the hall. Jazz finally snatched up her pistol and pointed it at them. They were moving so fast she was afraid she'd hit Cody, and she didn't fire.

They spun down the hall ahead of her, bounced each

other off the walls and tried to gain the advantage, and the impossible happened again. The walls, floor, and ceiling buckled, then burst and sprayed sheetrock and wood splinters everywhere. Jazz flinched backward as thick roots and vines spilled out of the widening cracks in the walls and floor. They writhed and slithered like tentacles reaching out for prey, and quickly filled the space in the hallway.

Jazz couldn't get through, and couldn't get a shot off as the living roots and branches grew into a barrier between her and Cody. She backed up, just out of their probing reach.

"Cody!"

"Go get Chaz! I got this guy!"

Cody and the Extractor separated, and the Extractor laughed. Jazz watched through the quickly closing space between the vines and roots as the Extractor spoke.

"I've been waiting for this moment for a long time, CJ."

Cody snorted. "Hiya, Cain. What, you've been waiting to die?"

"You're mine, CJ."

"I'll find you, Jazz!" Cody called out, and gestured toward himself with his fingers. "Come on, tough guy. Show me what you got."

The gap in the branches closed, and Jazz cursed, spun around, and hustled back down the hallway the way they'd come. She arrived at the landing at the top of the foyer stairs, and was about to try the hallway directly across from her on the other side of the landing when something amazing caught her eye through the huge panes looking out on the front of the grounds.

She gasped, mesmerized by the spectacle.

A cacophony of thunderous creaks and groans that sounded like hardwoods rubbing together accompanied the roiling mass of vegetation scuttling toward the front of the mansion. The blob of greenery was as big as a house and growing, and Jazz's eyes goggled as the floodlights shone on the figures riding in the forward center of the mass. The coiling vines and roots carried them aloft, bore them like a pair of wicker thrones parading the arrival of royalty.

Zeke scowled in his makeshift chair, and Dante barked, his tail wagging as if he'd discovered the best new game of all. A girl's sneering face as big as Zeke protruded out of a thick branch beside him. Her features appeared to be made of bark, but they flowed and rippled as the lush leviathan approached the mansion.

A battalion of mutant wasps each as big as a full-grown cat swarmed around the mass, their deadly stingers poised to strike. They darted downward, diving toward the four men guarding the front entrance. Jazz watched six Homestead security guards' bodies laying on the ground disappear beneath the forward edge of the mass, and wondered how many of their guys remained. The four men at the top of the portico steps had their hands full shooting at giant wasps and a roiling mass of trees and vines.

They shouted and cursed, and a pair of slithering roots reached out of the mass and snatched the legs of one of the defenders. The roots lifted the screaming man ten feet in the air upside down and ripped him in half like a giant wishbone.

Two of the men spotted Zeke and Dante, and turned their guns on them. A score of mutant wasps dove at them, confusing their line of sight, but the wasps either passed right through them or dissipated when they touched.

Two thick vines shot out of the mass and twined around the men like mighty pythons wrapping around their prey, and lifted them up. The men screamed as the vines squeezed. They burst from the pressure, and blood and gore sprayed out of their crushed bodies.

The remaining man on the steps shouted, "Fuck this!" and dashed back through the open front doors. From the landing atop the foyer stairs, Jazz shot him in the chest twice, and he dropped.

"Fuck *you*, buddy," she said, and dashed down the opposite hallway as the mass of greenery advanced up the portico steps.

Jazz pounded on closed doors, shouted for Chaz as she checked the doorknobs. They were all locked. A quarter of the way down the hall, she turned from one door to see a smiling figure turn a corner and stroll toward her with a pistol aimed at her.

It was Taja.

Jazz yelped and raised her pistol as Taja fired. Something tugged at her shoulder, knocking her backward. She squeezed the trigger, but the slide was open, the chamber empty. Taja laughed and holstered her pistol.

Jazz's hands trembled, her shoulder throbbing. Her fingers fumbled for the magazine release. She finally found it, ejected the spent magazine, and reached for a spare at her belt.

Taja seemed to fly down the hall at her. She dove feet first at Jazz and kicked into her chest like a sledgehammer. Jazz's pistol flew from her hands, clacking on the hall tiles behind her, and she jerked backward with the blow and landed on her back. Her head hit the floor hard, and sirens went off in her brain. She shook her head, trying to dispel the spinning stars, and glared up at Taja.

"Hi, Jazz." Taja leered at her. "I was hoping we would run into each other. This is going to be so much fun."

Chapter 33

Cody fought the battle of his life while tree roots and thick vines crawled through holes and cracks in the floor and walls. Cain was one of the best Extractors, and the one who had shot Cody when he'd first fled from Taja.

Cain kicked and spun and punched. Cody deflected the blows, looking for a hole in his flurrying attack. Cain delivered a lightning quick kick to Cody's head. Cody barely ducked and knocked aside his foot in time.

He caught Cain off balance and sprang at him right as Cain drew a knife with a wicked eight-inch blade. Cody grabbed his knife hand and they tumbled to the floor together in a blaze of kicking legs and grappling arms.

They rolled around, and Cody saw the sudden doubt in Cain's eyes. He rammed an elbow into Cain's nose, and slammed Cain's hand into a gnarled root protruding from the wall.

The effect was instantaneous. The root wrapped around Cain's hand. Cain shouted and tried to pull his arm free, and Cody rolled off him and sprang to his feet. Cain grabbed the knife with his free hand and slashed at the root, and it thrashed, grew, and wrapped around his knife hand. Cain howled as the root squeezed, tore through flesh, and crushed bone.

Cody darted down the hall, snagged his pistol off the floor, and spun and shot Cain in the head. The roots slithered off Cain's limp arms and receded into the crack in the wall. Cody huffed and shook his head. He'd been about to beat Cain hand-to-hand, and something—or some*one*—had just helped make the job easier.

He glanced back the way he'd come. He couldn't get through the mass of vegetation, so he headed down the hall.

When he reached a ninety-degree turn, he leaped forward and spun to face the new hallway with his pistol raised. The hallway was empty.

Evenly spaced doors flanked the exterior hall wall, but the interior wall sported only a single set of double doors midway down the hall. Warning signals blared in his mind as he glanced at the security cameras in the far corners. Feeling like time was running out, he dashed toward the double doors, shot the doorknobs, and kicked the doors inward.

He ducked and rolled inside when they flew open, ending up in a crouch. He spun with his pistol aimed at the shadowy interior of the room, looking for a target. Not spotting any movement in the gloom, he looked to a set of stairs leading to a room above him.

He heard a rustle from up there, and crept up the steps with his pistol aimed upward, ready to open fire.

The tang of trouble tickled his nostrils.

The room above was dark. He slipped past the banister at the top, and a light flickered on behind a large mahogany desk at the southeast end of the room. He spun and pointed his pistol at the smiling figure sitting behind the desk, feeling as if bullets were about to punch through his back and out his chest. Holding his fire, his finger tight on the trigger, he spun in a quick three-sixty. The room was empty except for him and the man behind the desk, and Cody faced him again.

Soulsnatcher still looked as old as dirt and dinosaurs, but he no longer looked like a prime candidate for the undertaker. He grinned at Cody, his ruddy cheeks suffused with a healthy glow that had been absent the last time Cody had seen him.

"CJ! Wonderful to see you again. I knew we would meet again one day."

Cody squeezed and fired, put six shots straight through him into the high-backed chair he sat in.

Nothing happened except for the chair bucking with the shots. It was as if Cody had just shot a ghost. Cody's nostrils quivered, itching.

Soulsnatcher didn't say anything for a few seconds. Then he finally laughed and stood. The chair didn't move with his motion.

"I knew you wouldn't be happy to see me, CJ, so I had one of my talented little friends create this elaborate illusion, projecting my real-time likeness from a safe location nearby. Disappointed? You shouldn't be. I did it just for you. Somehow I knew you would find me first."

"Dammit!" Cody growled. His spidey-senses were tingling.

"Really, CJ. Taja was right. You should come back to our side. The strong side. You were seduced by a false angel of mercy. You and I are really both the same, down deep inside."

"The fuck we are!"

Soulsnatcher pointed out one of the windows to a field at the back of the mansion. "See that helicopter down there? The helipad it's parked on is the roof of my emergency escape bunker. That's my ride out of here. You and Benjamin have sorely inconvenienced me, and you're going to pay dearly for it. Watch out the window. I'm waving goodbye to you, CJ."

"Oh, shit," Cody muttered as he figured it out. He fired at the window and dove toward it, knowing he didn't have time to dash down the stairs and out of the rooms.

The force of the explosion catapulted him through the shattering glass before he even heard its roar.

*****

Roberta lay in the unusually tall grass fifty feet from the wall, amazed by how the blades seemed to wrap around her and help conceal her as she picked out her targets. With her Barrett Model 82A1 semi-automatic .50 caliber rifle, she dropped a man with almost every shot.

She'd watched six of her friends drop from enemy fire,

and only saw two of the other six standing. Zeke and Dante had disappeared into the impossible churning jungle that she didn't want to think about now.

She glanced at Serena slipping into a downstairs window, and saw Marco sneaking around the grounds, waiting for the enemy to pop up out of nowhere. Focusing on the front entrance, she watched the ground roll like an ocean wave— *impossible*—and saw Cody and Jazz tumble toward the steps and confront two guards. Cody shot one and ran inside, and Jazz followed.

The other guard just seemed to disappear, sucked into the dirt like a snack for an underworld demon. Roberta couldn't think about that now either, or about the roots and vines exploding out of the downstairs windows.

Or about Kino. Something inside her had died with him, and she knew she would forever see him falling, and forever fall with him. But this wasn't about getting revenge, even though she ached for it. This was about rescuing the children, and getting rid of Taja and Soulsnatcher, so they could never do this again.

After that was done, Roberta could finally sink into the sea of grief drowning her, and suffocate in it. Until then, she concentrated on her task, and kept a wary eye out for the two main targets.

Four more defenders popped out of the front entrance, but the churning jungle blocked her shot before she could line up her sights on them.

She checked her perimeter and the wall behind her, then leaped up and hustled toward the east side of the mansion in a crouch. Over the sounds of shouting and gunfire, she heard an explosion from the rear of the mansion, along with the unmistakable sound of helicopter rotors.

"Oh no," she said, scowling. "You and Soulsnatcher aren't getting away that easy, Taja."

She hurried across the lawn, hoping she wasn't too late.

Her heart raced and she cursed as she saw a copter rise. She hit tile walkway and hauled ass to the southeast corner of the deck.

And collided with the Extractor rounding the corner from the other direction.

*****

Chaz wanted to die. He couldn't escape the small windowless room that the evil Tinga had thrown and locked him in after the explosions. He hoped it was Mother and the Guardians coming to rescue him, because he didn't know how long he could last this time.

His chest ached worse than ever. He didn't know if it was heartache, or if his fragile heart was finally giving up. The pressure felt like somebody as big as Kino was sitting on him, and that thought just made him start crying again.

The helicopter ride and the following plane ride in the dark night had seemed to last forever. He'd spent the whole trip worrying that someone would find the small object Kino had stuffed in his shoe, but no one ever checked. His heart felt like it was going to burst the entire flight, until he finally fell asleep from exhaustion. When he could no longer keep his eyes open and felt his lids fall, he'd thought it was for the last time.

He paced his room, unable to sit still, praying that Mother and the Guardians were coming for him.

The whole room started quaking, and he fell on his butt, certain it was the big one. The thunderous rumble he heard sounded like a mighty beast from Hell was trying to bust out beneath him.

The floor heaved upward, cracked in the center of the room, and canted at an angle. He slid a few feet, and the wall beside him split open in the sudden strobe flash of the flickering lights. Drywall cracked and burst apart, and he ducked. When he looked up, there was a three-foot-wide fissure in the wall, and a pretty golden-furred dog was poking its head through it.

"Hey, boy." Chaz crawled toward the dog and petted it. "Who are you?"

"Sadie, and she's a girl. Who's there?"

Chaz flinched at the English-accented voice and peered into the gloom. The lights quit flickering and stayed on, and a young black man emerged from the settling sheetrock dust.

"I'm Chaz. They killed Kino and kidnapped me and a bunch of the other kids and brought us here. Who are you?"

"I'm Jai."

"Hi, Jai, pleased to meetcha!" Chaz stroked Sadie's soft fur. Jai didn't seem to be looking at anything, but he smiled and thrust his hand out. Chaz took it and shook it, glad to find a friend in this dismal prison.

"I'm pleased to meet you too, Chaz."

"I like the way you talk."

Jai chuckled. "Thank you, Chaz. Do you see a way out of here, now that the place is apparently falling apart?"

Chaz waved a hand in front of Jai's face. "Wow, you're like blind as a bat, aren't you? And I never knew black guys were like... English or something."

Jai laughed. "I like you, Chaz. You speak your mind freely. And yes, I'm blind."

"Wow. I'm sorry. Have you been blind your whole life?"

"No, it was an accident, several years ago. And it's okay."

"So you could see once?"

Jai sighed, and his smile looked sad. "Yeah."

Chaz thought about that, and some of the pressure eased off his heart. He let go of Sadie. "Scoot back, I'm comin' in."

Jai moved back, and Sadie followed and stood at his side. Chaz crawled through the gap and faced Jai.

"Don't freak out or nothin'," Chaz said, and held his arms up. "But I need to... hug you."

Jai looked puzzled at first, but he nodded. "Okay." He bent toward Chaz with open arms, and Chaz embraced him and gave him his gift.

Thirty seconds later, Jai gasped and fell to his knees. Chaz slumped, but Jai caught him before he hit the floor, and Chaz looked up into his eyes.

"Oh my God," Jai said, and Chaz felt him tremble. "Chaz, I can see you! I can bloody see again! You're a healer!"

Sadie barked, wagged her tail.

"Sadie! You're a pretty girl." Jai looked back at Chaz. "I can't bloody believe it. Chaz, I'm so... what's wrong?"

Chaz felt the pressure again, and couldn't move. If Jai wasn't holding him, he would have collapsed. He wheezed, feeling as if the air was suddenly thicker.

"I think I... overdid it." His eyelids were slowly closing. "Mother..."

"Chaz!" Jai lowered him gently to the floor and kneeled beside him as the room seemed to get darker.

"I got a weak heart," Chaz said, and it came out in a whisper. He barely even felt the floor rumbling beneath him.

"Hang in there, Chaz. My turn." Jai grinned, crouched over him, and right as Chaz's eyelids slid shut and darkness descended, Jai put his hands on Chaz's heart.

Chapter 34

Jazz crawled backward a few feet, spun, and dove for her pistol. Right before she reached it, something hard and powerful slammed into her rear, and she flew forward and smacked her cheek into the wall. She rolled over and glared up at Taja, who stood smiling a few feet too far away to reach out and touch.

Taja kicked Jazz's pistol down the hallway behind her and took a stride toward Jazz. She stopped and looked down at Jazz's bandaged leg, and Jazz tried to grab Taja's ankle.

Taja kicked her hand away, sneered, and kicked her bloody, bandaged leg.

Jazz couldn't hold back the scream. The blow sent her rolling down the hall. She clutched her thigh, a crimson haze settling over her vision. She was about to pass out, but gritted her teeth and hung on. If she fainted, it was over.

She struggled to her feet with dark angels fluttering their wings in her mind, beckoning her to come join them. Blinking away the pain, she hobbled toward Taja, reached out to her.

Taja slapped her hands away and kicked her in the chest so hard it sent her flying several feet backward. She landed on her back and slid on the unyielding tile of the balcony overlooking the foyer. She lay there, struggling just to breathe.

As she looked up, Taja strode toward her, sporting a grim smile.

"You're the reason everything's fucked up, Jazz. And I'm loving making you pay for it. I saw your stupid, pathetic video. Pissy bitch. We fooled you all with Pablo, didn't we? Did I not warn you not to fuck with me? Did I not tell you what I would do to you if you did?"

Jazz struggled to one knee and tried to rise, but stumbled

against the balcony railing. She glimpsed behind her and saw the sprawl of quivering vegetation on the foyer floor, some of it crawling up the walls. Were Zeke and Dante still alive? Or had they been swallowed by the animated mass of foliage? Jazz turned and faced Taja. She was so close now, just a little closer...

She reached clutching hands out to Taja, and Taja laughed and spun around so fast Jazz couldn't track the movement. Taja's boot heel smacked into her chin, and she flew backward into the railing. She felt it give behind her, heard the wood handrail crack, and reached for Taja as she fell screaming, knowing it was over, knowing how Kino must have felt.

Oh Chaz, baby, no!

She landed on the corpse of the man she'd shot earlier, surrounded by a bed of lush greenery. She choked, tried to suck in air. Something was definitely broken, maybe beyond repair. Her left wrist was bent at an odd angle, and she spat up blood and maybe a tooth as darkness tried to overcome her.

Rolling off the man's body, she finally gasped in a sweet breath of air. Her head spun with the foyer walls and stairway. She lay on the floor and tried to move, angled her pounding head around to face the stairs, and watched Taja descend them.

The witch seemed to glide down the steps, as if everything was a dream, but it wasn't like Jazz's crazy dream from the night before when the dark man magically swooped down and rescued her and they fell in love and lived happily ever after. This was a nightmare. Taja strode up to her and sneered, glaring down at her. Where was her dark man when she needed him most?

"Sorry you fucking crossed me yet, bitch?" Taja said, leering.

"Sorry?" Jazz choked out. "I'll show you sorry."

Taja laughed and drew a wicked-looking knife with a long blade out of a sheath at her waist. She raised it above her head, thrust her other hand out, and grabbed Jazz's throat.

Finally.

Jazz laughed, spraying blood, and reached her good right hand up and grasped Taja's wrist. She didn't try to pry it off her throat, knew she couldn't, and didn't have to. Taja hesitated, her knife hand poised to strike.

"What the fuck are you laughing about, bitch? You're about to die."

Before Taja could slash or stab her, Jazz grinned and said, "This." She clenched Taja's wrist. "This is for Daddy, and for Kino."

Jazz gave Taja every bit of her power, everything she'd been saving up for twenty years. It flowed out of her like aftershock from an atomic explosion.

Taja's eyes bulged and her lips pulled back from her teeth in a horrified grimace. She dropped the knife, and it clattered to the floor. She ripped her arm off Jazz's throat and out of her grasp, staggered backward, and crumpled to the floor a few feet away. Wrapping her arms around her torso, she curled up into a fetal ball and groaned.

"What the fuck did you just do to me?"

Jazz rolled over and crawled on two shaky knees and one good hand toward Taja, looked down at her.

"Did I not warn you, Taja? Did I not tell you how sorry you'd be when I finally found you?"

Taja gasped and her eyes bugged out. "Oh no. What—"

"Mother said it was a curse. Ever since I started showing it when I turned eleven, she never touched me again. She left us a year later. Said I had cursed our whole family. But Daddy stuck with me. And we never told anybody about it, not even Chaz. Daddy always said one day it would finally manifest itself in a good way."

Jazz slowly rose, everything aching and burning and broken, but she smiled. Triumph softened the pain.

"I think it just did."

Taja moaned. "No, no, no, make it stop. What the fuck *is* this?"

"Mother said it skipped her generation. But it got me, and Chaz too. Just in radically different ways."

Taja could only moan and thrash around, as if dagger-toothed parasites were eating her up from the inside out.

"You don't even recognize it, do you, Taja? It's called regret. Remorse. Something you wouldn't know anything about. It must be worse than physical pain for you. Feel the sorrow, Taja. For every terrible thing you've ever done, everyone you've ever hurt, every family you've torn apart.

"For what you did to Cody. For killing Kino." Jazz hobbled a step backward. "For hurting my baby. Choke on it, bitch."

"No... make it go away, please."

Jazz turned away, heard shouts, and saw her dark man plunge through a set of double doors at the rear of the foyer. Bloody and covered in soot and ashes, he staggered up to her, his eyes and his gun on Taja.

Jazz had never seen anything look so good. Praying for Daddy and Chaz and all the children and all her new friends, she hobbled toward him and wrapped her arms around his neck. Before he could speak, she kissed him.

"Oh, Cody," she breathed when they parted.

He choked out a laugh. "I'm happy to see you too, Jazz. What the... hell did you do to her?"

She looked back at Taja, watched her writhe on the floor, and gazed into Cody's dark eyes.

"I made her sorry. Like I promised I would."

Cody looked at Taja, his jaw half-open. He winced, lowered his pistol, and started to say something, and Jazz kissed him again. When they drew back, his strong arms caught her and held her up, just like in her dream. He squinted at her.

"Damn, girl. I wondered why you kept saying that. Remind me not to ever piss you off."

"Don't ever piss me off, dark man."

"Okay."

Jazz smiled. "So where were you? What happened to you?"

"I got blown up, and fell off the roof. A series of roofs, actually. It's a long story. I'll tell you later."

"Damn, Cody."

"It's just a flesh wound. I'm feeling better."

Jazz shook her head. "If you say so. You look like Hell."

"Thanks. Same to you."

"So can we go find Chaz and Daddy now?"

"If we can get through this maze of roots and vines, yeah."

Jazz's eyes widened. "Hey. I just thought of something. Isn't that what Mara said she saw in her vision?"

"Yep. And I bet I know where they came from. But what about Taja?"

Jazz looked at Taja, then back at Cody. "She can't hurt anyone anymore, Cody."

"Make it stop, please," Taja whimpered.

They heard shouts coming from upstairs and a rustle from the balcony, and looked up. A tangle of vegetation opened up and churned out a barefoot human figure in scuffed brown chinos and a green blouse. It was female, but its skin looked like fluid bark.

The greenery behind her sounded like a chorus of maracas out of sync and spat out a man in a rumpled suit. He tumbled to the balcony floor and slammed into the rail. A vine snaked upward and snatched a pistol out of his shoulder holster and tossed it down the hall, and the man gazed up at the tree girl.

She shook her head. "You need to get a new job, Gordon." The vines wriggled around her. "Turn over a new leaf."

The man nodded. "Yes, ma'am."

The tree girl sneered at him. "You have to earn your place on your own."

The man swallowed, slowly stood, and nodded again. "Thank you, Kaylee."

He turned and descended the steps, breathing deeply as he watched the gathering below him. The tree girl approached the gap in the railing where Jazz had fallen through and looked down at them.

Taja still moaned and groaned. She was under the balcony, where the tree girl couldn't see her. The girl with the bark-face smiled, and her pulpy complexion rippled and became that of a normal, pretty teenage girl.

"Hey, Kaylee," Cody said, waving.

"About time, dark man," Kaylee said. "What took you so damn long?"

"Car blew up. Had to get another. Hopped-up vintage '68 Camaros are a bitch to find."

"Well, better late than never. Glad you could join the party. I've been real busy."

Cody grinned. "Yeah, I can see that."

"Who's your busted up friend?"

Cody gestured to Jazz. "Jazz, Kaylee. Kaylee, Jazz."

Jazz waved. Kaylee nodded and looked left, down the second floor hallway, and her eyes widened and her mouth dropped open. Excited shouts, laughter, and barking preceded the odd quintet that ran into view.

"Chaz!" Jazz squealed. She hobbled toward the stairs, and Cody took her arm and helped her along.

"Mother!" Chaz and Zeke hurried down the stairs, followed by Dante. The handsome young black man with them stopped at the top of the stairs, his eyes on Kaylee. The pretty Golden Retriever stopped beside him.

"Kaylee?" the young man said, his eyebrows raised. "Is that you?"

"Jai!" Kaylee squeaked, and ran toward him. She leaped

into his arms and they embraced.

"I can see you!" Jai laughed and picked her up, spun her around.

"Jai, what happened? How—?"

"My new friend Chaz healed me." Jai pointed at Chaz, who hurtled down the steps at breakneck speed.

"Oh, Jai!" Kaylee grabbed his face in her hands and kissed him.

Chaz practically flew into Jazz's arms. If Cody hadn't been supporting her, he would have knocked her down. She squeezed her precious boy, kissed him all over, and fresh tears streamed down her cheeks.

"Oh, Binky, I'm so happy."

"Me too, Mother. I was so scared, and worried. I thought I would never see you again. And you won't believe what just happened to me." He pointed up the stairs at the young man kissing Kaylee. "My new friend Jai just healed me."

"What?" Jazz's brow wrinkled and she looked up at Jai and Kaylee.

"He's a healer, just like me. My heart is *so* strong now, Mother. I feel like I could run up like a hundred mountains right now and not even get tired."

Jazz couldn't believe her ears. It was too good to be true. Her body shook with deep sobs as she squeezed him. Dante pranced around them, wanting to be a part of the celebration.

"Mother, you're hurt. Here."

"Chaz, wait—" Jazz felt a jolt and gasped. She actually felt the broken bones in her wrist knit together and heal, felt strength suffuse her. The pain in her leg, shoulder, head, cheek, jaw, and back faded, and disappeared.

"Oh, Binky, don't overdo it."

"It's okay, Mother. I feel like I can heal the whole world right now."

Maybe you can. Jazz squeezed and kissed him again.

Kaylee and Jai were walking down the stairs hand in

hand. Halfway down, Kaylee gasped. She let go of Jai's hand and dashed down two steps at a time, hurried around Jazz and the others, and stood scowling with her fists clenched a few feet from Taja.

Vines curled up from the floor and fluttered in the air around her as if a brisk breeze were whipping them into a frenzy, and they reached toward Taja.

"You evil bitch, did you kill my parents?"

Taja moaned, reached a hand toward Kaylee. "I'm sorry, Kaylee. Oh God, I'm so sorry…"

"Did you kill them?" The vines quivered around Kaylee like serpents coiled to strike.

"Please, I can't… it's killing me…"

"Ahh!" Kaylee growled. The vines pounced on Taja, squeezed her legs and arms.

"Do it," Taja said, closing her eyes.

"Don't, Kaylee." Cody put an arm on her shoulder. She turned to him, anger and tears battling in her eyes. "Don't stain your soul with that. Besides, what Jazz did to her is far worse punishment. Killing her would be merciful now."

Kaylee trembled, and the vines trembled with her. Tears spilled out of her eyes and rolled down her cheeks. She finally slumped, the vines dropped to the floor, and she reached up and threw her arms around Cody's neck. He wrapped his arms around her and held her.

"I kept praying you would come," Kaylee said, her eyes closed. "I knew you would come for me, dark man."

"Damn straight, girl." Cody let her go when several excited voices came from the second floor. Jazz and Chaz looked up with everyone else, and Jazz held her breath.

Serena sauntered into view, smiling and leading a gaggle of chattering children like a psychic Pied Piper. She cradled Andrea in one arm, and a smiling little Asian boy held her other hand, skipping alongside her. Lynette and Anthony and the other two missing Homestead children were with them, holding hands with five other children Jazz didn't recognize. Jazz's smile faltered when she didn't see her father with them.

The troupe headed down the stairs together, and Kaylee called out, "Jhin!"

The Asian boy grinned and let go of Serena's hand. He ran down the stairs and leaped into Kaylee's waiting arms. "Hi, Kaylee. I knew you would save us."

"Oh, Jhin, thank you." Kaylee squeezed him and spun him around, vines writhed upward around them, and Jhin giggled.

Jazz looked at Cody, and he held up a hand, signaling her to wait. Amid the excited chatter, a shout echoed behind them.

"You bitch!"

Everyone turned to see Roberta striding through the rear double doors. She had a bloody nose and a bruise on her cheek, and clutched her pistol in both hands, aiming it at Taja.

"I want my Kino back!"

"I'm sorry, so sorry, please help me..." Taja was blubbering now.

"Die, bitch!"

"Roberta, don't!" Cody shouted. He hurried over beside her and she looked at him, her face scrunched up in anguish.

"Why not? Cody, what... happened to her?"

"Jazz made her sorry, just like she kept saying she would."

Roberta frowned. "You mean... Oh my God." She looked over at Jazz. "Jazz?"

Jazz shrugged. "Having the power to make people feel regret isn't the kind of secret I wanted to share with my new friends. Or anybody else but my enemies."

Roberta slumped, shook her head, and looked up at Cody. "Lars... Soulsnatcher... got away."

Cody nodded. "I know. But he'll be licking his wounds for a while."

She nodded back, and she and Cody moved away from Taja and joined the others. Taja writhed and whimpered, reached a trembling hand out.

"Jazz, please." She retched. "How long?"

Jazz scowled at her. "I don't know, Taja. Daddy and I never tested it, after the incident with Mother, and we never heard from her again. And I haven't used it since, until now. It's a terrible power to have, but a worse one to receive, isn't it? Why don't you call me in about five years, and let me know if it still hurts."

"No, oh God, nooo…"

Jazz smiled and wriggled her fingers. "Ta-ta!"

The group walked away together and gathered in the foyer. Everybody jumped and turned when the crack of a gunshot rang out behind them.

Taja had apparently saved at least one round, and had put it to good use. Jazz realized only after the echo died that she should have asked her where Daddy was.

Roberta looked back at Taja's motionless body and nodded, her eyes flooding with tears. She holstered her pistol and sat down. Leaning against the banister, she closed her eyes, and her body started shaking.

Jazz's heart broke for her all over again. She knew how she felt. There was one unanswered question left, and she ached to know the answer, whatever horrible truth it may reveal.

Andrea climbed down out of Serena's arms and ran over to Roberta. She crawled into her lap and put her arms around her neck.

"Roberta, why are you crying? Everybody's safe now."

"I miss my Kino."

Andrea kissed her on the cheek and leaned her head against her shoulder. "I miss him too. But I'll stay with you, so you don't get lonely."

"Oh, sweetie. Thank you." Roberta wrapped her arms around Andrea and stood. She carried her over to the others and nodded at them with a renewed resolve in her eyes.

The sound of voices carried over from the balcony again. Marco strode into view, trailed by three of the Homestead security guards and three children Jazz didn't recognize. They descended the stairs together and joined the others.

Jazz held her breath and looked at Marco. "Daddy?"

Marco shook his head. "I'm sorry, Jazz. We checked everywhere that wasn't… overrun with…" He winced. "Trees and roots."

Jazz looked down, slowly letting out her breath.

Cody took her hand and squeezed it. "Jazz, maybe—" He flinched and snatched his cell off his belt. "Cody. Talk to me." He frowned, then smirked. "'Hey, butthead, put Jazz on the phone now'? Is that all you got to say to me, Mara?" He winced. "Okay, okay!"

He extended his cell to Jazz. "Here. It's for you."

Jazz's hands shook so badly she couldn't hold the phone, and Cody helped her raise it to her ear. Her voice quavered when she spoke.

"Hello?"

Chapter 35

"Jazz! It's Mara. I gotta tell you something. I saw something."

Jazz felt a lump growing in her throat, could barely speak past it. "What, Mara?"

"It was dark as hell, but there was this weird green glow. And there was an old man with a bandage on his hand sitting in the shadows surrounded by all these glowing, twisted roots and stuff. It felt like it was… I don't know. Underground or something. Does that mean anything?"

"Oh my God." Jazz nearly dropped the phone, and her hand flew to her mouth. "Yes, Mara, I think it does."

"Is everybody else okay? And Chaz?"

"Yeah. Chaz is… better. We have some new friends too. Mara, I gotta—"

"Good. Find him. Call me back and lemme know, okay?"

"I will." Jazz let Cody take the phone and looked at him. "Daddy's here. Somewhere. Underground."

"All right." Cody put the phone to his ear. "Call ya back, smartass." He turned to the others. "Search party. There's a basement here somewhere."

They spread out like a team that had rehearsed the drill before. Serena and Marco stayed with the children. Kaylee and Jai joined the search, and Chaz went with Jazz and Cody. Dante stuck by Chaz's side as if they were chained together. Roberta and the other security guards split up, and they searched the lower floors for a basement entrance.

Jazz heard a high-pitched voice shout her name after only a few minutes of searching. Kaylee burst around a corner and ran up to her, took her hand. Jai was right behind her, a goofy smile still plastered on his face, Sadie by his side.

"I think I know where he is, Jazz." Kaylee tugged on her arm. "I felt something moving in my… never mind. Come on."

Jazz's heart pounded as Kaylee led her away, and the others followed. Kaylee took them down a long hallway and up to a mass of twisted roots crawling out of the walls and floor.

"They never let me come down here," Kaylee said. "There was always a guard to stop me if I tried." Kaylee opened her palms, and Jazz saw the gashes in them. They should have bled.

They looked like stigmata.

Kaylee closed her eyes and extended her palms, and the twisted roots barring their way slithered and withdrew through the walls and floor. They revealed a door at the end of the hall, splintered open from the eruption of Kaylee's friends.

Jazz rushed forward, slipped past the doorway, and started down the stairs. Everyone followed right on her heels, ducking and dodging all the twining roots. They wouldn't have been able to see except for the green glow.

Kaylee came up behind Jazz. She smiled, closed her eyes, and raised her arms. The roots came alive and squirmed aside, and a figure stepped out of the gloom and smiled.

"Daddy!"

Jazz leaped into her father's arms. The bristles of a few days' growth of beard scraped against her cheek as she squeezed him. She kissed him, and he kissed her cheek and laughed. Chaz laughed and ran up to him and threw his arms around his legs.

Jazz laughed too, and the frosty fingers clutching her heart finally let go. She stepped back and admired him. A bandage was on his left hand, and he was definitely missing his little finger. Bruises were on his cheeks and under one eye. But he looked like Heaven to her. Jazz gazed into his eyes and finally danced again.

"I made her sorry, Daddy."

"That's my girl." He gave her a solemn nod, grinned, and picked Chaz up in his arms.

Jazz's heart fluttered. "I have some new friends I want you to meet."

She turned and saw Kaylee and Jai laughing and embracing. Dante was almost bouncing off the walls. Cody had a goofy grin plastered on his face that she hadn't seen before.

She wanted to see it again.

"Let's get the hell out of here," she said, and they did.

They called the others as they backtracked. When they all emerged through the front doors and out onto the lawn, happy friends big and small were there to greet them, giants all no matter their size.

Jazz turned to Cody and reached up to him, and he flinched. He snagged his cell off his belt and spoke.

"Cody." He grimaced. "Damn, girl, somebody's got to teach you some manners." He held the phone out to Jazz. "It's for you. Again."

Jazz took it. "Mara?"

"Jazz! Did you find him? Did I finally do good?"

"Oh yes, honey. You did real good."

"Good." Mara sighed. "Because I saw some other stuff I have to tell you about."

"Mara, what?"

"I saw this old guy sitting around a campfire with a bunch of children telling stories, and they were all like laughing and stuff. And plants and stuff were growing everywhere around them, you know, fruits and vegetables. It was all, like, Garden of Eden-ish. And there was a bunch of dogs, and everybody was happy. And ungodly healthy. What do you think?"

"Oh, Mara. Do you think it's Ben?"

"I think so. I hope so."

Jazz's heart soared. She was about to sign off and share the good news with the others when a thought crackled like chain lightning in her mind.

"Mara… what can Amanda do?"

Mara sighed. "She has the power of giving dreams. She mostly can only give nightmares, but she's been working real hard at giving good dreams, and she's getting better at it."

Ahh. The dream. "Well, tell her she did real good too, sweetie."

"Here. Tell her yourself."

Jazz heard a rustle, then: "Hi, Jazz."

"Amanda… you did good, honey. Real good. Thank you."

"You're welcome. We can't wait to see you all again, and meet some new friends."

Jazz winced and turned away from Cody. "Why did you do it, Amanda? I know how much you love him."

"That's why I did it."

"I don't understand."

Amanda sighed. "Jazz, Cody's been in love with you since he first saw you, before you even met him. I wanted to give him what he wanted most *because* I love him so much."

Jazz turned and looked into the dark man's eyes, those dual orbs that swallowed her whole. "Oh, Amanda."

"We'll see you all soon, okay? Tell Chaz I can't wait to see him again. Here's Mara."

Jazz heard another rustle as her heart did flip-flops.

"Jazz? I saw something else I have to tell you about."

"Oh God. What, Mara?" What more could she possibly say? There couldn't be any better news. Jazz held her breath and waited for the pendulum to swing low and make the fatal cut.

"I saw Roberta, and she was like all fat and happy and glowing and all that. I mean, she shined like the light of a million suns. Like something was growing inside her like all the plants and stuff everywhere, except it burned. But in a really cool way."

Jazz turned and looked at Roberta, and their eyes locked.

"What I mean is, she's..." Mara hesitated. "There's something really special growing in her. Like, right *now*. He's going to be an... um, amazing boy. And man. Do really great things and stuff. At least that's what I see. And we have to protect Roberta, and him. Does that make any sense? Did I do good again?"

Jazz almost choked. "Damn straight, girl. I have a big, cuddly teddy bear hug for you when I see you again, okay?"

She almost felt Mara nod and smile. "Okay. Bye, Jazz."

"Bye." Jazz handed the phone to Cody and strolled over toward Roberta, certain she was wearing the same goofy grin Cody had sported in the basement. Andrea held Roberta's hand, smiling at Jazz as if she shared an extraordinary secret. Jazz embraced Roberta and whispered in her ear.

"Mara says Kino left you a gift."

Roberta's jaw slowly dropped. When they stepped away from each other, she looked down and reached her hand to her belly and touched it, her other hand tightly gripping Andrea's.

Jazz suddenly realized that the greatest hope for humanity was not that heroes would be emulated or remembered, but that they would be reborn. She turned and faced Cody, took his hands in hers.

"I think it's time for you to take us home now, dark man."

There was nothing dark about the smile he gave her.

"Damn straight."

About the author

Colleagues and readers alike have dubbed Kerry Alan Denney as *The Reality Bender*. A multiple award-winning author, Kerry incorporates genre-blending elements of the supernatural, paranormal, sci-fi, fantasy, and horror in his novels and short stories. With joy, malicious glee, and a touch of madness, he writes reality-bending thrillers… even when the voices don't compel him to. Kerry lives near Stone Mountain, Georgia with his Golden Retriever Holly Jolly, a professional therapy dog, where he is currently writing his next novel. His post-apocalyptic sic-fi novel JAGANNATH will be published by Permuted Press February 2015.

For more information, please visit www.kerrydenney.com. Write him at kerrydenney@gmail.com.

Made in the USA
Charleston, SC
03 May 2014